Blood on a
Harvest Moon

David Anthony

The Crime Club
Collins, 14 St James's Place, London

William Collins Sons & Co Ltd
London · Glasgow · Sydney · Auckland
Toronto · Johannesburg

First published in Great Britain 1972

© 1972 by David Anthony

ISBN 0 00 231064 3

Set in Intertype Baskerville

Made and Printed in Great Britain by
William Collins Sons & Co Ltd Glasgow

To Elinor with an i

CHAPTER I

JOHNNY KING and I were cutting field corn in the bottom-land when the alarm bell on the barn rang two short bursts. Someone had just driven through the front gate, a quarter mile south of the house and nearly half a mile from us. From the bottomland we could see neither the driveway nor the house.

Johnny stopped honing his machete and stuck the whet-stone into his hip pocket. 'You expecting visitors?' he asked.

'No.' I finished knotting the twine around the shock of corn we had just finished cutting.

'Any chance of a squeal from your last job?' he asked.

'Very unlikely.' The job had taken me from Chicago to New Orleans and had got rough toward the end, but none of the injured parties had known me as Morgan Butler, gentleman farmer. 'All the same, I'd better check it out,' I said.

I shucked out of my blue denim jacket, hating to leave the field at ten in the morning. Another good day would give us fifteen acres cut in three days, right on schedule. Old Dame Nature had conspired as she rarely does in the growth of this corn, and my reluctance to break the rhythm of the harvest was like a superstition.

It was easily the finest stand of corn we had ever grown—twenty acres of stalks that soared to eight feet, boasting ears that averaged more than a foot in length. We had ploughed and planted the bottomland very early, risking the late spring rains that might have rotted the seed in the ground. But the Old Dame had co-operated. All summer long she gave us the rain when we needed it, and a fair time between rains in which to work the corn. The frost had come as if ordered on the first night of October. For six consecutive nights it had burned the corn. Then came Indian summer, the hot, hazy days that had cured the ears to a turn. We wanted to cut the corn in the final days of that golden heat, husk it, and get it into the barn before

the November rains. So the farmer in me resented the intruder before I knew who he was.

I said to Johnny, 'If it's okay, I'll ring the bell.'

'Check.' He was already twisting the stalks of four hills into the saddle that would form the centre of the next shock.

I hiked back through the stubble to the jeep we had parked in the shade at the edge of the field. We kept a carbine in a gun case in the jeep, the M-1 model, .30. It wasn't the best rifle for distance, but it had stopping power and gave you more range and authority than a handgun. I left the carbine on the back seat and drove up the hill to where I had a view of the house and barn.

A new red Mustang had just parked in front of the house, and a woman got out. I had only a glimpse of her before she reached the porch and passed from my field of vision. She was tall, fair-haired, and wore a yellow dress. Knowing she couldn't get in the house, I waited until I was certain she was alone. Then I drove down the hill.

She must have heard my engine, but she kept her seat on the screened porch until I parked the jeep and dismounted. As I approached the porch, she rose and opened the screen door.

'Hello, Morgan,' she said in the old voice.

There is no jolt like a face from the past that you once cherished. I felt a flush of tenderness toward her, an impulse to bow ceremoniously. For this was no ordinary intruder. I had married her, oh, so long ago, when she was twenty-two, divorced her three years later, and hadn't seen her in ten years.

I said, 'Hello, Elaine,' and walked up the steps to the porch.

I had the distance and objectivity of a decade, but it was poor insulation against the fact that the years had neither dimmed her lustre nor flawed her beauty. She was as tall as a woman should be, five-ten in two-inch heels. Her legs were long and exquisitely tapered—elegant legs, immoral legs. Her hair was the bright coppery shade of new pennies, her eyes mint-green. The nose was slender, the mouth contradicting it with a slight excess of width and plumpness

which rescued her face from primness. Her summer tan was a honeyed shade that seemed more like a glow from beneath the skin than a deepening of the colour of the skin itself. The yellow dress was cut on the bias across the thighs, draped to show a half inch of glossy, untanned breast. If she had aged at all, it was in the faint touch of cynicism I thought I detected around the mouth and eyes as she smiled under my scrutiny.

'Do I pass inspection, Captain Butler?' she asked. Her voice was throaty, as if she also felt some emotion from the past.

'*Farmer* Butler,' I corrected her. 'No rank here.'

'Yes, farmer. When I first heard about your farm, I could hardly believe it. In fact, my curiosity almost caused me to pay you a visit five years ago. I actually drove past your gate.'

'Why didn't you stop?'

'Cowardice. It wasn't only curiosity. You see, I had just promised a man I would marry him. I found out where you were and drove down from Michigan. But when I reached your gate, I balked. I knew that what I really wanted was your blessing. A bad idea.'

'Did you marry the man?'

'Yes. I'm Mrs Ralph Maynard, of Sweetbriar Falls, Virginia.'

Her casual manner slipped a little with these words that identified her. Her eyes made a jerky movement, a flicker of tension. Then she watched me with an avidity that pricked a nerve of memory, releasing ancient images of her vitality, her gaiety, her quick intelligence.

'Let's talk inside,' I said. 'It's cooler, and I want to get out of these sweaty clothes. How about a cold drink?'

'All right. Just bitter lemon, if you have it. It's too early in the day for the hard stuff.'

I served her the drink on the Virginia sofa in our living-room. The room is huge, with a high, beamed ceiling, a stone fireplace you could roast a boar in, and a picture window on the north side which gives a view of a handsome stand of timber. I showed Elaine a bathroom under the front stairs where she could freshen up, excused myself,

and went into the kitchen, where I opened a switch box and rang the bell on the barn for Johnny King's benefit, the all-clear. Then I ducked up the back stairs, showered, slipped into fresh slacks and a sports shirt, and returned to the living-room.

Elaine was standing at the picture window, looking out at the view. Smoke from her cigarette curled like blue memories above her head. 'How much of this do you own?' she asked.

'A hundred and twenty acres. All but twenty under the plough.' At the bar—a curved mahogany relic I had bought at an auction—I poured dry vermouth into a glass and twisted a piece of lemon over it. 'How did you learn about the farm five years ago?'

'From that man you used to work for in San Francisco.' She drifted over to the sofa. 'That man they called the Colonel.'

I sat in a chair across the coffee table from her. 'Colonel Edmund F. DeBlanc,' I said. 'Better known as the Bald Eagle. He was my battalion commander in the South Pacific years before I hooked up with him in 'Frisco. A tough old buzzard, with a heart like a piece of anthracite. What did he say about me?'

Elaine leaned forward and spoke as if her words had some special significance. 'He said you had quit the detective agency, but that you still took on an occasional job if the price was right. He called you a free-lance trouble-shooter and said he referred a great many jobs to you.'

I had to grin at that. Apparently the Bald Eagle had neglected to tell her that the jobs he passed on to me were ones his own agency wouldn't touch. They were either crooked deals or jobs so risky the Colonel feared his boys would report back with their heads under their arms. I screened the Colonel's offerings most carefully, aware that he had never forgiven me for my defection, which occurred when I took a job the agency had rejected. It had proved most lucrative. My fee had paid for the farm.

Elaine made an abrupt gesture, and again I caught a flash of tension. 'Morgan, do you still do that kind of work?'

'Yes, from time to time.'

'But why? Your Colonel gave the impression that it was dirty and dangerous work. Don't you make a living from the farm?'

Something in me resisted the investigation. 'I take the jobs to get me off the farm. To help cure me of my provincialism, my bourgeois conceits. As I recall, you used to accuse me of lugging around a trunkful of bourgeois conceits.'

She flushed. 'Ah, don't, Morgan. I said a lot of idiotic things during that last year, when things were going bad. I'm not very proud of some of my behaviour during that year either. Especially do I regret the way I behaved with the dashing Major Cartwright.'

This was more than I'd bargained for. 'Hey, don't apologize for old sins. My crack about the conceits was a joke.'

She gave me a crooked smile. 'All right, no apologies for old sins. But after what happened when you . . .'

'Don't avoid the word. You're talking about my crack-up.'

She nodded. 'I guess you knew that I went down to that hospital in San Diego three times, but they wouldn't let me see you.'

'I was pretty nuts there for a while, in and out of contact. I didn't want you to see me like that. Later, it didn't matter. If I learned nothing else in that hospital, I learned that you and the divorce had very little to do with the crack-up.'

That immobilized her. She said, 'I wish you had given me that message a long time ago. It would have been a nice gift.'

'Yes, I owed you that. But by the time I got out of the hospital and began picking up the pieces, you had left the Coast. It wasn't the sort of thing you can write in a letter —short of sending my case history—so I didn't try to track you down.'

'I went to work for Daddy,' she said.

I smiled. 'The Tycoon.'

'Yes. Both he and Mother were sorry about the divorce.

They were fond of you. They blamed me.'

'They were wrong.' I got up to fix us another drink. Elaine rose quickly and accompanied me to the bar, as if she feared the distance might break the mood we had created. So I knew that all this spadework into the past had its purpose : She had to establish a measure of intimacy or trust before she could tell why she'd come.

It took her another ten minutes. First she tried to be jaunty. Perched on the barstool, her face close to mine, she said, 'Put a slug of gin in it this time. A pox on the hour.' She drank. She lit a cigarette and inhaled deeply. The distracted way she primped her hair was as stimulating as a caress. She told me she had worked five years for the Tycoon. He owned a furniture factory in Grand Rapids, with outlets in the better department stores. Elaine's job was to visit these stores and set up displays of the furniture.

'I was a card-carrying career girl. I blame you for the fact that I stuck it out for five years. After you, I was gun-shy about men and marriage for quite a while.'

'I take that as a compliment,' I said.

'You should.' She put her glass down and her face became more solemn. 'You're different from what I expected, Morgan.'

'We all grow older.'

'I don't mean that. But from what the Colonel said, I expected to find you hard, bitter, on the make for the Yankee dollar. But you look healthy, genial, altogether a solid citizen.'

'Is that why you find it so difficult to hire me?' I said.

Her smile was sheepish. 'Yes. Am I all that transparent?'

'Well, you give off signals of a lady in distress. And for an ex-wife, you were too inquisitive about the wrong things.'

'Very astute of you.' Her mouth drooped a little. 'Yes, Morgan, I need your help. My husband, Ralph, has been missing for three days. I have reason to believe he's in serious trouble. I'm worried. I'm scared. I thought it would be easy to come here and hire you. But somehow you don't seem like a man for hire, in spite of what you said about those jobs you take.'

'So you decided to put it on a personal basis,' I said.
'Did I? Yes, I suppose that's true. Of course, I mean
to pay you. I insist on that.'

'If you hadn't, I would have,' I said. 'I don't do charity
work, and I certainly don't work for auld lang syne.'

Her nostril wings flared, and you could almost see the
frost in her eyes. 'All right, I'll give you a cheque! Where's
my purse?'

'Wait a minute! I haven't said I'll take the job yet.'
I walked over to a chair, sat down, and lit one of the short,
bitter stogies I enjoy. 'Tell me about Mr Maynard's disappearance.'

She hesitated, then crossed over and sat on the sofa. 'All
right. Maybe I did plan to cash in on auld lang syne. But I
couldn't take it to the police or to some seedy private
detective. I came to you for two reasons. I thought I
could count on you. And you don't have far to travel to
check this out.'

'You said your husband was in trouble. What kind of
trouble?'

Concern made her face look leaner. 'Morgan, I don't
know. Three days ago—around noon on Sunday—Ralph
got a phone call that upset him terribly. I heard him arguing on the phone with someone he called Milt. Then he
made a call for an airline ticket, told me he had to make a
business trip to New York, packed a suitcase, and took a
cab to the airport. He hadn't been gone ten minutes when
the airlines called to confirm his reservation—to Pittsburgh,
not New York. I felt uneasy, and I knew Ralph had made
a trip to his study while he was packing. I checked his desk,
and his revolver was gone. He took it with him.'

'Are you sure about that?'

'Absolutely! I'd seen it there only the day before. Now
let me finish. Ralph always calls me every night when he's
on a trip. It's a thing with us. But he didn't call that night,
or the next night. By yesterday noon I was pretty shook
up. I called his secretary on some pretext, and she said
he'd called the office on Monday, told her he'd gone out
of town for personal reasons and would be back on Wednesday morning. But he didn't show up this morning.

That's when I decided to come here. I flew to Columbus.'
'But obviously you have some kind of idea about where
he is. You can't expect me to pick up his trail in Pittsburgh.'
She nodded briskly. 'Three years ago Ralph got into a
financial bind with his business. He's a contractor and
sometimes owns a piece of a real-estate development he's
building. In this case, he had an option on some land, and
another partner failed to come through with the big money
at the appropriate time. Ralph stood to lose the land plus
the money he had already invested. He was over-extended,
couldn't get a dime from the bank. So he made a trip to a
place near Pittsburgh and borrowed a hundred thousand
dollars from someone—a personal loan. Yesterday I dug
back through his expense account records and found a
receipt for the motel he stayed in, the Fort Duquesne in
Crafton, West Virginia.'

'Have you tried to call Ralph there?'

'Yes. They have no Ralph Maynard registered, but he
could be using another name. Or he could be at a different
motel.'

'So far this is flimsy evidence that Ralph is in Crafton.'

'Is it? Then how about this piece of evidence. When he
came home from that trip to Crafton two years ago, I unpacked his bag and found his revolver. He took it that
time, too. I think that's the association I made when I
found he'd gone to Pittsburgh—the pistol—which is why
I went to see if it was gone from his desk.'

'Yes, that adds weight to the Crafton theory,' I said. 'I
gather Ralph doesn't usually pack a sidearm on business
trips?'

'No, of course not!'

'Then didn't it strike you as odd three years ago that
he took the gun just to get a loan from a guy?'

'Yes, and I asked him about it. I caught him in an
unguarded moment, while he was still jubilant about having
got the loan. He said something strange. He said he took
the pistol as insurance against the old maxim that there
was honour among thieves. But the maxim had proved to
be false, so the pistol was excess baggage. Then he called
the whole thing a bad joke and said to forget it. I thought

I had forgotten it. Until last night.'

For the first time her problem seemed real to me, as if this remark about honour among thieves was the spice that made it savoury. I chewed on my stogie for a moment. 'What about Ralph's financial situation now? Could he be after another loan?'

'He's never been so solvent,' Elaine said. 'He's cashing in on that development from three years ago. No, he's in trouble.'

'All right, he's in trouble. Let's get a fix on exactly what you want me to do about it. I take it I'm to trot over to Crafton, locate Ralph, find out what kind of jam he's in, if any, wade in, and bail him out. Is that a fair description of the job?'

Elaine wet her lips. 'Morgan, it's not that simple. You don't know Ralph. He's a self-made man, independent, rugged, and proud. He would resent the fact that I sent someone to intrude into his private affairs. I want you to use discretion.'

'Discretion,' I muttered. 'Listen, assuming I find him— and he's not already in dutch up to his ears—I can't just pussyfoot around and wait for something to explode.'

'But what if he doesn't really need help?' she said. 'What if there's a perfectly logical explanation for his behaviour?'

'Hell, you don't want a detective, you want a magician. The only way to find out if he needs help is to talk to the man.'

'Try to do it my way, Morgan. Please?'

Without working for it, she had put the catch in her voice and the smokiness in her eyes. It gave me a spasm of memory and left an ache like an old war wound in foul weather. I reacted against it. 'What if I turn up something ugly? Something against Ralph?'

'I'll take that risk,' she said. 'Can you go today? Now?'

'Yes.' I asked for a description of Ralph, and she promptly opened her purse and handed me a photograph. It was a colour print of Ralph from the waist up, and she had written his particulars on the back. He had a rugged face, all right, wide and solid, with black curly hair, shaggy brows, dark brown eyes, a nose that had been broken and

healed crookedly, and an overall look of a man who could face adversity without flinching.

'How much money do you want?' Elaine asked. She had her cheque-book out, her pen poised, a faint look of disdain on her face.

I almost told her that I would collect later. But it seemed wise to keep this transaction strictly on a cash basis from the outset. Money is the great purifier. To wrap a deal like this in coin of the realm relieves both parties of any emotional commitment. Better that look of disdain—her contempt for my affection for the sordid buck—than the tangled debt of gratitude and nostalgic guilt she might accumulate if the payoff weren't stated in advance. Remember, I knew this woman.

I said, 'Give me a thousand as an advance against twenty-five hundred for the job. But if it takes more than a week, or if it turns into hazardous duty, we'll renegotiate the fee.'

'Agreed.' She scribbled, ripped out the cheque, and handed it to me. 'I'm beginning to wonder if you're really the solid citizen I took you for.'

'You didn't come here to sweet-talk a gentleman farmer into pruning your shrubbery,' I said. 'You came to hire a hard-nose to deal with a piece of trouble.'

'So I shouldn't complain if I get what I'm paying for, is that it? All right, Morgan. I only hope I'm doing the right thing.' She looked at her watch. 'I can just make my return flight back to Washington. But first let me call home. We have an answering service. Maybe Ralph called in.'

I showed her the phone. She placed the call, talked with the answering service, and hung up. 'Nothing from Ralph, but his office is getting frantic.' She gave me her address and phone number. 'Morgan, call me no matter what you turn up. Promise?'

'All right.'

She was standing close to me. 'I'm just beginning to realize how rude I've been. I'm so preoccupied with this business, I didn't even ask if you've remarried.'

'The answer is no. But we don't have to exchange social amenities. I'm hired now. I'll do the job.'

She coloured a little, but her eyes didn't waver. 'All right, we'll keep it on a rude level. Call me.'

I watched her go down the porch steps and across the yard to the Mustang. She had those extra inches between the hips and neck that added gracefulness to her walk. The Mustang had barely cleared the yard when Johnny King came out of the wagon shed and crossed to the porch. He had come in for lunch.

He said, 'You get snazzy visitors for such a rustic fellow.'

'That was Elaine.'

He gave a low whistle. 'I admire your taste in wives, amigo.'

'Johnny, I've got to take off for a few days.'

'Another job? I thought you were going to lay off until the cold weather.'

'I couldn't turn this one down,' I said. 'I owe the lady.'

He nodded. 'How long?'

'No more than a couple of days, I hope.'

Johnny inspected the sky. 'The weather's supposed to hold. I'll finish cutting that bottomland myself. You watch your step. I'll expect you home to help with the husking.'

CHAPTER II

I HIT Crafton, West Virginia—a steel town on the Ohio River—at two that afternoon. If you enter from the north, as I did, you pass through a fogbank of sulphurous smoke from the blast furnaces. Next is the Bessemer, shrieking and belching a gaudy shower of sparks and greasy smoke as it turns upright. Then you pass the stacks of the open-hearth furnaces, burning green or yellow smoke. Glittering flakes of graphite coated my windshield for the next mile and a half of so-called city.

So you would hardly call Crafton a tourist attraction. A gas station attendant confirmed this observation when I stopped to tank up. He told me there were only two motels in the vicinity. Both were located on Crafton Heights, where the better-heeled citizens lived above the stench

B

in the valley. He recommended the Fort Duquesne, if I was a man who appreciated privacy. But I decided to do some phone work before I went out there. I got a fistful of change from the attendant and used his public phone booth.

You can sign a motel register with an alias, but when you rent a car you have to show your driver's licence. The Pittsburgh airport was forty miles from Crafton, and I doubted if Maynard had hitchhiked down. So first I got Pittsburgh information and asked for the numbers of the three largest car rental agencies at the airport. Then I dialled the first number on my list and made my pitch to the girl who answered, posing as a peace officer who had stopped Ralph Maynard on a speeding charge. My story was that Maynard claimed he had rented his car from her agency on Sunday night but had misplaced his rental contract. Naturally, I had to nail down the registration on the vehicle, and I hoped she could confirm his story. The girl checked her files and chirped in my ear that her agency had definitely *not* rented a car to anyone by that name on Sunday.

So I tried the second number on my list. This girl was also very eager to co-operate with the law. In twelve seconds she was back on the phone with her copy of the contract. Maynard had rented a light-blue Oldsmobile on Sunday night, and she gave me the licence number. I thanked the girl and hung up.

I drove the three miles out the pike to the Fort Duquesne and parked beside the motel office. The gas jockey had been right about the privacy. Each unit was a separate cabin, with enough space between them so that you could have a spat with your wife without drawing a crowd. Across the highway was a roadhouse where, according to the sign, you could dine, dance, and drink. All very convenient, but I was more pleased to see a certain blue Olds with the correct licence tag parked in front of cabin number 8. So the cabin I wanted was number 12, the front of which gave a fine view of cabin 8.

Twelve proved to be vacant, and while I was signing up the girl on duty turned her back to answer the switchboard. I flicked through her card rack and read the name

on the card for cabin 8 : Robert Mansefield. The initials clinched it. About then I decided to honour Elaine's request and get a fix on Maynard's activities before I took him to task for spooking his wife. It seemed reasonable to suppose that his mission wasn't terribly urgent, if he had been in town three days getting his teeth into it.

Duly registered, I backed the Merc into the slot in front of cabin 12 and took my suitcase inside. The cabin reeked from the pine-scented disinfectant they used to clean the bathroom. I opened the rear window. The screen that covered the frame was held in place with two hooks at the bottom. You could slip the hooks with a penknife. Removing my jacket, I rinsed my face, turned the easy chair so that it afforded a view through my front window, and took up the vigil. It was three thirty-five.

I smoked one black stogie. I watched a frenzied, whispered argument on the steps of cabin 10 between a pretty girl in a bargain basement dress and a middle-aged man in an Italian silk suit. It ended when the girl finally nodded and visibly flinched at the noise the key made when the man turned it in the lock.

At five after four Ralph Maynard came out of his cabin, wearing dark glasses and a light poplin jacket. I slipped into my coat while he was backing out, and when he hit the highway I had the Merc rolling fifty yards behind him.

Maynard was in no great hurry, but I hung in pretty close, cruising in the left lane with him in the right. I didn't want him jumping a traffic light on the yellow and leaving me in the lurch. When he hit Crafton's main drag, he turned south and moved with the traffic all the way through town. Three miles past the city limits, we came to a brand-new shopping centre with a macadam parking lot. Maynard turned into the lot. I whipped the Merc across the concrete apron of a service station on the right side of the highway and parked. The attendants were busy at the pumps and ignored me.

By then Maynard had parked in the lot and returned to the sidewalk. I didn't see him hail the cab. It came out of nowhere, stopped barely long enough for Maynard to jump in, and was in traffic headed north in seconds. I humped the

Merc over the kerb and rammed into the northbound lane a quarter of a mile behind the cab. It was painted red and had the company name in white on the side : KELSO'S CABS. The cab was making good time, but I was close enough to see it make a fast right turn off the highway.

As I made the same turn, I caught a flash of a gaudy orange sign I had read on the way south. It marked the entrance to a trailer court, where you could park a trailer or rent one on blocks. I gunned the Merc to the next bend and saw the cab turn left on a dirt road that ran along the valley floor. The paved road took you up the hill out of the valley. Reluctant to follow them on the dirt road and risk discovery, I drove up the hill, following the curve of the valley. I parked on a wide shoulder, took my binoculars from the glove compartment, and got out.

The cab was parked in a sumac thicket just off the dirt road below me. I scanned the terrain and located Maynard and the cab driver beside a creek. They talked for a while facing north. I tracked the binoculars across the creek and through the trees smack into the trailer court, about two hundred yards in front of them. Then I tracked the pair back to the cab. They drove farther up the valley, parked again, and walked toward the trailer court from the east. Ten minutes later they returned to the cab and retraced their course back toward the highway. Unless I misread the signs, they were reconnoitring the best approach to move in on someone in the trailer court.

I got back to the highway ahead of them, turned right, and parked off the pavement. The cab turned south, as I expected. I waited until I saw Maynard's blue Olds in my rearview mirror, then pulled into traffic ahead of him. I was seated in my cabin with the phone at my ear when he pulled into the Fort Duquesne.

I got an answer after two rings. 'Dispatcher, Kelso Cabs.'

'Hello, I'm calling about an incident involving your cab number seventy-three today. When I paid my fare, your driver accidentally slipped an extra twenty in with my change. I wouldn't want the guy to lose a day's wages.'

'That's very decent of you, sir. Cab seventy-three, you say? Hang on.' He rustled some papers. 'Hello? Say, you

must be mistaken. Seventy-three is in for a ring job. It wasn't out today.'

'Seventy-three is the number, friend. I'm sure of it.'

'Hang on.' I heard a squawk box in the background, then he said, '*My* mistake. The owner himself had that cab out today.'

'The owner? Would that be Mr Kelso?'

'That's him. Milton Anthony Kelso. Man, the boys will really razz him for short-changing himself.'

'Does he also own the moving-and-storage firm and the trucking line?' They were listed under Kelso's Cabs in the directory.

'That's him. You might call him a wheel in Crafton. Get it?'

I chuckled. 'Not bad. Well, with his loot he wouldn't miss a twenty, but I'll still send him a cheque.' I hung up.

Now I had the Milt who had called Maynard and given him the kind of news that caused him to grab a gun, lie to his wife about his destination, neglect his business, and crawl around in the brush spying on a trailer court. If Maynard was involved in something dangerous or illegal, I had enough information now to cause him considerable anxiety about going through with it.

On the other hand, it was possible to explain his behaviour without the sinister overtones. Suppose Maynard and Kelso were cooking up a secret real-estate deal involving the property the trailer court occupied. If it were lucrative enough, such a deal might distract Maynard from his conjugal and business responsibilities for a while. And if secrecy were essential, it would explain Kelso disguising himself as one of his own cabbies.

If you didn't take the gun too seriously.

But I took the gun seriously because Elaine did, so I couldn't sell myself completely on the real-estate theory. I bought just enough of it to cause me to postpone my talk with Maynard until I had a chance to shake down his cabin.

I waited two hours before I got a crack at it.

It was full dark at eight-thirty when Maynard emerged from cabin 8 and crossed the highway to the roadhouse.

I moseyed over there. It was the kind of place where the hostess wears a starched handkerchief pinned to her bosom. I went to the bar and ordered a dry vermouth. Through the latticework I saw Maynard alone at a table in the dining-room. As soon as he ordered dinner, I dropped a buck on the bar and left.

Maynard had left a dim light burning in his cabin, but the curtains were drawn. Since he hadn't double-locked his door on the way out, I decided to be bold and enter through the front rather than through the window in back. There was no one moving on the grounds as I crossed the lawn, but when I hit the gravel drive the door to cabin 10 slammed open and the pretty girl ran down the steps and jumped into the car in front of the cabin. The middle-aged man hustled after her in his shirt sleeves.

'Take me home!' she yelled. 'No more lies. No more nothing.'

They were too close to Maynard's cabin for comfort. So I hiked to my own cabin and holed up until the boy-friend got her calmed down and back inside. Maybe it took ten minutes.

I checked the grounds, then crossed to cabin 8 with the hard square of plastic in my hand. I took a firm grip on the doorknob, inserted the plastic between door and frame, and pried the lock back into its slot. The door opened easily and I was inside.

His cabin was laid out exactly the same as mine. A black attaché case was standing open on the desk. That was a careless move. I looked inside and saw the pistol, a .357 Magnum. For a sidearm, a Magnum is a piece of artillery. You can damn near stop a tank with one. Hoisting the pistol between two knuckles, I opened the gate and found it fully loaded. Just then the phone on the desk rang. I replaced the pistol. The phone rang again.

I picked it up and grunted, 'Yeah?'

'Ralph? This is your hack driver. Good news. We've got professional help for tonight, sent by way of AC. Come early, say a quarter to eleven. Same set-up. Got it?'

'Got it,' I growled and hung up.

So this was the night, and it didn't sound like any jolly

group of real-estate boys getting together for an honest swindle. I decided to hang around until Maynard returned and have that heart-to-heart chat.

I turned toward the easy chair, heard the silken, swishing whisper, then the ugly pulpy sound of the melon splitting when the padded ballbat hit the side of my head and let the dark in.

CHAPTER III

I DREAMED a painful, jumbled dream.

At first I was outside the dream, watching it leak from a crack in that vault in the catacombs of the mind, where all dark secrets are entombed. I throbbed with anxiety. It seemed unjust, because I had already opened that vault and aired it out during my tenure on the psychiatric ward of the Naval hospital in San Diego—aided by a master safecracker, a wiry old Navy commander named Dr Coffee. Before the crack-up I was a professional Marine, a captain, with sixteen years in the corps.

Then I was drawn into the dream, where I witnessed an incident that had occurred during that last summer before the crack-up. We were making an amphibious assault at battalion strength on the tranquil beaches of San Clemente in California. One of the landing craft capsized in the surf, and when they brought in the portable crane and turned it over, seventeen young Marines popped to the surface, buoyed up by their packs with the green camouflage rolls. We dragged them out of the surf and lined them up on the beach.

The Old Fox Coffee intruded into that dream, but I ignored him. I was captivated with a vivid technicolor movie of Elaine. She was kneeling on a sandy beach—sun-kissed, supple, and serene—jerking her swimming cap from her head, releasing a cascade of reddish-golden hair. I wanted to lick the salt water from her glistening skin. Then I entered the picture and dropped a *lei* around her neck. So it was Hawaii, where I met her in the summer

of fifty-four, a year after my return from the Korean War.

I had been a long time at war, and Coffee relentlessly harped on that fact. During my first eleven years in the corps—1942 to 1953—I'd spent nearly seven years in combat.

Then came Elaine, my antidote to the carnage, my health, my purity, my peace everlasting—a rotten assignment for any woman, a deadly one for a wife. But I sustained the fantasy for two years before she rebelled, like the spirited, intelligent woman she was. So we entered the third year of the marriage, the bad year.

And I was back inside the San Clemente dream, painfully aware of its significance. The seventeen Marines had drowned on the second day of a field problem scheduled to last a week. After the landing, we were to move into the hills of Camp Pendleton and play war. I knew Elaine had formed some kind of alliance with the dashing Major Cartwright, and I envisioned the two of them debasing her purity, mocking me in the heat of their trysts. So I had a plan to catch them together while they thought I was camped in the hills. My rage was a tropical fever in my blood, and I hate to think of what I might have done if I'd carried out the plan. But I was prevented from carrying it out by the freak accident that had killed seventeen men. This avalanche of death in time of peace turned a screw in my mind that made Elaine's behaviour unimportant. A month later we parted, and two months after that I was in a padded room in San Diego, a chanting inside my skull.

The dreams faded against the clear thought that I would never have stirred up these nightmares if Elaine hadn't paid that visit to my farm. I was regaining consciousness. My limbs were restored to me, and I felt the fabric of the rug against my cheek. I sat up, and the ache in my head broke into splinters, danced a little, and regrouped into a lively throb. I had a lump behind my ear. I felt it gingerly. The skin wasn't broken, which meant I'd been sapped.

As the grogginess passed I felt concern that Maynard would come back and find me in his cabin. But the furniture

didn't fit that notion. I recognized my suitcase and saw the chair I had shifted in front of the window. I felt in my pocket for the key to my cabin. It was gone. I went to the door and opened it. Number 12 was on the door, my door key was hanging in the lock, and Maynard's blue Olds was missing from in front of his cabin. Only then did I look at my watch : ten-thirty. The voice on the phone, Kelso, had said to keep the rendezvous at ten-forty-five.

I took a few deep breaths of the cool October air, and my mind began to function on most of its cylinders. Obviously Maynard had cut his dinner short and slipped back to his cabin while I was sweating out the fracas staged by the couple in cabin 10. He had heard me at the door, ducked into the bath, and when I was ill-mannered enough to take his phone call, he had slugged me and dumped me back in my own cabin. Likely he had also called Kelso back and got the message about the earlier time and the professional help.

I toted my head into the bathroom, ran some ice water on a cloth, and held the compress against the egg behind my ear. The relief made room for an idea. I called the desk clerk.

'Hello, Hollingsworth in twelve. I planned to meet Mansfield in eight for a drink, but his cabin's dark. Did he check out?'

'Yes, sir. Number eight checked out a little after ten.'

'Thanks. Guess he had to get on the road.'

I hung up, grabbed my door key on the way out, headed the Merc down the mountain, and I balled the jack. I passed traffic on the right shoulder, burned rubber on the curves, ran two red lights, and hit seventy at the city limits, headed south.

When I had passed the trailer court, I turned left on the narrow paved road. A bloated harvest moon hung in the sky above the valley, stained a bloody orange by the dust from Craft Steel. Near the entrance to the dirt road was a clearing where the state road boys kept supplies in a shack. I drifted behind the shack and parked. Then I applied pressure on two screw heads on the back wall of the glove compartment. The wall snapped open, and I took a Luger

out of its slot and started up the dusty road at a trot.

I had covered barely a hundred yards when I heard the metallic whomp from the woods ahead. It sounded like an explosion inside a fifty-gallon drum. At once somebody leaned on his horn. He wouldn't get off. The blast echoed from the hills, a monotonous, mournful trumpeting. I was moving straight toward it. Then I saw a glitter of reflected moonlight on metal in the trees off the road to my left—and the horn stopped. In the hush that followed, my footfalls in the soft dust were loud.

The glitter I had seen took the shape of a car parked off the road in a grove of trees. I halted forty yards from the car and waited. Nothing stirred in the immediate vicinity. A breeze carried strains of music from a radio in the trailer court. I moved to the left fender of the car. It was Kelso Cab number seventy-three. The back seat was empty. I eased to the driver's window. There was a hole in the windshield above and in front of the steering wheel. Jagged cracks radiated from the hole. The windshield around the hole was splattered, as if the cab had gone fast enough to smash a host of bugs. But the glass on the passenger's side wasn't splattered, which seemed odd. I took a better look inside. The goo on the windshield wasn't bugs.

It was part of a man, pieces from inside his skull. The rest of him was lying on the front seat, where he had fallen off the wheel, his head in the moonlight, a hole where his nose had been.

The metallic whomp had been a gun fired inside the cab. The muzzle had been held against the back of the driver's head. I wanted a better look at him, but then I heard a noise in the woods.

A girl's voice said, 'Over here, Bob! I see a car.'

I went to all fours. They were clumsy in the brush, and I could hear hoarse whispers. The girl giggled. The boy said, 'I tell you, it sounded like a shotgun.'

Keeping the cab between me and them, I crept through a growth of trees, hit the road about seventy yards from the cab, and began trotting. I hadn't made ten yards when the girl screamed. I kept running, ready to fling myself off the road if a car approached. But I reached the paved road

and started to cross when I heard the squeal of punished tyres, and a car without lights came hurtling down the hill with a whine in its engine.

I snatched my foot off the pavement and hit the dirt. The car went past with a whoosh. I couldn't see the driver, but the car was a light-blue Olds. I hustled to the Merc and got out of there.

A mile north of the trailer court a police car passed me headed south, with its siren wailing. At the edge of town I picked up a roast beef sandwich and a carton of coffee. Back in the Merc, I turned on the shortwave band and tuned in local police calls. All I learned before I got back to the motel was that the dead man was Milton A. Kelso, local bigwig.

At the desk in my cabin I ate my sandwich and tried to make sense of the night's events. I took the pessimistic view. After Maynard slugged me in his cabin, he must have assumed I was a sneak thief. Since he was in no position to call in the police, he dumped me back in my cabin. Maybe he called Kelso back to get that message about the professional help and the change in time. But then he changed the script. Instead of leaving his car in the parking lot, he had parked it on the hill above the spot he and Kelso had checked out that afternoon. If he left the motel at ten, he had time to cache the car and hike the mile south to where Kelso picked him up. Then when he and Kelso got into position off the dirt road, he could have shot Kelso and hiked up the hill to his car.

I didn't mean to convict the man before a trial, but this story fitted the facts as I knew them—with one exception. It didn't account for the whereabouts of the professional help, sent by way of AC.

I soaked the lump behind my ear with another iced towel. Then I crawled into bed and slept without dreams.

The next morning, over breakfast at the roadhouse, I read about the murder in the Crafton *News-Sentinel*. It was big stuff, covering the entire front page, with a photo spread inside. The story hinted that the police, headed by Detective Joe Millsop, had a basketful of clues. But the only one

mentioned was the slug from the murder weapon, which had ended up in a tree in front of the cab. The police had identified it as a slug from a .357 Magnum.

Another entry on the debit side of Ralph Maynard's ledger.

The police also reported finding a .38 revolver in Kelso's belt, loaded but unfired, and a 12-gauge shotgun in the trunk of his cab. Since the killer hadn't touched Kelso's wallet, the police doubted that robbery was the motive. Their scepticism was helped by the fact that someone had tried to break into Kelso's private office at three am. Kelso's office was above the garage from which his cabs operated. The prowler had slugged a mechanic, but the night watchman had scared the man off. The watchman got a look at him, and the description fitted Ralph Maynard like his skin. Of course, the police believed that the prowler was also the killer.

The rest of the story was the usual obit, ending up with the news that Kelso had left behind a widow and three children.

I thought I knew what Maynard was after in Kelso's office—papers that told about the loan Kelso had given him three years ago.

I had one cheerful report to give Elaine about her husband.

When I got up to pay my bill, I made one of those mental connections you have to make if you want to get ahead in this line of work. I got some change and called the business office of the local phone company. Identifying myself as Detective Joe Millsop, I asked to speak with the man in charge. I got a man named Miller who seemed impressed that the law had called on him.

'Miller, I'm investigating this Kelso murder and I need your help. But I want this kept on the QT. You understand?'

'Yes, sir. How can I help?'

I used my best cop's voice. 'I want the phone numbers of all long-distance calls Kelso made during the past week.'

'Certainly. I'll have that for you in ten minutes.'

'Not good enough!' I hollered. 'I need those numbers now.'

'Well . . . all right. Hold on.'

After a minute he picked up the phone. 'Detective Millsop? I've just learned that one of your people called in for that very information not an hour ago.'

'Aw, that was probably the sheriff's office. Confusion over jurisdiction, you know. You can give me the dope.'

'All right. I've got three long-distance calls charged to Mr Kelso in the past week. One to Pittsburgh on Friday. And two on Sunday, one to Sweetbriar Falls, Virginia, and one to Atlantic City.'

I jotted down the numbers as he rattled them off. 'Fine. Now keep this under your hat, Miller.' I hung up.

So Atlantic City was the AC Kelso had mentioned in his call. I got a long-distance operator and placed a person-to-person call to Mr Stanley Oglethorpe at the Atlantic City number. They put the connection through and a girl answered: 'Seabreeze Motel. Can I help you?' I hung up while the operator started about Oglethorpe.

I crossed the highway, checked out of the motel, and drove down to the trailer court south of town. Not that I hoped to learn much, but you have to touch all bases. You have to be tidy.

I drove in past the gaudy orange sign and back to the manager's office. It was a deluxe trailer mounted on blocks with permanent wiring hooked into it. I'd just stepped out of my car when a Dodge camper came from the camp, clashed gears as it gained momentum, and barrelled for the exit.

A cranky voice behind me said, 'He *knows* he ain't allowed to speed on these grounds. People get kilt thataway.'

The speaker was a wiry old gent in overalls and a ball cap.

'You the manager?' I asked.

'Cappy Ewing, at your service. Are you another reporter?'

'No, I'm looking for one of your transients, a fellow I ran into in town the other night. Said he had a rig for

sale cheap. I can't recall his name, but he hit camp last week.'

'What kind of rig was he fixing to sell?' Ewing asked.

'I don't remember. We were a little tight that evening.'

'You mean to tell me you don't even know if you came to buy a mobile wheeler or something mounted on a chassis?'

I shrugged. 'Either would do if it's a bargain.'

'Boy, you're easy to please.' Ewing plucked loose tobacco from a pocket and popped it into his left cheek. 'I only got three who might fit the picture. Two of them already pulled out.'

'Think you can recall their names offhand? That would help.'

'Shoot, boy, my memory's sharper than your razor. One party was two men in their fifties, Dunlap and Hanson, dragging a nineteen-foot Airstream Globetrotter. They left early today. Second party was that Dodge camper just missed running you down. Party of three in that, a married couple named Price and an extra man. Third party is an old couple named Jacobson in a twenty-two-foot Silverstreak. Any of them ring a bell?'

'The Globetrotter,' I said. 'Looks like I missed the boat.' I started for my car, then turned and said quickly, 'Did either of those that pulled out seem disturbed by last night's killing?'

'What's that got to do with you wanting to buy a rig?'

'Not a thing, old-timer. Much obliged.'

Well, I hadn't really expected to learn anything. I wasn't even certain that Kelso and Maynard had designs on anyone in the trailer court. It had just looked that way.

I drove southeast on back roads to Route 70. Near the entrance to the Pennsylvania Turnpike I stopped for gas and called Elaine Maynard. She answered after one ring.

'Elaine, Morgan here. Any word from Ralph?'

'Morgan, I thought you'd never call! No, I haven't heard from Ralph. Didn't you find him?'

'I found him, but he left town rather suddenly last night, before we had a chance to talk. I thought he might have called home.'

'He hasn't. What do you mean, he left town suddenly?'

'There's been some trouble here,' I said. 'A man was killed last night in Crafton. It's possible Ralph was implicated.'

'My God! Do you mean he's wanted by the police?'

'Nothing like that. I doubt they even knew he was in town.'

'But who was killed? Why would Ralph want to kill anyone?'

'Take it easy. I'll give you the details when I see you. I should be there in a few hours. Don't talk to anyone about this. If Ralph shows up, go along with any excuse he offers for his absence. It's possible we can clear this mess up.'

'All right, Morgan. I'll do as you say. I trust you.'

'Good girl. I'll see you about four.'

CHAPTER IV

I ENTERED the turnpike at New Stanton and left it at Breezewood, picked up US 70 to Hagerstown, then 81 south to Winchester. The last lap was a short run on state Route 50 to Sweetbriar Falls, which is not far from Fairfax, Virginia.

I am one of those who love to drive, over any surface and in any kind of weather. Especially do I enjoy driving my black Merc, a car I acquired in lieu of a fat fee from a casino boss in Vegas. He'd had the car designed to run skim money from Vegas to silent casino partners around the country. To all appearances, the Merc is of 1960 vintage. But the power plant is from Mercedes, as is the four-wheel brake system and the suspension. The special racing tyres are custom made. In addition to the gun box concealed in the dash, it has a compartment the size of a suitcase under the floor of the trunk, where I keep other tools of my trade. Given the pavement and the nerve, you can run this Merc at 150 mph, a fact that has helped me stay alive on more than one occasion. I put the Merc through its paces on the run to Sweetbriar Falls and

reached Elaine's house at three-thirty that afternoon.

It was a two-storied fieldstone Colonial with green shutters. Two giant willows anchored down a lawn so well manicured you could have played pool on it. I parked behind a silver-grey Jaguar-XKE. There were two other cars in the open garage, so the Jag looked as if Elaine had company. Elaine opened the front door before I reached it. She was wearing green hostess pyjamas with flared cuffs and a snug waist. The outfit made her look willowy.

She took my hand and said, 'Morgan, thank goodness.' She drew me into the vestibule and closed the door. 'Listen, I know you said not to talk to anyone about this. But I've confided in Ralph's half brother, Alex Crittenden. He just flew into Washington on business from the West Coast, and he usually stays with us when he's in town. I had to tell him. He's the only family Ralph's got and a good friend.'

'You did right,' I said. 'I take it Ralph hasn't checked in.'

'No, and I've run out of excuses for his office. He makes all the big decisions there, and they're frantic.'

We went into the living-room. It was a long room, done in green and gold, with a brace of sofas in front of the fireplace and a really first-rate oil painting of Elaine above the mantel.

A tall, elegant man rose from one of the sofas. Elaine introduced us, and Alex Crittenden gave me a strong handshake. Lean and six three, he had the profile and the glitter of a matinée idol from a bygone era who had aged gracefully. He was damn handsome, with a California tan that looked as if it had cost a hundred bucks a square inch. His dark wavy hair had just enough grey in it to give it character. His dress was on the flashy side for the East: a powder-blue sports coat, shirt with magenta stripes, and a silk tie.

He said, 'What's this stuff about Ralph being involved in a murder? I want you to lay it on the line, Butler.'

'That was my intention, Mr Crittenden,' I said.

'I warn you in advance that I'll be a hard man to convince,' he said. 'I know Ralph. Crusty exterior, tough as nails in his business dealings, but a gentle man. Just not

the violent type.'

I almost fingered the tender spot behind my ear. 'Why don't you listen to my story, then we'll talk about it,' I said.

'First I'd like to know exactly what your position is in this,' he said. 'Oh, I know you were married to Elaine once, and she came to you when Ralph pulled his disappearing act. But what makes you an authority? Are you some kind of private detective?'

'I used to be. I'm kind of retired from that work now, but I always offer my services when an ex-wife has lost her husband.'

Crittenden's jaw tightened. 'Okay, we can dispense with the wisecracks. Ex-husband or not, you're still hired help in my book.'

'Alex, not another word!' Elaine moved in front of him. 'I confided in you because I thought you deserved to know about this. But I didn't ask you to take over. I have absolute confidence in Morgan, and you can either respect that or leave.'

He flushed beneath the gloss of his tan. Then he sighed. 'I'm sorry. I don't know why I had to throw my weight around. Maybe I couldn't stand the idea of him accusing Ralph of murder.'

'I haven't accused anyone of murder,' I said

'My apologies,' he said. 'Tell your story, Butler.' He flopped back into a corner of the sofa and lit a cigarette.

Elaine sat on the same sofa, and I occupied the one facing them. I gave them an edited version of the events that had occurred in Crafton, omitting such details as the phone call I'd taken in Maynard's cabin and the Atlantic City number I had pried from the phone company that morning. I didn't milk it for drama, but I had an attentive audience even before I told about me getting slugged. As I wrapped it up, I handed over the Crafton newspaper I had bought that morning. They sat close together on the sofa and read it. Crittenden finished first. He got up, gave Elaine a reassuring pat, and went to the bar in the corner for a drink.

Elaine looked at me across the paper. 'It's bad, isn't it? Ralph's gun is a Magnum. I've heard him call it that.'

'Not so fast,' Crittenden said. 'I agree that it looks bad for Ralph, but so far the evidence against him is flimsy. You don't know that Ralph was the guy who slugged you. You don't know his gun was the one that killed this Kelso. Even assuming it was, there's no proof that he fired the gun. It's all supposition, right?'

'That's right,' I said cheerfully.

'But why didn't he come home?' Elaine asked. 'Where is he?'

'Take it easy,' Crittenden said. Both his tone and face conveyed a stability he hadn't exhibited earlier. He said, 'Butler, I don't mean to play the devil's advocate, but I think you could have handled the situation better.'

'How?' I asked.

'Well, as I understand it, Elaine asked you to find Ralph and help him. So why didn't you approach him and offer your services when you found him? Why all the coyness?'

'Alex, I asked Morgan to do it that way,' Elaine said. 'I didn't want him to interfere until he knew Ralph was in trouble.'

'All the same, Alex has a point,' I said 'I played it cosy, and the whole damn thing blew up in my face. I might have nipped his moonlight excursion in the bud if I'd braced him earlier.'

Crittenden flashed his impeccable teeth. 'Butler, I assume you haven't passed any of this on to the authorities yet. Do you have scruples that will compel you to do so eventually?'

This guy's personality sanded mine like an abrasive. 'We all have a few scruples lying around gathering dust,' I said. 'You answer one. Assuming Ralph shot Kelso and can get away with it, is he a man who can live with that, knowing you two share the secret?'

Crittenden drew back. 'How the hell should I know?'

'Which brings us back to the starting point,' I said. 'We need a heart-to-heart chat with Ralph.'

'So we just wait for him to call or show up?' he asked.

I hesitated. 'Do either of you have any idea of where he might go if he wanted to hole up for a while?'

Crittenden shook his head, but Elaine said, 'I know a

place. Alex, I don't think you know this, but Ralph is building a summer cabin on your dad's old farm in Pennsylvania.' She turned to me. 'It's about a hundred and fifty miles from here, near Cumberland. Ralph's been doing all the work himself. It's not finished yet, but the roof and sides are on, and you could stay there.'

'Is there a phone installed up there?' I asked.

'Yes.' She went to a desk in one corner and dialled.

Crittenden said, 'Funny Ralph never told me he was building on the old homestead. Not that I blame him. It's great country.'

Presently Elaine hung up and returned. 'No answer.'

'Maybe we ought to run up there,' Crittenden said.

'No, I think he'd answer if he were there,' I said. 'He'd know it was Elaine. He has to talk with her sometime.'

Crittenden pounded his fist on the arm of the sofa like a judge with a gavel. 'I just can't see Ralph shaking in a hole someplace like a scared rabbit. He's too much man for that.'

'I agree,' I said. 'I think he went to a certain place to see some people. But I prefer to check this lead out myself.'

'*You* prefer?' Crittenden said. 'Where do you get off making a decision like that?'

My distaste for the man put a chill on my teeth. 'A man's been murdered, and your brother is the logical suspect. We don't know how soon the Crafton police will get a lead on him, but it's a good bet they will. Ralph may have left prints all over that cab. So you could have cops pounding on the door any minute. You can't tell them where Ralph is if you don't know.'

'What do you think we are, a couple of kids?' he said.

'Wait, Alex,' Elaine said. 'I don't think it's just the police Morgan is concerned about. Maybe it would be dangerous for us to know where Ralph is. Is that it, Morgan?'

She had always been a smart girl. I said, 'Remember, Ralph took pains to keep his movements secret. A man that cautious must have good reason. I know there were more people involved in that Crafton caper than Ralph and Kelso. Who and how many, I don't know. Until I find out, it doesn't cost anything to be careful.'

'I hadn't considered anything like that,' Crittenden said,

eyeing me with respect. 'If it's like that, I'll string along.'

'When will you go to this place you mentioned?' Elaine asked.

'Right away. I just stopped to bring you up to date.' I paused. 'And to make sure you wanted me to go on with it.'

'Why shouldn't I?'

I shrugged. 'The situation has changed. Yesterday it was a case of a missing husband. Today it's murder. I might turn up some facts you won't want to hear.'

'I don't care!' Elaine said. 'I mean to know about this. Maybe he's trying to protect me. Maybe he's afraid I'll think less of him because he's done something underhanded, or even something evil. But that's not the marriage I thought we had. Yes, I want you to find him, Morgan. Make him understand that he's not alone in this. Offer to help, if you can do it in all conscience. You see, I don't have any conscience about him. I don't care what he's done.'

There was no Joan of Arc mist in her eyes. It wasn't histrionics, but a declaration of faith. She lowered her gaze. 'You should eat before you go, Morgan. I'll fix something.'

Both Crittenden and I rose as she glided from the room, and it wasn't just good manners. Crittenden's expression was rapt, like the face of a man focused on a better vision of the world.

He said, 'Butler, I haven't formed an opinion of you yet, one way or the other. But you just lost a few points in character. You were married to that woman, and you let her get away.'

'I was having similar thoughts along similar lines myself.'

'Did you ever marry again?' he asked suddenly.

'No. But I don't give Elaine credit for that.'

'I wasn't implying anything. I brought the subject up because I'm getting married myself in a few months. To a rare woman, a lady, and I mean lady in the original sense of the word. She made a few films years ago. Maybe you've heard of her, Christine Mellon.'

'I never go to the movies,' I said.

'This will be the first time for me,' he said. 'And I'm fifty years old. Maybe I'm a little anxious about it.'

I wondered if his lady hadn't suffered a little by comparison with Elaine. I had to adjust my feelings about the man. Just as I was honing the edge of a hearty dislike for the guy, he goes human on me. 'If you were eighty, you'd be anxious,' I said. 'Marriage is one contract without guarantees in the small print.'

He nodded absently. I wandered over to the bar and found a bottle of bourbon damn near as old as I was. I swiped an ounce and sampled it. You didn't want to contaminate it with soda or ice. The phone rang. Elaine must have answered it in the kitchen, for a dark, nimble maid entered the room and said that the call was for Mr Crittenden. He took the call at the desk in the corner. I could hear the voice on the other end squawking through the receiver. Crittenden interrupted with some curt instructions about wining and dining the gentlemen of the press. Then the squawking erupted again.

Crittenden said, 'That's your problem. Your studio promised to deliver the little minx. You said this promotional commitment was in her contract. Now we've promised a lot of people that she'll be there, and by God you'd better deliver. Don't tell me she has to go to Acapulco to get laid.' He listened to some more squawking, then said, 'Damn her astrologist, her psychiatrist, and her mother! Get tough! I want that glossy bitch there Saturday night with her plastic smile and her celebrated chest on display. Remember, if we cancel out now, the word will get around that we dropped the film because it was a bomb. You'll be lucky to get it into the third-rate houses as the bottom of a twin bill.' He listened. He said, 'The hell you say. It's a bold, artistic, and earthy exploration of the twisted morals of our age only if it gets the kind of reception I've sweated blood to give it. It's art, buster, only if enough of the right people say it's art. Otherwise it's just another skin-flick. You'll collect your quarters in the grind houses, but not enough to pay for the silicone shots to keep that star's talent pumped up. That's no idle threat, Herman, that's the word.'

He replaced the phone and gave me a half-embarrassed smile. 'Some business. I'm a film distributor, in DC to set

up a big première for Saturday night. But you try to delegate responsibility, and the flunkies start ricocheting off the walls. That's why I flew out early. But now this business with Ralph makes the whole thing seem so damned trivial, I even have to fake anger.'

'You did a good job,' I said. 'Maybe you're in the wrong end of the business.'

'Acting? I've done that, too. In the thirties I was a Hollywood bum trying to crash the gates. I landed a few parts in the horse operas they used to shoot in the wild and woolly San Fernando Valley. I usually got knocked off in the first reel. Once I had the distinction of being gunned down by Buck Jones.'

Suddenly I had one of those spasms of memory that teach you humility. This morning while I was prying Kelso's long-distance calls from the man at the Crafton phone company, I'd failed to see the significance of a remark he had made. He said the police had already called for those numbers. I had taken him at his word. Now I was sceptical. It was unlikely that the Crafton police would have moved that fast, if they would have checked Kelso's calls at all. But someone else might have wanted those numbers. If that were true, they not only had the Atlantic City lead, they had this house tagged.

Crittenden was looking at his watch. He said, 'Damn, I really ought to run into the city for a couple of hours.'

'Could you put it off?' I asked.

He looked at me sharply. 'Why?'

'I think Elaine should have company for a while. I mean someone who will be suspicious of any strangers who drop around.'

'Do you mean she's in danger? Are you serious?'

'Yes. I think somebody got a lead on this house. There's a chance they also know as much as I do about Ralph's whereabouts. Which means I won't wait for food. Can you stick around?'

'If you say so.' He moved closer. 'Level with me, Butler. Are you holding information that might convict Ralph of that murder? Could you be trying to whitewash him for Elaine's benefit?'

'You're an odd one,' I said. 'When I walked in here, you all but accused me of trying to railroad him for the murder. You were sore about it. Now I'm trying to white-wash him, and you're still sore.'

He looked embarrassed. 'I guess you gave me a scare, and my imagination took over. Sorry. I just hate being in the dark like this about Ralph and whatever he's done.'

Just then Elaine entered the room. 'Potluck dinner in ten minutes.' She stopped abruptly. 'What's the matter?'

'I've decided not to stay for dinner,' I said. 'The quicker I get on the road, the quicker I'll be able to report back.'

Crittenden decided to assist my white lie with a smoke-screen. He stepped forward and shook my hand with an excess of heartiness. 'Butler, when you see Ralph, tell him I'm behind him, with money, influence, the works.'

'I'll tell him if I see him,' I said. 'But I don't guarantee anything. This is in way of being a long shot.'

Elaine's posture was intense, as if something hard and unfeminine had taken shape inside her. 'Maybe I should coax you to stay,' she said. 'But I want that report. Come on, I'll walk you out to your car.'

She slipped a hand into the crook of my arm and we walked out. Her grip tightened on my bicep. 'Morgan, when I came to you I didn't know it would be this bad. Is this what you meant by hazardous duty? Do you want to renegotiate the money part?'

'I'll charge you what it's worth when it's finished,' I said.

'You're a cynic, Morgan. Do you know the definition of a cynic?'

'I know one definition. A person who knows the cost of everything but the value of nothing.'

'That's it. Good luck.' She swayed from the waist. She was a woman who needed to be held, but I wasn't the man to hold her.

I backed out of the driveway, and before many miles had passed I realized that she had mentioned my fee for the same reason I had insisted on one in the first place— to keep this from being personal between us. We were both fakes. No amount of money could prevent it from

being personal. I didn't know her side of it, but after that sideshow of dreams I'd had in Crafton, I knew my motive. Years ago I had used her and abused her. I had battered her spirit and dented her self-esteem. So I was indebted to her. If I found Ralph Maynard, dusted his troubles off him, and tucked them both snugly back inside their marriage—maybe the debt would be settled.

CHAPTER V

I CHECKED into the Seabreeze Motel in Atlantic City at eight pm, with a .25 Mauser on my hip.

Indian summer or not, it was the off season in Atlantic City—mecca of the jolly conventioner and the wage slaves who swarm in annually with the little women and the kiddies for their two weeks of sun and surf. So I got the glad hand. A fifty-year-old boy in maroon livery trotted into the lobby with my bag. The desk clerk gave me a smile that all but caressed my wallet. With a straight face, he said that he just might be able to accommodate me even though I had no reservation. He flicked through his room cards and produced a room with an ocean breeze and a view of the motel pool. This time I registered under my own name. The bellhop got the key to 312, and we went upstairs.

The room had about as much personality as the inside of a refrigerator and a temperature to match. I turned down the air conditioner while the hop showed me how the closet door opened. He was bald, with savvy eyes and the name Stanley embroidered on his coat.

I peeled a ten-spot from my money clip and tossed it on the bed. Stanley gave me a sharp look. 'Hey, we don't hustle here.'

'Since when?'

His mouth twisted into a fishy grin. 'Since last month, when the bimbos migrated to Florida for the winter trade.'

'Forget that. That money isn't for a woman.'

'Oh, you want information.'

I showed him Maynard's picture. 'I'd like to know if this man is at the Seabreeze. He might be registered as Robert Mansfield.'

Stanley looked at the snap. His eyebrows twitched like nervous caterpillars. 'You think I'd milk for a lousy sawbuck?'

He knew he had what I wanted, so the price had gone up.

'I thought we could do business. Forget it.'

'Don't go huffy on me,' he whined. 'Maybe I should know why you're interested. I wouldn't want to get a guest in trouble.'

'All right. The guy's wife thinks he's stepping out on her. She thinks he came here to shack up with his girl-friend.'

Stanley looked sceptical. 'You wouldn't be trying to set up a frame, would you? We had one last year, and it damn near gave the boss another heart attack. What happened, this guy steps into the elevator one night, and this chick pops in to ride up with him. Frisky bit of fluff, wearing a white raincoat. Well, she sprains her ankle getting off the elevator, and this sap helps her into her room. Then she shed that raincoat—naked as a jaybird under it—and swarms all over that man. Bang, the door bursts open and two guys jump in, a private dick and a photographer popping flashbulbs. The chick was San Quentin Quail. They tried to hang a statutory on him.'

He told it fervently, his eyes glittering like motor oil.

'Nothing like that involved here,' I said. 'I just want to get a line on the man's girl-friend. His wife doesn't want a divorce. She just wants to get something on him.'

'Okay, I'll buy in.' He pinched the ten-spot and tucked it into his shirt pocket. 'Your boy's in four two two, one floor up, which is one reason I believe this shack-job story.'

'I don't get it.'

Stanley just watched me, working his jaw.

'You said *one* reason, which means you have two,' I said.

'Two is correct. And worth another sawbuck, believe me.'

I peeled off another ten. 'Tell it. COD, Stanley.'

'Okay. Him being on four is the clincher, because technically that floor is closed. The boss closes four down in the slack. So your boy paid plenty to get up there, like a man who wants mucho privacy.'

'That's one reason.'

'Here's the other. I think I've spotted his girl-friend.'

I had to play out the charade to keep him from getting suspicious. 'Tell me about her, and you've earned the ten.'

'What I thought. Well, she is *some*body's sweet bit of fluff, I kid you not. She checked in this afternoon, very smart, very dolled up—all by her lonesome, and arrived by cab. I also know this fluff was in the bar the same time as your boy tonight. I can't swear they were together, but you could check it out.'

I feigned excitement. 'What's her room number?'

'I don't know, but she's here on three. A glossy blonde, about five five and stacked. You can't miss her.'

'Stanley, it's a pleasure doing business with you.' I held out the ten. He gave it a tug, then looked up in surprise when it didn't come out of my grip. 'No working both sides of the street.'

'Never entered my mind, a cheap trick like that!' he said.

I released the bill. 'Good man. Stay pure, Stanley.'

He left. I unpacked the minimum and took a long shower to sluice away the grime and muscle fatigue from the long drive. Then I dressed in grey slacks, a dark-wine turtleneck, and a tweed jacket. I felt loose, nimble. I had hit Crafton three jumps behind the action. Here I felt less like an orphan.

The first order of business was to get the lay of the land. Dousing the lights, I opened the drapes and the sliding glass door, and stepped out to the balcony. The smell of salty sea spiced with kelp tingled in my nostrils. It wasn't wafted in on the breeze. It was part of the mist that dampened my face and made soft haloes around the amber lights on the balcony. The surf out beyond the boardwalk was a muted roar. Three floors below, the lighted pool was a rectangle of shimmering blue with steam rising from it. It was empty. Apparently the October chill

discouraged moonlight dips.

I prowled the balcony. It ran the length of the motel and down both sides. The deck chairs scattered around were all empty. In one corner was a closed staircase, which gave you access to the pool directly from the balcony. The heavy iron door to the stairway was unlocked. I climbed to the fourth floor. That door was locked, and it wasn't a lock you could slip with a plastic card. I went back down to three and found a door that led into the hallway from the balcony. I took the automatic elevator up to four. It stopped, the grillwork opened, but the accordion steel doors remained shut. Maynard had really bought himself a piece of privacy.

A prong of scepticism began to vibrate in my mind like a tuning fork. I descended to the lobby and stepped out. Stanley was sitting in a niche beside the desk. He raised his brows but I shook my head and went out through a door with a BAR sign above it.

The bar wasn't an integral part of the Seabreeze. You had to cross a narrow alley to enter the bar through a side entrance. It also had an entrance from Pacific Avenue, and a third entrance from another motel, the King Neptune. The place was about half full. Canned music caressed the eardrums, and the lighting was the kind that made most of the patrons look ten years younger than they were.

I parked at the bar and ordered a dry Martini and a steak sandwich. Then I went to the phone booth and called the Seabreeze. When the desk man answered, I asked for room 422.

He said, 'That room is unoccupied, sir. Who did you want?'

'What do you mean, unoccupied?' I said with a bluster. 'He said he was in four twenty-two. He checked into the King Neptune—'

'There's your problem,' the clerk said. 'You got the wrong motel. This isn't the King Neptune. This is the Seabreeze.'

'My mistake.' I hung up, not liking it.

While I was eating, Stanley eased into the waitress's slot at the bar and ordered a bucket of ice. He murmured,

'The fluff's name is Carol Mitchell. She's in three thirty, on your floor.'

'Good man. But how do you know my boy is in four twenty-two?'

He looked hurt. 'I saw him with my own eyes, is all. I took his luggage up at seven this morning when he pulled in.'

'You work long hours, Stanley.'

'Last night I worked a double, both the four-to-twelve and the graveyard shift. The regular night man is on a drunk.'

'Why didn't you tell me the fourth floor was sealed up?'

Anxiety pinched at his nose. 'But it ain't. Even if they lock the elevator door, you can use the stairway on the balcony.'

'That door is locked, too, Stanley. I want the key.

'No can do! That's getting in too deep for me. No, sir!' He scooped up his tray and took off.

I finished eating and went up to my room. Obviously Maynard's concern about security didn't include a fear of being seen, or he wouldn't have been loafing around the bar earlier. So it stood to reason that he was on four either because he feared that someone would try to get to him while he slept or because he wanted privacy for a meeting. I opted for the secret meeting.

Since no casual visitor to four could get up there by way of the elevator, I figured they would have to go up by the balcony stairs. So I doused my lights, opened the glass door an inch, and waited. I began the vigil at ten-fifteen. The visitors came at eleven.

There were two of them. They gained access to my balcony through the door from the hallway, three rooms north of my room. I heard footsteps on the concrete, and they passed through my field of vision in the fog, a broad man in a business suit and a shorter man in a trench coat. I couldn't see their faces. They mounted the stairs and I heard a key scrape metal. *They had their own key.*

I got up and stepped out to the balcony. The mist had become a briny cotton fog. Overhead, the footsteps came back down the balcony, stopped, and someone lightly

rapped on glass with a key or a coin. The
heard muffled voices, and the door closed

Just then I saw movement farther dow
I started down that way and saw a blun
swiftly past the yellow square of light from a ro
shape vanished in the fog. I walked down to where
first seen movement, with the .25 Mauser in my hand. I
came across a deck chair with a blanket on it. The cushion
was dry and warm. Warily, I went to the end of the balcony, turned the corner, and walked the width of the
motel. No sign of life. Apparently they had ducked into a
room.

Standing immobile in the fog, I fell into a brief trance,
absorbed with the sensation you sometimes have in a
dream, that I was re-enacting a prior event with different
furnishings, and if I knew the truth about that first one
I would be able to avoid the ugly consequences of this
one. A second later the hallucination passed. I'd had them
before and tended to distrust them. Yet an aftertaste lingered, making me prickly with apprehension.

I returned to my room and waited for an hour. When I
heard sounds overhead, I moved stealthily out to the spot
on the balcony beneath Maynard's room. A voice said
something unintelligible.

Another voice answered, 'Sit tight one more day, Ralph.
Send your wife a telegram. Tell her you'll be home Sunday.'

The first voice spoke more words I couldn't make out.

A third man spoke harshly. 'Screw your business! You'll
be out of business the way Kelso went out if we don't play
this right.'

They lowered their voices for more talk, then the sliding
glass door closed overhead and I heard the two men
moving back toward the stairway. I ducked into my room,
killed the lights, and let myself out into the hallway. I
sauntered to the elevators, pressed the down button, and
was standing near the hallway that led to the balcony
when I heard that door open. I was lighting a stogie when
a man hove into view from that hall, the one in the trench
coat. Apparently the other one had gone down the stairs to
the lobby.

I blew out my match and dropped it into a canister of white sand. 'Good evening,' I said. 'Hope you don't mind a little cigar smoke in the elevator. I thought I was making this trip alone.'

He smiled. 'No sweat. I'm addicted to the weed myself.'

I had a couple of inches on him, which made him five ten. He was a trim man who might have been any age from forty to fifty. His hair was cropped close to his head, dark brown and wiry, with grey at the temples. He had a tiny V-shaped scar on his left cheek. His smooth and muscular face set off his military bearing. He didn't look like any kind of hood—but, then, who does these days?

The elevator arrived and we dropped to the lobby. He gave me a curt nod and headed toward the garage exit. I was tempted to follow, but I would have been too conspicuous. So I went out the front entrance and stood on the sidewalk until he drove out on Pacific. He drove a new green Buick, and I made a note of his licence tag. Then I drifted back inside, alert for any sign of the other man. He didn't show. Maybe he was residing in the motel on another floor.

It looked like Maynard was bedded down for the night, so I had a nightcap in the bar and went up to bed.

CHAPTER VI

I WAS awakened by a sound I'd heard a thousand times but couldn't identify immediately—a hollow thonk followed by a vibration with more rattle than rhythm. It was nine am. I had overslept. On the farm we were in the fields by seven.

I heard the sound again. It was a springboard. I got up and opened the drapes. The balcony hid the pool from view, so I couldn't see who had gone off the board. I didn't care. I was focused on a man sitting on a chaise longue near the edge of the pool. He wore bathing trunks and sunglasses. It was unmistakably Ralph Maynard. Last night you couldn't get close to him with dynamite, and

now he sat taking the sun like any tourist.

I got dressed, tucked the Mauser into a pocket, and went out on the balcony. The swimmer was a girl in a blue shark-skin suit and a white bathing cap. She reached the ladder near the springboard and climbed out, high of breast, moving with that subtle undulation of the hips that teen-agers imitate but never achieve. She stood poised on the board, took the one prancing step, and did a half gainer that dropped her into the pool with about as much splash as a dime would make. It didn't bother her that she per-formed for an audience of one. I decided to make it two.

But the show was over by the time I got downstairs. The girl was parked on a deck chair across the pool from Maynard, peeling off her cap. Maynard was absorbed in a newspaper. He was one of those men with extra meat and muscle everywhere—on his jaw, his wrists, his chest, thighs, and calves. His black body hair glistened in the sunlight. I got close and said, 'Hello. Ralph Maynard, isn't it?'

His right hand twitched as if it might dart under a towel on the cushion beside him. Otherwise, his control was admirable. He said, 'Sorry, buddy, you've got the wrong man. We've never met.'

I perched on the chair beside him, the Mauser con-cealed between my hands. 'You're wrong, Ralph. We met at the Fort Duquesne in Crafton, when you gave me a lift from your cabin to mine. I needed help because you'd just sapped me. That jog your memory?'

The left side of his mouth peeled open, but again his poise took over. He made a show of sitting up. Now he had the hand under the towel. He said, 'You're talking in riddles, buddy. Suppose you identify yourself and state your business.'

'Before you get tricky with your right hand, look here.' I showed him the bore of the Mauser between my fingers.

'Jesus Christ!' he said in a hoarse whisper. 'Who are you?'

'Morgan Butler. I was married to Elaine once. She thought you were headed for trouble in Crafton and figured I might be able to help you. Obviously it didn't work.'

It was too much for him to digest in one lump. His face

looked bleached with the effort. He said, 'Morgan Butler? Why should she go to you? Wait! Can you prove that's who you are?'

I showed him my driver's licence and some credit cards.

'Yeah, she said you lived in Ohio,' Maynard said. His hand came from under the towel. 'I thought you were a farmer. What qualifies you to do what Elaine asked you to do?'

'I used to do detective work. Private stuff.'

'Damn, this is all I need,' he said. 'She shouldn't have meddled. Say, how did she know to send you to Crafton?'

I told him about the airline confirming his reservation to Pittsburgh, and about the old receipt from the motel in Crafton.

He gave a dry laugh. 'Done in by the businessman's bondage to the tax man. That was one scrap of paper I shouldn't have saved for the deduction. Now let me get this straight. Elaine hasn't seen you in what—ten years? And I'm supposed to believe you would run this errand just because she snapped her fingers?'

I could hardly explain the personal debt I owed her. So I snarled at him, 'Don't be an ass. I'm doing this for one reason only, coin of the realm.' I threw Elaine's cheque on his lap.

He looked at it and handed it back. His expression was bleak. 'You're like me, something of a bastard. She hasn't been very lucky with her men.' His words were tainted with self-loathing.

'Maybe we can make it up to her before we're old and grey.'

For some reason that hit Maynard where he lived. He lowered his head and raised it again. The flesh of his face seemed to sag from the bones. 'You made a crack about me sapping you in Crafton. Hell, I never even saw you over there.'

The words rang true, but there was something false about him, as if a smaller man cringed and leered within the big man's body.

'I'll tell about the sapping in its place,' I said. I gave him an account of my day in Crafton. This time I included

the phone call I'd taken in Maynard's cabin from Kelso.

'But there wasn't any professional help!' he said. 'That was a trick. I would know if they'd sent help.' His gaze flicked up toward his room, as if he recalled last night's conference.

'Maybe someone's not playing straight with you,' I said.

'What do you know? Damn, I wish she hadn't meddled in this.'

'Forget Elaine for now,' I said. 'I'm still curious about who laid me out and moved me back to my cabin that night.'

'It wasn't me,' he said. 'I didn't leave that restaurant until almost ten. My car and gun were gone, but you weren't in my cabin.'

'You claim somebody swiped your car and gun?'

'Yes. I had a feeling of disaster, corny as that may sound. I was supposed to meet Kelso at eleven in that parking lot where you saw us earlier. I tried to call him, but no luck. So I checked out, and took a cab to that parking lot. My car was parked exactly where it was supposed to be.'

'What time did you reach the car?' I asked.

'I can't remember exactly. I know—' His mouth went slack with incredulity. 'Christ, you don't think I killed him?'

'It stacks up that way. Your Olds came out of that valley not ten minutes after Kelso got shot. I saw it. Kelso got it with a three fifty-seven Magnum, probably your gun. Then a few hours later you broke into Kelso's office. Maybe you were after a piece of paper telling about a loan Kelso made to you three years ago.'

Maynard's features had hardened as he absorbed the punishment. 'I thought you were hired to help me,' he said in a flat voice.

'If you killed him, you need a lawyer, not a wet nurse.'

'I've got news for you, Butler. I don't need either one. Go back to Ohio and rotate your crops, or whatever it is you do. This is not advice, buddy. This is the word.'

I lit up a stogie. 'Maynard, if I quit a job every time I got threatened, I wouldn't have one nickel to rub against another.'

'You don't understand.' Now he had gravel in his throat.

D

'I'm firing you. I'll square it with Elaine later.'

I lashed out, 'You're on the spot, Maynard! I can tie you in with Crafton and Kelso. That watchman can identify you as the clown who tried to break into Kelso's office. Now you talk turkey to me, or I'll blow the whistle on you and your whole damn crowd!'

The belligerence faded from his face. 'What crowd?'

'The crowd you met with last night—the dapper guy with the scar and the big worried boy. Holding a council of war, weren't you?'

His face had the impassive cast of a man tuned to his innermost thoughts. He said, 'You won't turn me in. You wouldn't do that to Elaine. Tell me, how much of this does she know?'

'Most of it. She knows about Kelso, and the fact that you left Crafton smelling like something less than a rose.'

'How did she take it?' he asked.

'Like a trooper. Loyal to the bone marrow. Oh, yes, your half brother Crittenden was there. He's in your corner, too.'

'Alex would be.' He shook his head in wonderment. 'I never dreamed Elaine would send a bodyguard after me.'

'You should have checked in from time to time,' I said.

'Yeah. But now I'm worried about a wire I sent her this morning. I told her I'd dropped down here from New York on business and would be home Sunday. More lies, and she knows it.'

'Did you give her this address?'

'No, I didn't want her telephoning.' He took a deep breath. 'Butler, trust me a little. Go back to Sweetbriar Falls and tell Elaine you're satisfied that I'm innocent of that business in Crafton. Tell her I'll be home Sunday to explain. Do it, Butler.'

'No dice. I can't reassure Elaine in good faith unless I'm satisfied personally about Crafton.'

His eyes roved, brooding. 'I can't satisfy you without opening up the whole can of worms. Can't you see how it is?'

'All I can see is that you're in bad trouble, and it's far from over.'

'Trouble?' He snorted a savage laugh. 'Man, it's a nightmare.' He shifted, and I mean he shifted all over—his eyes, his gut, his hands. Even his jaws did a grinding act. Again I had the impression of a second person dwelling beneath his skin leaking deceit through his pores. He said, 'Let's make a deal. I'll tell you enough to convince you about Crafton. But I mention no names, and you can't tell anyone about it, not even Elaine. I need your word.'

'If I buy your story, you have my word. Now tell it.'

But at that moment a party of four bounced into the pool area, making enough noise for twelve. The two men were pushing fifty. They sported paunches and those comic straw hats with miniature beer cans and other doodads fastened to the crown. The two women were on the sunny side of thirty, but they shrieked like teenagers. They all did a circuit of the pool, the men chasing the girls with hoarse shouts. Finally the plumper of the women allowed herself to be caught, and the men wrestled her into the water. Across the pool, the blonde swimmer regarded their antics with distaste.

'Let's go to my room,' Maynard said. 'I could use a drink.'

'Fine, I'll carry this for you.' I scooped up his towel and the object beneath it, a .38 automatic with walnut grips.

'Trusting soul, aren't you?' Maynard said, leading the way.

We circled the pool, mounted the stairs, and he unlocked the steel door. When we reached his room, Maynard made a beeline for a fifth on his bureau. 'Does scotch suit you?' he asked.

'Too early for me,' I said. I thumbed the clip from his .38, checked the empty chamber and tucked gun and clip into a drawer.

Maynard slipped on a robe and sat on one of the beds. 'This trouble started over twenty years ago, just after World War Two. Kelso, myself, and a couple of other guys were working for a construction outfit in Texas—all young bucks a year out of the service. The company was building a factory in Mexico, just across the border. Kelso drove a cement truck, hauling the stuff from Texas down to the

factory site. One day he told us about a shady character who had offered to pay him to smuggle a package of heroin from Mexico in the cement truck. Kelso had turned the guy down twice, and he'd jacked the fee up to twenty thousand. So Kelso was willing to risk it, but he wanted the three of us to go along in case this character—let's call him Mr X—decided to pay off with a gun. We agreed to split the fee four ways.

'One of us rode in the truck with Kelso the night he made the run. The other two followed in a car. But Kelso had lied about why he wanted us along. He wasn't worried that he wouldn't get paid. He was afraid that a scheme he had hatched might fail to come off. This Mr X was already on the run from the federal law. This heroin deal was to be the big score that would let him hide out in style. Well, unbeknownst to the rest of us, Kelso had turned him in. The feds picked him up trying to cross the border. We'd already made the drop and picked up the money. We had two hundred grand to split instead of twenty. Fifty thousand, tax free, was a lot of money in forty-seven. We couldn't work up much sympathy for the crook we swiped it from—not after they put him away for twenty years.'

'And nobody worried about the day of reckoning,' I said.

He shook his head. 'Kelso was the only one he knew, and he didn't figure Mr X would trace him to Crafton, not after twenty years.'

'But Mr X found him.'

'God knows how, but he did. Last Saturday he got into one of Kelso's cabs and pumped the driver about his boss. The driver told Kelso about it. The cabby had dropped this guy at the trailer court, and Kelso spotted him there. Then Milt called me, and I went to help.'

'Yeah, you took a gun,' I said. 'Your buddy Kelso was armed with a shotgun and a thirty-eight. Did you plan to kill Mr X?'

Maynard had a lot of sweat on his face for a man in an air-conditioned room. 'We were prepared to kill him if it came to that. Hell, Kelso had him tagged as a psycho back in forty-seven. What would he be like after twenty years in prison? But I swear we didn't want to kill him. What we

really wanted was to buy him off. Kelso was in touch with those other two guys from Texas. We were each going to ante up fifty thousand. We thought the money would be more important to this guy than revenge. But we never got the chance to make the offer.'

'You think he tumbled to you, is that it?' I said.

'What else? From what you've said, I think he tailed me back to my motel on Wednesday afternoon. He must have waited in my cabin and slugged you by mistake. Then he dumped you in your cabin, took my gun and car, and went to meet Kelso. That way, he could frame me for Kelso's murder, and he'd have us both.'

'How would he know what time to keep the appointment?'

'That phone call! Suppose he had called Kelso and bluffed him into thinking he was sent to help us. Kelso would have told all.'

'It's possible,' I said. 'Let's go back to where you found your Olds in that parking lot that night. What did you do?'

'I drove up that road south of the trailer court, but I didn't take the dirt road. After that raid on my cabin, I was cautious. I drove up the hill and parked above the trailer court. I saw the cab down there and started down. Then I heard the shot.'

'Did you see anyone leave the cab?'

'No, too much foliage on that hillside.'

'What did you do?'

'I climbed back up and got the hell out of there. When I heard on the car radio that Kelso was dead, I went to his office.'

'What were you after?'

'It wasn't any document about any loan,' he said. 'I wasn't worried about what the police might find. I was afraid Milt might have left something that would lead Mr X to me or one of the other boys from Texas. But I never got past the watchman.'

'The other boys from Texas, were they your visitors last night?'

He hesitated. 'Yes, and we still want to pay this man

off. Maybe that strikes you as cold-blooded, after what happened to Milt. But we can't go to the police. Look at the fix we'd be in.'

I said, 'Maynard, I'm not here to persuade you to go to the law. But after Crafton, I think it's a mistake to try to negotiate with this man. I also think it's suicide for three businessmen to go up against a psychopathic killer. So why don't you bring me in on it—all the way in. I've had experience with boys like Mr X. Let me be your middle-man. I'll go up against him, if necessary.'

Maynard shook his head. 'My partners would never agree.'

I wasn't crushed at his refusal, but I'd promised Elaine I would make the offer. 'Tell me more about these partners of yours.'

'I trust them, if that's the point. Why do you ask?'

I shrugged. 'That call about the professional help troubles me. Suppose these buddies of yours didn't like the idea of paying off Mr X. Suppose they did send a gunman to Crafton to eliminate the one link between Mr X and them —Kelso.'

'And frame me in the process? That's crazy! Look, we're waiting now to see if Mr X did turn up a lead to one of us. We want to make contact and put our proposition to him.'

'Oh, he got the lead. He should have been here before me.'

Maynard jerked to his feet. 'Jesus, but I'm dense. I didn't even think to ask how you knew where to come.'

'Same lead.' I told him about the phone numbers I'd conned from the man in Crafton, and why I doubted that it was the police who had already taken the numbers. 'It means your Mr X has got a line on you personally. Home address, name, the works.'

'You knew this, yet you came up here instead of staying with Elaine? God damn you, Butler!' He was ready to swing at me.

'Take it easy. Yesterday I didn't know about Mr X. For all I knew, you shot Kelso. Besides, I tipped off Critten-den. He promised to stick around and guard the fort '

'But Alex can't handle a man like that. He's a killer!' He snatched the phone from its cradle, hesitated, then slammed it back. 'Butler, do me this favour. Go down to your room and call Elaine. Make sure she's safe. Then call me back. I've got to report this other business to my friends. You understand.'

'All right. But how do I get back to you? The switch-board downstairs denies that you're on the premises.'

'I'll call you,' he said. 'Come on.' He opened the glass door and led me down the balcony.

At the metal door I said, 'One more question. Why did you take a gun that time you went to Crafton to borrow money from Kelso?'

Maynard flashed a jerky smile. 'I was worried about a rule we laid down back in Texas. We were never to make contact, especially about money. There was always the chance that one would go broke and blackmail the others. But Milt didn't raise that old rule.' He had the door un-locked. 'Remember our deal. You lay off. After I call you about Elaine, you go back to Virginia.'

I nodded and stepped through the doorway. Maybe it was only the sensation of passing from sunlight into shadow, but I had an acute, chilling doubt that he would ever make it home.

I wouldn't dignify the feeling by calling it a premoni-tion. It was a gut reaction, and in my guts I was soured on him. For I hadn't believed a damned word of Ralph's story about the Great Heroin Caper on the Mexican Border. No more did I believe that four hard-nosed businessmen had agreed to hand over 200 G's to a psychotic ex-con because he waved a pistol at them.

CHAPTER VII

I never did reach Elaine in Sweetbriar Falls—because she was already in Atlantic City. But I didn't learn that until later.

The telegram Maynard had sent was all the incentive she

needed to make the trip. She had put in a bad night, and when the telegram arrived with the bald-faced lie about a business trip, she had to confront Ralph. She consulted with Alex Crittenden. Since they didn't know that Atlantic City had been my destination, it was easy for them to persuade each other that they had to find Ralph and warn him that his enemies knew his identity and his home address.

They took precautions to make sure they weren't followed. Crittenden chartered a private plane by phone, backed his Jag into the garage so they wouldn't be seen loading suitcases, and drove to National Airport by a circuitous route. They landed at Bader Field in Atlantic City around noon, rented a car, and checked into the Montclair, one of the grand old hotels on the boardwalk.

Then they set out to find Ralph Maynard. Using the telegraph office that had sent the telegram as a hub, they checked out every motel and hotel within a five-block radius. To cover the ground faster, they split up, each armed with a photograph of Ralph and the alias he had used in Crafton. Their plan called for them to meet at three to eat and map out more terrain to cover.

Not until after this meal did it occur to Elaine that I might be trying to get in touch with her. She called her answering service in Virginia and left word that she was at the Montclair. I didn't get the message until four-thirty, when I placed my seventh call of the day to her home. I made the call from a pay phone in the bar, where I'd gone for a beer and sandwich. I promptly called the Montclair, but all I got was another message—Elaine was out and due back at five.

I didn't go back to my room to wait for another call from Maynard asking if I'd made contact with Elaine. I'd had a skinful of his cloak-and-dagger tactics. Besides, my loyalty was to her, and I figured he could sweat it out the way she had. So I hiked over to the Montclair and waited for Elaine in the lobby.

The place had the flavour of musty elegance. A great many old people sat in the lobby, most of them stout old ladies with jewelled wrinkled hands, living on the insurance of the dearly departed. When Elaine entered at five-thirty

with her copper hair and elegant legs, she was vibrant motion in a drab place. I intercepted her, and she flashed me a wry smile. I saw fatigue in her eyes.

'You were going to wait until you heard from me,' I said.

'Ah, don't scold, Morgan. I've had a rotten day. If I'd known you were here, I wouldn't have come. Did you find Ralph?'

'We talked this morning. I'll give you a report in the bar.'

We entered the bar and found an empty corner booth. 'Make it a Bloody Mary,' Elaine said. 'I need the nourishment.'

While we waited for the drinks, she told me about her day.

'So Alex is here with you,' I said.

'Yes, he's been great, a real friend in need.' The drinks arrived. Elaine took a pull from hers and leaned close. 'Now tell me about Ralph. Don't spare me. I want the truth.'

'I don't know the truth. All I know is the fairy tale he invented to get me off his back.'

She paled a little. 'How do you know he lied?'

'Let's say his story put a great strain upon my credulity.'

'No sarcasm, Morgan. Please.'

'All right. His yarn was all about how he and three other guys chiselled a professional crook twenty years ago, and how this bad guy is now seeking revenge. It stinks to high heaven.'

I expected her to deny vehemently that Ralph would ever have chiselled anyone. Instead, she said, 'Why does it stink?'

'No crook would have set himself up the way Ralph told it. I know about this sort of thing. He lied.'

'Does that mean Ralph might have killed that man Kelso?'

'He denies it, and maybe he's telling the truth. But he admits that he's in big trouble, and it looks dangerous.'

'Did you offer to help him?' she asked.

I nodded. 'He turned me down. He's got help, a couple of old pals who are in this jam with him.'

'What kind of men are they?'

I shrugged. 'Ralph swears they're straight. He trusts them.'

Elaine lit a cigarette with ragged movements. 'What do you plan to do now?'

'Go back to the farm and husk corn in the sun,' I said.

She spat a stream of smoke from the corner of her mouth. Her face looked almost grotesque for a second. 'So you're quitting.'

'There's nothing to quit. Didn't I make myself clear? Your loving husband turned me down. He was adamant.'

'But a man's been murdered, Morgan! Doesn't that bother you?'

'Not unless Ralph killed the man. Do you think he did?'

She hesitated, then spoke in a husky voice. 'No, I don't.'

'Then you've got no prbolem. My advice is to go home. Whatever he's mixed up in, his need for secrecy is a part of it. He knows what he's up against and claims he can handle it.'

She seemed gorged suddenly with a coarse, brazen emotion. 'That's not good enough for me. To hell with you boys and your masculine mystique. I won't spend another night like last night. He lied to you, but he won't lie to me. Will you take me to him?'

Her passion was as strong as incense in the booth. I felt envious, enamoured. 'Sure, I'll take you. But what about Alex?'

'No problem. He just came in.' She signalled to him.

Crittenden may have been out pounding the pavements in a hot sun, but in a burgundy blazer and white turtleneck he still looked as if he'd just stepped out of a *New Yorker* ad. When he saw me, he said, 'I should have known you'd come to the right place. I trust you had better luck than I did. I feel footsore and foolish.'

'Morgan talked with Ralph this morning,' Elaine said.

'That *is* good news.' Crittenden sat down and ordered gin and tonic. As soon as the waiter was out of earshot, he said, 'Well, did Ralph explain that business in West Virginia?'

'Ralph pleads innocent,' I said. 'He said the killer was a character with a legitimate grudge against Kelso and him.'

'Who is this mysterious character?' Crittenden asked.

'Ralph wouldn't give his name. Nor did he give me the real story of how they happened to make him an enemy.'

'I don't understand,' Crittenden said.

'Ralph won't let Morgan help him,' Elaine said. 'He's on a very private mission. He wants to keep it a deep, dark secret.'

Her sarcasm was an astringent to Crittenden's cheerfulness. He scrutinized each of us and said, 'What's up? I feel like the gent who came too late to the party to get in on the fun.'

'You're just in time,' Elaine said. 'We're going to see Ralph.'

'Do you think that's wise?' Crittenden asked.

'Why not?' she said. 'We came up here to see him.'

'Yes, but we didn't know then that Butler had talked with Ralph. If Ralph is all that insistent about secrecy, we might foul him up by interfering. What say, Butler?'

'I made the same suggestion,' I said. 'The lady vetoed it.'

'That's right,' she said. 'I choose not to honour his secrecy.'

Crittenden shrugged. 'He's your husband. Butler?'

'I'm just hired help, remember?'

I paid the bill, and we took the elevator to the basement garage where Crittenden's rented car was parked. We all sat in front, with Crittenden at the wheel. I gave directions to the Seabreeze.

'The Seabreeze?' Elaine said. 'But I checked that motel out later this afternoon. They said Ralph wasn't registered.'

'They were paid to say that,' I said. 'Which is why I want you two to let me work on the desk clerk when we get there.'

They agreed, and when we reached the motel they took seats in the lobby and I approached the desk alone. The clerk was the same one who had checked me in, and he greeted me by name.

I said, 'I need your help in a small matter.'

'You name it, Mr Butler.'

'I've got a friend staying here incommunicado, in room four twenty-two. Maynard by name. He asked me to report back to him. So please call his room for me.'

The clerk's smile vanished. 'You must be mistaken about the room. This is the slack season, and our entire fourth floor—'

I slammed my hand on the desk hard enough to raise dust from an ashtray. 'Don't give me that song and dance! I was in his room this morning. Now hop on the board and call him!'

Suddenly a door jerked open ten feet down the wall and a big man in a wrinkled suit barked, 'What's the commotion, Frank?'

'Mr Duncan, I'm sorry,' Frank said. 'But Mr Butler here insists that a friend of his is on four. I've told him that's impossible, but he's absolutely belligerent about it.'

'I'll talk to him,' Duncan said. 'Come into my office, Mr —Butler, is it?' He ducked back inside, leaving the door ajar.

I gave Elaine and Alex the hold sign and followed Duncan into his office. He was already behind his desk, ensconced in a black leather chair. He was a beefy man with thin black hair and a blotchy complexion. He wheezed with each breath.

'Sit down, Mr Butler,' he said. 'Frank's a good desk man, but tact is not his long suit. Now what seems to be the problem?'

I recognized his voice. I had heard it while standing on my balcony in the fog. No wonder Maynard's visitors had had their own key. I sat across the desk from Duncan and took out a stogie.

'Sorry, have to ask you not to light that,' he said, tapping his chest. 'Had a coronary occlusion last spring. Fancy term for heart attack. Now they tell me I've got a touch of ephysema.'

'I'll bet they told you to stay out of the pressure cooker.'

Duncan gave me a patronizing smile. 'Why, do you mean to put me in the cooker?'

'You're already in it, Duncan. You were in a sweat last night, but your blood pressure must have really started to

percolate after the news Maynard gave you this morning.'

Duncan tried the smile again, but it was sickly. 'So far, you're talking Greek, buddy. Who's Maynard?'

'Save the bluff, Duncan. I saw you boys visit Maynard last night. Hell, Ralph must have told you about me. Why the dumb act?'

He drummed his fingers on his desk, then gave it a whack. 'Okay, so I know Ralph Maynard. So he came to town on a very hush-hush business deal, a transaction in which I am involved in a small way. So I stashed him on the fourth floor, where he could conduct this business on the QT. Now what's all the fuss about?' There was a hardness beneath the beef I hadn't detected earlier.

'Is that your story?'

'What's the matter with it?' he asked.

'Didn't Ralph tell you who I am?'

'Why should he?' He looked confident, and that bothered me.

'Suppose you call Ralph down here,' I said.

'Like to oblige, friend, but Ralph checked out an hour ago.'

'Where did he go?'

'He didn't say. Home, for all I know.'

'You're a liar, Duncan. You know where he is. You boys are stuck together in a deal, all right, but the adhesive isn't money. It's murder. You were very articulate on the subject last night. Remember? You told Ralph he'd go out of business the way Milt Kelso went out if he didn't play this right.'

Duncan flushed to the colour of burgundy. He took some deep breaths as if he needed them. 'The doc tells me to be patient, but you're an irritating bastard. You'd better scram.'

'When you produce Maynard, I'll leave,' I said.

'We'll see about that!' He put a hand on the phone.

'Call the law,' I said, grinning. 'I'll tell them a tale that will get them on the teletype to Crafton, West Virginia.'

'Now who's bluffing?' he said. 'You won't shoot your mouth off because you're working for Maynard's wife. She'd get sore.'

'You're wrong, Duncan. Elaine Maynard is sore enough right now to call in the militia. She's out in the lobby. Shall I bring her in? Of course then she'd know you're part of the conspiracy.'

In an icy, bitter voice, Duncan suggested that I perform an anatomical impossibility. Then he said, 'Oh, Christ,' jerked open a drawer, and came up with a pint of bourbon. Uncapping it, he took a belt with a practised flip of the wrist. 'That's the one drink I'm allowed each day.' He offered me the bottle. 'Drink up.'

The plastic smile that accompanied the gesture turned him into a caricature of the jolly innkeeper oiling a guest's ruffled feathers. A thought glided through my mind like a buzzard's shadow. If this is the calibre of Maynard's team, he's in a bad way.

'No, thanks. Listen, Duncan. You must know I'm no threat to you and your crowd. Maynard must have briefed you.'

'Some briefing. You were supposed to go home and hold his wife's hand. Instead, you show up with the wife foaming at the mouth.'

'It couldn't be helped,' I said. 'Maynard sent her a telegram, and she came looking for him.'

'But she doesn't have to find him. Tell her he took off for parts unknown. It's for her own protection. Use your head, man!'

'It's too late for that,' I said.

'Damn women! Well, I'll have to call first.'

I clamped a hand on the phone. 'No calls. We go upstairs.'

'He's not upstairs. He's at my house in Pearl Beach, a few miles south. I have to set it up. There's another man involved.'

I took my hand off the phone. 'All right, go ahead.'

He lifted the receiver and dialled. After a long time, he thumbed the receiver and dialled again. We sat through a dozen rings.

'This better not be a stall, Duncan.'

'Something's wrong,' he said. 'I tell you, they weren't

supposed to leave the house.' His face was splotchy and worried.

His concern made my scalp prickle with the same sensation of alarm I'd experienced on the balcony the previous night when I suspected that someone else was spying on Maynard. Now it made sense. I had felt that I was re-enacting the events in Crafton—while I stalked Maynard, we were both being stalked by a third party.

'We'd better run down to your place,' I said.

His eyes were hot. 'You're thinking of what happened to Kelso, but you're wrong! McCloud and Maynard are both armed and ready.'

McCloud. I filed the name. 'Then why don't they answer?'

'You're right. Let's go down there. But can't we leave Maynard's wife out of it?'

'She goes. Maynard's half brother is here too. He goes.'

'Jesus, Butler. Okay, but play it my way. Tell them the yarn I tried to sell you—Maynard's in town on business, and I have a piece of the action. Will you do that much?'

'It's a deal.' I didn't add that I preferred it that way.

'One more thing. You and I go in my car. They can follow.'

'All right. Come on.'

'Wait, have you got a gun?' He took a .38 revolver from his desk and tucked it under his belt. His jaw was resolute, his gut sucked in, and his shoulders back. A gun will sometimes do that for a man, especially if he rarely handles them.

'I'm all right.' I wasn't armed, but he didn't have to know.

We went out to the lobby. Duncan nodded to Elaine and Alex and stopped at the desk. I crossed the room and briefed Elaine and Alex, describing Duncan as he had requested. I added that Duncan had allowed Ralph to move his base of operations to Duncan's house, which was only a few miles away.

At once Elaine said, 'Are we going down there?'

'Right now. I'll ride with Duncan. Alex, you fall in

behind when we come out of the garage.'

'It's your show,' Alex said.

Duncan joined me en route to the garage and ushered me into an orange Porsche. He over-revved the engine and lurched out of the garage, travelling south. He picked up Atlantic Avenue at Albany and tooled through Ventnor and Margate. Alex stayed close behind. It was early dusk. I had glimpses of the sun at every intersection, a dazzling red ball ready to dip into the ocean.

'Two more blocks,' Duncan murmured.

Then I saw a puff of black greasy smoke bloom in the sky to our left, accompanied by a red glow that was not part of the sunset. As I started to speak, a dirty white Dodge camper came hurtling out of a sidestreet ahead of us. It was travelling too fast to make the right turn with ease, but the driver fought through the turn. The tyres squealed as the back end skidded across the double yellow line, then shimmied back where it belonged. Duncan swerved his Porsche unnecessarily. I had a glimpse of the driver of the Dodge as we passed. He had a white, pasty face, like a man startled by the sudden exposure of a flashbulb up close.

'What the hell's the matter with him?' Duncan asked.

'There's a fire down that street,' I said. 'A big one.'

'Hey, that's my street!' He geared down for the turn.

Now the flames were licking high above the roof of the last house before the beach on the right side of the street.

'Jesus H. Christ, that's my place!' Duncan said.

CHAPTER VIII

It wasn't Duncan's house that burned so spectacularly. It was his garage. Tar shingles gave off the black smoke, and glowing embers shot upward a good fifty feet, endangering the house. The garage door had been blown off its hinges. There was a car inside, burned black, a jagged hole where the gas tank had been.

I saw all this as Duncan skidded to a stop across the street from his house. A dozen people had emerged from

their homes and stood in stilted postures along the block. As we clambered from the car a man yelled, 'Mr Duncan! I've called the fire department.'

'Good man!' Duncan bellowed, peeling off his jacket. He had the presence of mind to jerk the .38 from his belt and wrap it in the coat before he flung the bundle into the car. 'My house will go if we don't get water on that roof,' he said.

The heat was terrific. Even at forty yards it shrivelled the skin on your face. 'Get your neighbours to hook up their garden hoses,' I said. 'Get as much water on your roof as you can.'

'Right! What about you?'

'I have to check on your guests.'

He seized my arm. 'Do you smell what I smell?'

'Yes. We'll work out a story later. Now get cracking.'

Alex's rented car was parked a few cars back. I trotted back there as Elaine got out of the car.

She said, 'Is that Duncan's house? Is Ralph in there?'

I grabbed her and manhandled her back in the car. 'Shut up and listen. The law will be here soon, and this could get messy. I don't want you two involved until I know the score. Alex, take her back to the hotel and sit tight until I call.'

'No, Morgan,' Elaine said. 'Please.'

'Get going, Alex, while you can still get off the street.'

I could hear the lusty wail of a siren very close. Alex backed into a driveway to make his turn. I crossed the street at a run. A random stream of water sprayed me as I bounded up the porch steps. The interior of the house was cooler than outside, but the popping and cracking from the fire was intensified. Light from the flames threw a gaudy pattern on one wall. There wasn't much smoke. Nothing in the living-room looked out of place.

I started toward a doorway, when I saw the parallel tracks in the nap of the rug. They came from behind an easy chair and led down a hallway. I looked behind the chair and saw a throw rug where none should be. I looked under it. The bloodstain was about the size of a skillet and still damp. I dropped the rug and followed the heel tracks

E

left by the guy who had shed the blood when he was unceremoniously dragged from the room.

The tracks led down the hall to a room containing a pool table and other sporting equipment, then across the waxed floor to a door that gave access to a patio. A glass panel in that door had cracked from the fierce heat just beyond it. But I'd passed a bedroom where I'd seen luggage on a bed. I backtracked and stepped inside. It was Ralph Maynard's luggage—the suitcase and attaché case I'd seen in the motel in Crafton. I hurried back to the game room and took a better look through the glass panel on the door.

The side of the garage was a wall of flames, but there was a dark hole in the wall where the side door led into the garage. I could just see into the car. A black, charred figure of a man sat upright in the front seat. I spotted two objects on the flagstone between the house and garage. One was a man's shoe, curled with the heat. The second object, a man's wallet, was much closer. Water was dripping from the eaves of the house now, and the wallet lay only a foot beyond where the water hissed on the patio.

I opened the door, jumped out there, grabbed the wallet, and scampered back inside. The heat had seared my face like a whip lash. I opened the wallet on a table in one corner. The plastic cardholders had melted, and the edges of the currency were singed. But some credit cards were still intact. It was Ralph Maynard's wallet.

I heard quick, hard steps, and Elaine entered the room. 'Morgan, where's Ralph?' she asked in a sharp voice.

I got up, shielding the stuff on the table. 'I told you to get back to your hotel. Where's Alex?'

'Parked around the corner. Morgan, I have to know!' She pulled a cute manœuvre and grabbed one of the cards from the table. 'That's Ralph's wallet. Where did you find it?'

'Outside. But it doesn't prove anything.'

'You're a liar! He's in that garage. I can smell him.'

'There's a body in there, but we don't know who it is.'

She yelled something, but I didn't hear her because a siren split the air with a roar that made the floor tremble.

I grabbed her by the elbows. She jerked violently once, then sagged against me. She said tonelessly, 'He's dead, isn't he?'

'It looks that way. Now will you get out of here?'

She shivered once and locked icy fingers around my wrist. 'I knew it was evil. I knew he would never make it home.'

'Wait a minute.' I stuffed the cards back into the wallet, went to the door, and tossed the wallet back outside.

'Why did you do that?' she asked.

'I want the police to find it the way it was. Now, come on.' She moved rigidly, but she let me guide her down the hallway. Heavy boots thumped on the front porch, so I made a left turn through the kitchen and out a side door. A walkway led to the street.

'Why can't you go back with me?' Her voice was sulky.

'I have to see the police. Maybe I can piece this together.'

Her mouth twisted cruelly. 'What difference can it make?'

The street was a tableau of ornate fire equipment, through which men in hip boots and black slickers moved briskly, unrolling flat white hoses. A fireman shouted orders through a bullhorn. No one paid any attention to us as we moved up the street.

I gave Elaine a shake. 'Listen, when you get to the hotel, call your answering service at home. Tell them not to answer your phone for any reason. Can you remember that?'

She nodded. 'Morgan, come soon.'

'As soon as I can make it.'

I watched her out of sight, then crossed the street and made a circuit of the fire apparatus, looking for Matthew Duncan. I found him propped against a tree on the lawn across the street from his house. His heels were dug into the turf, his fist pressed against his chest, and he sucked air in grotesque parody of a fish.

I hunkered down beside him. 'Duncan, what is it?'

He whistled through his teeth. 'Angina pectoris. Partial blockage of an artery. My dynamite's in the car. Get it, Butler!'

'What dynamite?'

'Nitroglycerin pills. Glove compartment.'

'Hang on there.' I ran across two lawns to his Porsche, found the bottle of pills, and trotted back. Duncan extended a hand palm upward, and I shook one tiny white pill into it. He slipped the pill under his tongue and leaned back.

Behind us the crowd made a noise like an audience at a fireworks display, and I turned as the roof of the garage collapsed. A second later the first hard, bright stream of water shot out from the firemen's hose, making a thonking noise when it hit the car. The corpse would be a wet cinder before they finished.

'Butler, what's the score over there?' Duncan asked. His voice was surprisingly firm and his colour was better.

'That stuff works fast,' I said.

'We don't call it dynamite for nothing. Give, man! Who roasted in that car?'

'The evidence points to Maynard. Whoever did it shot him in the living-room, dragged him to the garage, and built a fire.'

'Mother of God.' He took a deep breath. 'What about McCloud?'

'No sign of him. I do know this. McCloud drove a Buick from your motel last night. That car in the garage is a Ford.'

'Maynard was driving a Ford, a rental.'

'Was McCloud's Buick a rental?' I asked.

'Yes. He flew down in his own plane.'

'From where?'

'Never mind. We'll get to that later.'

A patrol car pulled up behind the fire engine. Two officers got out, and the fire chief began to give them an earful. No doubt the chief had smelled plenty of cooked meat in his time.

'We've got to have a story for the law,' I said. 'Who did it, Duncan? Who are you men really afraid of?'

'I can't tell you that.'

I leaned close. 'If Maynard's dead, I don't have anyone to protect. So you'll tell me, or I'll talk to the police. You choose.'

His eyes looked oily, slitted. 'I didn't mean I wouldn't tell. But later, man, later. We haven't got time to open that

ball of wax for the police. We have to concoct something.'

I gave it some thought. Lying to the law is an ill-advised luxury. Usually I give them all the truth I can spare, holding back only those scraps that might incriminate me. They may later find my story incomplete, but never inconsistent. Consistency pleases them.

'Here's our story,' I said. 'Forget McCloud for now. If they find his body under a bed, he's a stranger. Can you do that?'

'Yes, but I doubt if he got McCloud. Mac's too good.'

'Yeah, I remember the build-up you gave him and Maynard.'

'Okay, so he tricked McCloud away from the house.'

'I can think of one other possibility,' I said.

He shrunk back. 'You're crazy! Mac wouldn't kill Maynard.'

'Forget it. Here's what you tell the law. Ralph Maynard is an old buddy. He called you the other day and said he needed a place to hole up, to avoid being served a court summons. You trusted the guy, so you hid him on your fourth floor.'

'Not half bad,' he said. 'That gets me off the hook with the staff. But how do you figure in it?'

'I'm Mrs Maynard's ex, from years gone by, which is true. She got worried when Ralph disappeared. She found the name of your motel scribbled on a pad, so she called the motel. But they denied Ralph was registered. Then she asked me to run up for a look. I got in last night and talked with Ralph today by the pool. He told me a different story from the one he told you, but you and I didn't have any reason to compare notes until later.'

'What story? Oh, that business about the Mexican border.'

'Yes. By the way, was there any truth at all in that yarn?'

He gave a sickly grin. 'Maybe ten per cent.'

'You owe me the other ninety, remember. I mean to collect.'

'I gave my word, didn't I?' He looked insulted.

By then the fire was pretty well out and they were easing

the big truck off the street. A tow truck headed into the street.

'Here's the rest of our story,' I said. 'Maynard was irked that I had flushed him out. He asked you for a new cubby-hole. You sent him here to your place. When I came by this evening I put pressure on you by telling you the tale he'd told me—about this hardcase gunning for him. That scared you enough to make you agree that we ought to have a talk with him. Have you got all that?'

'Yes, but what about the wife? Do we mention her?'

'No, she's out of it. I don't want them talking with her.'

'I only hope they buy the story,' Duncan said.

'We'll find out soon enough.'

Across the street, the tow truck was dragging the Ford and its grisly cargo from the garage.

CHAPTER IX

WE got to tell our story fifteen minutes later, seated around Matthew Duncan's dining-room table. We told it to Jim Cunningham, chief of the Pearl Beach police, a big, raw-boned redhead with pale-blue eyes and a grip like a crimping bar. He was dressed in civvies.

After introductions, Cunningham sat down and began to fiddle with a tape recorder. He said, 'I hope you gentle-men will tolerate this contraption. I've got a lousy memory.'

But we were interrupted by a patrolman who stuck his head in and told Cunningham that the lab crew and ambulance had arrived. Cunningham went into the living-room. I listened as he gave specific instructions to the lab crew. He was also very particular about how he wanted the ambulance spotted on the lawn. By then I was wishing we had rehearsed our story better.

Cunningham was unlike any cop I had ever met. There was not an ounce of bluster, grimness, or cynicism in his make-up, and he exercised his authority without effort. He had the size and the slightly battered look of a man who had played pro football for a dozen years, say at line-

backer, and had retired in his prime to take up police work. His manner implied that it was tame stuff but enjoyable if you didn't take it too seriously. He was neither jolly nor patronizing, but his hardness was tempered by an amiable quality that put you at your ease. I guessed his age at forty-five.

There was something else about him that troubled me. I couldn't shake the feeling that I knew the man, that I'd served with him in a war or in San Francisco. But I didn't actually recognize him, so I decided it was just his style, that his mannerisms reminded me of someone else.

Presently Cunningham returned and got the tape recorder working. He put the mike in the middle of the table and had us confirm the fact that we had reached the scene after the fire had started.

Then he said, 'We've got a nasty piece of business here. Let me lay it out for you. There's a body in that car outside. Mr Duncan, it looks as if the victim was shot in your living-room, then stashed in the car before the fire was started. We've also got luggage and a wallet that might belong to the victim. Did you have a houseguest, Mr Duncan?'

'Yes,' Duncan said. 'A man named Ralph Maynard, an old friend.'

Cunningham nodded. 'The luggage and wallet belong to Maynard. Suppose you tell me how he happened to be here, Mr Duncan?'

Duncan told his end of it convincingly. His agitation was genuine, and his speech was flavoured with the incredulity of a man to whom fate has dealt a swift one below the belt. His voice weakened near the end. 'So I thought everything was on the up-and-up, until Mr Butler showed. Should I tell what he said about Ralph?'

'We'll let Mr Butler tell that,' Cunningham said.

'Well, it made me uneasy,' Duncan said. 'So when I couldn't raise Maynard on the phone, I thought we'd better run down here.'

'What time did Maynard leave your motel to come here?'

'Five o'clock, I would say.'

'And Mr Butler showed up at what time?'

'Maybe six-thirty.' Duncan looked at me, and I nodded.

'I'm troubled by Maynard's motive for moving from the motel,' Cunningham said. 'You say that he feared Butler might reveal his whereabouts to someone who would serve him with a court order. Didn't that strike you as flimsy reasoning?'

Duncan wiped sweat from his brow. 'Ralph was a respected citizen in his neck of the woods. You wouldn't doubt his word.'

Cunningham fired a quick one. 'Was he afraid of Butler?'

Duncan looked astonished. 'No, nothing like that. He seemed annoyed that Butler had found him, but he wasn't scared.'

'It seems to me you went to an awful lot of trouble for this old friend, considering that you haven't seen much of him in recent years,' Cunningham said. 'You did say that, didn't you?'

'Yeah. But back when he was single, he used to take his vacations up here, and we'd go out on the town.'

'Maybe you used to fix him up with one of your shady ladies?'

Duncan squirmed. 'I don't mess with that stuff anymore.'

'Correction.' There was iron in Cunningham's voice. 'You *do* still work the skin trade, but you do it within the rules laid down by my colleagues up the beach.'

Duncan shrugged. 'That's got nothing to do with this.'

'Maybe not, Mr Duncan, but let's keep the record straight.'

For a moment the only sound was the hum of the tape recorder. Then Duncan said, 'Look, I'm a little under the weather.' He fingered his chest. 'Had an angina attack outside a while ago. If you're done with me, could I lie down in my room?'

'By all means, Mr Duncan. Should you call your doctor?'

'No, all I need is a Librium and a little sack time.'

'You go ahead.' Cunningham raised his voice. 'Sullivan, Mr Duncan's going to his room for a rest. I don't want him disturbed.'

Duncan mumbled his thanks and left the room.

Cunningham gave me a smile. 'Maybe I shouldn't have

made that crack about the ladies of ill-repute. Duncan's motel is in a convention town. He couldn't stay in business if he couldn't give certain customers the right phone number when they get the itch. That doesn't make him a pimp in my book, but he does have to abide by the rules. One rule specifies that his tarts don't cross the boundary into Pearl Beach. Two years ago a woman on this street raised a stench because Duncan had one of his shady ladies living here in his home. We leaned on him, and she moved out.'

'So maybe you thought Maynard didn't come to the house alone.'

He grinned. 'The way Duncan told it, Maynard seemed awfully touchy about his wife finding out where he was. That, Mr Butler, is your cue. I'd be grateful if you'd start with your address and occupation.'

I complied, then I spoke my piece as I had outlined it to Duncan. I began with a lie. I told him that my divorce had been an amicable one and that Elaine and I had retained an interest in each other's welfare over the years. So when Ralph had been missing for three days, she had called and asked me for help.

When I had finished, Cunningham gave his head a shake and said, 'You're a hard man to focus on, Butler. Oh, I had you down as an outdoors man. You've got that kind of tan, and your hands are horny enough. But I wouldn't have guessed you a farmer.'

'Why not?'

'Oh, manners, bearing, polish. I would have pegged you a construction engineer with one of the big outfits, at home in the field in a hard hat but also at your ease in the better hotels.'

'Sorry to disappoint you.'

'I can bear up under it,' he said. 'There's something else that troubles me about you. You didn't put on an act.'

'I don't get it.' Like hell I didn't.

'Well, the average citizen seldom gets involved in a murder. When he does, and he has to tell me about it, you get one of several reactions. Their jaws unhinge and they blabber. Or they become very earnest and sincere. Or

they run scared, tell you nothing, then suddenly decide they need a lawyer. When I don't get one of these standard reactions, I figure either that the citizen has been in my line of work, or he's worked the other side of the street. Murder doesn't rattle him, and he's glib with the law.'

I took time out to light a stogie. I don't think Cunningham even blinked his eyes. He didn't have to. He had exceptional presence, and I could feel its weight. 'All right, I served sixteen years in the Marine Corps, resigned as a captain. That's where I got the spit and polish. Later I worked for the DeBlanc Detective Agency in San Francisco. They trained me to be glib with the law.'

'I know the DeBlanc organization,' he said. 'Years back when I was in another line of work, I spent some time on the Coast. High-powered outfit, as I recall. Plush offices, well-heeled clients, good pay. And you gave all that up for the plough?'

'I'm a simple guy at heart.'

'Yeah, just a country boy.' An odd smile flirted around his mouth. 'Well, this explains why Mrs Maynard might ask you to investigate her husband's disappearance. So he left home on Sunday. By Wednesday she's in a sweat, and that's when she finds his gun missing. She has a lead to the Seabreeze but can't get any co-operation over the phone. So you come up to check it out.'

'That's right.'

'Tell me what troubles me about that, Butler.'

'You're missing four days. Maynard left home on Sunday, but he didn't check into the Seabreeze until Thursday.'

He nodded. 'Any idea where he spent those four days?'

'Maybe he was holed up someplace else in Atlantic City.'

'That won't wash. Maynard's car rental contract was in his luggage. He rented that Ford at the Philadelphia airport Thursday morning. Nice bit of coincidence, him showing at the Seabreeze just hours ahead of you. When that was your only lead.'

'Don't you believe in coincidence?'

'If they don't get too frequent and too convenient,' he said. 'What kind of handgun did Maynard's wife say he was packing?'

'She didn't say. You know how women are about guns.'

'Did you ask Maynard about his gun this morning?'

'I did. That's when he told me that story about him and his pals chiselling that hardcase on the Mexican border years ago.'

'What did you think of that story?'

'Pure fabrication. But I don't doubt that he was scared.'

'Scared, on the run, and armed. You being a friend of the family, why didn't you offer to help him out of his scrape?'

'I did. He insisted that he could handle it. All he wanted me to do was go back to Virginia and lie to his wife.'

'But your loyalty was to her. You told her the full story, and she gave you this ultimatum to give to Maynard.'

'That's right. I didn't get in touch with her right away. She'd taken some sleeping pills and had the phone turned off. When I did contact her, she blew her top. I was to tell Ralph to call her, or they were finished, kaput. But I never saw him again.'

He sat absolutely still, as if he were listening to music. Then he said, 'Tell me the part you've left out.'

'What part?'

'You're a professional. You came down here looking for a man. The garage was on fire and the stench in the air wasn't autumn leaves. You didn't just sit on the lawn and wait for us.'

A guy this good could make you nervous. 'Yes, I looked around. I saw the bloodstain, the heel tracks, the luggage and wallet.'

'You looked in the wallet?'

I didn't have to admit that, but I did.

'Then you told Duncan. Is that when he had the angina attack?'

'No, he was already racked up with that when I reached him.'

He listened to a few more bars of his private music. Then he said, 'Okay, you've had time to think it over. Any conclusions?'

'A couple.' His asking my opinion put me a little off balance. 'If that body was burned to make identification

impossible, it was careless of the killer to leave the wallet and baggage behind.'

'What else?'

'Well, that was a big bloodstain, but nary a drop of blood between those tracks in the hallway. I doubt if the killer wrapped the body to keep from spoiling the hall rug. So the victim must have been dead for a while before he was moved.'

'Now add it up.'

'It's not Maynard, but we're supposed to think it is.'

'Either that, Butler, or it was staged to make us jump to that conclusion, so we'd beat the brush for Maynard.'

'That's a little too thorny for me without more proof.'

'For me, too,' he said. 'But I don't like the other version either. Suppose someone was gunning for Maynard and followed him here from the motel, but Maynard got lucky and won the shoot-out. There are plenty of things you could do with a body besides burn it. He could have run it out to the swamps. He could have waited until dark and dropped it off a pier. Why burn it?'

'I don't know.' An idea stung me. 'Of course, all this is so much hot air if the body didn't burn beyond recognition.'

He looked pleased. 'All too true. Okay, you know Maynard. Got the stomach for a look at the remains?'

He was full of tricks. 'Why not?'

'Let's go.'

I followed him down the hall and out the back door. They had rigged up two arc lamps in the yard, and they gave plenty of light. A couple dozen charred studs were all that was left of the garage. A few blackened bottles and cans floated in several inches of water inside the garage. The Ford had been dragged halfway down the drive, and the ambulance was parked at right angles to it, blocking the view from the street. They had thrown an old tarp over the stretcher from the ambulance, and the body was on that. The ambulance driver and a patrolman were standing near the arc lamps, upwind of the body, for the breeze was coming in from the sea. A medical man in a loud sports coat was leaning over the stretcher.

The dead do not disturb me. They say that in war you

never get used to the dead, but they lie. Oh, I know it is
customary for the young men to come home from the war
and, when asked the inevitable whispered questions, to
insist that they never adjusted to the dead. But they are
merely laying claim to their humanity. It's my experience
that most men didn't worry much about the dead. Once a
man dies, he is gone, and what is left is so much cold meat.
You can mourn the passing of the man if you knew him
and cared, but to get sentimental about his carcass or
squeamish about what the nasty shell did to it seems to me
misplaced emotion. So I wasn't upset by what was on the
stretcher, and I saw no reason to stage an act for Cunningham's benefit.

The smell wasn't bad, because they had sprayed him with
a preservative. My first look answered the question I had
posed to Cunningham—he was impossible to identify. You
couldn't even tell if it was a man or woman. All you had
was black and red seared flesh oozing body fluids of various
colours.

'It looks too small to be Maynard,' I said. 'He was over
six feet and husky.'

The doctor said, 'They all shrink in that kind of heat.
The car seat was saturated with gasoline. Tremendous heat.'

'Any chance of identification through his teeth?' I asked.

The doctor snorted. 'Very little. No bridgework.'

'How about a lodge pin, stuff in the pockets?' I asked.

'Nothing but a few coins,' he said.

'If size means nothing, I can't help you,' I said.

Cunningham shrugged and we went back inside. The
chief paused in the living-room to talk to a man and when
he joined me asked again if I had seen Maynard's gun
when I talked with him.

I grinned. 'So you found the slug?'

'We found two. The one on the easy chair was hardly
damaged. Answer the question.'

'All right. Maynard didn't deny that he had a gun, but
he didn't show it to me. We didn't discuss the make.'

'Think about that description you got from Mrs Maynard. Could she have been describing a three fifty-seven
Magnum?'

My surprise must have shown.

'Means something, does it?' he asked.

'Just that a Magnum is a lot of gun. Two cannonshots like that. The whole neighbourhood must have heard them.'

'You'd think so, but just five people heard them. None of them thought they heard gunshots, unless you count the old geezer who thought it was a shoot-out on the TV his kids were watching. Two different women thought they heard firecrackers. A couple of boys throwing a football on the beach decided they were backfires. And none of these people can place the time accurately. Between five and five twenty is the best I can do.'

'But Duncan said Maynard didn't leave the motel until five.'

'Even so, Maynard could have hustled down here before five-twenty and got himself shot.'

'Or in time to do the shooting,' I said.

'That makes me wonder just whose side you're on, Butler.'

'No side. When murder happens, I take a position of strict neutrality. I don't owe Ralph Maynard that kind of loyalty.'

'But what about Mrs Maynard, who used to be Mrs Butler?'

'Do you think I'd try to cover for Maynard for her benefit?'

'Suppose it was Maynard who roasted,' he said cheerfully. 'You might feel duty-bound to find out who did it on your own.'

'I'm not that dumb. What could I do in a week that you and your men couldn't accomplish in a day?'

'But what if the widow asked you? As a personal favour?'

His blue eyes were as innocent as a choir girl's.

'So you think there's more between Elaine and me than I've told.'

He said nothing. He was all blue eyes.

'Maybe you think she hired me to kill him for his insurance.'

He still gave me the silent treatment. There always

comes the time with a cop when he deliberately makes you simmer, then waits for you to boil.

'All right, I've sat here and let you play on me like a harp for over an hour. I don't mind the melody, but the lyrics have gone sour. If you don't like my story, hold me while you check it out.'

He chuckled. 'No offence meant. But you'll have to admit that you went to a lot of trouble for an ex-wife after ten years. I don't run into that kind of loyalty every day.'

'You don't meet women like Elaine Maynard every day,' I said.

'I don't doubt it. Besides, I did check you out, and you look good. You were seen going into that bar off the Seabreeze at four. You had a sandwich and a beer. You placed a call on the pay phone around four-thirty.'

'Another effort to get in touch with Mrs Maynard,' I said.

'I have to buy that because the switchboard gal at the Seabreeze confirms that you tried to call the lady six times today. Okay, that call in the bar didn't light a fire under you. You had another beer, left the bar, walking, about four-forty-five. See how it gels? You could watch Maynard's room from yours. So he had to wait until you were out of the way before he could move from the motel. Of course, I'd like to be able to account for you between five and six-thirty, but you can't have everything.'

'I told you I took a stroll on the boardwalk and finally raised Elaine Maynard on the phone after six.'

'That's the one piece I can't confirm,' he said. 'We haven't been able to raise the lady at all. We've tried several times.'

'Maybe she's out to dinner,' I said. 'Hey, are you going to hit her with this before you know who the victim is?'

'That is a problem,' he said. 'Actually, it might be better for you to break this to her. I'd hoped to talk with her before you did, but the only way I can make that happen is to hold you. I've decided against that. Come on, I'll run you back up to the Seabreeze. I want to have a look at that room Maynard occupied. They haven't cleaned it up yet, which could be a break.'

I got to my feet. 'What about Duncan?'

'He's dead to the world. I think he took something stronger than a tranquilizer. Christ, he's got enough drugs in his medicine chest to open a pharmacy. Let's go. I need the fresh air.'

CHAPTER X

Two reporters and a photographer were camped on the front lawn when we came out. Cunningham parried a couple of questions, then told them that the man who had burned in the car was presumed to be a houseguest of Mr Duncan's from out of town. But they hadn't made positive identification, so the houseguest's name was being withheld to avoid alarming his next of kin.

The tallest reporter made a sound of disgust. 'Come on, Jim. You can do better than that. What about the shooting?'

'We believe the man was shot,' Cunningham said. 'But I never anticipate the coroner's report. Tomorrow I'll give you the full picture. If we decide he was murdered, you'll know about it.'

'Maybe it was suicide,' the short reporter said with a sneer. 'The guy shot himself, then cremated himself to save funeral expenses.'

'I don't know you,' Cunningham said, a chill in his voice

'I'm Foster, AC *Sentinel*,' the man said.

'Where are you parked, Foster?' Cunningham asked.

'Blue Chevy over there.'

'You're in a fire zone. Move it.'

'In a minute. Listen, I want—'

'Move it now, little man.' Cunningham had lowered his voice, but his words rang like hailstones on a tin coffin.

Foster hesitated, then turned and went down the walk.

Cunningham addressed the other two. 'You men know I don't give out facts until I'm sure of them.'

'Sure, Jim. We understand.'

The pair moved aside as the chief and I walked down to his car, an unmarked Plymouth. He headed north on Atlantic Avenue.

He said softly, 'Where do they get the notion that any clown with a press card can make a cop roll over and do tricks?'

'Some cops worry about their press notices,' I said.

'Not in Pearl Beach. Not lately. Those TV newsboys have the same arrogance. Had an armed robbery suspect last year. The TV boys thought they could stick their camera in his ear and treat him like a freak on display. I taught them otherwise.'

He said, 'Will you stand still for a personal question, Butler?'

'Go ahead.'

'You served sixteen years in the corps and resigned a captain. Why didn't you stick four more years and take that retirement pay?'

'I couldn't cut it anymore,' I said.

He changed lanes and passed a bus. 'Why did you quit DeBlanc?'

'Same reason.'

'So you retired to the farm. Nothing but ploughing the old furrows and bringing in the sheaves. Quite a change for you.'

'Sometimes I listen to the corn grow.' This wasn't just small talk. There was an inconsistency in me that bothered him. 'My turn to ask one. What kind of work did you do before Pearl Beach?'

'Government work. Mostly overseas.'

'CIA?'

'No, a different outfit. Not that well known.' His tone implied that it would not become better known through him.

'You retired pretty young yourself,' I said.

He chuckled. 'I'm like you. I couldn't cut it anymore.'

Then I had an idea about him. Pearl Beach was his farm. In this suburban resort village he cultivated the tranquil life, spiced with just enough challenge to allow him to exercise his talents in a mild way.

F

I wouldn't have had this notion about him if he hadn't been so persistent about the exact nature of my retirement. Nor would I have had it if I hadn't experienced that feeling of kinship from the beginning. In dismissing it, I had misread him. That battered look wasn't from pro football. It was the look of a man who has gone to remote places and done work that was dangerous and dirty and not in the least romantic. And done it for a long, hard time. No wonder he made me uneasy. Oh, he had good manners and some quaint ideas about human dignity, but I didn't want him for an adversary.

Cunningham parked in the garage at the Seabreeze and we entered the lobby. A slender man in civvies rose from a chair and gave the chief a nod. Cunningham introduced him as Evans, Atlantic City homicide. Evans said he had a man watching Maynard's room and they could go straight up. Cunningham asked if I cared to join them.

'Not me. I need a drink, a bath, and a meal, in that order.'

'Fair enough. I hope you plan to stick around for a while.'

A left-handed way to give me an order. 'You know I do.'

They left, and I crossed the alley to the bar. I didn't need the drink. I'd just had enough of Cunningham for a while. The bar was doing a brisk business, the Friday night crowd. I found an empty stool and ordered bourbon.

I hadn't lied about wanting food and a bath, but first I had to see Elaine and Alex Crittenden. It was after nine, which meant they had been waiting three hours. I paid my tab, wheeled around, and almost collided with the desk clerk from the Seabreeze.

'I've got a message for you!' he said in a hoarse whisper. 'I'm to give it only to you.' His fist was clenched between us.

'Relax and hand it over,' I said.

'I'm just doing my job. I don't want any trouble.'

'You won't get a kickback, Frank. Give.'

He slipped a paper into my hand and said, 'You can reach him at that number on the hour or half hour, until ten tonight.'

I started to offer a tip, but he said, 'No money. Call it

loyalty to Mr Duncan. I take it he's all right?'

'He's fine. Taking a nap. You know about the fire?'

He nodded, edging away. 'Good evening, Mr Butler.'

I opened the note. It said. *Enjoyed our chat by the pool. Call me.* The phone number wasn't familiar, but since I was to call at a specified time, it was probably a pay phone.

I felt no great surprise to learn that the charred corpse in Duncan's garage was not Ralph Maynard. For some hours now I had suspected that this Atlantic City kill was Crafton, West Virginia, repeated—with only the furniture and the geography changed.

It was too early to make the call, so I decided to call Ralph from a phone on the boardwalk en route to the Montclair. I went out to the street. The night was cloudy, balmy with the kind of breeze that often means rain. It was only two blocks to the boardwalk. By the time I reached it, I knew I was being followed.

I turned right on the boards, the wrong direction for the Montclair, and paused occasionally at a store front to get a peripheral view behind me. He was there, but I couldn't get a good look at him. He anticipated my stops and blended into the crowd, or dropped behind one of the electric carts in which old folks rode majestically down the centre of the boards. But I got an impression of a slender, quick man, and I thought of Evans, the cop Cunningham had introduced me to.

I gave my tail a quarter mile of brisk walking before I found what I wanted, a pier on the seaward side which had a flight of steps leading down to the beach about twenty yards back. A building on the pier would shield me from my shadow's view long enough to get me down the stairs. I halted at a store front, which made him stop, waited for a clearing in the throng, then moved across the boards, behind the building, and down the stairs. When I hit the sand, I trotted back under the boards, turned right, and jogged for two hundred yards. There I found an exit to a side street, walked into the garage of a big hotel, crossed the pavement, and took the elevator to the lobby. It was nine-thirty.

I found a bank of public phones and dialled the number

on the note from Ralph Maynard. He answered after the third ring.

'Butler?' His voice was hoarse, guarded.

'Yes.'

'I want to know what happened with the police at Duncan's house,' he said. 'The desk clerk said you were down there.'

'That's right. Who burned in the car, Ralph? McCloud?'

'Did Duncan give you that name? Has he talked?'

'Only to me, and not much of that. Who killed McCloud, Ralph?'

'He was dead when I got to the house. I swear it!'

'But you stashed him in the garage and burned him, didn't you?'

He hesitated. 'Yes, I did that.'

'Why? The killer must have known who he killed.'

'That's just it, he didn't. Except for Kelso, he didn't know us. And Mac didn't have any ID on him. He had his wallet hidden in his car, as a precaution.'

'So you grabbed the chance to get this killer off your back.'

'Yes! He had a lead on me, remember? So I burned McCloud.' His voice cracked, but he said, 'Did the cops buy it?'

'They're reserving judgment. But your fire was a success, Ralph. McCloud is not much more than a cinder.'

'Shut up, damn you! I had to do it. You don't know.'

'There's a lot I don't know. For instance, why was McCloud so easy to kill? Didn't you warn him that Mr X was in town?'

'Yes. But McCloud didn't even get his gun out. I don't see how he could have got to Mac like that. Broad daylight, too.'

'Who, Ralph? Let's have his name.'

'I can't tell that. You say Duncan didn't talk?'

'We invented a yarn for the police.' I filled him in on that.

He said, 'Thanks, Butler. Listen, do me another favour. I need money. I left my credit cards in my wallet.'

'Don't be stupid. Turn this mess over to the law. The

head cop on the case is a good man. He'll listen.'

'After what I did to McCloud? Sure he will.'

'So you committed a rash act. You'll get a slap on the wrist. You've got to stop running some time. Where will you go?'

'I've got a place to go—don't worry. But I need money.'

'But two of your friends are dead now. If you're clean, come in for your own protection. That old crime can't be that bad.'

'The hell it isn't.'

'I warn you, I may have to tell the law all I know.'

'Do you think that's a threat to me? Sweet Christ.'

'What about Elaine? Does she deserve this treatment?'

'No, but that won't work either. What about that money?'

'All right. I'll get it. Meet me later tonight.'

He was silent for a while, then he said. 'Forget it. I don't trust you enough. So long, Butler.' He hung up.

I called the Montclair. Crittenden answered the phone.

'Butler, it's high time. Where have you been?'

'Sweating out a police interrogation. How's Elaine?'

'She's bearing up. Say, did you confirm—'

'Not now. I'm on my way over there.' I hung up.

Ten minutes later I rang the bell of suite 815 at the Montclair. Alex opened the door. He was in shirt sleeves, solemn as a deacon.

Elaine was standing near the windows. She wore a dark-blue lounging outfit and held a highball glass. There was a rigidity about her posture and her face looked brittle. She said, 'Hello, Farmer Butler. I hear you were oh so clever with the nasty police.'

Alex shrugged and said, 'She's had a few, and she won't eat.'

'But I'm not drunk,' she said. 'A certain memory has a very sobering effect. I keep thinking of what you told me down in the bar, Farmer Butler. You said Ralph knew what he was up against and that he could handle it. Remember?'

'He did pretty well,' I said. 'He didn't burn in that fire.'

Alex said, 'Are you sure?'

'Absolutely. I just talked with Ralph on the phone.'

Elaine lost her balance, took a quick step to catch it, and settled carefully on the edge of the sofa. 'Morgan, I'm so sorry.'

'You were right to rap me. I haven't done much of a job.'

'But what good news!' Alex said. He was animated and wore a smile. 'It's like having a weight lifted.'

Elaine lost her balance, took a quick step to catch it, and settled carefully on the edge of the sofa. 'Morgan, I'm so sorry.'

Elaine lifted her chin, her eyes brilliant with moisture. 'But if Ralph wasn't the one who . . . died, then who was it?'

'One of Ralph's partners,' I said. 'A man named McCloud.'

'But if the police know that, then what do—?'

'The police don't know the victim was McCloud. Let me fill you in from the beginning. First, the owner of the Seabreeze, Matt Duncan, is another of Ralph's partners. I learned that this evening.'

'Did he tell you what this trouble's all about?' Alex asked.

'No. He was reluctant to talk about it, and we were crowded by the law. I'm supposed to get the story from Duncan later.'

'What did you tell the police?' Elaine asked.

So I told them the story Duncan and I had concocted for the law. By the time I'd finished, Alex's elation had faded. 'That Magnum again,' he murmured. 'Do you think Ralph shot McCloud?'

'He says not. All Ralph did was drag the body out to the garage and start the fire.'

'You're crazy!' Alex said.

'He admitted it. He claims this killer doesn't know his victims by name. So when Ralph walked in on the body, he saw the chance to pass the victim off as himself.'

Elaine said, 'But what a ghoulish thing for Ralph to do.'

'But a smart move,' I said. 'It could keep the killer away

from Sweetbriar Falls. He wasn't thinking only of himself.'

She made a sharp negative gesture. 'Don't try to justify him to me. What a hellish thing to put me through.'

'Take it easy,' I said. 'He's scrambling for his life. He can't worry about consequences. In fact, he left his credit cards behind. He's in need of money.'

She looked at each of us in turn. 'So you think I'm being selfish?' We said nothing. She caught her lower lip between her teeth. 'Maybe I am, but how could he burn that man? Everything he's doing is turning him into a stranger. That's what I can't bear.'

Alex moved closer and said, 'How long can Ralph get away with that stunt he pulled? Is this McCloud liable to be missed?'

'He'll be missed,' I said. 'He's a man of substance. He even flew down here in his own plane.'

'From where?'

'Duncan wouldn't say. Wait. Ralph won't leave town until he's briefed Duncan on the facts.' I picked up the phone and dialled.

A hearty voice answered. 'Officer Sullivan, Pearl Beach police.'

'Sullivan, this is Butler. I left with the chief tonight. I'm calling to check up on Duncan. Is he up and about?'

'Still out. Probably for the night.'

'Are you going to baby-sit?' I asked.

'Jim wanted the premises covered. Guess I'm elected.'

'Fine. If Duncan wakes up, tell him I called.' I hung up.

'Duncan's under police guard. But we can get a fix on McCloud. His plane must be at Bader Field, where you two landed today. Maybe I'd better run out there.'

'Let Alex do it,' Elaine said. 'He has to fly back to DC tonight, then on to the Coast. He's neglecting his business.'

'To hell with that,' Alex growled. 'My business can suffer. I can't run out on Ralph. And I certainly can't leave you alone.'

'But, Alex, I heard you on the phone today,' she said. 'You stand to lose thousands if you don't get back. Besides. I'm hardly alone. Morgan will help me cope.'

Alex gave me a rueful smile. 'Butler, I didn't mean that you weren't reliable. I guess I assumed you were calling it quits.'

'I can't. A cop gave me a personal invite to stick around.'

'And you forget, Alex, Morgan's getting paid,' Elaine said. 'Even if he hasn't given very good service for the money so far.'

The rudeness of her speech was tempered by a look she gave me that spanned twelve years. It was at once whimsical and shrewd. She knew we had substituted the money for any strong emotions that might arise between us, but she knew it was the emotions she could rely on.

But Crittenden responded to her words. 'Hey, I thought that line about you being hired was a gag. Do you mean to say that money changed hands?' He looked like a gourmet who had sipped bad wine.

'Yeah, I really am hired help. But the fact is, I'm officially involved and you're not. I think you should go take care of your business. We'll keep you posted. Tomorrow I have to produce Elaine for this cop. If you're here, you'll have to go under his guns.'

'Do you think I can't fool him?' Alex said.

'That's not the point. I've kept you out of this because Elaine and I may be watched. Suppose Ralph tries to get in touch. I told you he needed money.'

'Oh, I get it. I'd be able to help. Yes, that makes sense.'

'Then you'll go?'

'Yes. How should I handle that business at the airfield?'

We decided that he should pass himself off as a friend of McCloud's. He would say that McCloud was ill and had to leave his plane at the field longer than planned. Alex would offer to pay the hangar fee. Having established his honesty with the colour of his money, he would ask for McCloud's home address so he could send a telegram to McCloud's wife. Alex took his bag and departed.

Elaine said, 'Was I out of line with that remark about money.'

'I got the message. I admit the money's a fraud.'

'So you are doing this for auld lang syne?'

'Do you think anyone else could have lured me away

from that field of corn? We farmers take our harvest seriously.'

'I suppose you think I asked that question out of vanity?'

'No, you're worried about what this might cost, aside from money.'

'Oh, please! Now who's vain?'

'All right. We've talked four times. Each time you've made a pitch about how devoted you are to Ralph. I'm beginning to wonder who you're trying to convince.'

She took a hard drag on her cigarette but said nothing.

I said, 'Tomorrow Chief Cunningham will be very curious about how things are between you and Ralph.'

She snubbed out the cigarette. 'Should I tell the truth?'

'Why don't you try it on me first.'

'All right. For the first three years it was a fine marriage. Then Ralph began to change. Bizarre as it sounds, I associate the change with his financial success. Oh, he was doing well when we got married. But he didn't get into the big money until that real-estate deal paid off, about two years ago.'

'How did he change?' I asked.

'Small ways at first. He began to show flashes of cynicism. He ridiculed people and ideas I thought he respected. He would lash out at someone without provocation, a waiter, the gardener. He was hardest of all on people who deferred to him because of the money. There were times when I thought it was the money he held in contempt. But that's silly, when you consider how hard he worked for it.'

'How about you? Was he harder on you?'

'No, I was exempt. Here's something else. It was about then that he started building that cabin in Pennsylvania. It was supposed to be a hobby, something he did for pleasure. Well, last summer we took a week of our vacation up there, living in a camper. We'd planned to spend most of the time swimming and fishing. But he worked twelve hours a day on that cabin. He mixed concrete, cut pipes for the plumbing. He had blisters on his hands, sore muscles, but he wouldn't stop. It wasn't a pleasant thing to watch.'

'You have had a rough time of it lately.'

'Yes, but not so rough that I've wanted to call it quits.'

Her eyes brooded. 'Morgan, I could use another drink.'

'No, you could use some food. We have to rehearse your story for Cunningham. I don't want you hung over when you face him tomorrow.'

Her mouth softened into a demure smile. 'All right, I'll eat. I never could anaesthetize myself with booze anyway.'

She got a menu and asked if I would join her if she ordered the crabmeat salad for two. I said yes. She called it in and went into the bedroom. The phone rang, and I answered it.

'Butler, Alex Crittenden. Listen, it worked like a charm. I've got McCloud's address.'

'Fine. Give it to me.'

I jotted it down. The name was Robert T. McCloud, the address on East 73rd Street in New York City. 'Good work, Alex. You all set?'

'Yes, I take off in five minutes. I'll call you tomorrow.' He paused. 'Damn, I still feel as if I'm running out on Ralph.'

'What could you do except help us sweat it out?' I said.

'Okay, I'm convinced. You do well by Elaine, you hear?'

'Scout's honour.' I hung up.

Presently the waiter arrived with the tray. He had scarcely departed when Elaine emerged from the bedroom. Her face looked pink and healthy, as if she had scrubbed it with cold water.

She said, 'I'm ready for my nourishment and my lesson.'

She served the salad at a table near the windows. I began by telling her exactly what I'd told Cunningham; then we ran through her side of the story. It was midnight when we finished. By then she had eaten her share of the salad and was on her second cup of coffee. We had moved to the sofa, and she was smoking.

She said, 'You told Cunningham one lie I wish had been true.'

'Which one?'

'That part about us having kept in touch over the years, because we were interested in each other's welfare.'

'Why?'

'Why do I wish it were true? Well, I would have made that visit to your farm five years ago when I was tempted. I needed your blessing for the pending nuptials. I was troubled by the fact that the love I felt for Ralph was different from the way it was with us.'

'Maybe it was only the difference between twenty-two and thirty.'

'Yes, that was my rationalization.' She averted her face. 'Well, all of this must sound very girlish and foolish.'

My curiosity about her was as intense as if she were a stranger. 'Not at all,' I said, rising. 'But I'd better go.'

She tossed a skein of hair from her eyes and rose in one motion. Her posture was awkward, her mouth crooked and lovely. I seized her wrist and pulled her close. She was no stranger. The kiss was warm and intimate, full of an old, familiar sweetness. When it ended, she put her head on my shoulder and said, 'This is no good.'

'Speak for yourself. Personally, I found it very stimulatting.'

'No, I meant that I'm vulnerable with you. With other men, my marriage is my armour. It doesn't work with you. Maybe because we were married once.' She extricated herself and retreated to the sofa. 'But that kiss cheered me up considerably. Do you mind?'

'No, it's a service I offer my more attractive clients.'

She smiled. 'You can't cheapen it. It was spontaneous and warm and I needed it. But I do think you'd better go now.'

'Yes. Get your sleep, and remember your lines for to-morrow.'

CHAPTER XI

THE phone in my room at the Seabreeze began to ring as soon as I entered. I answered it.

'Butler, Jim Cunningham. Hope I didn't wake you.'

'Not at all,' I said. 'You work late.'

'Only when I have a murder case as tricky as this one. Listen, I called to ask if you'd made contact with Mrs Maynard.'

'Yes. She'll be up tomorrow.'

'What did you tell her?'

'Just that Ralph was missing again. I didn't want to give her the full brunt of it over the phone. Did you make the body yet?'

'Nope. Okay, see you tomorrow.'

'Hold on. Did you put a tail on me tonight, by any chance?'

'No. Somebody bird-dogging you?'

'Maybe I imagined it.'

'Not you, Butler. You would make sure, one way or the other. Which raises an interesting question. Who would want to tail you?'

'A mystery to me. All he got was a tour of the board-walk.'

'Didn't you shake him?'

'Why should I?'

'No reason. See you tomorrow, Butler.'

I replaced the phone, stripped down, and took a long shower. Afterward, I was still too keyed up for sleep, and I had to admit that a steamed libido was partly to blame. I could still taste Elaine's special flavour, and I had more than a few erotic memories of that woman gone nimble and sultry with passion.

So I poured myself three fingers of Jack Daniels, put on slacks and a sweater, and retired to a chair on the balcony. Beneath the mist that had moved in you could feel the chill and threat of rain. I thought of the farm. By now Johnny King would have finished cutting the corn. One rain wouldn't hurt it in the shock. But several days of drizzle, and it would begin to mildew. I shrugged that out of my mind and began to think about Ralph Maynard.

The remarks Elaine had made about his behaviour troubled me. What do you do with a man who slaves for twenty-odd years to get into the chips, then despises his success? It was poor testimonial for the American Dream. I groped for my glass beside the deck chair and heard the

clop-clop of wooden sandals on the balcony.

I caught a flash of bare legs in the panel of light thrown on the balcony from a room down that way. Then she materialized out of the mist, a brunette of medium height in a white beach robe. She had a towel over one shoulder and a swimming cap dangling from one wrist. I hadn't expected traffic along the balcony, so there wasn't much clearance between my chair and the rail. That didn't bother the girl. She said, 'Hello, there,' sashayed through sideways, and clopped on down the pavement. A moment later I heard the thonk and rattle of the diving board.

She swam twenty minutes without a break. She did the crawl, the backstroke, and one lap of the butterfly, which can take it out of you. The scene had an ethereal quality— the blue-lighted pool with steam rising from it, and the sleek creature moving effortlessly through it. Maybe it was her style, but suddenly I recognized her. She was the girl who had swum that morning, then sunned herself while I talked with Maynard. But this morning she had been a blonde.

Finally she came out and sat on the edge of the pool. She threw her head back to jerk her cap off, but she held it in an awkward position too long. She was looking for me, but from her angle I wasn't exposed against the light. I waved. She waved back.

That exchange gave me an idea about her. Soon I heard her on the metal stairs. The sandals beat their tattoo down the balcony but faltered when she entered my light. Her face glowed from exertion. 'Hello again,' she said.

'You're very good. That takes a lot of stamina.'

'I'm afraid I overdid it a little. I got a chill.'

'You need a hot bath and a stiff drink,' I said.

'The bath's a cinch, but not the drink. No room service after midnight.' She made a movement as if to depart.

I took my cue. 'Join me for a nightcap. I'm all alone.'

She hesitated, giving me an earnest appraisal. 'I'm tempted. So am I alone, although that wasn't the way I'd planned it.'

I rose. 'Let me get you the drink.'

'Well, I could use one. But would it be forward of me to suggest that we move inside out of this air? I *am* cold.'

'Absolutely not.' I opened the glass door and stood aside.

Again she hesitated. 'Believe me, this is the first time I've let myself get picked up on a motel balcony.'

'Why cheapen it? Call it hospitality for a weary swimmer.'

She flashed a rueful smile. 'Sorry. I'm soured on a certain guy, and I take it out on you.' She entered the room.

I picked up my glass and followed. She sat on the chair in front of the desk. I fixed her drink in the bathroom, and when I returned she was vigorously towelling one leg. She had opened the robe to do it, and I caught a glimpse of sleek breasts. She was wearing a bikini tonight. I gave her the drink. 'I'm Morgan Butler.'

She saluted me with the glass. 'Carol Mitchell.'

But of course I had already known her name. She was the girl Stanley, the bellhop, had classified as somebody's sweet bit of fluff. Also, she was probably the eavesdropper I had flushed from the balcony when Maynard was holding his meeting last night. Add to this the fact that she hadn't taken her midnight dip until I had come out to the balcony, and you have more coincidence than I can take.

She was older than I had thought outside, close to thirty. Her face was more striking than pretty, but you would remember it long after you had forgotten the pretty ones. Her eyes were dark and vivid, her cheekbones high, her nose a shade off-centre. She exuded a promise of great vitality tempered by shrewdness, a gypsy air.

I sat on the bed. 'So you're soured on a guy. He stand you up?'

'Twice in two days,' she said. 'I like to swim, mind you, but a workout like that is not my idea of a heavy date. I thought it would tire me enough to sleep.'

'Twice in two days,' I said. 'He must be sure of himself.'

'No more, he's not! When he called tonight with another big-shot excuse about a meeting in DC, I gave him a piece of my mind. I told him that if he didn't show up tonight, I'd be long gone when he did arrive. And I assured him that I wouldn't leave alone.'

'Were you serious?'

'About being long gone? Sure. About the other man?' She shrugged. 'I wanted to hurt. I hinted that the man would be younger and more virile than he. At his age, he's sensitive about that.'

I got up and made us another drink. When I returned she had moved to the easy chair, where she sat with one leg draped over the arm at a rakish angle. She said, 'So it's not just a soggy swimmer you're entertaining, but a woman scorned. Hope you don't mind.'

'Not a bit. I gather your man is with the government.'

'He aspires to be. Right now he's a gilt-edged lawyer, very distinguished, very rich, very married. Ah, it's an old story.'

'Let me guess. You've given new meaning to his life. He'd like to get a divorce, but he's afraid of smudging his reputation.'

She gave a self-deprecating laugh. 'I told you, an old story.'

'If he's that worried about his reputation, he's taking a risk meeting you here,' I said.

'Oh, he doesn't come here. He has a secluded bungalow in Longport. I cool my heels in this plastic tourist trap until his nibs hits town and calls me down for his little romp. Sorry, I didn't mean to go vulgar on you.' She seemed suddenly aware of her provocative posture. She swung the leg off the chair arm and sat up. 'Lord, I come in for a drink, then bore you with this drivel.'

'Carol, we all have to unload when we get into an emotional bind. And maybe there is something to that old saw about finding a stranger more *simpatico* than a friend.'

'That's sweet of you.' She lowered her gaze. 'I have a confession. I've seen you around, and I was on the balcony a while ago when you came out. I'd pretty well decided to go down to the bar and find someone *simpatico*. So, you see, my swim wasn't just a sedative. I was flirting, in a clumsy way. Do you mind?'

This burst of candour made me wonder if she might not be on the up-and-up. For ten seconds. 'Not at all,' I said, hoping my grin was sufficiently wolfish. 'Personally, I think it's a smart move.'

'So do I!' she said, with a toss of her head.

Now we were conspirators against the tyrant who was exploiting her. I said, 'You know, you don't strike me as the usual secretary-type who gets herself into this kind of jam.'

'Hah, that's what I thought!' she said fervently. 'If anyone had told me a year ago that I would be humiliated like this by a man—any man—I would have laughed in his face.'

She took a hefty drink and elaborated. She was a writer on a news magazine in New York. She moved with a sophisticated crowd, earned good money, did the smart things, and rarely met unattached men who were as astute or self-sufficient as she was. So she was ripe for her lawyer when she met him. He was wise, generous, cultured without being feminine—a finished man. In his presence, her smartness and independence seemed shallow, trivial. She fell hard.

During her recital I made her yet another drink, and she moved to the foot of the bed, catty-corner from me. She became caustic. Beneath the lawyer's veneer of charm she had detected, of late, contempt for her devotion. 'I have to end it,' she said. 'You reach the point where you either place a value on yourself, or you become an emotionally dependent creature worthy of contempt.'

She talked well, this girl, but she was even more eloquent at what the psychology boys call non-verbal communication. She gave me some very humid looks with those gypsy eyes. She had a trick of darting her tongue over her lips after each sip from her glass. She treated me to candid views of breasts, midriff, and thighs.

I decided it was time to learn what she wanted from me. The way to begin was to offer what I knew she didn't want. I said, 'I agree, end it. But have you got the nerve to finish what you started?'

'What do you mean? I told you I would be gone when he gets here tomorrow. That should be plain enough.'

'Not to the arrogant man you've described,' I said. 'That's letting him off too easy.'

'Funny you should say that. I did have another idea. I

planned to wait for his call, trot down to the bungalow, then at the critical moment I would tell him off and get out.'

'Why don't you do it?'

'Too insecure, I guess. I'm afraid he'd talk me out of it.'

'If that's true, then your other plan sounds pretty feeble. How do you know you won't come running the next time he beckons?'

'I don't.' She finished her drink. 'Yes, I see what you mean about letting him off too easy. It has to be something drastic.'

'Yeah, like the threat you made on the phone tonight.'

'Oh, you mean another man, younger and more virile.' The boldness was back in her eyes and her smile was full of allure.

'Don't forget *simpatico*.' With that, I leaned forward, seized her by one ankle, and pulled her flat on the bed. She didn't even flinch. I stretched out beside her, my face inches from hers. Her lips parted and I kissed her. She stiffened as I caressed her supple belly, but then she relaxed and kissed back avidly.

Then she said, 'This is what you meant about having nerve.'

'Uh-huh. Have you got it?'

'Yes! Damn him! But won't you feel as if I'm using you?'

I gave what I hoped was a lecherous chuckle. 'I don't mind being used a little, for such a worthy cause.'

We kissed and touched some more. She did a playful thing with her knee. I unbuttoned the halter of her bikini and pulled the damp fabric from between us. Her breasts were cool and buoyant. When I touched them she tracked my naked back with her nails beneath my sweater. So I dropped my hand under the band on the bottom of the bikini.

She seized my wrist. 'Darling, wait. This is not the place.'

'Why not? We won't be interrupted.'

Her face was full of purpose. 'But don't you see? If we're going to cuckold him, he has to wear the horns.'

G

'I still don't get it.'

'We'll go to his bungalow, use his bed, drink his wine. I'll leave dainty underthings in conspicuous places. He'll get the word.'

So her assignment was to lure me to that bungalow, and I doubted that our tryst would be as private as I was led to believe. I gave her a lazy smile. 'You are a vengeful little devil.'

'He deserves it, and I'll truly be free of him. Will you go?'

'Try and stop me now.'

'Good!' She pulled the robe over her shoulders and retrieved her halter. 'Darling, I'll be quick. I've got this delicious glow on, and I don't want to lose it. Give me ten minutes.' She had gone a little elfin on me, but I kissed her again and let her go.

I was ready when she knocked, fully dressed, with the .25 Mauser in the hollow behind my ankle, held in place by the kind of elastic band an athlete wears when he's got a sprain.

CHAPTER XII

SECLUDED was hardly the word to describe the location of this mythical lawyer's bungalow. Isolated was more accurate. The house stood at the end of a long private driveway, on a point surrounded by a growth of pine trees. A squall blew in from the sea before we reached the house, with violent gusts of wind that tumbled raindrops like silver shot through my headlight beams.

'Oh, I like the rain,' said Carol Mitchell. 'We'll have a cosy fire and hot toddies, and we'll luxuriate on the bearskin rug.'

She was still giving me the build-up. She had been on this vivacious kick from the moment she'd returned to my room at the Seabreeze. Even her garb was lively— a chic vinyl raincoat, polka-dotted, with hat to match. At first I'd thought she was naked under the coat, but she had opened

it and proved me wrong. She wore a snappy cocktail gown of pale-blue silk with a miniskirt and no bra. After the exhibition she had moved in uninvited for a kiss. When we parted, I knew I'd been frisked for a weapon.

I parked in the driveway. 'Do we break in?'

'No, there's a key under the mat. Do you have a flash-light?'

I got the flash from the glove compartment and lighted our way up the porch steps. While she knelt for the key, I jerked the Mauser from under my sock and slipped it into a side pocket. Then I held the light while she unlocked the door, took her arm in a firm grip, and said heartily, 'After you, sweetheart. Find us some light.'

As I eased her over the threshold, I nudged the door open with my elbow and scanned the room with the flash. No movement. She wiggled out of my grip, and a second later three lamps went on. I closed the door. The house smelled as musty as the inside of a trunk.

We were in the living-room. It was furnished with Early American reproductions, and did have a bearskin rug in front of the fireplace. You could see directly into the dining-room through a wide doorway, and on one wall of the dining-room was a door to the kitchen. A second doorway from the living-room led into a hallway.

'You like?' Carol said. She flicked off the rain hat, slipped out of her coat, and hung it over one shoulder.

'Cosy,' I said. 'Very cosy.'

She raised her voice. 'Why don't you build a fire? There's wood in the basement. You'll find the doorway down that hall. I'll inspect the larder.' She drifted toward the dining-room.

Moving swiftly, I slipped my left arm under hers and seized her right bicep with my left hand, locking her arms behind her. She yelled. Her purse, hat, and coat tumbled to the floor. I jerked her up on her toes and tickled her neck with the Mauser.

I said, 'This little gun is hell on spines at this range. Call your partner out, and we'll talk.' I turned her toward the dark hallway, the place she had wanted me to enter.

'I swear to God I don't know what you're talking about!'

she said. 'There's no one here but us.' She strained and popped one of the thin cords supporting her gown. I caught a flash of breast.

'You're a sweet liar,' I said. 'You went to a lot of trouble to get me down here to meet someone. Now get him out here.'

'You're crazy! We're alone in this house.' She heaved again and snapped the other cord. 'What are you accusing me of?'

'Murder is the word, and you're in it up to your neck.'

'You *are* crazy.' But her voice was hoarse, lacking conviction.

'Okay, if you won't call him out, we go in after him. But we go with this gun against your spine.' I nudged her forward.

'Wait!' she said. 'All right. I'll call him.' She took a deep breath and called, 'Harry? Come out, Harry.'

Nobody moved in the hallway, but a floorboard creaked behind me. Before I could turn, encumbered as I was, a hard voice said, 'Hold it, Buster! Now you've got a gun on your back, and it's more gun than you're holding. Let her go and drop yours. Do it now!'

I chanced a look over my shoulder. He was a tall, bony man with a sharp face, standing in the doorway to the dining-room. He held a .38 automatic equipped with an ugly black silencer.

'Shoot me, and your girl-friend's bound to get it,' I said.

'That would give me two dead ones, but you'd be one of them.' His voice was as tough as his sentiments. 'Make up your mind.'

'You win, just don't shoot,' I whined.

'Then you better move!'

'Okay, okay.' I put the safety on the Mauser and tossed it on to the sofa. Then I seized Carol by the waist with both hands, pivoted, and threw her at him, a hundred and ten pounds of sinewy girl flailing her arms.

He jerked his gun arm up instinctively, and I was right behind her. I caught the wrist of the gun hand with both hands, made a quick half turn that locked his elbow in my armpit, and turned his arm in its socket. He yelped with

pain. I could have broken his arm, but I applied just enough pressure to open his hand. The gun rattled against a baseboard. I jerked him off balance and spun away from him. The girl had ended up on her knees against the dining-room wall.

The tall man swung a left hook, but he wasn't planted well enough to give it accuracy. I bored in, locked my wrist, and drove my right fist into his solar plexus. He was moving toward me, and it felt as if I'd driven his navel against his spine. He jack-knifed with a sound like a parrot screeching and fell heavily on his side.

I had to step fast to get out of his way. Luckily I stepped in the right direction. The girl had crawled to her handbag and was clawing inside. Her mistake was in watching me as she did it. I lunged forward and knocked the bag from her hand. A dozen objects scattered across the rug, including a stubby .32 automatic. She pounced, grabbed my left wrist with both hands, and sunk her teeth into the heel of my hand.

It hurt like hell. I tried to shake her off but she hung on, making harsh sounds through her nostrils. So I cracked her on the jaw with my fist. Her eyes went glassy and I was free. She sagged back out of reach and crumpled to the floor.

All of this might have taken thirty seconds.

I started forward to pick her up, when a hoarse, guttural voice said, 'You'll pay for that, you son of a bitch!'

The voice belonged to a man coming out of the hallway. He was grotesque in appearance and a little awesome. He was completely bald, his dome so shiny it looked like scar tissue. His complexion was pink and grey, and his face had odd lines in it, like a young man wearing crude make-up to age him. At first he looked like a caricature of a TV wrestler, but what looked like blubber was really spectacular muscular development, the kind you get from lifting weights four hours a day from puberty on. He wore only a striped T-shirt and slacks, and his muscles rippled obscenely as he moved. He didn't have a gun. He didn't need one.

I backed toward the fireplace. He moved forward with a rocking gait, his arms hanging down, his hands open. His

eyes were as dark and shiny as the business end of a pair of blackjacks—and looked just as lethal. There were three guns in the room, but I couldn't get my hands on any of them quick enough to do any good.

So I fought him. I shifted, feinted, and gave him my Sunday punch in the belly. It was like hitting a tough leather sofa with steel springs. Too late I realized that he had let me hit him. By then he had made a nimble movement and chopped a right to the side of my head. It almost tore my ear off and set the bells to ringing. I went to one knee. He picked me up and hit me over the heart with the same right fist. It didn't travel eight inches, but it was brutal. My back hit the wall hard. I felt sick and in shock.

I came off the wall much slower than I went on it. The bald man had not a vestige of emotion on his face. He was as indifferent as a butcher carving beef. He flicked his left into my face twice, and blood began to flow into my right eye. His fists were like cement. I didn't need an odds-maker to tell me I was overmatched. So I tackled him. I hit his thighs squarely with my shoulder, and I felt the impact all the way to my tailbone. He turned sideways with a grunt and brought both fists down into the nape of my neck, a vulnerable nerve centre. The impact drove me to the rug. He hit me there again, and I was paralysed. I couldn't breathe properly, and I seemed to be staring into an eclipse of the sun, bright yellow around a solid black core.

The girl yelled, 'No more! You'll kill him.' Her voice came from afar. I closed my eyes to protect them from the eclipse.

I must have been out for at least twenty minutes. When I felt something cool on my forehead, I thought it was the night air. But it was just a cold towel the girl was holding against my head. She was now wearing a sweater and slacks, and she sported a nifty bruise where I had clipped her on the jaw.

'Sorry I had to slug you,' I said. 'But you bite hard.'

She didn't answer, so I had a look around. I was on my back on an old bed in the basement. A naked bulb burned in a socket above me. This corner of the basement was a

storehouse for junk. I was surrounded by old furniture, a rug, trunks, broken athletic equipment, even a dressmaker's mannequin. The bed was an old brass relic, and the mattress was bare. My right wrist was handcuffed to the bedpost. A folded quilt that smelled of mildew supported my head.

Carol Mitchell jerked the towel off and I saw blood on it from a cut over my eye. The man called Harry was sitting in a chair beside the bed, rifling my wallet. His gun was on his lap. Mr Grotesque, master of the sweet science, was seated at the foot of the bed. He was wearing a faded ball cap, which altered his appearance enough to remind me that I'd seen him before. He had been driving the Dodge camper that had almost collided with Duncan's Porsche.

Harry said, 'Okay, Mr Morgan Butler. Now we can talk.'

I grinned at him. 'How's your belly, Harry?'

His mouth twisted. 'A damn sight better than yours is going to be when we're finished with you, wise guy.'

'Stop it,' the girl said. Her face had a cool, chiselled look. Nothing of the gypsy about her now. 'Mr Butler, you were right on one item. We wanted to ask you some questions. I think you've had sufficient proof that we can get rough if we don't get answers.'

'Suppose I do answer your questions,' I said. 'What then?'

Harry snorted. 'You're in no position to bargain, buddy.'

'Wait, Harry,' Carol said. 'If you co-operate, you won't be harmed,' she said to me. 'That I can promise you.'

'No offence, lady, but after your performance tonight you don't inspire one whole hell of a lot of trust. I've known some tarts in my time, but none as glib or brazen as you.'

Mr Grotesque growled. 'Watch your mouth, Butler.'

But I was watching Carol. She said, 'Obviously I wasn't clever enough. You weren't fooled. So here's your first question. If you knew this was a trap, why did you walk into it?'

'You know damn well why,' Harry said. 'He was hired to find us. He's a professional hardcase. Your average citizen

doesn't pack a hideaway gun or handle himself the way this guy did.'

'Is that true?' Carol asked. 'Were you hired to find us?'

'I didn't even know you existed until tonight,' I said.

'Prove it,' Harry said.

'Wait, let's start at the beginning,' she said. 'What are you doing in Atlantic City?'

'I came to see a man named Ralph Maynard. His wife hired me. She thought he was in trouble. You know who Maynard is, don't you?'

The girl and Harry exchanged quick glances. She said, 'Never mind who we know. Just keep talking.'

'Okay. I can only tell you what I told the law tonight.' Then I gave them exactly the same yarn I'd given Cunningham, from the amicable divorce to the fire in Duncan's garage. I had a reason for not revealing that I'd been in Crafton, West Virginia.

After I finished, Harry said, 'Who burned in that car?' I shrugged. 'The police think it was Maynard.'

'What about the other guy at Duncan's house?' he asked. I feigned surprise. 'I didn't know he had another guest.

'You're lying!' the girl said. 'You rode down in the elevator with him last night, after his meeting with Maynard.'

I grinned at her carelessness. 'So that was you on the balcony last night. Sorry I scared you off.'

'Sorry, hell,' Harry said. 'You were hired to guard that meeting. Or else you're one of them. What do you say, Iceman?'

'Don't call him that!' Carol said, and her tone was fierce.

'Would you rather I used his real name in front of this gink?' Harry asked. 'Well, what about it?'

Iceman was not a bad name for the bruiser. He stared at me and said, 'No way to tell, except for the one with the scar.'

'Let's check that out,' Harry said. He got up and peeled both coat and shirt off my left shoulder. 'No scar.'

'If he were one of them, he would have attended that meeting,' Carol said. She gave me a cynical smile. 'So my performance tonight was a flop. But you pretended to fall

for the act, and you brought a gun. That puts you on their team. Look at the facts. You were seen with that man in the elevator. You talked with Maynard this morning. And tonight Duncan drove you to his house. So I go along with Harry. You were hired, but not by any nervous wife.'

Now I knew they had trailed McCloud to Duncan's house last night. Also, they knew Duncan was in on it. 'You're wrong,' I said.

'Is she?' Harry said. 'Then where did you go tonight on the boardwalk? You worked hard to keep it a secret.'

'Was that you on my tail? I shook you because I don't like being shadowed. No other reason.'

'You're a liar,' Harry said. 'You went to report to someone. We want to know his name.' He showed me the bore of the .38.

'I can't tell you what I don't know, Harry.'

'We think you do know,' Carol said. 'Or you would have told the police about that meeting Maynard had with Duncan and that other man last night. Why didn't you tell the police about that?'

'For the same reason I didn't tell them I saw yonder Iceman come barrelling out of Duncan's street in a Dodge camper after that fire got lit,' I said. The girl stiffened, and I had their attention. 'I didn't know what kind of trouble Maynard was in. So I told the police as little as possible to protect him. And I can prove his wife hired me. Her cheque is in my wallet, behind my driver's licence.'

Harry dug it out, looked it over, and passed it to Carol. She said, 'Maybe he's telling the truth.'

'Just because of that cheque?' Harry said. 'Hell, the guy's wife was probably taking orders from hubby. She's in on it, too.'

'I don't think so,' Carol said. 'I can't see Maynard telling his wife the truth about this. No decent woman would forgive him. These are all very respectable men, with very decent wives.' The scorn in her voice would have cut through a steel plate.

I said, 'Something puzzles me about you three. You've asked a lot of questions, but I notice you've avoided the big one.'

'What big one is that?' Harry asked.

'Murder. Somebody killed Ralph Maynard in Duncan's house around five today. Were any of you on the premises?'

'Damn you!' Carol said. She pounced forward and leaned over the bed. 'The last thing we want is more killing.'

'Shut up,' the Iceman growled. 'You talk too much.'

She straightened slowly. 'I know. But every plan we—'

'That's enough,' Harry said. 'Look, let's say this clown is what he says he is. What are we going to do with him?'

'Can't we just leave him like this?' she said.

'No good,' Harry said. 'He'd bust out of there in an hour. I say let's give him a shot that'll lay him out for eight hours.'

'I'm opposed to that,' she said. 'He got hit awfully hard. A dose that size, I'd be afraid for his heart.'

'Then I'll give him the shot myself,' Harry said. 'I have my neck to think of.' He started for the stairs.

'No, I'll do it.' She motioned to the Iceman. 'Get the box.'

The Iceman lumbered up the stairs. Harry finished jerking my shirt and jacket off my left arm. He did it roughly and with relish.

A cold sensation settled in my stomach. 'I hope you know what you're doing with that stuff,' I said to Carol.

'Don't worry. I was an RN back when I was young and pure.'

The Iceman came back all too soon, toting a medical kit. Carol took out a bottle of alcohol, cotton, a syringe, and a small medication bottle. She dampened a piece of cotton with alcohol.

'Do you want me to hold this zootsuiter?' the Iceman asked.

Carol raised her eyebrows at me in query.

'I'll take it,' I said. I didn't have much choice.

She swabbed a spot on my muscle and filled the syringe. Then she squeezed my bicep with her left hand and pricked me with the needle. I felt a cold spray on my arm, and she winked. She hadn't given me the full dose! But she pretended to jerk the needle out, then wiped my arm with the cotton. 'Let it take you under. You'll sleep for eight hours

and have very little hangover.'

'Drop the bedside manner,' Harry said. 'We got people to see.'

The men went up the stairs, and Carol started to follow.

'Wait,' I said. 'Why are you after Maynard and the others? What crime did they commit?'

Her face had that chiselled look again. 'Why should I tell you anything? However you slice it, you work for them.'

'But Maynard's dead now.'

'Is he? Suppose I told you that Maynard was the one who killed that man in Duncan's house?'

'Can you prove it?'

'Harry was watching the house when Maynard went in. Then Harry heard the shots. A little later Maynard drove a Buick out of the garage and ran his Ford in. *I* saw that. He left in the Buick well before the fire started, but Harry thinks he rigged a candle.'

'Do you trust Harry all the way?' I asked.

Her lip curled. 'To hell with you.' She crossed the basement and went up the stairs. The lights went out and minutes later a heavy motor roared to life outside. Their headlight beams swept past a dirty window high on the basement wall.

I was in the dark, chained to a bed, with a camel's hump of pain at the base of my neck, and already dopey with the small dose of knockout serum the girl had injected into me. I was sorely tempted to sleep off the drug and worry later about getting free.

But beneath my torpor a beetle of anxiety chewed on a nerve. Why? Unlike Harry, I had no people to see. But I groaned myself to a sitting position, then eased down to my knees beside the bed. Happily, they hadn't taken my stogie lighter. I got it burning. The bed was a solid piece of work. The other half of the cuffs was fastened to the main post, a hefty piece of brass that extended to the floor. Two other rods served as braces for this big one, one above the mattress line and one below it. Maybe I could muscle these supports from their sockets, but my big obstacle was the steel L-shaped beam that supported the mattress. This beam was fastened to the main post by a heavy clamp

screw that hadn't been off since Roosevelt's first term.

I inspected the household junk within reach—a bag of golf clubs, a trunk of books, a box of Christmas decorations —but found no tool that would help pick the lock on the cuffs. I did find an old belt buckle that might help in dismantling the bed.

I rapped the clamp with a golf club to loosen it and began working on the big screw with the buckle. I worked by touch to conserve the fuel in the lighter. Enfeebled as I was by Carol's needlework and the Iceman's mauling, it took twenty minutes to get the clamp loose. I leaned against the trunk to rest before I tackled the brace. I felt like an old man with hardened arteries.

I must have dozed, but I jumped awake at the sound of a car. Headlight beams swept across the basement. Now I knew why I had felt the anxiety. In a crevice of my mind had lurked the suspicion that they had let me off too easy. I came off the floor fast, scalded by adrenalin. Seizing the golf club, I stood on the bed and smashed the overhead bulb. No doubt my visitor expected to find me unconscious, ready for the kill. Bless Carol for her squeamish heart. I scrambled off the bed, seized the dressmaker's mannequin, and flopped it on the mattress. By the time I'd covered it with the quilt, footsteps were thumping overhead. I went to my belly on the cement and crawled under the bed.

The door at the head of the stairs opened, and I heard the click of the light switch. A dim bulb in the stairwell went on. The light didn't fall on the bed, but it must have revealed the bed and my draped mannequin in silhouette. Footsteps descended half the stairs and stopped. That placed him roughly twenty feet away. I could hear him breathing.

I heard a metallic click, a hammer cocking, followed by a thunderous roar and belch of flame. The bed jumped above me. He fired three more rounds, very fast. I gave the bed a jerk, grunted a low moan, and let it trail off. I waited. The smell of cordite reached me. I ached for a look at him but didn't dare move. I expected him to come over and inspect his handiwork, close enough for me to get a crack at him. Instead, he walked back up the stairs, turned off the light, and left the house.

CHAPTER XIII

THERE is a point of exhaustion I reach that puts a hoar-frost on my brain and a tropical fever in my blood. My mind is lucid, my reflexes lousy, and I feel happily remote from the human race. Add to that a stiffness in my torso that feels like a whalebone corset, and you have the shape I was in when I got back to the Seabreeze.

It was five-thirty am, an hour when I should have been able to slip up to my room with no one the wiser. But there were two police cars at the kerb outside, and when I entered the lobby a cop braced me. 'Pardon, sir, are you a guest?'

'Yes, room three twelve.' I showed him my key.

'Hey, you wouldn't be Morgan Butler, would you?'

'Yes. What does that buy me?'

'A talk with the brass. Have a seat by the cigarette machine.'

I sat down and lit a stogie. I wasn't eager to learn what the ruckus was about. That chill on my brain made me a patient man.

Presently Jim Cunningham appeared and sauntered over. I said, 'Little out of your jurisdiction, aren't you?'

'You look like hell,' he said. 'Where you been all night?'

I grinned around my stogie. 'Been out on a date. Hot stuff.'

'Uh-huh. Did she give you that cut over the eye before or after she tried to chew your hand off?' He sat down beside me.

'The hand is her work. The job on the eye was done by her boy-friend. She had two boy-friends. One had a gun.'

'You're not telling me you got rolled?'

'Rolled is too tame a word, Chief. I got vamped, beat up, knocked out, grilled, and shot at.'

He gave me a smile so deadly it looked sutured in place. 'Speak American, Bub. I'm not in the mood for a snow job.'

'Let's talk in my room. Can you negotiate some coffee?'

He sent a bellhop for coffee, and we went to the elevator. He said, 'Anybody fill you in on this mess?'

'Not yet. Looks like somebody knocked over the front desk.'

'You're wrong. About an hour and a half ago, somebody cold-cocked the night clerk. The Atlantic City boys found Duncan's office torn up, but the thief didn't even rob the clerk's cash drawer.'

We were in the elevator. 'So it wasn't robbery,' I said. 'That still doesn't explain what you're doing here.'

'The first thing the clerk told the law was that the robbers didn't get the money Duncan kept in a lock box in the safe. They didn't get it because Duncan himself picked it up at three am.'

'But I thought you had Duncan under guard.' I unlocked the door to my room and we entered.

'So did I,' he said. 'But he slipped out of his bedroom window about two-thirty. Took off on foot down the beach.'

No wonder he was sore. There was one drink left in the bottle I had used to woo the gypsy swimmer. I drank it, shuddered, and began to strip down. 'I need a shower, or I'll pass out on you.'

He picked up a glass. 'Lipstick. You did have a date.'

'That's it, keep your hand in. Rifle my luggage.'

I went into the bathroom, shed my shorts, and soaked my bruised back and neck under the hot spray. Then I turned on the cold and let it beat on my face until my eyeballs ached. After a little towel work, I examined the gash over my eye. It was a nasty one.

Cunningham stuck his head in and said the coffee had arrived. He gave a low whistle. 'The nape of your neck looks like a ripe eggplant. He rabbit-punched you.'

'It felt more like a kick from a mule,' I said.

'Always the bucolic touch. Snap it up, will you?'

When I came out, he was parked in a chair, working on a carton of coffee. I got into my robe and straddled a chair in front of him.

He said, 'Tell me about last night's big adventure.'

'That can wait. We have something to iron out first.'

He gave a sour grin. 'So it's time for our showdown.'

'Showdown is too strong. What I had in mind was a trade.'

'What have you got to trade? And for what?'

'I offer information and my services in return for your co-operation. I'm banking on the fact that you run your own show.'

He looked amused. 'What makes you think I need your help?'

I lit a stogie. 'You need me because the killing at Duncan's house is only one incident in a complicated series of events. I know some of the pieces, and I've met some of the people involved. This much I'm sure of. We're not going to solve your murder until we unravel the whole mess. We're not going to do that in Pearl Beach. You have a limited jurisdiction, a limited budget. You can't send out an investigator to track down leads. I'll do that work.'

'Butler, I'm beginning to wonder if that guy didn't knock a screw loose last night. I'm not in the habit of enlisting civilians to do police work. Least of all would I enlist a half-baked farmer whose only claim to fame is that he used to install bugs in executive washrooms for DeBlanc's jittery corporate clients.'

'Put the needle away, Chief. I admit I've kept my hand in over the years. DeBlanc still hands me an occasional job.'

'But you're not licensed to do work like that, are you?'

'No, but I don't go around breaking the law.'

'I'll bet you bend it a little from time to time.'

'Only when it's malleable. Look, we don't have to fence. Check me out with DeBlanc. He usually gets a feedback on my work.'

'*Kick*back is more like it. He had the rep for being horny for the buck. What about you? I'll bet you charge plenty.'

'Yes, I'm expensive. But I earn my money.'

'Not this time, though. This one is a sentimental journey, as I recall. A personal favour for the ex-Mrs Butler.'

'No, I lied about that. She pays, just like the rest.' I got the cheque out again. It was getting a little dog-eared.

Cunningham unfolded it. 'You mercenary son of a bitch.' He said it with a hint of admiration.

The cheque was in my favour because, as a professional,

he would have no confidence in a man on a sentimental journey. I was getting great mileage out of one cheque. He gave it back and said, 'For your information, I've already checked with DeBlanc. He gives you a good score, but that doesn't satisfy me. Obviously that yarn you told me last night was the bunk. How much did you leave out?'

'When I tell the rest, you may want to lock me up.'

His expression went a little bleak. 'If that's true, you have a lot of crust telling me anything. Why the change of heart?'

I took my stogie from between us. 'Yesterday I thought I could handle my end of this alone. But it's too big for one man.'

'I didn't think it was only that *I* needed *your* help,' he said. 'But you still haven't explained why you think I'll co-operate.'

'Let's say because you're a certain kind of maverick.'

'You fascinate me. What kind of maverick am I?'

'The kind who won't let the TV boys stick a camera into a suspect's ear.'

'You'll have to do better than that, friend.'

I took a long drag on the stogie. I felt like blowing the bitter smoke in his face. 'All right. You're not just a cop with a murder to solve. Somebody came on your turf and despoiled it. You take it as an insult and a challenge. You will exact retribution, and you won't be squeamish in the way you go about it. You'll use just about any method or any person that can help, including me.'

He ran a thumb along his jaw. 'You left something out. You didn't say whether I was married.'

'If you are, she'd fit the picture. She'd likely be an Eskimo with a tattoo of a seal on her chest.' I felt reckless.

For a second he watched me the way the cobra watches the mongoose. Then he said, 'But us mavericks don't like to take on a partner. It cramps our style. Or didn't you know that?'

Ignoring the sarcasm, I dug the clipping on the Kelso murder from my bag and tossed it to him. 'That's where it started.'

He unfolded the clipping and read it through twice.

'Last Wednesday night and a three fifty-seven Magnum,' he said. He got out a pen and pad. 'Tell it. If I have questions, I'll interrupt.'

I talked for the better part of an hour. When I finished, Cunningham read through his notes and said, 'By all that's holy, Butler, I should lock you up. If you'd told me about Duncan last night, I might have pried the whole story out of him.'

'Not a chance. The crime he and his buddies committed was too big. The rap for it would be greater than any threats of yours.'

'Maybe so. But if I'd known the identity of the dead man, we would have locked Duncan up while we checked McCloud out. Also, we would have had an APB out on Maynard.'

'Okay, that's a black mark against me. But you're still ahead of the game. You have McCloud's home address, plus a make on the car he rented, which Maynard is probably driving. In fact, I think Maynard contacted Duncan last night. They probably left town together, with Duncan's bankroll to finance them.'

'I'll buy that,' he said grudgingly. 'We learned that the phone in Duncan's bedroom is no extension. It's a separate line, unlisted number. That's how Maynard got in touch. But if they left town together, I wonder how far Duncan will get?'

'Why do you say that?'

'Get off it! Maynard left home with a three fifty-seven Magnum, and both Kelso and McCloud were killed with a Magnum.'

'Yeah. The hell of it is, I believed Maynard when he said he didn't sap me in Crafton.'

'I don't get your logic.'

'Well, I figure that whoever sapped me killed Kelso. For a while last night, I thought it had to be one of Carol's boy-friends. So I deliberately didn't tell them I'd been in Crafton.'

'Wasn't that risky?'

'A little. If one of them had sapped me, he would have challenged my story. But they bought the story.'

H

'The one who came back with the gun didn't buy it. Tell me more about the one they called the Iceman.'

'I'd bet my eyeteeth he's served time. He has that zombie look, a case of arrested development. And he called me a zootsuiter. When was the last time you heard that expression?'

'Early forties. Yeah, that dates him. Now let me tell you one. The man I had on duty at Duncan's house found him missing at four this morning. Sullivan followed Duncan's tracks down the beach a ways, then spotted a couple parked in a vehicle overlooking the beach. He asked if they had seen a man, but they claimed they'd just pulled in. Very lovey-dovey, this couple, and Sullivan had his mind on other things. The point is, their vehicle was a Dodge camper.'

'So they knew Duncan had busted out. He was their only lead. That would make them desperate enough to raid his office.'

'I agree. Okay, get dressed. I'll make some calls, and then we'll go to Duncan's house. Maybe we can make a deal at that.'

I eavesdropped on his phone work while I packed, and he was efficient. He dispatched a lab crew to the house in Longport. He gave descriptions of Harry, Carol, and the Iceman and requested that the Iceman be checked out for a prison record. He put out an APB on the Dodge camper and McCloud's rented Buick. He put in a teletype request for a wirephoto blow-up of the slug that had killed Kelso. And finally he told someone to call the New York police direct and get a report on one Robert T. McCloud.

When he finished, we went down to the lobby. I paid my bill and we drove to Duncan's house in my car.

Cunningham said, 'If we do make a deal, you won't be any good until you get some sleep. You'd better get a few stitches in that eye, too.'

'Have you got a doctor handy?'

'I called one while you were getting your gear from the bathroom. Dr Sam Marshall, a good man. He'll meet us down there.'

Dr Sam Marshall was sitting in a chair on Duncan's

porch when we arrived. Cunningham introduced us and ushered the doctor and me inside and down the hall to a bedroom.

'You better look at his hand, too, Sam,' Cunningham said. 'A girl chewed on him last night.' He left us alone.

Sam Marshall had me remove my jacket and stretch out on the bed. He examined me, gave me a local above the eye, and put the stitches in. I was almost dozing when I felt a second needle in my arm. I asked what it was for, and the good doctor said it was a tetanus shot, standard practice for bite wounds. I suspected that it was a sedative Cunningham had asked him to give me on the sly, but I was too weary to protest.

CHAPTER XIV

ELAINE MAYNARD woke me up at three pm. 'Morgan, I've brought you coffee.' Her eyes were tender, solicitous.

I sat up and drank some coffee. She asked how I felt.

'Much better. I slept eight hours. Must be getting old.'

'You needed it, according to Chief Cunningham. He told me about last night, including the fact that they tried to kill you.'

'All that means is that you owe me more money. I warned you that my rates would go up if this involved hazardous duty.'

'Don't make jokes! Listen, you said you were doing this for me. Now I want you to stop. Go back and finish your harvest.'

I had the macabre thought that I was involved in a much grimmer harvest. That made me the Grim Reaper. 'I can't quit now. I've made a deal with Cunningham. How did you fare with him?'

Her smile was rueful. 'He's a very persuasive man. He came to the hotel and said you had told him the whole story, and he wanted to confirm it. I made him tell me several things only you and I knew. Then he put me through the wringer, if that's the phrase.'

'Yes, he's thorough. But a good man, which is why I came clean with him. I know I should have consulted you first, but—'

'No, you did right. We can't protect Ralph any longer. I accept that. You'd better finish your coffee. Cunningham is waiting for you in the living-room.' She got off the bed.

I drained the cup. 'How about groceries? I'm starved.'

'Dinner, sir, is in the works. To save time, the chief decided to raid Matt Duncan's freezer. The only catch is that I have to cook. But I think the chief wants me out of the way while you talk.' She leaned and kissed my forehead, then left the room.

I took a quick shower, dressed, and went into the living-room. Cunningham was on the phone, propped on the sofa smoking an ugly bulldog pipe. He saluted with the pipe and pointed to the other end of the sofa. When he hung up there was zest in his eyes.

'How do you feel?' he asked.

'Almost human. What about our deal? Do I work for you?'

He nodded. 'It's a bootleg play for me, but I've decided to take you on. I do need an investigator who will go out and beat the brush. The way things have been popping, I can't wait for the other city police forces to do my legwork. They co-operate, but in their own good time. So it's a deal, but there are a few ground rules.'

'Fire away,' I said.

He gave me a badge and a card which identified me as a special deputy. He said, 'This allows me to give you confidential police info with a clear conscience. It also permits you to pack that Luger you keep behind the glove compartment in your car.'

Yes, a thorough man. I said, 'What else?'

'You're under my orders. That means you report to me regularly. No holding out in the interests of recent employers.'

'I agree. Go on.'

He grinned lazily. 'On the other hand, I want you to play your own game. You may have to lean on some people. Use your own judgment. I wouldn't want you to think I

was cramping your style.'

'I get the message. You said things were popping.'

He flicked open a notebook. 'Those slugs fired at you last night came from a Magnum, the same one that killed McCloud *and* Kelso.'

The stitches over my eye felt as taut as piano wires. 'So one of Carol's boy-friends did pick up that Magnum in Crafton.'

'Or Maynard had it all along and followed you from the Seabreeze last night. By the way, that house they rousted you in belongs to a reputable party, a widow vacationing in Europe.' He turned a page. 'Let's move on. It seems your unholy three did pick up a hot lead in Duncan's office.'

'How so?'

'They busted into McCloud's townhouse in New York early this morning, locked Mrs McCloud and the help in the pantry, and rifled McCloud's safe. This McCloud was really in the chips. He *owned* an office building in Manhattan, plus other real estate.'

'But why raid McCloud's house? They must know he's dead.'

'Maybe they were after information on where Duncan holed up,' Cunningham said. 'Stuff like these items Sullivan rescued from a fire Duncan left burning in his bedroom fireplace last night. The sap forgot to open the damper.'

He handed me an eight-by-ten glossy of a honey blonde in a low-cut gown seated at a piano keyboard. The photo was signed : *To Matt, with love, Beverly.* A printed legend on the back identified the picture as a publicity still from the Blue Pelican, a nightclub in New York. The girl's full name was beneath the legend : Beverly Sherwin. Cunningham gave me a dozen charred snapshots of the same girl taken on the beach beside Duncan's house. The girl was slender but well endowed. Yet even in the torchy photograph she gave off an aura of innocence and naïveté that made her cleavage seem a sacred place.

'Is this the tart you once caught living here with Duncan?'

'Hardly looks the part, does she? But after she moved in, several ladies on the street had anonymous calls about her

occupation. They complained to us, and we talked with Duncan. He fumed, but he moved her out. Probably back to New York.'

'Have you got her address?'

'The New York police are working on that.'

'Okay, what about our quartet of businessmen—Maynard, Kelso, McCloud, and Duncan? Have you found a common denominator?'

'Not yet. But their ages suggest that they might have served together in the war. I'm having their service records checked out.'

'Let's get back to Mrs McCloud,' I said. 'Did you have the New York law break it to her about the demise of her husband?'

'No, I saved that chore for you. Maybe she has info that can help. She called Duncan's private number three times today, trying to locate McCloud. We said he was out on business. So you break the news to her. If it shakes her up, you might learn something.'

'I'll talk to the lady. What else do we know about her?'

'Not much. She runs some kind of talent agency. Probably a tax write-off for McCloud. She doesn't need the scratch.'

I picked up the photos of the Sherwin girl. 'Okay, New York it is. If you turn up this girl's address, I'll leave tonight.'

Just then Elaine entered and announced that dinner was ready. It was a simple meal—steak, broccoli, and a salad—but for me the atmosphere was enhanced by Elaine's regal presence. She held herself proud and ate sparingly, her gaze a little abstract. She seemed to be holding herself intact with a masonry of pride and sorrow, and doing a fair job. Scrupulously, she didn't ask if Ralph was officially suspected of murder. We were having coffee when Cunningham received the phone call that gave him the Sherwin girl's address in New York City. He gave it to me.

I said, 'I'll leave as soon as I drop Elaine at her hotel.'

Elaine had already rinsed the dishes and put them in the dishwasher. She nodded to the chief and said she would wait in the car.

After she had gone, Cunningham gave me the name of a cop to contact if I needed help in New York, Captain Jack Masters. He walked me to the door and reminded me to keep him posted. I told him I would, then walked out to the Merc and headed north on Atlantic Avenue. Elaine was silent until I'd parked at the Montclair.

She said, 'Morgan, I almost forgot. I talked with Alex at noon. He called from the Coast while I was talking with Cunningham. I told him we were co-operating with the police, and it upset him. He said he would call back at five, and he wants you there. It's almost five now. Will you come up and wait for his call?'

I said I would. She held my arm on the way up in the elevator. When we entered her room, she asked if I'd mix her a drink. I made her a stiff one, a weak one for me. The phone rang and I answered. An operator chanted that Mr Crittenden was calling person-to-person from Beverly Hills for either Mrs Maynard or Mr Butler. Elaine took the bedroom extension. I identified myself and Alex came on.

'Butler, what's this garbage about you yapping to the law? That isn't the way we planned it! You promised me—'

'I promised nothing! Duncan and Ralph both blew town last night. I warned them that I'd call cop if they didn't co-operate.'

'To hell with that,' he said. 'I thought we agreed to play it Ralph's way until we found out what he was up against.'

'I met that crowd last night.' I gave him a summary of my adventure, including the fact that someone had tried to kill me.

He digested this and said, 'That does put a new edge on it.'

'Alex, we have to face it. Ralph is in trouble for burning McCloud's body. He's a fugitive and has to be treated as such.'

'Yes, but who killed those men? Isn't that the question?'

'It is, and we have to know before there are more killings.'

'Okay, I'll go along. What's your next move?'

'We've placed this Iceman and his pals in New York. I'm headed that way now.'

'I know you'll do your best. How's Elaine?'

She said, 'I'm fine, Alex. But I can't speak for tomorrow.'

'Buck up,' he said. 'I'll fly to DC late tomorrow. I want to line up a good criminal lawyer. We can brief him on what we know so far about Ralph's trouble.'

'All right, Alex,' Elaine said. 'See you late tomorrow.'

We all hung up, and she joined me in the living-room. She said, 'Morgan, take me with you to New York. Please.'

'I'm sorry. You'd only be in the way.'

'Please! I have a dread of being alone. I know it's cowardly, but when I'm alone I feel trapped in a Dali painting. Everything's distorted. I guess I'm not equipped for this sort of thing.'

'Nobody is. Look, go home tonight. Call a friend.'

'Oh, that's a pretty picture. What would I say? "Wendy, I need company because my husband's a fugitive on a murder charge." That would go over big.' Her voice had gone a little shrill.

I seized her arms. 'Take it easy.'

She stared at me intently for a moment, then eased forward against my chest. Slowly the tension left her and she sagged against me. I kissed her forehead and her eyes. She found my mouth with hers. It began as a chaste kiss, but in seconds it was sweet and carnal. I despised the fact that her capacity for joy was being burned away by brutality. I felt gorged with the masculine conceit that I could restore her and give her peace through intense pleasure. But it would be exploitation of a crude order, a form of rape.

I said, 'Is this the real reason you want to go along?'

She jerked away, her face pale and hurt. 'That's cruel. I'm beginning to think you are the way that Colonel De-Blanc described you—coarse and barbaric.'

'Well, it's a coarse line of work,' I said cheerfully. 'You meet lots of ugly characters. You meet guys who torture their wives in various ways. You meet guys who kill other guys and sometimes burn them up. Yeah, barbaric is a good word.'

Her face was taut with anger. She opened her mouth to speak, then closed it, and sat abruptly on the sofa. 'Oh, I see. You're warning me that I'm very down on Ralph because he's making me suffer, and you think I might use

you to take revenge and regret it later.'

'Is that what I'm doing? I thought I'd insulted you.'

'Yes, and I deserved it. It was better than a slap. All right, Morgan. I'll go home tonight. You go. But be careful.'

CHAPTER XV

Two and a half hours later I entered Manhattan through the Lincoln Tunnel, drifted north for a few blocks, then pulled into a motel between Ninth and Tenth avenues. They had knocked down a dozen squat tenements to build the place, and it gleamed among the squalid brownstones like a diamond stickpin on a Bowery bum. I had stayed at the same motel the last time a case brought me to New York. It gave me access to my car and a quick exit from the city.

I got the usual antiseptic room for too much money, and as soon as the bellboy left I got Beverly Sherwin's phone number from information and called her apartment. A woman answered in a breezy voice. 'Beverly's boffo bash and passion pit!'

I heard laughter, strident music, and other party sounds in the background. I said, 'Beverly Sherwin?'

'She's in the kitchen, fondling ice cubes. This is Irene Cassidy. Can I help?'

I took a chance and told her I'd been invited to the bash and was calling to confirm the address.

She gave it to me, then said, 'Hey, you're not in Bev's new show, by any chance?'

'No, but I'd like to be.'

'You and eighty other guys. They all want to play that knock-down-drag-out nude scene with her in the second act. I even know a few chicks who would like to play that scene with her, and I don't mean on the stage.' She gave a bawdy laugh.

'Present company excepted, of course.'

'Oh, fun-nee, fun-nee! What is your name?'

'I'll introduce myself when I arrive.' I hung up.

The party made the situation delicate. If I went up and flashed my badge with the party in progress, I doubted that the girl would let me in. It was a cinch she wouldn't let me in if Duncan was there. But she would tip him off, and he would fly the coop. So my best bet was to visit Miss Sherwin after the party was over. That gave me several hours to kill.

I picked up the phone and called Mrs Robert T. McCloud. From Cunningham's description of her affluence, I expected to have to wade through at least one butler and two maids. But the crisp voice that answered turned out to be the lady herself.

'Mrs McCloud, my name is Butler. I'm with the police.'

'Not again. I answered all your questions this morning.'

'I'm not calling about this morning. It's about your husband.'

'My husband's out of town on business.'

'I know. He was in Pearl Beach, New Jersey, until yesterday. I'm with the Pearl Beach police. Your husband was involved in some trouble down there. I'd like to talk with you about it.'

'What kind of trouble? So far, you haven't said anything that would persuade me to give you one minute of my time.'

'All right, how's this? Yesterday a man was murdered in the house where your husband was a guest. No one's seen Mr McCloud to talk to since. On top of that, the owner of the house has vanished.'

'How do you know my husband was staying at this house?'

'It's the same house you called today, trying to contact him.'

She was silent for a few seconds. Then : 'Let me get this straight. Are you accusing my husband of murder?'

'No, but—'

'But you think he might be able to shed some light on the guilty party, or some such jargon. Well, he's the one you want to talk with, not me. Why didn't you ask for him when I answered the phone?'

I had to think fast. 'His Cessna Skyhawk is still parked at

Bader Field in Atlantic City. I doubt he would go home without it.'

'Oh, come on! You're not suggesting he was kidnapped?'

'Mrs McCloud, this business is too complicated to discuss over the phone. Can't you spare me fifteen minutes?'

'Not tonight. I'd like to co-operate, Mr Butler, but I have to see a client. It's clear across town, and I'm already late.'

'You're not much worried that your husband may be in trouble.'

'Robert? Obviously you don't know him. If someone's giving Robert a hard time, they're the ones to worry about. Now I must go.'

'Wait. How do you plan to get across town and back?'

'My chauffeur will drive me, and I'll take a cab home. Why?'

'Let me chauffeur you. I can get to your place in ten minutes. We can talk on the way.'

'That's a very unorthodox suggestion for a policeman to make.' She sounded amused.

'I'm an unorthodox policeman,' I said. 'How about it?'

'Well, if it means that much to you, come ahead. But ten minutes is as long as I'll wait.' She hung up.

I checked the clip in my Luger and drove to the McCloud house on East 73rd Street with a minute to spare. It was a three-story townhouse behind a spiked, cast-iron gate that must have been ten feet tall. I started to ring the bell when a burly man in a chauffeur's uniform stepped from the shadows and asked my name. I identified myself. He grunted, unlocked the gate, and led me into an entrance hall the size of a handball court. A gleaming mahogany staircase curved upward at the rear of the hall, and hanging down the stairwell was a chandelier with a thousand prisms of glass. My escort grunted me into the living-room. It was a sizable room with a vaulted ceiling, but its austerity had been reduced to character by a skilful decorator. The drapes, paintings, and fabrics created an effect of comfort and warmth.

Mrs Robert T. McCloud rose from a wing chair near the fireplace. She wore a modish pantsuit flamboyantly styled

along the lines of a Spanish *caballero* outfit. The black silk pants were low on her hips and snug all the way to her knees, where they flared to her shoe tops. Each flare was inset with a scarlet pleat, matching the scarlet sash she wore. Her short jacket was black with scarlet buttons and her blouse was white. It was masculine garb, but it emphasized rather than disguised her sex, from curve of breast and hip to coy instep. She was a tall woman, and supple, with dark hazel eyes and chestnut-coloured hair worn to her shoulders.

She said, 'Mr Butler, my decision to let you drive me may have been a trifle hasty. After my experience with those hoodlums this morning, I have to be careful. May I see your credentials?'

'Certainly.' I produced my badge and deputy's card.

She frowned over the card. 'But according to this, you just started to work for the Pearl Beach police today.'

'That's right. That murder I mentioned is part of a case I was already working on, so they assigned me as a special deputy.'

'But isn't that unusual?' she asked.

'It's an unusual case. So far, two men have been killed, and last night they almost got a third.'

She glanced at the bandage over my eye. 'Were you the third, by any chance?'

'Yes. I tangled with those three who raided you this morning.'

'Which one did that to your eye?'

'The big guy with the pasty face. They call him the Iceman.'

She appraised me with intelligent eyes. 'So there is a connection between them and Robert. I thought so when they ignored the valuables and asked for Robert's papers.' She flashed a sudden smile. 'All right, Mr Unorthodox Policeman, you've earned yourself a driving job. Max, tell Linda to get my coat.'

This last was directed at the chauffeur, who had moved to one side and taken the stance of parade rest. He said, 'Mrs McCloud, with all due respect, you don't have to talk to this fellow.'

'Max, I'll be the judge of that. Now do as I asked.'

'Yes, Ma'am.' He gave me a nasty look and left the room.

'Don't mind Max,' she said. 'He feels guilty because he was out when those hoodlums came this morning. Are you ready?'

We went into the entrance hall, where a maid helped her into a sable coat. Then I escorted her outside to the Mercury and requested our destination.

She said, 'The West Side. Riverside Drive, in the nineties.' She opened her purse and read the exact number.

My heart jumped. It was Beverly Sherwin's address.

Before I could speak, she said, 'Mr Butler, exactly what is the connection between Robert and those callers I had this morning?'

'We're not sure. We suspect that some years ago your husband was involved in a deal with this character I called the Iceman. We think the Iceman served a prison term for his part in the deal.'

'So it's revenge they're after.'

'That's our guess. Let me try a few names on you. Milt Kelso. Ralph Maynard. Matthew Duncan.'

'Wait, I know that last one—Duncan.'

'You should. It was his house you called three times today.'

'I didn't know *that*. Robert gave me that number over the phone on Wednesday, in case I had to get in touch with him.'

'You mean you haven't talked with him since Wednesday?' I asked.

'No, why? Oh, I see. Not very wifely behaviour on my part. You think I should call him every night when he's away and exchange sweet endearments. Sorry, ours isn't that kind of marriage. Neither of us is bound by the usual conjugal straitjackets. We each have our own work, friends, amusements, quite apart from the other. That's the way we prefer it.'

'What about love?'

She had a husky laugh. 'Love? Robert would gag on the word. There should be another word for people like Robert

and me. Respect. Admiration. I don't know the word. How did we get on the subject of my marriage anyway? It has nothing to do with your case.'

She was right, but it had everything to do with the fact that her Robert was dead and I had to break the news to her. I was a little dazzled by this woman. But there was an element of pity in my admiration which neutralized the impact of her beauty and wealth.

I made a left turn off Fifth into Central Park. 'Let's get back to Matt Duncan. You said his name meant something to you.'

'But I can't recall why,' she said. 'It must have been something trivial, a phone message I took. What does he do?'

'He owns a motel in Atlantic City. The Seabreeze.'

'Sorry, that doesn't ring a bell.'

So I tried a different tack. I asked if she knew what papers the Iceman and his crew had taken that morning. She couldn't help me. They had forced her to open the safe in Robert's study. They had ignored the cash and jewels in the safe. They were interested only in a strongbox of Robert's to which only he had a key. She didn't know what was in it. As soon as she opened the safe, they whisked her to the kitchen and locked her in the pantry with the help.

We were almost through the park. I said, 'You didn't leap to your husband's defence when I said he might have been involved in a shady deal at one time.'

She made a sound of amusement. 'I know Robert's made a lot of money over the years, and I'm sure you don't make that kind of money without cutting corners. That's what I thought you meant by a shady deal. But I told you, I don't pry into Robert's affairs.'

'You don't care how he makes it, as long as you get your cut. Is that it?'

'No, Mr Butler, that is not it!' she said. 'I'm not dependent on Robert's money. He wouldn't be interested in a woman he could buy. I told you I have my own work. It's a lucrative business, and I was doing well before I even met Robert. I run a small talent agency for actors and writers. Last year I cleared over thirty thousand. So I'm my own girl as far as money is concerned.'

'Sure you are. I would guess that coat you're wearing set you back all of last year's profits.'

'You'd be right. Yes, this coat was a gift from Robert, if that's what you mean. He's also given me a mink and a grey fox, not to mention a tidy sum in jewellery. But they're just trappings. I could give them up tomorrow with no sweat. Robert knows that. The admiration and respect I mentioned earlier work both ways.'

I turned into Riverside Drive. 'Okay, I stand corrected.'

'Mr Butler, I don't give a damn for your opinion. For some reason, you made me angry and I sounded off. I think you had it coming. There's the building. Let me out by the mailbox.'

'I'll park,' I said. 'We're not finished yet.'

I made a U-turn and parked. She was silent until I turned off the engine. Then she said, 'You're mistaken. We are finished. I've had enough of your cheap insinuations. You have a talent for opening people up. I'll give you credit for that. Now good night.'

But I reached across her and grabbed her door handle. She stiffened, and her face looked enamelled. 'Let go of that door!'

'Not until I know the connection between you and Beverly Sherwin.'

She seemed to wilt a little at the neck. 'Who *are* you?'

'I'm just what I said I was. If Beverly's a client of yours, it is one staggering coincidence. She's in this thing, too. We think that man Duncan is hiding in her place right now.'

'You can't be serious. Beverly is a sweet, sensible girl. Oh, I know she got in a jam years ago when she worked at that nightclub, the Blue Pelican, but—' She grabbed my arm and spoke slowly, 'Now I remember where I heard Duncan's name. Not from Robert. From Beverly. Duncan helped her when she was in that trouble years ago.'

'How did you happen to acquire her as a client?'

'Robert told me about her. He said she was the friend of a friend. No doubt the friend was Duncan, but he didn't say so. Anyway, she was out of work and supposedly talented. I don't take on cabaret singers as a rule. But I took her to lunch, and right away I knew she had something

besides poise and looks. She radiates a kind of purity that seems to come from the soul.'

'I've seen her pictures.'

'Then you know. Well, I pulled a little coup. They were casting a new soap at one of the networks, and they needed a nineteen-year-old girl with that angelic quality. Beverly was twenty-three at the time, but I got them interested, and I staked her to the best acting coach and voice teacher in town. She worked like a trouper, got the part, and did so well they had to expand her role in the next story projection. Now she's got a part in a play that could take her to Hollywood.'

'Yeah, she does a terrific nude scene in the second act.'

Her teeth gleamed in the poor light. 'No! There's no way you could know that. That play's still in rehearsal, off Broadway.'

I laughed and told her about the Cassidy girl on the phone.

'Yes, that sounds like Irene. She's in the soap with Bev.' Her voice became more crisp. 'What do you intend to do?'

'Get inside Beverly's apartment. I want Duncan.'

'Do you suspect him of those murders you mentioned?'

'No, he's more like the next potential victim.'

She lit a cigarette. 'What if he's up there? Suppose he lied to Bev, and he's using her. Would you charge her with a crime?'

'I'm not after her scalp. I want Duncan.'

'That's not good enough. If I get her to co-operate, I want you to keep her out of it altogether. Do you have that authority?'

'I have it. But what would I get in return?'

'My help. I'll take you to that party and pass you off as a friend from, oh, say, California. With that tan, who would doubt it?'

'Do you go to bat like this for all your clients?'

'No, this is extreme. But there's something about Beverly that makes helping her a natural gesture. Of course, it isn't all altruism. I'm protecting my ten per cent, remember.'

The cynical remark didn't ring true. I said, 'If we're to pull this off, I'd have to have a job. We could say I

work for a man named Alex Crittenden, a film distributor based on the Coast.'

'Yes, I've heard of Crittenden. So we have a deal?'

'Yes, but your girl has to be on the up-and-up.'

'She is. And please call me Susan. These people know me as Susan Wolfe, the name of my agency. Shall we go up?'

'Not yet. Do you know if there's a doorman on duty over there?'

'Yes, until midnight I think.'

'I want a chat with him before we go up. Five minutes.'

'All right, Morgan—if we're old pals, I should call you that.'

I crossed the street and entered the lobby of the apartment house. A sign in the vestibule informed you that the doorman went off duty at midnight and all visitors had to buzz a tenant to gain entry after that hour. The lobby was empty, but there was a tiny office in one corner with the door ajar. Inside, an old man was sleeping at a desk, his head resting on his folded arms. He wore blue uniform pants and a wrinkled white shirt. A leather sap protruded from his hip pocket through the slats in the chair. I relieved him of the sap, then went back and slammed the door.

The old guy jumped. 'Hey, what the hell!' He blinked at me.

'What's the idea of sleeping on the job?' I asked roughly.

'What business is it of yours? You're not the super.'

I waved the sap. 'You know it's against the law to pack this.'

His hand darted for his hip pocket. 'That's for my own protection. There was a thug prowling the premises earlier, a hell of a bruiser. Hey, would you be the law?'

'You guessed it.' I flashed my badge and let him see my shoulder harness. 'I want the story on that prowler.'

He curled his lip in disgust. 'If that ain't like New York's Finest. You show up five hours after I call it in.'

'I'm in no mood for guff, old man. Don't make me get nasty about this sap.' I slapped it into my palm.

His eyes followed it. 'Okay, just sounding off. I saw this bruiser just after I came on duty at four. He was coming

I

down the stairs in the north wing. Nobody uses those stairs since we put in the new elevators. He was big, man. Built like a gorilla.'

'How was he dressed?'

'I don't know. Slacks, sweater, and a ball cap.'

'What did he do?'

'When he saw me, he took off down the hallway past the elevator. He got out to the alley behind the building through a back door.'

'Any complaints from the tenants about a robbery?' I asked.

'Nary a one. The super checked the doors, but no damage.'

I looked at a chart on the wall that listed the tenants by apartment number. 'How about the Sherwin girl in seven-A?'

He blinked. 'You mean the actress? No, she was out when it happened. I saw her come in about an hour later with bundles.'

'Was she alone?'

'Yes, but she's got plenty of company right now. Big party up there tonight. You think that gorilla was after her?'

'We've had complaints.' I threw the sap on his desk. 'Keep that out of sight. I have to call in, then I'll go up and join the party for a while. Just to be on the safe side.'

'I'm for that,' he said fervently. 'She's a peach of a girl.'

I went outside and crossed the drive to my car. I had my hand on the door handle when Susan Wolfe said, 'Over here, policeman!' There was an odd note of scorn in her voice. It took me a moment to locate her on a bench beneath a big tree, with the Hudson River and the Jersey shore behind her. I walked over.

'What's the matter?'

'I've been doing some thinking, and something doesn't add up.'

'Like what?'

'You said Duncan and Robert were together in some kind of crooked deal. You called Duncan a potential victim. You said Duncan was missing and Robert was missing. You're

interested in Duncan's whereabouts, but you
single question about where Robert might I
hide. I think you know where he is.'

'Yes, I know where he is. He was killed
house in Pearl Beach late yesterday afternoon.

I heard the sharp intake of breath. 'Why didn't you
tell me?'

'I meant to tell you later.'

'Yes, after you'd used me.'

'That was your idea, sweetheart. Let's not twist things.
Do you want me to drive you home now?'

'No. Just leave me alone for a while. Please.'

'How about a shot of brandy? I've got some in the car.

'No! Just take a walk.'

I took a walk up the drive. Autumn leaves crackled
underfoot. The night was crisp and clear, but you could
feel the dampness from the river. Suddenly I experienced
a warm rush of memory from the first time I had lived in
New York City, when I pulled a year of recruiting duty
here between my wars. The year was 1948 and I was
twenty-three, a first lieutenant. I had an apartment on West
End Avenue, and my girl and I used to take long walks
along the drive on autumn nights. She was a student at
Columbia, a rangy redhead with an extraordinarily beautiful smile and freckles on her shoulders. She had a lazy
way of moving until you got her on a tennis court, where
she was a whiz. She had passionately campaigned for Harry
Truman all that fall.

Why the sudden attack of nostalgia? I recognized the
symptom. That was one of the times in my life when I
could have made a decision that would have kept me out of
this line of work I call my avocation. If I had married that
girl—and I'd had the notion—I would have left the corps
and taken up another line of work. I wouldn't have had my
second war and the aftermath—the marriage to Elaine, the
crack-up, the job with the DeBlanc Agency, et cetera, et
cetera. But every man has several of these mileposts he can
retreat to and dwell on when things get rough. I turned and
hiked back to Susan Wolfe.

She was still sitting on the bench. She said, 'Morgan, I'd

ike that drink of brandy now.' Her voice was low, vibrant.

I got the flask from the car, sat down beside her again, and served her the two-ounce cap from the flask brimful. She knocked it back and squeezed my wrist while she swallowed.

She said, 'It's hard to believe he's dead. He was the most . . . indestructible man I've ever known. How did it happen?'

'He was shot in the chest, in Duncan's living-room.'

'That's odd. Did he know he was in danger?'

'Yes, and he was armed.'

'Then whoever did it was either very good or Robert's friend.'

'Why do you say that?'

'Because Robert had reflexes like a cat, and he was an expert shot. He was fifty-two years old, but physically he was in better shape than most men of thirty. He worked out every day of his life: swimming, boxing, squash, handball. No, Robert knew the man who killed him.' She dug a cigarette from her purse and lit it. The hand that held the lighter was steady. 'Did you do any good over there?'

It took me a moment to focus on her question. 'Yes, that man I called the Iceman was seen nosing around this afternoon. He and his pals must think Duncan is there. Susan, can't I take you home?'

'Not yet.' She turned and brought her face to within six inches of mine. I felt her grip on my jacket. She said, 'Butler, you said you'd been working on this case before Robert was killed. Is it something you mean to see through to the end?'

'Yes, all the way.'

'Another thing. I assume the police signed you on because you know your business. Have you done this sort of thing often?'

'Often enough.'

'Are you good at it? I know I sound like a damn producer asking for credits. But are you really good?'

'Susan, I'm an expert.' No other answer would have satisfied her. Her voice was so fierce it had gone hoarse.

'And finding this Duncan will help solve those murders?'

'Yes.'

She rose abruptly and flicked the cigarette away. 'Then let's go find Mr Duncan.'

I got up and took her arm. 'Are you sure you can pull it off?'

'Just you watch me pull it off.'

I had to say it. 'So you didn't love him, eh?'

'That's not it. I'm only doing what he would have done for me if our positions were reversed. Are you ready?'

'Let's go find Mr Duncan,' I said. I certainly didn't feel pity for her now.

CHAPTER XVI

IN the elevator Susan said, 'Suppose Duncan is at the party. Will he make a scene when he sees you?'

'I doubt it. He's a sick man, bad heart. If he's there, I'll greet him as an old friend. I think he'll play along.'

The door to 7-A was ajar, and the party was holding forth in two big rooms, one on either side of the entryway. The room on the right contained a piano, a dart board, and a black leather bar with stools—all of which were getting a strenuous workout. A young couple at the piano were performing, posing as a team assigned to write songs for a Hollywood musical of the thirties. The boy had golden locks to his shoulders and the girl was garbed in buckskin, a Jewish Pocahontas. Their satire was biting, sprightly, and they had an appreciative audience. The dart-throwers were a black with an Afro hairdo and a young white who looked like a newly minted Wall Street broker. They were talking heatedly, and each threw his darts as if to strike home a telling point. The people at the bar were high and animated, tossing conversation around like a medicine ball.

The guests in the living-room were more sedate. Couples and small cliques sipped drinks and talked in low voices. In one corner a husky girl stroked the hair of a pale blonde who looked as if she'd just come off the farm. Two sweet young things sipped wine and darted eyes at a wrinkled man

of sixty between them on the floor. The man appeared to be reciting a monologue.

'No Duncan,' I said. 'It seems a very mixed bag.'

'They're from Beverly's two worlds,' Susan said. 'Her soap and the off-Broadway play.' She touched my arm. 'There's Beverly.'

Beverly Sherwin entered the living-room through a doorway diagonally across from us. There was nothing theatrical about her entrance, but the effect was dramatic. Voices stopped, heads turned, glances were speculative, admiring, envious. Beverly was smaller than I'd assumed from her pictures, no more than five four and a hundred and ten. But her size had nothing to do with the impact she had. She had silky blonde hair well below her shoulders, without adornment of any kind. She wore pants and a bolero jacket that appeared to be made of white lace, through which her black briefs and bra were discernible. The white pants were sculpted low on her hips, giving you eight inches of exquisite flesh to admire. On any other woman the costume would have brought a leer to the mind, if not to the lips. But this woman gave off an elusive quality that evoked only appreciation. There was nothing frail, cute, or tawdry about her, nor was she sultry. This is not to say that she was not alluring, but her sensuality seemed locked inside an imperishable sweetness that conveyed the promise that if you were lucky enough to have any of it bestowed on you, all your sins would be wiped clean.

Beverly was followed by a husky young man wearing a virile guardsman's moustache and a Nehru suit. He moved well, but in the girl's wake he was a tanker lumbering behind a clipper ship.

Beverly and Susan exchanged greetings with a dainty touch of cheeks, and we had introductions all around. The man with Beverly was Tony McGraw, the director of her play, a little number called *Marathon Madness*. He had a nice smile and a hearty handshake. Beverly's grip in mine was brief, but her smile was memorable. You wanted to take it home and press it in a book like a rare flower.

She said, 'Welcome, Mr Butler. I hope you're only in the distributing end of the film business. If you're in produc-

tion, everybody here will start performing for you. A pure reflex.'

'Not everybody,' I said. 'I can't see you hustling yourself.'

It was a calculated remark, referring to what Cunningham had told me about her. But I detected no reaction on her part.

She laughed. 'Don't you believe it. I'm an ambitious girl.'

I shook my head. 'I'm no producer, but I think it's safe to say that if you wanted Hollywood, you could have it.'

'Speak to my very astute agent.' She squeezed Susan's arm.

Susan said, 'I told you that when you go out there, you'll go on our terms. None of this starlet routine and a chintzy five-year contract. And if *Marathon* is the hit I predict it will be, we can dictate the terms.'

'Speaking of which,' Beverly said, 'I've got some publicity stills from the play I want to show you. I'm a little uneasy about a couple of them. Exposure is one thing, pornography quite another. Come on, they're in the bedroom. Tony, get Mr Butler a drink.'

The girls moved off down the hall. My gaze must have lingered on them too long, or maybe something showed in my face.

For McGraw said, 'Maybe you need that drink. A little dry in the mouth, aren't you?'

I grinned as if he'd caught me out. 'They haven't invented the drink to cure this thirst. Is she your girl?'

'No. I once made the mistake of getting involved with an actress I was directing. It makes for a lousy working relationship.'

'You're a man of principle,' I said.

'No, just ambitious. *Marathon* is one hell of a play, and I want it to be perfect. To get back to that thirst. I know booze won't cure it, but it eases the pain.'

'You sound like the voice of experience. That rule about not dating your actresses must be hard to enforce of late.'

'It is for a fact. Butler, what say we hit yonder bar?'

The tempo in the rumpus room had increased by a

drink's worth. McGraw and I found a place at the bar and ordered. The bartender was a pro obviously hired for the evening. The name Carl was sewn above his pocket. He was brawny, with a phlegmatic face, as out of place in this crowd as a piece of garlic on a sundae. We got our drinks and imbibed. The racket in the room prohibited serious conversation, and after a while a fellow stopped by and challenged McGraw to a game of darts. McGraw introduced me to a willowy woman on the barstool beside me before he left.

She was dressed in a stylized version of an Indian sari, draped over one shoulder and under the other arm. She sported a gaudy emerald on the draped shoulder. Her hair was silver, so beautifully shaped and fine that it had to be a wig. Her face had a lacquered look, as if she'd sprayed her make-up on from a can. I hadn't caught her name, but I mumbled a greeting and started to turn away when she plucked me by the sleeve and said, 'Did I hear right? Are you in the film huckstering business with Alex Crittenden?'

'Well, I work for the man. Do you know him?'

'Know him? That is to laugh. I knew him before he had the proverbial pot or the window to throw it out of. Why, sir, I knew him in Hollywood back when the Sunset Strip was something you did against a picture window at Malibu for a late afternoon tryst. Not to say that the boulevard wasn't there. I don't go that far back. But it was not the cesspool it is today. God, what a corruption.' She made a gesture of disgust and almost fell off her stool.

A young man standing behind her caught her with a hand on the small of her back, and she said, 'Thank you, Lester.'

'Yeah,' he said, without altering his expression, which I would have called an adolescent sulk.

The woman gave me the exaggerated wink of the drunk. 'Lester is irked. He always gets irked when I get stewed in public. And I am stewed, make no mistake. But not so stewed I don't remember Alex.'

'And a late afternoon tryst at Malibu,' I said.

'Clever boy! Yes, we trysted. Or you might say that Alex jousted and I trysted. He was my knight in shining armour

and a swordsman of no mean repute, as we used to say. No doubt he had his press releases to live up to. Look, when you see Alex, tell him Molly Prescott said hello.' She tilted her head and a rapt expression came over her face. 'Funny, I wanted to speak to him when I saw him today, but—'

'You saw him today?' I said. 'Where?'

She flinched at the sharpness in my voice, then squinted at me. 'Ah, *where* is a tough question. Just tell him I saw him in the bar of a fabulous hotel, a hotel where he once wooed me. He was with a blonde, *très décolleté*, and he looked very sinister.'

Behind her back, Lester made a universal gesture, indicating that she was a little cracked. I said, 'I'll tell him, Molly Prescott. You weren't out on the Coast today, were you?'

She stiffened. 'Are you serious? I haven't been off this island in ten years. Well, I must go in and sneer at the soap sellers, the heart throbbers. Coming, Lester?'

He eased her off the barstool and held her until she had her equilibrium. 'You go ahead. I'll bring fresh drinks.'

'You're a sweetie, Lester.' She moved off sedately.

'Pardon my ignorance, Lester,' I said. 'But who is she?'

His sulk turned into a scowl. 'No reason why you should know her. She was a starlet back in the thirties, bit parts mostly. She married rich just before the war, migrated East, did some Broadway stuff, lost her husband in the war, married rich again. Now she clips coupons and backs plays. She's the big angel for *Marathon Madness*.'

'Do you think she saw my boss today? Or did she make it up?'

He shrugged. 'She leads quite a fantasy life. That stuff about your boss might have been just to get my goat. When she gets loaded, she likes to throw these red-hot lovers from the past at me.'

'What are you to her?' I asked bluntly.

He gave me an ugly grin. 'I'm the guy who holds the coupons while she clips them.' With that, he took the drinks and departed.

I waited a few minutes, then eased out of the room and down the hall to a door which I assumed was Beverly's

bedroom. I turned left and ambled on down to the kitchen, where I paused and listened for a minute to two men and a woman who were vehemently butchering the work of a European film-maker. Both the men had beards and the woman had a face that needed one.

I moved back down the hall to a closed door that interested me. I tried the knob, but it was locked. My interest mounted. To my left I watched Beverly and Susan leave the bedroom and head toward the rumpus room. I hustled down to the bedroom, entered the bath, and locked the door. As I'd hoped, a second door in the bathroom led to the room that had aroused my curiosity. I unsnickered a bolt on the door and tried it. It was also locked with a key. Kneeling to get a look at the lock, I spotted a tiny pill near the baseboard, surrounded by splinters of glass.

Somebody rapped hard on the bathroom door. 'Anybody home?'

It was a man's voice. 'One minute.' I tucked the pill into my shirt pocket, ran water in the sink, and opened the door.

Carl, the bartender, was standing there. 'Sorry to rush you, but I've got to get back.' His gaze flicked toward the other door and he frowned. I'd left the door unbolted.

I went jolly on him. 'Hey, I know I've seen you somewhere before. Haven't you worked in some nightclubs around town?'

'I've worked around,' he said grudgingly. He moved past me with a manœuvre that allowed his arm to caress my Luger. His eyes tightened. 'What's your line of work, buddy?'

I patted the Luger. 'You saw the lady I walked in with?'

'Yeah. I know who she is.'

'Her husband is paying me to escort her around town. He's got some nasty enemies who've been making threatening noises.'

He thought it over. Then he said, 'I knew you weren't one of them when I saw you packing iron. You need a better tailor.'

'Thanks for the tip. Hey, I know where I've seen you. Didn't you once work at the Blue Pelican?'

'Yeah, I worked at the Pelican. But I gave it up. Now I work a soft afternoon berth and pick up extra bread at shindigs like this.'

'Not a bad deal. Well, I've got to get back on duty.'

I drifted down the hall and located Susan Wolfe in the living-room. Minutes later she perched on the arm of my chair.

She said, 'Beverly's tense about something, but she claims it's only man trouble. Any sign of your Mr Duncan?'

'Yes.' I showed her the tiny pill. 'I gave Duncan one of these yesterday. Nitroglycerin. Plus the fact that Beverly has a back room locked up. Plus the fact that the bartender is an old pal of hers from the Blue Pelican. He's guarding that back room.'

I felt her nails on my wrist. 'What do we do?'

'Do you know if Beverly has an extra door key stashed someplace?'

'Yes, she keeps one in her bedroom.'

'You swipe it. Then we'll bide our time and get out before the party breaks up. You can make some excuse to Beverly.'

'Easy. I'll imply that you're an old flame and we want to spend some time together.'

'Sounds like an excuse she's heard from you before.'

A frosty smile hovered around her mouth. 'Mr Butler, my morals can hardly interest you. We've formed a partnership to do a piece of work. I think you'll find me reliable and resourceful. But let's not engage in dreary battles of who will dominate whom, with barbed innuendoes and amorous insults. Are we understood?'

'You are a conceited wench,' I said. 'What makes you think I want to play games with you, in or out of bed?'

'Why, I do believe the gentleman's angry,' she said.

'I never get angry at grieving widows.'

'So that's what rubs against your moral grain. You didn't get the typical response. I didn't blubber. Maybe I misjudged you. I thought you knew that helping find Duncan was my way of grieving.'

I took a deep breath. 'I withdraw the insinuation. Truce?'

'Truce, by all means.' She rose, haughty with tension and

very desirable. 'I'll circulate, then I'll get that key.'

She got it, and when the guests began milling around the buffet dinner, Susan and I left. We went down to the drive, got settled in the Merc, and had a nip of brandy. Then I asked her to tell me about the trouble that had brought Duncan and Beverly together.

'All right. The trouble began, oh, three years ago, at the Blue Pelican. It was Bev's first big job and she was doing very well, until the night an ugly little man named Dangler took a fancy to her. He was a gangster, one of the old breed, and people were scared of him. One night he pro- positioned Beverly. He offered her the works—from luxury apartment to a Mercedes. She turned him down, but every night for a week he came in and raised the ante. When she refused his last offer, he almost stuck his lighted cigar in her face. But he left, and she thought she was done with him.'

'But Mr Dangler wasn't done with her,' I said

'Not by a long shot. Vicious stories began to circulate about her. One had her on drugs, the hardstuff. Within a week she got her walking papers from the Pelican, her agent dropped her, and the police picked up her cabaret card. Needless to say, she became a social leper. Then she had a call from Mr Dangler.'

'I'll bet his offer had been reduced by a few shekels,' I said.

'Worse than that. All he offered now was a thousand bucks for a week-end with her, after which he would set her up as a lady of the evening, Park Avenue variety. Then she knew she was in real trouble. A musician friend lined up a job for her in Atlantic City. She actually snuck out of town on a bus and took the job under an assumed name. It was a third-rate club, a big comedown for Bev, but she stuck it out. She had a room in a motel—Duncan's prob- ably—and I gather he was smitten. But he treated her with total respect. Well, this set-up lasted a month. Then one night Bev sat down at the piano bar to do her act, and Mr Dangler was perched on a stool. He said something that terrified her. She never told me what it was. Bev appealed to Duncan. He moved her to his home and offered to marry

her. But Dangler harassed her even in Duncan's home.'

'I know about that part. Go on.'

'Here's the ironic part. Less than a week after Bev moved to Duncan's house, Mr Ugly Dangler was found in the Jersey swamps with a big hole in him. The story came out that a Jersey gang had long since warned him never to set foot on their side of the Hudson. I guess they didn't make allowances for a man sick with frustrated lust.'

'Was that your diagnosis or Beverly's?' I asked.

'Hers. And that ends my tale. She didn't want to marry Duncan, so she came back to New York and we hooked up. You know how.'

'She's had a very chequered career, this client of yours.'

'Yes, she seems to bring out either the best or the worst in men. But you can hardly blame her for that.'

We had more brandy. Then we smoked and listened to the radio while guests trickled down from the party.

'How will we know when they've all gone?' Susan asked.

'When Carl leaves,' I said. 'Let's hope he leaves alone.'

'Why?'

'Just wait.'

Carl appeared ten minutes later, but he wasn't alone. Beverly was with him, and between them they supported a hefty man who looked as if he were feeling no pain.

Susan whispered, 'Somebody really got loaded.'

I waited until they passed beneath a street light. 'I don't think he's drunk. I think he's dead. That's Matt Duncan.'

'How can you tell from here?'

'Let's call it an educated guess. You don't hire an unsavoury character like Carl just to get rid of a drunk.'

'But isn't it a crime to move a body like that?' she asked.

'Stop worrying about your client. She's not in jail yet. She's just flirting with it.'

'You don't have to get nasty.'

We were silent while Carl manhandled the body into a black Chrysler parked on the other side of the drive. Beverly and Carl got into the front, with Carl behind the wheel. He headed north.

'Hang on,' I said. I made a U-turn, gunned up a small grade, and spotted them waiting to make a left turn on to

the West Side Highway at 96th Street. When they made the
turn, I followed them to the highway. Carl jockeyed over to
the fast lane and burned rubber. I didn't want to be conspicuous, but I had to shove the needle up to eighty to
keep them in sight. Minutes later Carl switched three lanes
from left to right, doused his lights, and whipped off the
highway on the 158th Street ramp.

It was a piece of luck. I knew the exit and the streets
around it. Years earlier I had come here often to play tennis
on the courts beside the river. I doused my lights before I
hit the top of the ramp. The Chrysler's tail-lights were garish
red beacons at the foot of the hill. But instead of driving
straight up the hill to 158th Street, he made a sharp left
turn. It was a tricky manœuvre. It would put him on the
southbound ramp. At the bottom of the hill, I braked and
made the same left turn. I was all set to gun it up the other
ramp when I spotted a flicker of tail-lights on a service
road that ran north along the Hudson under the highway.

'Why are you stopping?' Susan asked.

'They took that dirt road.' I backed into the road, spun
back to the exit ramp, and sped up the rough brick road.

'Aren't you going to follow them?' she asked.

'They would see us. I'll go in on foot.'

At the top of the hill I made the ninety-degree right turn
and parked in front of a garage used by the city mainten-
ance people. I killed the engine. 'Some stairs over there
lead down to that park by the river. Now I use shank's
mare. Wait here.'

'Oh, no, you don't,' she said. 'If this ends up with Bev
being charged with a crime, I want to see the whole thing.'

'You might snag your sable,' I said.

'That's easily fixed.' She shrugged out of the coat, but-
toned her neat little jacket, and got out of the car.

We crossed the street to the stairway. Susan's heels
echoed eerily as we descended. At the bottom we stood
beneath the skeleton of girders supporting the West Side
Highway. The steel and concrete overhead vibrated with
each passing car. Noise and flashes of light seemed to rico-
chet down into our catacomb. The river smelled like freshly
peeled shrimp and crude oil.

The bulbs in the lamp-posts in the park h[...] by vandals. But the orange glow of the city [...] gave us adequate light. We followed the narr[...] past a row of handball courts, two tennis [...] paved area surrounded by benches. Here the [...] east for thirty yards, then turned north ag[...] parallel to the railroad tracks. We were cutting through a playground to intersect the road when a car door slammed not forty yards away. We were screened from the road by shrubbery. I took Susan's arm and we drifted to the corner of the playground. We heard Beverly speak in a low, plaintive voice.

Carl said, 'To hell with that noise. The longer it takes them to identify him, the better for all concerned.'

Beverly said something I couldn't quite catch.

'Don't go soft on me!' Carl said. 'You're the one in the fix. I'm sticking my neck out a mile to get you off this griddle, doll. So you'll play it my way, and no arguments.'

'All right. But let's stop on the way back for a drink,' Beverly said. 'I couldn't drink at the party, but now I need one.'

'There's plenty left at your place,' Carl said. 'We'll go back there and toast the dearly departed.'

'I'd rather stop at the Inferno. It's on the way.'

'You wouldn't be trying to get rid of Old Carl, would you?' he said. 'Listen, we've got things to talk about. We don't ever want anyone to get wise to this night's work, now do we?'

'No, of course not.'

'Then you listen to Carl. We go to your place. Come on.'

The car door slammed, and the Chrysler glided back the way it had come. Susan grabbed my arm and spoke sharply. 'What kind of a policeman are you, to let them drive off like that?'

'Easy, lady. They won't skip the country. Besides, what happened to all your concern about your precious client?'

She took a deep breath. 'I guess I felt a touch of horror. Whatever Duncan was, he was good to Beverly.'

'That's not what really worries you,' I said.

'Then tell me what worries me, clever man.'

'You're worried about how he died. Let's go look.'

'You're right. That is what worries me. All right, let's go.' This last was uttered with a touch of bravado.

I used my pencil flash to light the way. We found Matthew Duncan stretched out on a park bench, fully clothed and quite dead. I gave her the light to hold and went through his clothes. They hadn't left him so much as a matchstick. I opened his clothes and inspected the body, examining ears, eyes, scalp, neck, and torso. I even sniffed at his mouth. All I found was an old scar on his left bicep, likely the one Harry and the Iceman had tried to find on me.

'What's the verdict, doctor?' Susan asked.

'Looks like natural causes. Probably his heart.'

'Then it's not much of a crime, is it? If he told Beverly he was mixed up in a murder, then died of a heart attack, you can't blame her for doing this. In a way, what she did took courage.'

'Don't you ever stop working? Let's go hear her side of it.'

'What? Surely you're not going to leave him like this?'

'Why not? Mr Duncan couldn't care one way or the other.'

CHAPTER XVII

I DROVE back to Beverly Sherwin's apartment much faster than the law allowed. Some of the starch had gone out of Susan Wolfe. I doubted that she had ever seen a dead man outside a casket, and I suspected that the sight of Duncan had given to McCloud's death a reality it had lacked for a few hours.

But I offered her neither comfort for the one nor condolences for the other. One word along that line, and I would be taking away her strongest protection, her pride in her own toughness, her independence. It had served her well so far.

I left the West Side Highway at 96th Street, stopped at a red light, and spotted Carl's Chrysler parked at a fire hydrant on the drive. Carl and Beverly were inside, silhouetted against the headlights of the traffic flowing down the hill. They were arguing.

I nudged Susan. 'The body-snatchers. That changes our strategy.'

'I see them! But what do you mean about strategy?'

'I was going to use you to get us into her apartment. But now I'll go up ahead of them. You wait in the car until they go in. Then step into the vestibule and give her buzzer three rings. That will alert me. Wait five minutes, get upstairs, and ring the doorbell. Insist that Beverly let you in. Don't give up.'

She agreed to the plan. Minutes later I parked south of the apartment house and hiked up to the entrance. I had to push four buttons before a tenant answered over the intercom. 'Yeah?'

I read his name above the button. 'Telegram for Mr Schulman.'

'Hell, bring it up and slide it under the door.'

His buzzer snarled and I was in the lobby. I took the elevator up to seven and entered the apartment with the key Susan had swiped from Beverly's bedroom. I locked the door and went down the hall to the room that had been locked during the party. It contained an old desk, a filing cabinet, a bookcase, a bed neatly made up, a bureau, and a portable TV set. I saw no evidence that Duncan had ever been in the room. I began a more detailed search, when the buzzer in the aparement rang three times. Carl and Beverly were on the way up.

I cracked the door to the room and got my Luger out. They entered, and light from the living-room leaked into the hall.

Beverly was speaking. '—a sick joke. I don't find it amusing.'

'You know it's no joke,' Carl said. 'Or I wouldn't be here.'

'I brought you up here to prove what a liar you are! I know you threw Duncan's wallet down the incinerator

K

with the other stuff.'

'You're wrong. It's hidden here in your pad. Where you'll never find it in a year. And your fingerprints are all over it. Which means I can prove to the law that he died here any time I take the notion. One phone call. You hid a man wanted for murder.'

'You can't be that cold-blooded. I thought we were friends.'

'Don't make me laugh. At the Pelican you were Miss High-and-Mighty. You never gave me the time of day.'

She was silent for a moment. Then she said, 'All right, forget the past. Tonight you did an ugly thing for me. But you got well paid. A thousand dollars is awfully good pay for one evening.'

'Don't con me, doll. That grand came out of Duncan's wallet. So far, this little caper hasn't cost you a dime.'

'What are you getting at?'

'Your salary. You must make a grand a week on that TV show.'

She laughed off key. 'Barely half that, once you deduct my agent's commission, my acting lessons, my—'

'You'll have to learn to economize, like us common people.'

'What do you mean?'

'You've just picked up an extra expense—Old Carl. But I'm not greedy. I'll settle for five bills a month.'

'No! First prove that wallet is here. Show it to me!'

He chuckled. 'I knew you'd want proof, so I hid another item in a different place. Would Duncan's watch persuade you?'

'Get it.'

'You sit tight.' Carl went into the kitchen, banged around, and returned to the living-room. 'Read it and weep, doll.'

'You filthy, rotten blackmailer!' she said.

I heard flesh strike flesh. It jerked a sob from her. There was a brief scuffle, then a harder slap. 'Keep a civil tongue in your head when you speak to me,' Carl said, panting.

She spoke in a weary voice. 'You ruined my blouse.'

'I'll ruin more than that if you don't mind your manners. Look, I don't *need* your money. I'm liable to turn you in

for the kick of seeing you get busted. How would you look after five years in a laundry at the state prison for women?'

She murmured something in that plaintive tone.

'That's better,' he said. 'I'll tell you something else. Any time you want to take the five bills out in trade, Old Carl might be willing. In fact, I could use a down payment along those—'

He was interrupted by the doorbell. 'Who's that?' he asked.

'I don't know. It's the doorbell, not the street buzzer.

'Don't answer it.'

'I have to. They can see the lights. Maybe it's the super.'

'Then get rid of him. I'll wait in the back hall.'

Carl entered the hallway and stood with his back to me. Beverly went to the door and I heard her voice raised in query. I couldn't hear either end of the discussion that followed, but I assumed Susan was doing her stuff. Finally I heard Beverly unlock the door. Carl didn't like it. He backed down the hall toward me, his head cocked, listening. When he was three feet from me, I stepped out and jammed the Luger into his kidney. He grunted.

'Get frisky, Old Carl, and you'll be keeping Duncan company.'

'Butler?' he croaked.

'That's right.'

'Jesus, you scared me out of a year's growth.'

'You'll be lucky if that's all you lose tonight, black-mailer. Clasp your hands in front of you. That's right. Now, if you want to feel pain, separate those hands. Hold still for a frisk.' His only weapon was a limber little sap. Apparently saps were the vogue in New York this year. 'Now we join the ladies. Move it.'

We entered the living-room just as Susan and Beverly entered from the entryway. Beverly paled and said, 'Susan, is this your work?'

'Partly. Mr Butler is a police officer, and I advise you to trust him.'

'She's lying, doll,' Carl said. 'Cops don't pack Lugers.'

I rapped the corner of his jaw with the sap. It put a glaze on his eyes, but he didn't break the grip of his hands.

I said, 'Cops don't beat helpless prisoners either. Sit, black-mailer.'

'Blackmailer?' Susan asked.

'That's his game. Carl stashed Duncan's wallet in the apartment, evidence that could stick Beverly with two crimes—aiding and abetting a fugitive, and dumping that body.'

'See what your meddling has done!' Beverly said to Susan.

Susan ignored her. She flung her sable aside and came over beside me. Maybe it was her costume, but she seemed to regard Carl the way the matador regards the bull. 'So he's a blackmailer. But can't we wreck his scheme by find-ing that wallet?'

'We don't have to find it. Carl's going to get it for us.'

'Screw you!' Carl said through clenched teeth.

I snapped the sap into his face and broke his nose.

'Hey, Butler, that was a little rough,' Susan said.

'Rough is the way Carl likes it,' I said. 'He was roughing Beverly up when you rang. His way of getting amorous.'

'That's true,' Beverly said. She lifted a skein of hair and turned her face toward the light. Her cheek was swollen and bruised.

Susan took a close look. 'Get an ice pack on that. You can't go in front of the camera Monday looking like a Times Square chippy.'

'Wait,' I said. 'Was Duncan dead before Carl arrived tonight?'

'Yes,' Beverly said. 'I called Carl to get him out of here.'

'All right. Go get your ice.'

She left the room and Susan returned to my side. 'I have an idea,' she said. 'How would it be if you and I swore we saw Carl loading Duncan's body all by himself?'

'You could never make that stick,' Carl said.

'You're wrong, Carl,' I said. 'We could say that we saw you slug Duncan and manhandle him into your car. You were rough, and he died on you. Oh, we could make it stick, blackmailer.'

'Stop calling me by that name!'

'Why? That's your trade, isn't it?'

'No. Man, I earn a good living. Look, I wouldn't have taken money from Beverly. I was just showing off. All in fun.'

'So hiding that wallet was your idea of a gag?' I said.

'Yeah, along that line. Bev and I go way back.'

'I heard all about that. Get the wallet, Carl.'

He wiped blood from his mouth and chin. 'I need a screwdriver.'

I took out my camper's all-purpose knife and opened the screwdriver shaft. 'Go to it, Carl. I'm right behind you.'

He led me into the bathroom, where he unscrewed the light fixture above the sink and produced the wallet. 'Do you mind if I clean up a little?' he asked.

I nodded. He sponged the blood from his face gingerly with a wet cloth, and we returned to the living-room. Beverly and Susan were on the sofa. Beverly held an ice pack to her cheek. I had Carl sit at a small table in one corner and sat down across from him. I wiped the wallet clean, the leather, hardware, and plastic card cases. Then I threw it in front of him. 'Pick it up, Carl.'

His eyes were as bitter as the pits from the olives in the thousands of Martinis he had served. He shrugged and picked it up.

I said, 'Now put a set of prints on every card case.'

Blood rushed into his face. 'I will like hell!'

I hefted the sap. 'Do it, Carl.'

His glance flicked over to the women. It hurt him to knuckle down in front of them. But he opened the wallet and printed it.

'Now I want the thousand bucks you took from the wallet.'

'Hey, that's not fair,' Beverly said.

'Shut up!' I said. 'Let's have the loot, Old Carl.'

He took his wallet out. 'You don't leave a man much, do you?'

Duncan's thousand was easy to spot—twenty new fifties. I removed them, returned the wallet, and he put it away.

'Go home, Carl,' I said. 'You're in the bag now. If you ever bother this girl again, you'll be the one who sweats out five years in prison. Now scram.'

He got up and walked to the doorway, where he tried to salvage some pride with a final word : 'I still say you're no cop.' He left.

I spent a full minute lighting my stogie to my satisfaction.

Susan Wolfe pinched an earlobe between two scarlet nails and said, 'Watching you spring into action is quite an experience.'

Beverly lowered the ice bag. 'Mr Butler, I don't know why you didn't let him keep the money. God knows, he earned it.'

'I'll tell you why,' Susan said. She watched me with the shrewdness of an old cat. 'Morgan wanted all of Carl's memories of tonight to be painful ones. All loss, no profit.'

I said nothing. I smoked and studied Beverly Sherwin. She rose abruptly. 'I need a drink. Anyone else?'

Susan ordered brandy, but I shook my head. After Beverly had left the room, Susan made a clicking noise with her tongue.

She said, 'Let me revise my theory about why you were so hard on Carl the Louse. It was a performance, wasn't it? You broke him down and stripped him to impress Beverly with your ruthlessness.'

'Maybe I'm just the sadistic type,' I said.

'No, but that's what you want Beverly to think. You want her scared and pliable.'

'All I want from her is the truth about what happened with Duncan. You should want the same thing. You have a stake in this.'

'Yes, but I don't like your methods. I wonder if Carl wasn't right about one thing. You're not really a cop.'

'You'll find out how much of a cop I am if Beverly doesn't come clean,' I said. 'She'll serve time.'

'That's just another form of blackmail, isn't it?'

'But when I do it, it's legal. What are we fighting about?'

The question seemed to startle her. 'I don't know. Ragged nerves, maybe. I seem to have forgotten our mission. Another truce?'

'Agreed.'

Beverly returned with the drinks, wearing a taut, brooding expression. She served Susan and stood with her high-

ball glass held beneath her breasts. She said, 'In three hours it will be six am, twenty-four hours since Matt Duncan called. Everything that's happened since is a little jumbled in my mind. Take Carl. I really thought I could trust him. In the old days he was always jolly with me, even protective. So when I came back from shopping yesterday and found Matt dead, Carl seemed the only one who could help. And for a while I thought it had worked. We had gotten rid of the ugliness. So when he began to spout that evil blackmail business a while ago, one part of my mind refused to believe it. But just now in the kitchen I had a glimpse of what Carl would have done to me in months to come if you two hadn't been here. I got the shakes, and I felt terror like hot wires. So I thank you. End of speech.' She made a humble gesture with the glass and drank. 'What now?'

It was the kind of talking jag that is often the prelude to hysteria. I gave her my warmest smile and said, 'Now we sort out those jumbled events you mentioned. Then you'll take a sedative and sleep the clock around. Sit down here at the table.'

'Do I get the third degree?' A coyness flickered in her eyes as she took Carl's seat and folded her hands. 'The weird thing is, Matt swore there was no way anyone could connect him with me.'

'No mystery there,' I said. 'We traced you through some snapshots he took of you that time you stayed at his house.'

'I see. Do you know why I was staying at his house?'

'Yes. Susan filled me in about that gangster.'

Beverly looked at Susan. 'That was sweet of you, dear.'

Susan's voice crackled. 'Listen! Robert was murdered in Duncan's house yesterday. Butler is investigating the murder. That takes precedence over all girlish confidences. Do you understand?'

Beverly gave her a long, incredulous look, then a spasm crossed her face. For a second I thought she would fold up. But she said, 'Oh, Susan, I am sorry. Did Duncan do it?'

I said, 'No. He ran because he was afraid he would be next.'

'That explains a lot,' Beverly said. The impact of murder

seemed to stabilize her. 'Duncan was scared. He—'

'Wait, I want it in order, from the beginning,' I said.

She nodded, and she told it fairly well, all things considered. Duncan had phoned at six am and begged her to put him up for two days. She owed him too much to refuse. She was troubled about the party she had scheduled, but Duncan promised to remain out of sight. So she put him up in the back room, and he slept until noon. Over lunch she asked about his trouble, but he was evasive. He told her only that he expected a call from a man named Ralph Maynard. After lunch, Duncan relaxed in his room while Beverly ran some errands. When she returned, Duncan was trying to place a long-distance phone call. He was very excited. Finally he gave it up, his face grey and haggard. He sent her for his nitroglycerin pills, dissolved one under his tongue, and appeared to recover. But he was extremely agitated. He asked the operator to keep placing the call every hour. But he was worried about not being in shape to come to the phone. So he had Beverly write down the name of the man he was calling and the message she was to give him if she had to take the call.

'Did you save that piece of paper?' I asked.

'Yes, it's here in the end table.' She got it for me.

I read it. The party Duncan had tried to call was Gilford Sims, in Jericho, Tennessee. The message read: *Tell Maynard I saw Trader Horn in Atlantic City. Maybe he got to the Warden.*

'Did he add anything that would help identify these names?'

Beverly said, 'Funny, I asked about that, because the message was so vague. But he said that Maynard would understand it.'

I put the cryptic message away. 'Okay, tell the rest of it.'

'All right. I had to go out again. When I got back, a little after five, he was dead.' Her hands formed two hard fists. 'Here's the ugly part. Someone deliberately let him die.'

'How do you know that?'

'Duncan must have had another heart attack in the bed-

room. He kept his nitro pills and pain pills in there. But someone had taken those bottles into the bathroom and crushed them on the floor. Whoever it was also locked the bathroom door. I saw where Duncan had beat on the door with my stapling machine.'

'That practically makes it murder,' Susan said.

'I know,' Beverly whispered. 'I almost called the police. But I was scared. So I called Carl, instead.'

'How did Carl know Duncan was wanted for murder?' I asked.

'He saw an item in the *Post* about a man killed in Atlantic City and Matt being wanted for questioning. Mr Butler, what now?'

What now, indeed. A part of my mind relaxed, and Beverly Sherwin's face inflated in my vision like an image on the silver screen—lavender eyes, silky lashes, delicate bones —enchantment. I hardly knew the girl, yet of the three men I knew who had become involved with her, Dangler and Duncan were dead and Carl was badly bruised. Men died around her, but I doubted if she ever caught so much as a whiff of the shroud and the mouldy earth. I detected the smell of nervous perspiration from her. Her halo was tarnished.

She said, 'Well, what's the verdict, judge?'

I got her back into focus. 'The verdict is that I don't want you to spend the rest of tonight in this apartment,' I said.

'May I ask why not?' she said.

'You may. There's a good chance Duncan died before the Iceman got anything out of him. If that's true, they have to find out if he gave you information to pass on, like this message. So I think they'll be back. I want to be here to greet them. Alone.'

'If you're trying to scare me, you're doing a first-rate job,' Beverly said. 'But where do I go?'

'You go home with me,' Susan said. 'I'll have Max pick us up in the basement garage. Is that the way you want it, Morgan?'

'Yes. Say, you are resourceful.'

'I'm glad you noticed.' She dialled the number, cupped the mouthpiece, and said to Beverly, 'You'd better pack a few things.'

Beverly left the room. Susan finished giving instructions and hung up. She said, 'Well, Mr Unorthodox Policeman, can I assume—'

'Your client's off the hook. You do work for that ten per cent.'

She stiffened. 'What's the matter, your work not going well? Three dead men and nobody to put the cuffs on? Hey, maybe that's why you worked old Carl over. Frustration.' She lifted an arm to fluff her hair, turning her head archly. Her breasts moved saucily, as she intended. It was a gesture both brazen and contemptuous.

She was standing too close when she did it. I hooked two fingers into her sash, jerked her forward, and kissed her hard. She neither resisted nor participated.

When I released her, she said, 'What was that for?'

'Maybe I just wanted to see what you tasted like.'

Her expression was all mockery. 'No, you were after a response of some kind. I think you're still looking for the grieving widow.'

'But all I find is the plastic mannequin, programmed by IBM in the vaults of the Chase Manhattan Bank.'

'My, he tells jokes, too. Now, may I get my ten per cent and leave?'

'I hope the two of you will be very happy,' I said.

CHAPTER XVIII

IT was pushing four am when they left. Twice I heard the hollow rattle of a loose manhole cover on the drive as cars passed over it. It was a melancholy sound, very appropriate to the hour.

I poured a glass full of dry vermouth, drank half, and called Jim Cunningham in Pearl Beach. His hello was husky with sleep. I identified myself. He said, 'Jesus, you keep hard hours. What's up?'

'I found Matthew Duncan.'

'Alive?'

'Nope. Dead since yesterday evening. His heart, I think.'

'Where did you find him?'

'He's on a park bench beside the Hudson River. I want you to contact the law up here and have them pick him up.'

'Why haven't you called them?'

'I don't want to spend hours explaining why I was in that park. You can plead ignorance. Tell them your hotshot deputy saw someone dump the body, then took off after the guilty party.'

'How do I explain why you called me instead of them?'

'Tell them I had a third party report it.'

'All right, I'll bluff it. But I hope you don't mind telling me how you got to that park. Just to satisfy my morbid curiosity.'

'I'll tell. But there's a certain party I want to keep out of it. I made a deal to get some co-operation.'

'Oh, you're a hotshot deputy, all right. Can you guarantee that the coroner won't find a hole from a Magnum in Duncan's hide?'

'Nary a hole. You have my word.'

'Ha! Tell me about it. Pretend I'm the chief of police.'

'Okay. I'll start with Mrs Robert McCloud.' I told it chronologically and factually, omitting only the trivia.

When I'd finished, Cunningham said, 'You have put in a busy night. That McCloud woman is one cool customer.'

'I noticed. Jim, will you contact whatever law they have in Jericho, Tennessee, and get a fix on this Gilford Sims?'

'Number-one priority. You think Maynard is with Sims?'

'That's the way I read that message Duncan left. Sims was to warn Maynard about somebody named Trader Horn, a character Duncan must have spotted in Atlantic City.'

'But that doesn't wash. Duncan rode to New York with Maynard. If Duncan saw this gink in Atlantic City, he'd have told Maynard.'

'Maybe he saw somebody, but didn't figure out until later that it was this Trader Horn.'

'Pretty thin. Let's pass that for now. This case is turning into a comic opera. Trader Horn. The Warden. The Iceman. Any ideas?'

'Just one. I would add Gilford Sims to that list you're checking out with the Defence Department. Any word on that yet?'

'Too early. But I've got a man down there cutting red tape.'

'Good. Add this name to the list. Alexander Crittenden.'

'Maynard's half brother? Why?'

'He was seen in New York yesterday when he was supposed to be on the Coast. He could have been in the Army with those others.'

'Okay. But you know what troubles me? Three of the five are dead, and Maynard has led a very charmed life. By God, I'd better call the law in Jericho, if only to give Sims some protection.'

'You could be right about Maynard. Any leads on the Iceman?'

'Not yet. How long are you going to hang around waiting for that bruiser to waltz in and knock you around some more?'

'I'll give it until noon. It's a good hunch. Check me out. They rousted me in Atlantic City, then broke into Duncan's motel office, then McCloud's townhouse. They're desperate for information, and I think they've hit a dead end. They'll show up here.'

'Good luck. But if they don't show by noon, you plan on a trip to Tennessee, depending on what I turn up about Sims.'

'Fair enough. I'll be in touch.' I hung up.

I experienced a glow of exultation, which I couldn't for the life of me justify. Jazzed up, I prowled the apartment. In Beverly's office I found a copy of her play, *Marathon Madness*. It was the story of several people involved in a marathon group therapy session at a mountain retreat. I read a few pages, and it wasn't half bad. So I got a full glass of vermouth, put it beside my Luger on the nightstand, and stretched out on the bed to read the play. I'd just finished the first act when the doorbell rang. It

strummed my nerves like a chord on a flamenco guitar.

I picked up the Luger and moved down the hall and had a look through the peephole. Susan Wolfe stood there, wearing a dark mink coat instead of the sable, toting a leather shoulder bag that clashed with the mink. She was alone, so I opened the door.

She said, 'Don't shoot. I'm a friendly.' She appeared to have undergone a subtle transformation. Her voice was mellow, and her eyes and mouth created an effect of humility. I invited her inside.

I locked up again and turned on lights in the living-room. She deposited the leather bag on the sofa—with considerable care, I thought—and removed the mink. The transformation was complete. She had shed the *caballero* outfit. In its place she wore a snug cashmere dress of hunter's green, decorated with gold embroidery. She sat poised on the sofa, elegant, proud, enigmatic.

'You don't seem very surprised to see me,' she said.

'I was expecting company. You could be it, for all I know.'

'Hey, surely you're not suspicious of me?' she said.

'Not if you have a good reason for being here.'

'I have several reasons. Won't you put that gun away?'

'Sure.' I put the Luger in the drawer of an end table and sat down in the easy chair beside the table. 'Fire away.'

'All right. The first reason is a piece of information I wanted you to have. Remember that message Duncan left about the Warden? Well, Robert was the warden of an Army stockade in the South Pacific during World War Two. I don't know exactly where.'

'When did you happen to remember this little item?'

She coloured a little. 'When you read that message. But I was feeling spiteful toward you then. I'm sorry about that.'

'You could have given me this dope over the phone,' I said.

'That brings me to reason number two. It occurred to me that if that gang means to question Beverly, they'll call first to make sure she's here. If you answer, you'll scare them off. But if I were here, I could pass myself off as Beverly on the phone.'

'That makes sense,' I said grudgingly. 'What else?'

She hesitated, then a little of her briskness came to the surface. 'I don't mean to pry, but I really am in the dark about your position in all this. You said you were involved before that chief deputized you. Does that mean you were hired by someone?'

'Yes.'

She waited for me to say more. When I didn't she made a shy gesture and said, 'Would it be unethical for me to hire you, too?'

'Ethics don't enter into it. It just isn't necessary. I've already told you I mean to see this case through to the end.'

'Maybe you consider my money tainted because Robert's a crook.'

'Don't work yourself into a lather. I never held with the view that money could be contaminated by the people who handle it.'

'How tolerant. Then maybe you just don't want to work for me.'

'Why do you want to hire me? So you can order me around?'

Now her expression was solemn. 'No, Mr Butler. I seriously doubt that anyone orders you around, even if you're on their payroll. I think you operate from a very private code of your own. You're like Robert in that respect. You don't consult people. You don't need a committee to make a decision. You encounter a situation, and you act. You want something, and you go after it. It's a rare trait and an admirable one. Do you resent the comparison with Robert?'

'No, but you talk too much, and too much of it's about me.'

'That's why I want to hire you. I thought it would entitle me to the answers to some personal questions about you.'

'Such as?'

'Well, how did you get into this line of work? Where do you live? What else do you do?'

'What makes you think you have to pay me for those answers?'

'Habit, pure habit. I'm a New Yorker. Here money is the substitute for everything. Money oils the hinges, calks the cracks, greases the skids. Money buys privacy, pleasures, privileges. It isn't just a medium of exchange, it's a form of communication.' She stopped, as if embarrassed at the vehemence that had crept into her voice. 'I'm still talking too much. If I offended you, I'm sorry.'

'I'm not offended. I'm just waiting for you to tell me the real reason why you changed costumes and came back over here.'

I meant to needle her, but instead of indignity she responded with a quaint smile. 'I was getting to that. Oh, those reasons I gave were sincere. But they were part and parcel of another motive. I took Bev home, gave her a sleeping pill, and she went out fast, emotionally exhausted. I almost took a pill myself, but I despised the impulse. What a hollow way to treat the death of a man with the vitality of Bob McCloud. Then I thought of all the other hollow acts I have to perform—buy a cosmetic job from an undertaker, a stranger who never knew him. Buy a mass-produced casket, a ditto headstone, the phony prayers. Bob would hate me for the travesty.'

'So I'm a substitute for a sleeping pill? I don't get it.'

'Wait.' She opened the leather bag and produced a fifth of liquor and two glasses. 'I decided to hold a private wake for Robert, a ceremony he would appreciate. A wake is very appropriate. He was half Irish. I brought a fifth of Bushmill, good Irish whiskey. You can't hold a wake alone, so I hoped you might join me.' Her smile would have converted a Nazi to Judaism.

It didn't quite reach me. I was as thorny as a cactus with suspicion of this woman. Her entire performance seemed out of character. Too recent in memory was the pseudoseduction worked on me by the gypsy Carol. I had a quick flash of insight : With all Susan's talk of widowhood and wakes, she had come here to persuade me that McCloud was dead, which meant that he might be alive. The charred corpse may have been a more complicated conspiracy than we suspected. Or she could be setting me up for someone.

I said, 'You can't be this hard up for drinking companions. You must have friends who would be happy to send Robert off in style.'

Her eyes were moist, lustrous. 'Yes, I have friends. But not one would have used that phrase, "send him off in style." Oh, I made a mental list of our friends. The hell of it is, Morgan Butler, in this city most of your friends are fellow hustlers. You make friends because you can do something for one another—socially, politically, artistically. You are always hustling, at every luncheon, dinner party, bridge game. If I called one of those friends at four am to join me in a wake, he would ask what to wear and who else would be there. Not a pagan in the lot. Not an ounce of spontaneity in a carload. Oh, they're decent enough in their own way. But if I made a sweet fool of myself, there's not one who wouldn't use it against me later. I won't have that kind of restriction. The trouble with this goddamn city, Morgan, there's not enough money or mercy to go around.' She made a shy gesture with the bottle. 'So I ask again, will you join me in a wake?'

Under pressure, she had shed the polish that made her come across as a pampered woman armoured against the crudities of life. Her face revealed something warm and tender that could be crushed. She said, 'You see, I need a salty individual, a man with character.'

'What makes you think I have character?' I asked.

'Oh, the way you behaved tonight. Okay, so there's risk involved. But at least you won't be my hangover for months to come. Will you booze it up with me, Mr Morgan Butler?'

'I'd be honoured.' I felt sodden with shame for my suspicions. A paranoid suspicion is what you substitute for intelligence when things go badly for you. Now I felt bolstered by her trust. I took the bottle from her and poured the glasses brimful.

She raised her glass with a jaunty motion. 'Let's drink to Bob McCloud, deceased. He could be seven kinds of a bastard. He could be ruthless, lusty, vain. He started as a coal miner's son in Harlan County, Kentucky, and he made a million bucks. He had good taste in wine, clothes, cars

and, if I do say so, in women. He also had a lifelong fascination with the sordid and the seamy side. He would go on binges, sexual as well as alcoholic, and he always told about it afterward. But whatever else he was, he was a man.'

We touched glasses. I said, 'Hallelujah,' and we drank.

We had another round, and Susan decided the wake should be spiced with music strictly in the American grain. From that bottomless shoulder bag she pulled several tape cartridges and inserted one in Beverly's stereo. First we had down-home Dixieland jazz, Sidney Bechet playing 'Big Butter and Egg Man,' Bunk Johnson's 'Sobbin' Blues,' and Coleman Hawkins' rendition of 'Stompin' at the Savoy.'

At one point we drank a toast to their marriage. It had lasted a decade because, Susan informed me, she had always been more mistress than wife, no mean feat since it is the task of the mistress to heap scorn upon the marriage and provide a haven from it. But she'd had the talent to pull it off. Anyway, acting was part of her heritage. The only child of a show business couple, she'd been born when they were both past forty. They had always been embarrassed about their tardy fecundity. 'Which is why I've always felt a trifle illicit,' she said.

Later she kicked off her pumps and we danced to 'Body and Soul,' and 'Blue Reverie,' from Benny Goodman's 1938 jazz concert in Carnegie Hall. Her body grew more pliable. We had another drink, and the whiskey glistening on her mouth made it appear sultry. I kissed her. Her tongue caressed mine with delicate stabs of pleasure.

When it ended, I said, 'A great improvement over our first kiss.'

'Yes, you rat. Programmed by IBM, indeed.'

'You had it coming. You were giving me the business.'

'I know. I wanted you to insult me. I was afraid that if you said one kind word to me, I'd come apart at the seams. But when I was alone with that sleeping pill, I knew I had to come back. I know you have character, because of what you did for Beverly.'

'To hell with that.' I kissed her again. Her tongue was even more nimble, her flavour spicy and hot.

She shoved her head against my chest and said, 'Whoa.

I didn't mean for this wake to include a seduction.'

'You made no rules. Don't start acting the grieving widow now.' I picked her up and carried her into the bedroom.

On the way she said, 'That's just it. I don't feel like the widow. Or the wife. Or the mistress.'

'Stop being so damn analytical. Call it your answer to those widows in India who throw themselves on the funeral pyre.'

She looked enchanted. 'That's lovely! You be my pyre.'

She came out of the cashmere dress like something ripe and glistening from a ruptured pod. On the bed she surged in my arms as if we rolled in ocean surf. Our hands collided as we touched. Soon she was all silk and sinew, rippling around me, and at the peak of her pleasure she gave a sob of voluptuous delight.

We were quiet for a while, then she smiled lazily and said, 'A pyre to put out a fire.' We laughed, and then we settled down into the tropical aftermath, savouring each other. We drank wine, smoked, talked, kissed, and fondled. Susan grew languid, lovely in the oil of her sweat. There was no talk of guilt or shame or who had used whom. We felt proud, heartened, strengthened.

Until then I hadn't realized how weary I had grown of defending myself against the sly barbs and stiletto thrusts of the emotions aroused in troubled women—from Elaine to Carol Mitchell to Beverly Sherwin—which was why I'd been so wary and sceptical of Susan.

I held her by one earlobe and said, 'Fair Lady, you have restored my equilibrium with all your mystical powers.'

'No euphemisms, please. Debauchery is what you needed.' She moved her breasts against me in a spectacular way. 'Why, I do believe you're on the verge of debauching me again.'

I was, and I did, for a long, euphoric time. Afterward, we slept until the phone rang. It was the call we had been expecting, the serpent who always intrudes into Eden.

At the second ring, Susan propped herself on one elbow and nodded. As pre-arranged, I put the phone between us.

Susan answered it, holding the receiver so we could both hear.

A crisp feminine voice said, 'Is this Beverly Sherwin?'

'Yes, who is this?' Susan asked.

'You don't know me. My name is Elaine Maynard. My husband brought a mutual friend to your place yesterday, Matthew Duncan.'

I shook my head and Susan said, 'You must be mistaken.'

'You're the one who's mistaken,' the woman said tartly. 'I know Duncan was in your apartment. I also know where the police found his body. There's an item in the *Times* about it. I think the police would love to know where he died. Now will you co-operate?'

Susan said, 'Exactly what is it you want, Mrs Maynard.'

'That's better. I didn't mean to get nasty, but you must know that my husband is in the same trouble Duncan was in. Here's my problem. Ralph and Duncan planned to get in touch with a friend who could help them. Ralph told me to call Duncan at your place and get the address, so I could join him. With Duncan dead, I'm stymied.'

I scribbled *be coy* on a pad. Susan said, 'I agree that you're in a tough spot, Mrs Maynard. But I don't see how I can help.'

'I have to know where Ralph is! Surely Duncan made some calls from your place. Or maybe he left a message for Ralph.'

I scribbled again, and Susan said, 'I do recall a message of some kind. I'd have to look for it. Can I call you back?'

'No, I'm at a pay phone. I'll call you in ten minutes.'

'Make it twenty,' Susan said. 'I have to find that message.'

'All right, twenty minutes.' The receiver clicked in my ear.

Susan replaced the phone. 'How was I?'

'You were fine.' She looked naughtily nude with a strand of hair draped over one breast. 'You were superb.'

She smiled. 'I didn't mean that, rogue.'

'I know what you meant. You shower while I make coffee. We've got to concoct a little strategy for the lady.'

'It's a deal. I gather that wasn't Mrs Maynard.'

'No, indeed. That was my playmate from Atlantic City, the Iceman's little helper, Carol Mitchell.'

In fifteen minutes we had finished a pot of coffee and had our strategy mapped out. We were seated at the table in the living-room, the phone between us. Susan said, 'But what makes you so sure that she'll bite? She can't prove she's Mrs Ralph Maynard.'

I grinned. 'You saw her in action. This is no choir girl. She'll assume she can bluff the message out of you, once she gets you alone. Or she might bring the Iceman along. He's persuasive.'

She gave a little shiver. 'Enough said. All right, sir, I shall carry out your instructions to the letter.'

She lit a cigarette and the phone rang. Susan answered, paused, and said, 'Yes, I've got it. But I've had some second thoughts, Mrs Maynard. I can't give you this information over the phone. I know there is danger for the men involved, so I have to be careful. How do I know you are Mrs Maynard?'

She listened, mugging at the static she got from the other end. Then she said, 'No, you can't come here. I have to go downtown. In fact, I have an appointment in midtown at one. I could meet you around noon.' There was more crackling from the earpiece.

Susan said, 'No, I must be adamant about this identification. Why should you object?' She paused, then: 'Of course I'll be alone. Do you know the main branch of the public library on Fifth? Fine, let's meet in Bryant Park, behind the library. There's a bust of Goethe in the southeast corner. I'll meet you there. I'll be the blonde in the blue-tinted fun fur. Noon sharp.' She hung up.

I looked at my watch. 'Ten-thirty. Time for me to get back to my motel and dress for the occasion. You go straight home.'

Her mouth drooped at one corner. 'Ah, men. Duty calls, and the party's over. Tossed aside like an old shoe.'

I sensed that she needed the levity to dilute something bitter that had crystallized in her. 'That's the risk you party girls run.'

She made an airy gesture. 'Yes, an occupational hazard.

But Daddy always said to exercise your God-given talent.'

'If it's any consolation, you're the best in your line.'

'No compliments. We prefer strictly commercial transactions.'

'It came close to having that stigma, remember?'

Her sudden laugh was warm and gay. 'Yes! *I* almost hired *you*. At least you spared me that, Mr Morgan Butler.'

She was all right again. At the door she kissed the corner of my mouth. 'You be careful. I won't make any girlish pitch about seeing me again. But call before you leave town. Please.'

'I'll call you.'

CHAPTER XIX

AT a quarter to twelve I occupied a bench about forty yards north of the statue of Goethe in Bryant Park. I wore a brown suede jacket, sunglasses, and one of those caps the sports car buffs affect. I sat behind a copy of the New York *Times*.

There was a nice crowd in the park, including tourists with cameras. The bright sun brought them out and the chill in the air kept them moving. On a flight of stairs below me, two bearded vagabonds were playing folk music on guitars.

Precisely at noon Carol Mitchell walked briskly up the steps past the guitar players, bareheaded, wearing a red plaid coat. She was a blonde again. She lingered near the music lovers, casing the area around Goethe. It was sparsely occupied. So she strolled over and sat on a bench about four axe handles south of the statue.

During the next fifteen minutes, she smoked three cigarettes and brushed off two young men who tried to pick her up. She began to get edgy. She got up and moved to a stone wall which overlooked a field of grass with a promenade around it. Suddenly she turned and examined every bench in sight. But I was slouched behind my paper.

Then she decided to scram. She wheeled and stepped out

smartly, exiting from the park on 42nd Street, headed east.
I used a narrow walk adjacent to the library and trailed her
to Fifth Avenue. She crossed the avenue, as if headed for
Grand Central. I followed, closing the gap. At the Lincoln
Building she pulled a cute trick. She darted inside and
down a stairway that led to the subway complex under
Grand Central. But I got down there in time to see her drop
a token in a slot, click through a turnstile, and clatter downstairs. It was the entrance to the shuttle to Times Square.
Tokenless, I snatched open an exit door and bulled my
way down steps past people who had disembarked from a
train. Carol boarded a forward car. I ducked into one well
behind her. The doors closed, and we shuttled to Times
Square.

No doubt it was an escape route she had worked out
ahead of time, and it was a good one. For on the other
end, I lost her. She left her car at a run, well ahead of the
pack. I got jammed in a flow of humanity moving in six
directions at once, catching only a flash of blonde and
red. She could duck into any of a dozen tunnels. But I
followed my last sighting and got to the Broadway line, the
downtown platform. A train thundered in. I could see
through its windows to the uptown platform. Carol came
from behind a pillar over there. Now she was a brunette,
clad in a white coat. The red plaid was reversible. I hit
the nearest flight of stairs, took six long strides down a cor-
ridor at the top, and three more down to her platform. I
just did make the train.

It was a local, and Carol got off at the first stop, 50th
Street. She moved down the platform as if she no longer
expected pursuit. I followed. She took the exit to the south
side of the street. I chose the north side. She turned south
at the corner of Seventh Avenue, walked down to 49th, and
waited at a bus stop. I backtracked to a cab parked on
Seventh, handed the driver a five spot, and told him to
follow the next cross town bus if I said go.

He looked in the rearview mirror. 'What's the pitch,
Mac?'

'Police work.' I flashed my badge.

'No squawk from me. But that bus only goes to Tenth.'

'You get the five either way. See the girl in the trench coat? If she gets on the bus, you tag along. When she exits, I leave you.'

Presently the bus lumbered into the kerb, and Carol boarded. The driver made a quick right turn, and we followed. Carol rode to Tenth, disembarked, and started walking north. I had the driver haul me several blocks past her, do a right turn, and let me out.

There were no tourists with cameras in this neighbourhood. It was a section of grubby tenements, hole-in-the-wall stores, and marginal industries. I risked a look around the corner, just as Carol crossed the avenue a block away.

I sauntered south fast enough to watch her progress down the side street. She passed three tenements with huge white X's painted on the windows—condemned buildings. Then she stopped in front of a low building which bore the legend MARTY'S AUTO REPAIR and entered through a small door mounted in the garage door.

I crossed the avenue, entered a greasy spoon on the corner, took a booth that gave me a view of the garage, and ordered lunch. I had run them to roost. I'd give them time to decide she hadn't been followed. My order arrived. I ate like a man stoking a furnace.

Then I saw a bizarre sight. A hefty girl in jeans and a poncho walked up the steps of one of the condemned buildings and rapped on the two-by-fours nailed over the doorway. The door behind the barrier opened. The girl ducked between the boards as nimbly as her bulk permitted and entered. Talk about a low-rent district.

But I was grateful to the plump hippie lass. She had shown me a way to enter Marty's Auto Repair without making a frontal assault. I left the diner and strolled past the condemned tenements. Chubby had entered the second one. I approached the third, which flanked the garage. This doorway had the same NO TRESPASSING sign over the two-by-fours, and the door was secured by a steel plate screwed to both door and jamb. But the screws on one side of the plate had been loosened. This building had also housed vagrant guests. I ducked through the barrier and entered, closing the door behind me.

The hallway was dark, but I used my pencil flash to light my way to an apartment at the end of the hall. The door was ajar, so I entered. The place had once been a two-room apartment. Now it was an animal's lair, the human variety, reeking of decay. The floor was littered with débris and pieces of old mattresses. On one wall was a giant poster of Che Guevara. Beneath it, scrawled in red paint, was the legend KILL THE PIGS! In one corner were some empty sterno cans and a rusty hatchet. I picked up the hatchet and went to the rear window. Marty's garage formed one wall of a court behind the tenements, and on that wall a stairwell led to a basement door. I lifted the sash and dropped to the court. The basement door was made of steel and boasted a padlock the size of my fist. But the hasp holding the lock was imbedded in old wood. I worked the hatchet blade beneath the hasp and pried it off the wall. Armed with my pencil flash, I stepped inside.

I saw an old, rusted boiler, a network of pipes and ducts. A rat the size of a mole scurried out of my light. I crossed to the stairway and mounted quickly. The door at the top was unlocked. It opened with only a faint creak. I smelled old grease and carbon tetrachloride. I tucked the light away and got out my Luger.

Light filtered into the garage from a filthy skylight. On one side were two rusty hulks that had once been automobiles. The walls were festooned with tyres, mufflers, and other spare parts. In the middle of the floor I saw a grease pit. Beside it, grimy with road dust, was the Dodge camper. The back wall of the garage supported a jerry-built second floor. Up there a light burned behind a frosted-glass door. Access to this office was gained by a flight of metal stairs fastened to the left rear wall, broken by a landing. Stealthily, I ascended the stairs to the landing. It ran deeper than I had thought, no doubt back to a toilet. I could smell it. I started up the next flight of stairs when a shadow loomed on the frosted glass above me. The door opened, and exposed in a bright light was the Iceman. He stood looking back into the room.

He said, 'Stop your bellyaching! I'm only going out for a sandwich and coffee. You can sit here and dream up

another harebrained scheme while I'm gone.' He slammed the door and zipped up his jacket, but not before I saw the automatic in his belt.

I ducked back around the corner of the landing and stood with my back to the wall. The stairs vibrated as the big man descended. I put the Luger away and eased Carl's sap from my hip pocket. If I braced him with the gun, he would bellow a warning or go for me, and someone would die too fast to do me any good. He hit the landing and passed me, reaching for the railing. I stepped forward and cracked him solidly behind the ear with the sap, goaded by a surge of the same fear and frenzy the caveman must have felt when he clubbed *Tyrannosaurus rex*. Then I blundered. His knees buckled and I feared he would bust his skull on the steel stairs. So I grabbed him with both hands, letting the sap dangle around my wrist on its thong.

But he didn't go down. His hand was locked in place on the railing. He pivoted awkwardly, snorted once, and hooked me in the ribs. It was a love tap for him, stunned as he was, but it jolted me backward. He bulled forward, flailing his arms, operating purely on brute willpower. I clawed the Luger free, but one of those anvils he called fists struck my elbow and sent the Luger flying. I gave ground, trying to get the sap back into my hand.

But he caught my right wrist with his left hand, my throat with his right, and slammed me against the wall. I bulled my neck muscles, but his grip was a steel clamp threatening to crush my larynx. I hit him twice in the gut with my left, with no effect except for a pain in my knuckles. My brain was seared with flashes of yellow, like the windows on a subway train hurtling past. Then I knew that what I had hit was the gun under his jacket.

I lurched sideways along the wall. His jacket was hiked above his belt. I got a hand on his gun, jerked it free, and chopped the butt into the back of his head. He snorted with pain. I chopped again, a terrific clout. The iron grip on my throat relaxed, and he rocked back on his heels. In frantic haste and fear I hit him hard in the chest. He took three stiff-legged steps backward, hit the railing, toppled over, and made a fearful crash when he landed.

I heard a yelp of consternation from the office and quick footfalls. I didn't hunt for my Luger. I slapped the butt of the .38 into my right hand and moved to the corner. The automatic was the one Harry had used in Atlantic City. The silencer was still screwed over the muzzle.

The door above opened outward and Carol stood on the threshold. It was a mark of her confidence in the Iceman's prowess that she hadn't doused the light. But she held her .32 automatic in her hand. She called, 'Vince? What happened?'

I spoke hoarsely through my sore throat, 'Vince can't hear you, sweetheart. Drop the gun.'

She held it tightly and said, 'Who is it? Maynard?'

Apparently the rasp in my voice disguised it. I lined the .38 on the frosted glass behind her and squeezed off a round. The pistol popped, the glass cracked, and a huge shard splintered at her feet. She dropped the gun. 'Good girl. Now I'm coming up there.'

When she saw me, she spat my name in a bitter voice. She had that bony, chiselled look on her face. 'What did you do to Vince?'

'All in good time. Back into the office.' She obeyed. The room was furnished with an old desk, a Coleman lantern, and two camp stools. A satchel on the desk contained extra ammo clips, a large manila envelope, and two pairs of Harry's handcuffs. I looked at the ID in her purse. Her real name was Rita Sutton.

'Where's your boy, Harry?' I asked.

'We had a fight and I fired him. He's long gone.'

'Without his gun? You don't mind if I don't believe you?'

'That's your privilege.'

I tucked Rita's purse and gun into the satchel, hefted the Coleman lantern, and ordered her down to the landing. I made her wait while I retrieved my Luger and tucked it under my arm.

She said, 'If you've killed Vince, I swear to God—'

'Shut up! You'd better start worrying about yourself. The law wants you for armed robbery, felonious assault, and suspicion of two murders. You can be salted away for a long, long time.'

'I thought you were an errand boy for an ex-wife,' she said.

'Not anymore. As of yesterday I represent the law officially. Now let's go down and see if I killed Vince.'

Not only was Vince not dead, he was trying to move when we reached him, spread-eagled on his back in a bed of sawdust, cellulose, and the kindling he had made of the packing case he had landed on. Rita went swiftly to her knees and examined him. She asked if she could get the first-aid kit from the camper.

'First we take a few precautions,' I said. Thirty feet back under the overhang from the second floor was a sturdy work-bench. I hung the Coleman lantern above the bench, then knelt beside Vince and cuffed his hands together with a pair of Harry's cuffs. Then Rita and I went to the camper and got the first-aid kit.

She gave Vince a whiff of smelling salts. He groaned and heaved his shoulders. She talked to him soothingly. I had her move him to a box near the work-bench, where she began swabbing his head with cotton and alcohol. He sat with his head bowed, his elbows on his thighs. The scene had the flavour of caricature, the trainer trying to whip the bruiser into shape for the next round.

That image inspired me to take another precaution. While he was still groggy, I uncuffed his right wrist and chained his left to a massive old engine on the work-bench that had to weigh three hundred pounds. It was queasy work.

Rita said, 'I know he has a concussion, maybe a fracture.'

'He'll get medical care from the police surgeon,' I said.

'No, I won't,' Vince said. His voice was low, savage. 'I've spent more than half my life in the bucket for a crime I didn't commit. I won't go back. You'll have to kill me first.'

'Don't, Vince,' Rita said.

'Screw him! I want him to know the score.'

'Then tell me about the crime they framed you for,' I said.

'Go to hell. Why should I tell you anything?'

'I'll get the story one way or the other,' I said. 'We'll

get a make on your prints.'

'From a dead man's prints,' Vince said.

'Wait,' Rita said. 'How do we know you're really a cop?'

'That's easily proven.' I offered her my card and badge. She looked at the card. Her face hardened. 'Why did you enlist in this thing? To protect Maynard, even if he's guilty?'

'If you can prove Maynard committed a crime, do it,' I said.

'Careful, Rita!' Vince said. 'You can't trust this geezer.'

She was watching me intently. 'Like the man said, Vince, he'll get the story one way or the other now. Besides, he's been in on most of this. He saw how scared they got, how they armed themselves. It's the closest thing to proof we've got so far.'

'Correction, I've been in on all of it,' I said. 'I was in Crafton. I saw you leaving town the day after Kelso got it.'

'So that's what you meant about two murders,' she said. 'You're better qualified than I thought to fit this together.'

'Rita, what the hell are you doing?' Vince said.

'Maybe we're making a deal, Vince,' I said.

'Not so fast,' Rita said. 'How seriously do you take that badge?'

'Seriously enough to take you two out of circulation if I don't like your story. This time I have the whip hand.'

'But when we had you in the same fix, we let you go. Remember?' Her eyes reminded me that she had spared me the needle.

'Yes, that's a plus for you. But it's cancelled out by the fact that someone returned after you left and tried to kill me.'

'I swear to God it wasn't us!'

'Can you alibi both Harry and Vince?'

'Not for every minute, but you have to understand that we don't want to kill anyone. That's not our purpose.'

'What is your purpose? Start with Vince. What's he to you?'

'He's my brother. He's already suffered as no man was

meant to suffer on this earth. I won't have any more of it. I'll see him dead and in hell first.' She vibrated with intensity.

'Take it easy.' I turned to Vince. 'Why don't you just tell me your story, big man?'

'You can read it,' Rita said. 'I typed up his testimony from the transcript of his trial when I tried to get his case reopened. The manuscript is in my satchel.'

'No, I prefer to get it straight from the horse's mouth,' I said. I wanted to make him relive the experience with the telling, if only to fire up his emotions. I wanted him less wary, vulnerable. 'Tell it, Vince. It's the only way you two will get off the hook.'

Vince massaged his throat with his free hand, as if flexing his vocal cords. 'You better keep your end of the deal.'

'Good man. Let me take one more precaution.' I grabbed the last set of Harry's cuffs and chained Rita's left ankle to a pipe that anchored the work-bench to the concrete floor. Then I moved my stool close to Vince. I didn't want Harry Price creeping up on my blind side. 'Go ahead, Vince,' I said.

CHAPTER XX

VINCE wet his lips and said, 'Okay, it started back in the fall of forty-four. I was just nineteen, a tail gunner on a Navy torpedo plane, working off the carrier *Yellowjacket* in the South Pacific. My pilot was Ensign Charlie Hamilton. He could really lay those tin fish in there. He had guts to burn. He proved it during the battle of Leyte Gulf, in October of that year. We made seven sorties against Jap shipping in two days. Charlie wouldn't dump his fish until he could see the gold fillings in the Nips' teeth.

'Okay, on the third day we ran into a hornets' nest of zeros on the way back from the target. We got shot up bad. A cannon shell chewed up our instrument panel and wrecked our navigational equipment. We ducked into a

rain squall. When we came out, we were low on fuel and lost. We spotted a group of islands, and Charlie decided to crash land in the lagoon near the largest. He misjudged the approach, and the plane broke in two. We both got busted up. Charlie had a broken leg, smashed ribs, and a concussion. I had a broken arm and a slew of cuts. We just made it into the water before the plane went down. I got our life jackets inflated. I don't know if I could have dragged Charlie into the beach. But I was ready to try when an outrigger came out from the island. I could hardly believe my eyes. The island wasn't even on the charts.

'Well, it turned out there were eight natives and a white man living on the island. The white man was a Dutchman named Wilhelm Hoekveld. He'd been an overseer on a plantation on Luzon before the war. He was about fifty, a chunky guy with a round red face.

'The island was small, maybe half a mile long and a quarter mile wide, with a volcanic cone in the middle and a nice growth of palm trees. There was a freshwater spring on the island. The houses were all built under the trees. They had a few staples, but mostly they lived on fish, vegetables from a garden, and the animals they slaughtered from small herds of goats and pigs.

'They also had medical supplies, and the Dutchman was a damn good doc for a layman. He set my arm and Charlie's leg and patched us up all around. But this Hoekveld was an odd geezer. He told us he and the natives had come to the island to avoid the Japs back in forty-two. But soon I noticed that they kept funny hours. During the day they stayed off the beach and the sea. They did their fishing before dawn or at twilight. Even after we told them that the Americans were back, they didn't build a signal fire. One day I spotted a Navy PBY and started to signal it, but Hoekveld stopped me with a pistol. He said he had a private reason for not wanting to leave the island yet. But he would leave soon, and after that we could signal the planes. Charlie and I were in no position to argue with the man.

'Besides, life on the island was plush. The natives waited on us hand and foot, and it felt good to be out of the war.

After my arm healed, life got even better for me. Four of the natives were women, one a boy. So three of the women were mated. The one who wasn't was a fifteen-year-old with big dark eyes and black hair hanging to her waist. She went by the Spanish name Juanita. After a while, she began taking me for walks and moonlight swims, and before long she became my woman. Don't look so surprised, Butler! I didn't always look like this.'

I grinned but kept silent. I didn't want to distract him.

Sutton rubbed his jaw with his fist and went on. 'We lived on that island for five months. Hoekveld had a radio receiver powered by a hand generator, and we listened to the news every night. We knew that American troops invaded Luzon in January, that the Marines assaulted Iwo in February, and that Manila fell to us later that month. The Dutchman was pleased. He said it wouldn't be long now.'

Sutton took a deep breath and said, 'Then the butchers hit us. They came before dawn one morning. By chance, Juanita and I had slept in a hut near the spring, in the middle of the island. We were awakened by small-arms fire coming from the beach. I made Juanita stay put and climbed up the hill to the highest point on the island. I saw a PT boat anchored in the lagoon. Several men were herding Hoekveld, Charlie, and the natives out of the compound. There were three bodies on the beach, the native men. The raiders were all dressed in Navy fatigues—blue dungarees and blue shirts—and wore black rubber hoods, like a frogman's garb, and goggles.

'Just then the native boy broke away and began running. One raider fired his carbine and the boy dropped in the sand. I didn't know what to think. If they were US Navy, how could they commit murder? I told Juanita to stay put and moved through the brush down to the housing compound. I picked up a club and crawled to within fifty yards of where the raiders had taken their prisoners—to a clearing in the forest near the beach.

'There were bamboo racks in the clearing where we dried fish. The raiders had lashed Hoekveld and Charlie to one rack and the native women to another. They were all naked

to the waist. I counted four raiders. I didn't know they had sent three others out to make sure there was no one else on the island. The four raiders at the racks were trying to pump Hoekveld. He was shaking his head, protesting. Then the one in charge gave an order. A second one whipped out a bayonet and slashed one of the native women in the chest. Her scream damn near curdled my blood.

'But the Dutchman was stubborn. He kept shaking his head. So one of those butchers jammed the muzzle of his carbine into Charlie Hamilton's face. Hoekveld screamed: 'There is no gold! I swear it!' So they shot Charlie twice in the face. Blood spurted on Hoekveld.

'Then I heard Juanita scream from behind me. She burst into the compound, stark naked, running, shiny with sweat. Right behind her came a raider toting an M-1 rifle at port arms. He caught Juanita and knocked her down with his rifle butt. There was brush between me and the raiders near the beach—and I didn't know there were two more coming from the spring—so I took off toward the man who had hit Juanita, armed with my club. He never saw me. He was getting ready to mount her when I hit him on the head. He was out cold. He had his sleeves rolled up, and I saw the tattoo on his forearm, a tiny American flag and the words CRAFTON, W. VA.

'I grabbed his rifle just as his two buddies came into the compound from the spring. I snapped a shot at them, and they ducked back up the trail. Then I stripped the cartridge belt from the guy I'd knocked out and got Juanita to her feet. By then two of the bastards from the beach reached the compound. One armed with a Thompson fired a burst at us. I went to one knee and fired three rounds at them. Juanita began to run. The one with the Thompson fired again, and three slugs stitched Juanita across the back. I shot the man with the Thompson in his left bicep, and he went down. By then I was getting carbine fire from the two on the trail. One round hit me in the left thigh. The slug went clear through—no bone damage. So I took off running, got to the woods, and took another trail to the volcanic hill. I climbed to the top. My wound was bleeding, so I made a compress from my shirt and tied it in place with

my belt. I had four clips of ammo, each holding eight rounds, and two rounds in the rifle. I had a canteen of water, no food, no shade, and it was a blister of a day.

'It didn't take them long to find my bloody trail. But when they started up, I sent them hopping for cover with the M-1. It was some four hundred yards from their position to mine, too much range for accuracy with the carbines and the Thompsons. I had the advantage of terrain and weapon. They tried sniping, but they were afraid of the M-1. Finally they left two men to keep me on the hill, and the rest went back to finish their business on the beach. I heard more screaming and figured they were working on Hoekveld. I couldn't see them from the hill, but I had a good view of the PT boat in the lagoon.

'Late that afternoon, after the screaming stopped, I saw them loading small boxes into a rubber raft and floating the raft out to the boat. I figured that was the gold. After that, I heard more shooting. Then they held a conference on the beach. I thought they were getting ready for another try at me, but I was wrong. At dusk they boarded the PT boat. I counted them. There were seven, one with a bandage on his left bicep. The boat got underway and headed south.

'I waited up there all night and came down at dawn. My thigh hurt like hell, and I had a king-sized thirst. I went to the spring, but they had dumped crude oil in it. Back at the compound they had destroyed everything—the garden, the dry stores, the coconuts. They had even slaughtered the animals and thrown them into the sea. But I found a shoat they'd missed. I shot him, gutted and bled him, and put him to roast over a fire while I examined the dead.

'Everybody was dead. Hoekveld had been butchered before he talked, and they had put a bullet in his head. Then I found something that surprised me. They had left behind a Thompson submachine-gun and a carbine. Damn careless of them, I thought. I kept the weapons as evidence, hoping the serial numbers would help the authorities track them down.

'I spent the next few hours getting myself in better shape. I shot down some coconuts still in the trees and drank the

milk. Then I rummaged in Hoekveld's house and found
the medical kit. I smeared both holes in my leg with antiseptic salve and wrapped a new bandage around the thigh.
Then I had a meal of roast pork and took a nap. That
afternoon I did more exploring and got more surprises.

'First, I found our outrigger canoe and sail intact. I'd
figured they had destroyed the boat. Then out of curiosity
I went to the place where they had found the gold, a cave
in the volcanic rock near the spring. The cave looked empty,
but as I started to crawl out I found a wooden box they
had overlooked. I pried off the top and found two gold
bars inside. *More evidence for the authorities,* was my
reaction.

'Then I had to decide whether to stay on the island
until I could signal a friendly plane or take the outrigger
and make a try for Luzon, which I knew was in American
hands. I debated it for two days, while I buried the dead,
took the canoe out for a trial run, and caught some fish.
Finally I decided to go for Luzon, mostly because I doubted
that I would be picked up for weeks, and by then the
raiders would be long gone from the area.

'I got a map from Hoekveld's house that showed my
position and the main islands of the Philippines. I outfitted
the boat with coconuts, the medical kit, and plenty of
dried fish—and set out early one morning. I had over two
hundred miles to go, and with luck I figured I could make
it in five days.'

Sutton gave a harsh, guttural laugh. 'I had plenty of
luck—all bad. The second day out I hit a tropical storm
that took my sail and most of my supplies. I barely man-
aged to keep the boat from overturning. Then for a day I
drifted beneath low clouds and lost my bearings. By then my
leg was infected, and I was feverish, without water or coconuts. I was out of my head, off and on, for two days. When
an American light cruiser found me, I was far gone, unconscious. They found the box of gold and the weapons,
which I'd lashed to the boat, and they listened to my
raving about murder and gold on the island. When I came
out of it and told my story, I could tell by their faces that
they didn't believe me.

'They transferred me to a Navy hospital ship in Manila Bay, and the Navy sent a team of investigators to the island in a PBY. They dug up the bodies, took the bullets out, looked the island over, and came back. They compared the slugs from the bodies with rounds fired from the weapons I'd brought from the island, and they found that the carbine and the Thompson accounted for most of the dead. A commander came by with a stenographer and took down my story. He treated me like something that had crawled from under a rock. He told me that I was the one with the gold and the weapons, and he couldn't buy the idea that the raiders had left them behind for me. Also, he pointed out that there were no PT squadrons operating within range of the island that couldn't account for their boats on that particular day.

'I travelled back to Pearl Harbor under guard. At Pearl, they put me in the hospital brig, and when I was physically fit they held a preliminary hearing and then a general court-martial. They had testimony from the doctor and pharmacist's mate from the cruiser that had picked me up. Both of those jaspers were convinced from my babbling that I had killed several people. Not a damn soul believed my story, least of all my defence attorney. They handed down a sentence of a dishonourable discharge, forfeiture of all pay, and from twenty years to life in the Naval prison at Portsmouth.

'I served twenty-two years and seven months.'

CHAPTER XXI

WHEN Sutton finished his story, I felt dehydrated and oddly embarrassed, like a drunk who has fried the tissues of his brain in alcohol and sin. I said, 'They suckered you. They laid out the bait and you took it.'

He nodded. 'I was green. No more brains than a lizard.'

'Didn't your wound count for anything at the court-martial?'

'They made a monkey out of me,' he said. 'The prose-

cutor got me to admit that maybe I could have made it back to an American base if I'd worked at it. Since I didn't, they figured I'd learned about the gold from Juanita, then waited until I could kill them all and make my escape. They took a dim view of the fact that I was shacking up with a fifteen-year-old native girl while my buddies were out fighting the war. Bunch of blue-nosed, gold-braided bastards!'

'Yes, that would have prejudiced them. So they racked you.'

'The old purple shaft. They stuck it in and broke it off.'

'You must have been pretty sore.'

'Sore?' He gargled a laugh. 'That first year in Portsmouth you could have fried eggs on me. I spent most of that year in solitary. I couldn't adjust. I puked my food so much, the acid from my stomach ate the enamel off my teeth. These are false ones, upper and lower. But finally I decided that I would get out one day and find those killers. Then I would justify the brand they had put on me, a black-hearted murderer. So I became a model prisoner. I took all the hard labour those monkeys could throw at me. I lifted weights. I did exercises in my cell at night. I went out for the boxing team. In fifty-two I took the heavyweight title, and I held it for twelve years. They called me the Iceman.' He looked perplexed, as if he'd forgotten his point.

'Well, you finally got out,' I said conversationally. 'How many of those raiders did you find and kill?'

'Stop it,' Rita said.

'You be quiet.' I was watching Vince.

He was unruffled. 'I get your drift. But you're wrong. I made a deal with Rita. We decided killing was too good for them. There's no statute of limitations on murder. So we decided to expose the scum and put them in the iron bucket. An eye for an eye.'

'How did you plan to perform this bit of magic?' I asked.

'Let me answer that,' Rita said. 'I sold Vince on that idea a year before he got out of Portsmouth. I'd already identified Milt Kelso as the raider with the tattoo, even though he'd had it removed. He was a fat cat, and I thought

we might scare a confession out of him. Then the government would have to reopen the case, go after the others. At least that's what one lawyer advised me.'

'You took Vince's story to a lawyer?' I asked.

'Three in eight years,' she said. 'Each one charged me a stiff fee for some cheap advice. Get new evidence.'

'So you've been working on this for eight years. But you must have been just a kid when it happened.'

'I was seven,' she said, her face gaunt with bitterness. 'Oh, for thirteen years I believed what everybody believed, that he was a murderer, a wartime deserter. I watched it kill my folks. Dad was a schoolteacher in New Carthage, Indiana, a town of five thousand patriotic souls. The story of Vince's trial was big stuff in the local papers. Life became pure, unadulterated hell for the Sutton family. We moved three times that first year, but the scandal followed us. Finally Dad took a job in a rubber factory in Akron. Oh, the hell with it.'

'Tell it all!' Vince said. 'Tell how Dad put the shotgun in his mouth and blew his brains out. Tell it all!'

'No, we mustn't play on Mr Butler's emotions.' She turned to me. 'Suffice it to say that little Rita survived. And one day she decided to go to Portsmouth and see this wicked brother. Well, he told me the truth, and I believed him. Now are you satisfied?'

'Not yet. How did you locate Kelso without the tattoo?'

'A combination of persistence and luck. I spent a month in Crafton, sorting out the better-heeled businessmen and looking up their war records in the local paper. Then one day I was up at the country club to look over a couple of likely candidates, when I saw a photo of Kelso taken back in forty-seven, before he'd had the tatoo removed. He'd made a hole-in-one or something. I almost blew it. I wanted to work on him myself. That would have been a mistake.'

'So you hired a pro,' I said. 'Where did you find Harry?'

'Actually, he came to me. One of those lawyers tipped him off that I needed someone. He's an ex-cop turned private detective, so he knows the rules of evidence.'

'Did you call the lawyer and ask if he did send Harry?'

'No, but he had a letter from the guy. Look, you can't

fault Harry. He had a fine plan for cracking Kelso. It wasn't his fault somebody killed the man before we got him where we wanted him.'

'You blundered,' I said. 'According to Ralph Maynard, one of you tried to pump one of Kelso's cabbies, and the guy reported it.'

'Maynard lied! We didn't have to pump anybody. We knew our man. We waited for him to show himself, but we never saw him.'

'Somebody saw him. He was killed within shouting distance of your trailer. Now I suppose you'll tell me that the three of you were sitting there playing Old Maid when it happened.'

Her eyes slewed away from me and back. 'No, but—'

'Where were you, Vince?' I asked.

'Out getting my ashes hauled, hotshot. I hadn't had a woman in over twenty years. So when Rita and Harry went out for groceries, I caught a bus down to Water Street. I really tied one on.'

Rita said, 'It's true. Harry and I spent hours hunting him.'

'Separately, I'll bet.'

She nodded. 'So we can't alibi each other. But if you'd seen Vince when we found him at midnight . . . well, he was a mess.'

'Drunk as a skunk,' Vince said. His false teeth made him look grotesque. 'That hootch can hit you after a twenty-year layoff.'

'We didn't kill Kelso,' Rita said. 'We didn't want him dead.'

'And you didn't kill McCloud in Pearl Beach?' I said.

'No. I told you about that. Harry heard the shots.'

'But neither of you were with Harry at the time?'

'True, but—'

'And you had nothing to do with Matthew Duncan's death?'

'That wasn't murder. He died of a heart attack.'

'Yeah, but somebody gave him a nudge. Right, Vince?'

'No, please—' Rita began.

'Stop begging the son of a bitch!' Vince said. 'He don't

want the truth. He wants to pin those murders on us. Can't you see it?'

'Nice smokescreen, Vince,' I said. 'But you were seen leaving the Sherwin girl's apartment, and the timing was just right.'

His forearm jerked, and the heavy motor on the bench moved an inch. I lifted the .38, but Rita said, 'Take it easy, Vince.'

'I've had a bellyful of this pistol,' he said. 'He talks like that chintzy two-striper who prosecuted me at Pearl.'

'Give it a chance,' she said. 'Tell him the truth. For me.'

Vince calmed down. 'Okay, I went up there to throw a scare into Duncan. We thought he could tell us where Maynard was, or at least give us a lead on the seventh man.'

'The seventh man?' I looked at Rita. 'You can account for six?'

She nodded wearily. 'The score sheet's in my purse. Five are dead. That leaves Maynard and the seventh.'

I felt Old Dad Time nipping at my heels. 'Finish it, Vince.'

'Okay. I had the girl's apartment staked out when she went shopping. It took me a while to duck past the doorman, and when I got upstairs her apartment was unlocked. Seemed fishy, but I went inside. I heard a funny noise from the rear of the pad. I went back there. The noise stopped just before I opened the door to this back room. Duncan was curled up in front of a door, holding a piece of junk he'd been banging the door with. I couldn't feel a heartbeat. But I think someone was behind that door. I heard a noise like someone walking on sugar. So I shagged out of there, but fast.'

That sugar could have been ground glass, but of course Vince might be trying a little deception. I said, 'Sit tight while I check that score card.' I took a notebook from Rita's purse. The list was on the first page :

1. Milton Kelso—murdered.
2. Ralph Maynard—?
3. Robert McCloud—murdered.

4. Matthew Duncan—dead.
5. PFC Kenneth Watson—KIA, war (paper from McCloud's safe).
6. PFC Andrew Marshall—KIA, war (paper from McCloud's safe).
7. ?????

The Watson and Marshall KIA's were confirmed by copies of official War Department communiqués clipped to the notebook.

'So you've accounted for all the raiders but one,' I said.

Rita nodded. 'All we have left is your pal, Ralph Maynard, and the unknown number seven. One of them is the killer.

'What makes you so sure?' I asked amiably.

'It's the only logical explanation,' she said. 'One of the seven decided to kill off the others. But he was smart enough to wait until Vince was free. Vince is the perfect fall guy.'

'If you're right, this killer is one clever boy. He's made sure Vince was in the vicinity when someone died. If he follows the pattern, he only has to manipulate you one more time, and he's home free. I'd be careful, if I were you.' I got to my feet.

'Does this mean you're not taking us in?' she asked.

'We made a deal, didn't we?' I acted offended. 'Besides, Vince says I'd have to kill him. I'm not that much of a cop.'

She gave a tentative smile. 'Then get this cuff off my leg.'

'That wasn't part of the deal. I have places to go, and I don't want you people on my backtrail.' I raised the .38 and blew out all four tyres on the camper, then tossed the gun into the grease pit.

Vince didn't bat an eye, but Rita said, 'God damn your soul!'

'Fortunes of war, sweetheart.' I took her notebook and the typed manuscript of Vince's story and walked to the front door. The street was empty, so I ducked out and flagged a cab at the corner.

Five minutes later I was in my motel room. I grabbed

the phone and called the East Side precinct that had handled the robbery of McCloud's house. I got the assistant on the case, a Sergeant Samson.

I said, 'Sergeant, I've got a fix on the gang that raided Bob McCloud's home yesterday. Two men and a girl. You interested?'

'Hell yes, but first I want—'

'No questions,' I snarled. 'Take this down.' I gave him the address of Marty's Auto Repair and described the layout. Then I said, 'You'd better move fast. They're getting ready to blow town. And a word of warning. The big guy is tough. He's Vince Sutton, a graduate of Portsmouth Naval Prison. He's sworn never to go back, and he means it. I would play it close to the belt.'

'Okay, buddy, but I want your name.'

'Just call me an interested citizen.' I hung up.

I hoped my big act in the garage had gone over and that Rita had believed I didn't plan to turn them in to the law.

I got a pint of brandy from my bag, had a snort, and picked up the phone to call Cunningham. Somebody knocked on my door. I gently replaced the phone and snaked out my Luger. Maybe Harry Price had seen me leave that garage and had tailed me home.

CHAPTER XXII

I stood near the door and called, 'Who is it?'

'Susan Wolfe. May I come in?'

I opened up. She was bareheaded, wearing an oyster-white foul-weather coat and a pale-blue scarf knotted at her throat.

'Sure.' I closed the door behind her and put the Luger away. 'That's the second time you've shown up when I expected trouble.'

'That's hardly an enthusiastic greeting,' she said. 'Aren't you going to ask how I knew where you were staying?'

'You peeked in my jacket this morning and saw my motel key.'

'Yes. Look, Morgan, I know it was gauche of me to come here after we agreed that you would call. But I had to come.'

'I hope we don't have as many reasons to wade through this time before you tell me why.'

She flushed and seemed to stretch with tension. 'Why all the venom? Didn't the girl show up?'

'She showed. All told, I've had a fruitful afternoon.'

'Then what's the matter?'

'Damn it, woman! I have nothing but warm feelings for that wake we celebrated. I'm also grateful for the help you've given me. But I'm working, and I'm on a tight schedule.'

Anger congealed in her face. 'All right, this won't take long. After last night's . . . bacchanal . . . I was afraid I'd left you with a misapprehension. One thing has to be clear. Not only do I want Robert's killer found. I want to know *why* he was killed. What did he do that would make someone kill him? It must have been something very bad. I guess I have to know how bad he really was.'

'You weren't very interested in his sordid past last night.'

'That was before I knew he was dead! Before I knew you were after his killer. Somewhere along the line you'll learn—'

'I already know.'

Her lip curled. 'Then you lied to me.'

'I didn't know last night. But today I learned why a lot of men have died.'

Susan backed up and sat on the bed. She looked meek, chastised. 'So that's the new thing between us.'

The idea pinched a nerve that made her look blurred for a second.

She gave a self-conscious laugh. 'Aren't you going to tell me?'

'Can you take it?'

Her nostril wings flared with each breath. 'So it's that bad. Morgan, I have to be able to take it. Let's have it.'

I was seized by the weird sensation that this woman had displaced Elaine, not only in bed, but in this act that required me to inform her of the corruption she had shared without knowing it. I grabbed Rita Sutton's manuscript and tossed it to her. 'Read this.'

It took her five minutes. Then she laid the manuscript aside and looked at me solemnly. 'You've learned who this Vince Sutton is?'

'You met him yesterday morning. The Iceman.'

She tried a smile that didn't work. 'And I'm supposed to believe that Robert was one of these raiders?'

'I think he was the head man. He was the warden of an Army stockade, remember. The dates still have to be checked out.'

'But this alone is hardly proof,' she said.

So I showed her the other papers that had come out of McCloud's safe, plus the list Rita Sutton had compiled, and I backed them up with salient facts about Crafton and Atlantic City.

She picked up the pint of brandy from the nightstand and took a drink that put a huskiness in her voice. 'So he took his share of the loot and parlayed it into a million bucks. Last night I called him seven kinds of a bastard. I hardly did him justice. Tell me, Mr Morgan Butler, if you had known all of this last night, would you have helped send him off in style?'

It was a loaded question. She was really asking if I would have found one Susan Wolfe repugnant, a woman who would have inspired loathing instead of desire.

I said, 'That wake we celebrated was something between us. You are a spectacular woman, in and out of bed.'

She looked in pain. 'But I was married to him for ten years.'

'Yes, and he had a message tattooed in hieroglyphics above his naval: "I am a murderer," and you didn't break the code. Hell, he wasn't a contract killer for the Mafia. He was a guy who did a nasty thing for money a long time ago and got away with it. Any mark it left on his character was painted over long before you met him.'

This time her smile worked. 'I'm not sure your logic is sound, Morgan, but I like your sentiments. You're good for morale.'

'My turn to ask one,' I said. 'Now that you know how bad he was, are you still willing to help find his killer?'

'But he is tracked down. It's this Sutton, isn't it?'

'I don't think so. I think the killer is one of McCloud's raiders from the Philippines.'

Her eyes narrowed. She snatched the notebook from the bed and scanned the list Rita had compiled. 'Then it has to be Maynard. Or that other one, Sims in Tennessee. Which one is it?'

'I'm trying to keep an open mind.'

'Wait! Are you telling me you didn't arrest those Suttons? You must have found them, if you got these papers.'

I looked at my watch. Three-ten. 'They should be in custody now. But answer the question. Will you help me?'

She didn't hedge her response by asking what the help consisted of. She said, 'If you were still after Sutton, the answer would be no. I couldn't fault him for killing them all. But if it's one of Robert's so-called colleagues in crime, yes, I'll help.'

'Fine. I may want you to run that batch of papers down to that cop in Pearl Beach I told you about. He should have them right away, and there are two other places I have to be.'

'One of them being Jericho, Tennessee?'

'Yes. Can you drive a stick shift?'

'That's all I ever drive. Yes, I'll make that trip if it will help. I have to go there anyway to make arrangements about Robert.'

'Sit tight.' I placed the call to Jim Cunningham.

His deputy answered, and then Jim came on. 'High time you checked in, Butler. I began to think you had run into trouble.'

'No trouble,' I said. 'What's the word on Gilford Sims?'

'I'll get to that. The big news is that we hit paydirt with the service records. Maynard, Duncan, Kelso, McCloud, and Sims—they all served in the South Pacific at the same

time in the war. But here's the flaw. Only Duncan and McCloud served together.'

'I can eliminate that flaw,' I said. 'McCloud was warden of an Army stockade on Luzon, early forty-five. The rest of the boys probably pulled a hitch as prisoners. And you've got to update our list. The gang had seven men in it.'

'How do you know all of this?'

'Today I picked up a biography of one Vince Sutton, alias the Iceman. He was framed for robbery and murder by this gang during the war. I'll send it down by messenger. You should read it.'

'Why not bring it yourself? Hell, man, you've cracked it. Where's Sutton now?'

'I hope he's in jail, along with his sister.' I told him how I'd chained the Suttons and turned them in to the law.

'I don't like it,' he said. 'Okay, so you didn't want to shoot the maniac. But you should have waited until the law showed.'

'I couldn't get locked into that play,' I said. 'I've got a date in Tennessee. Maynard and Sims are the only ones left alive.'

'I gather you don't believe that Sutton is our man.'

'That's my gut reaction. Consider that McCloud kill. He was armed and on his guard. Sutton didn't walk into that house in broad daylight and shoot him twice in the chest.'

'Okay, who did shoot him?'

'I don't know. What's the story on Sims?'

'Just listen. You'll recall that I was worried because Maynard was en route to see Sims. So this morning I decided to call the law in Jericho and have them put a watch on Mr Sims. I called the county sheriff. You'll never guess who he turned out to be.'

'Gilford Sims.'

'Bingo. Well, I did a fast shuffle. I couldn't tell Sheriff Sims my suspicions about citizen Sims. So I gave him the squeal on Maynard, big murder suspect, likely on his way to Jericho.'

'How did the sheriff take it?'

'Deadpan. He took the description and will alert his

troops. But when I mentioned sending a deputy down there, he got his back up. I got the impression that you would be most unwelcome.'

'All the more reason to go. Sims has to be the seventh raider.'

'Maybe. But you don't go to Tennessee until I say so. I'm checking this Sims out. He's no run-of-the-mill corn-pone cop.'

'How are you checking him out?'

'An old *compadre* of mine in DC has made an appoint-ment for me with the Congressman from Sims' district. I plan to fly to DC on the evening shuttle. Why don't you meet me down there? I don't want you hitting Tennessee until I get the word on Sims.'

'Fair enough. Then I will deliver these papers in person. And this will give me a chance to visit Elaine Maynard. I have to fill her in on Ralph's gory past. I gave my word.'

'You are a brute for punishment, friend.'

'I also have a question to put to Alex Crittenden.'

'If it's about him being in the Philippines in forty-five, forget it. He was never in the service—Four-F. His contri-bution to the war was a USO tour of Europe in June of forty-five. I got that from Elaine Maynard today, and DC confirms it.'

'That still doesn't explain why he was in New York yesterday.'

'Ask him. By the way, we've confirmed that it was McCloud who burned. We got some X-rays of an old fracture from his doctor.'

'I never doubted it. One more thing, while you're checking on Sims, find out if he's been out of Jericho this past week.'

'That's at the top of my list, deputy.' Then he gave me the name of the motel he would stop at in DC, and we broke it off.

I said to Susan, 'You don't have to make the trip, after all.'

'I heard. I also heard that Elaine Maynard is the wife of Ralph, one of Robert's raiders. Is he the killer?'

'If he's not, someone's gone to a lot of trouble to make it

look that way,' I said.

'And this wife is the one who hired you in the first place?'

'Yes. But that was before murder happened. Ralph was acting like a man in trouble. She hired me to ease him out of it.'

'And now you may have to ease him straight into jail. Hardly what she bargained for. Do you think she'll pay her bill?'

I had a bad five seconds, a sensation as humiliating as the first time they had wrapped me inside an ice-cold sheet pack on the nut ward in San Diego. The spasm must have shown on my face.

'What's the matter? Hey, I do believe Elaine Maynard is something more to you than an employer.'

'Yes, I was married to her once.'

'So my gallows humour was in the worst possible taste. Sorry.'

'You didn't know.'

She studied me gravely. 'I know this. Last night's wake wasn't as one-sided as I thought. You put something to rest, too, didn't you?'

'You're talking too much again. Look, I need a Xerox copy of Vince's story. Can you help me?'

'That's easy. My office is just across town.'

'Good. Then will you drive me to the airport and keep my car for a few days?'

'On one condition. That you promise to call me and tell all when this thing is finished.'

'It's a deal. Let's go.'

The flight from New York to Washington took just long enough for me to take a good sour look at myself. The investigation was prompted by the remark Susan had made, pointing out the ironic fact that Elaine had hired me to help Ralph rather than hang him—and the noxious effect the words had had upon me.

Clearly my desire to repay the old debt to Elaine had led me to violate one of the basic tenets of this line of work I call my avocation. I had let personal feelings destroy

my objectivity. Early in the game I'd emotionally committed myself to the task of scrubbing Ralph clean of his troubles and returning him to Elaine, not merely unscathed but innocent. The operative word was innocent. In the face of all evidence, I had never seriously believed that Ralph Maynard had gone beyond the pale and committed a crime too serious to be corrected. Not the man married to the goddess I had once adored.

There was the rub. Despite all those skull-busting sessions with the feisty Dr Coffee, I still genuflected before that image of Elaine I had created in Hawaii—the goddess, the golden girl who could bestow the love that anointed and purified. She had come to the farm like a shimmering vision, elegant and unflawed, and she had worked the old magic on me. I had responded like a knight of old, selected by the lady of the manor to slay the ugly dragon.

I had never realized that the goddess was something of a fraud—a joint product of my imagination and her deep seated need to be adored in that way, to reign over that munificent image of herself. For she had chosen me as eagerly as I had her on that Hawaiian isle, and she had conspired with me to sustain the illusion.

But marriage to a goddess is a rarefied existence for a mere mortal, giving you about as much sustenance as a mirage on the Sahara. So in our third year I began to neglect her. I went on hunting trips in the Sierras and spent much time in the hills of Pendleton, playing at war—just as Ralph Maynard had taken her up into the Pennsylvania mountains last summer for the idyllic vacation but instead had worked twelve hours a day like a common labourer on his house. The demons were nipping at his heels, driving him to toil and sweat. Those old stains on his hands were blood, buddy, and all the ambrosia administered by the fair goddess had failed to scour them clean. I knew, because I'd been there and back.

An old rule of geometry seemed to apply—things equal to the same thing are equal to each other. Ralph and I were equal in our ability to stimulate Elaine and cause her emotions to burn at their highest pitch. Now I had the

crux of it. I had resisted the belief that Maynard was guilty and irredeemable because I didn't want to equate myself with evil.

May Zeus have mercy on my soul.

CHAPTER XXIII

I LANDED at Washington National Airport at dusk in a cold drizzle. Inside the terminal I inquired about flights to Jericho, Tennessee. Nashville was the closest airport, and I had a choice of two flights to that city. The first was a milk run that left DC at nine, with stopovers at Richmond, Raleigh, and Knoxville. The second was a non-stop departing an hour later but arriving earlier. I made a reservation on the non-stop, rented a car, and drove to the motel where Cunningham was staying. He'd left a note telling me he was in Georgetown and would be back in an hour. So I left him a copy of Sutton's story and drove to Sweetbriar Falls.

As I approached the Maynard house, I saw three people on the porch—Elaine and a man and woman in rain-coats. I cruised past and waited at the kerb until the visitors got into their car and left. Then I made a U-turn and parked in the driveway. Elaine answered the door promptly. Her expression was neutral, inscrutable.

She said, 'Hello, Morgan. I knew you would show up tonight. It's like a pattern. I hired you on Wednesday, and roughly twenty-four hours later you reported back. Next you left for Atlantic City, and we met up there a day later. Then I saw you off to New York about this time yesterday. So you were due. Come in.'

She enunciated clearly, but the effect was stilted, as if she recited lines. I followed her into the living-room. 'I bet you'd like a drink,' she said. 'You might pour me some sherry.'

'All right.' I poured her sherry, bourbon for me, and sat across the coffee table from her. 'Are we alone?' I asked.

'Yes. I gave the maid a week off. Alex is in Washington,

N

talking to a criminal lawyer about Ralph. I just had a
meeting with Sam and Wendy Brewer. Sam is the general
manager of Maynard Construction. He has six nervous
clients waiting for decisions only Ralph is authorized to
make. Today Sam insisted on an explanation for Ralph's
absence. To hear him tell it, the entire corporate structure
is on the verge of collapse. So I concocted a credible false-
hood that would enable Sam to take over with a clear
conscience. After all, we must preserve the corporate structure.'

'I take it Sam believed your story.' I caught myself
bracing for still another recitation.

'Oh, yes. It reeked just enough of scandal to satisfy Sam.
I told him that Ralph's half brother was in serious trouble
and that Ralph went to California to help him. I implied
that Ralph was helping hide Alex from the authorities, and
they were both incommunicado. Sam knows that Alex is a
big shot in the film industry, and Sam is the kind of self-
righteous citizen who thinks that all they do in Hollywood
is dream up new forms of corruption with sex and drugs.
I'm sure he's convinced that Alex is wanted on a morals
charge and that Ralph is the noble brother risking his
reputation to help him. Ironic, when just the reverse is
true.'

Now I understood why her speech and mannerisms were
so stilted. Every word and gesture conveyed stoic control
over rage and despair. But I didn't feel a rush of anger
against the forces that were brutalizing her. Her magic no
longer worked on me.

I said, 'I wouldn't say that the reverse was true. Ralph
is wanted for something more serious than a morals rap.'

She frowned. 'Of course I didn't mean to imply—Oh,
I see. You have more news about Ralph. Every time we
meet, you have another ugly thing to tell me about him.
What is it this time?'

I eased the Xerox copy of Sutton's story from my pocket
and tossed it on the coffee table. 'Remember Ralph's yarn
about the guy he double-crossed in Mexico? This is what
really happened.'

She made no move to pick it up. 'Tell me what's in it.'

'No, you read it. The other day you demanded the truth. Now you've got it, and you'll damn well read it.'

She paled a little. 'You needn't be nasty about it.' She picked up the story and read it. After she finished, she sat for a while as if in a stupor. Finally she said, 'So he was one of those seven. No wonder he couldn't stand success. His whole life was built on blood money. Where is he now? Is he dead?'

'Not that I know of. Do you want him dead?'

'What a cruel thing to say! I assumed that the man who wrote this was the one who killed those others, and—' She caught her lip between her teeth. 'Lord, I *did* have the thought that if he didn't make it home, this story wouldn't come out. Think of the harm it will do to his firm's reputation, to the people who work for him.'

'And to you and your reputation,' I said.

'Yes, why not me? Does that make me some kind of monster?'

'No, I would call that a fairly normal response,' I said.

'You mean selfish. I heard the contempt in your voice.'

'Maybe I was thinking of a speech you made in this room just last Thursday. You said you would stick by him, no matter what he's done, that you had no conscience about it.'

She averted her eyes. 'Noble words, weren't they?' She dropped the story back on the coffee table as if she handled carrion. 'They didn't prepare me for this at Vassar, I guess. I need a drink stronger than sherry—say, three fingers of brandy.'

I didn't move, so she jerked up out of her seat and went to the sideboard. She poured brandy into a heavy highball glass and then wheeled around suddenly. 'Who are you to defend him anyway? He's a fugitive, with all kinds of charges against him. Right?'

'True, but I'd like to hear his end of it before I put the noose around his neck. Tell me, why are you so afraid of him?'

That last question was just something that popped into my head, but it almost cost me an eye. Elaine made a choked sound and flung the heavy glass at my head, spray-

ing an amber arc of brandy. Pure reflex made me jerk in
the right direction. The glass nipped my ear and chopped
into the wood panelling behind me. I took the brandy in
my face and chest. I groped for a handkerchief.

Elaine said, 'Oh, Morgan, I'm so sorry! I could have
hurt you seriously. You should see the dent in this wood.'
I felt her weight on the sofa. 'Here, let me.' She wiped
my face. Hers looked feverish. 'Morgan, why did I do it?
I'm not like that.'

'I hit a raw nerve,' I said.

She became motionless. A pulse in her throat throbbed.
'Yes,' she whispered. 'I am afraid of Ralph. I told you
about his erratic behaviour, but I didn't tell all of it. One
night he hurt me and cursed me in vile language. He was
drunk. He didn't even remember it the next day. That's
what scared me. It was as if the savage in him was slowly
getting the best of the civilized man.'

'You make it sound like a cheap horror movie,' I said.
'The werewolf running amok, and you the dainty, innocent
victim.'

'Why are you doing this to me?' she asked.

She recoiled, but I grabbed her and held her in place.
'You didn't throw that glass for fear of Ralph. I'm
not Ralph.'

I felt a muscular contraction in her body, and compre-
hension came into her eyes. 'Sweet Christ. Yes, I feared *you*
that way, too. It's grotesque, because now I recall an
ugly thought I had about Ralph not long ago. I worried
that he might crack up, like you did.'

'Maybe he did, in his own way.' I released her.

She drooped against the back of the sofa. 'First you, now
Ralph,' she said. 'It's not just coincidence, is it, Morgan?'

'How should I know?' I couldn't damn her because I'd
married her to give peace to my soul and she hadn't per-
formed that miracle.

She watched me avidly. 'You know *something*. From the
minute you entered this house tonight, you've been stalking
me.'

'Next I'll be blamed for you throwing that glass at me.'

She flinched. 'No, that was me cracking up a little. I

suddenly felt ugly, deformed. I had to blame someone.'

'Let's blame Ralph. He's caused all the grief.' I got up. 'I'd better rinse the brandy out of my hair and change shirts.'

The phone rang, and Elaine jumped. 'Morgan, will you get it?'

I crossed the room and answered the phone. It was Cunningham. I told Elaine it was for me, and she went into the kitchen.

I said, 'Fire away, Jim. Did you get my package?'

'Just finished reading it. Sutton tells a grim little tale. It's a lot of motive for a vendetta, which brings me to my first news item. Sutton and company eluded New York's Finest.'

'I didn't think that was possible. What happened?'

'A fluke. That pair was still chained in the garage when the law arrived. But they pulled into that street with a siren going and flushed out a gaggle of hippies holding a freakout next door. Big drug cache. One hophead panicked and fired off a gun. The patrolmen had a small riot on their hands. By the time they got it under control, our friends had flown the coop.'

'I'll bet Harry Price slipped in and got them out,' I said. 'Too bad. What about Sheriff Sims? Did you get your report?'

'Yes, and Mr Sims does pack a lot of clout in Jericho County. According to his Congressman, Sims is the local resident saint, a combination of Robert E. Lee, Daniel Boone, and Gangbusters. He runs a crack outfit, with modern equipment, bright young men, and no deals with anyone. He keeps that county so clean, even hustlers and hoboes give it a wide berth. He's also a lay minister in the Baptist Church and the guiding light behind every good cause in the county. There is no evidence that he ever spent a nickel more than his salary.'

'Sounds like he got religion at an early age,' I said. 'Could your informant tell you if Sims has been up north lately?'

'This Congressman just came back from campaigning the county. Sims has been in court all week as a witness on

a case. So much for background. Now get this. Sims just called with a hot lead on Maynard. He's found the motel where Maynard stayed, has a fix on his rental car, and is tracking him down. How does that grab you?'

'I'd say Sims plans to give Ralph to us on a platter. Hardly sporting of him, if Ralph went down there to warn him about Sutton.'

'Yes, but a nice out for Sims if Ralph went down there gunning for him, and Sims scared him off with all his hired help.'

'Maybe. But I won't be satisfied until I've talked to Sims.'

'Ditto. But right now we want Maynard. Sims has promised to call tonight with definite word on his whereabouts. If he's on his way home, we'll meet him. Can I reach you there later tonight?'

'Unless they kick me out,' I said and hung up.

It was just a way to sign off. I didn't mean to be prophetic.

I got my suitcase from my car, went up to the guest bathroom, and got cleaned up. When I returned to the living-room, Alex Crittenden was parked on a sofa with Sutton's memoirs on his lap and a grim look on his face. Elaine was standing by the mantelpiece. The hostility in the room was like static electricity.

Alex waved the pages at me. 'Elaine tells me you accept this convict's story as gospel.'

'It fits the facts, Alex. That's the test.'

'And you actually believe Ralph was one of these . . . marauders?'

It was a quaint word. 'That's right.'

'Suppose you enlighten me with some of your so-called facts.'

'First you enlighten me about something. How is it you were seen in New York yesterday when you were supposed to be in Hollywood?'

Incredulity made his face look gaunt. 'You're crazy! Who said I was in New York?'

'An old flame of yours. You knew her as Molly Prescott.'

He frowned. 'Yes, I knew a Molly Prescott. We made a

film together once. I hear she's become a Park Avenue lush, with a passion for booze and tennis bums. But I haven't seen her in years.'

'I didn't say you saw her. I said she saw you.'

'She lied. I can prove I was on the Coast from early yesterday until midnight last night. But I don't have to prove it to you.'

'Morgan likes to throw his weight around,' Elaine said testily. 'That policeman's badge has gone to his head. A while ago he all but accused me of conspiring with someone to kill Ralph.'

I was astonished that she could so easily distort the facts, but I saw by her face that she believed it. We were alienated now, at last, as the divorce had failed to alienate us.

I said to Crittenden, 'I haven't accused you of anything. I just said this woman claimed she saw you in New York yesterday.'

'Oh, Christ,' he said. 'All right, for the sake of your suspicious mind, exactly where did the lady see me?'

'Some bar in a big hotel. You were with a blonde and you looked sinister. She claims you once courted her in the same hotel.'

Suddenly Crittenden began to laugh. I don't mean he chuckled. He put his head back and laughed from the gut. Finally he stopped and said, 'Good old Molly. Of course she saw me in New York.' He laughed some more. 'Butler I hate to do this to you. You see, Molly saw me on TV yesterday, in the umpteenth re-run of *Rangeland Renegades*, a horse opera, *circa* nineteen thirty-nine. I was a tinhorn gambler, in league with Black Bart to fleece the homesteaders of their land. Sure I was sinister. I wore a black hat and a sneer I'd practised until my jaws ached. And it's true I once courted Molly in that same bar. Earlier that year we made a cheapie, with me as the shy cowpoke and Molly as the dancehall slut with the heart of gold. Let's see, if that re-run was a network screening, it'll be in the local TV guide. Elaine, is there one around?'

She produced it from a magazine rack. Alex flicked it open and said, 'Here we are. They even gave me billing

here. Biggest part I ever had.' He handed me the magazine.

The entry for *Rangeland Renegades* called it a Western starring Buck Jones and Victor Ritchie, made in 1939.

'The egg on your face is showing, Butler,' Crittenden said.

'Maybe I'll stop listening to lady drunks. Sorry.'

'Forget it.' He made a magnanimous gesture. 'Let's get back to this convict's story. It's a bitter thing to accept about Ralph, but if it's true, then obviously Sutton is the one who killed Kelso and McCloud. He's the man with the motive. Don't you agree?'

'But I talked with Sutton yesterday. He denies it.'

'Let me get this straight,' Crittenden said. 'You talked with this convict in New York, and you didn't have him arrested?'

'I tried, but he's a hard man to arrest. He got arrested back in forty-five, and he didn't like the experience.'

'Butler, I don't believe you're being altogether candid.'

'That works both ways,' I said. 'I understand you just came from talking with a criminal lawyer about the jam Ralph's in.'

His eyes got cagey. 'That's true. So what?'

'Unless you hired a fool, he should have advised you to dump me. If Ralph gets charged with these murders, I'm the witness who can couple him with both Kelso *and* McCloud.'

Alex grinned sheepishly. 'You do have a brain. Yes, the lawyer told me to send you packing. He didn't just advise it. He made it a condition of his taking the case.'

'And you tried to milk me before you canned me. For shame.'

'To hell with that, friend. Ralph's the only family I've got.' He got out a cheque-book. 'Now let's get down to brass tacks.'

I looked at Elaine. She said, 'Alex and I discussed this while you were upstairs. I've agreed. It's a legal necessity.'

'What were the terms of Butler's employment?' Alex asked. He spoke with zest, as if his cheque-book gave him a lift.

'I gave him a thousand dollars as an advance against

twenty-five hundred,' she said. 'But I promised more if he got hurt.'

'You did get knocked around,' he said. 'Not to mention your expenses. What do you say to an additional five grand? I call that a handsome settlement.' He wrote the cheque as he talked.

'Far too handsome,' I said. By then I had Elaine's much-travelled cheque out. 'I can't even accept this. I didn't do the job I was hired to do—bail Ralph out of his trouble. Remember?'

'But that wasn't your fault!' Elaine said.

'Quiet!' Alex raised a hand. 'Butler, is this your cute way of saying six grand isn't enough for your silence?'

'No, the point is that I've developed a conflict of interest. I may have to take Ralph in. I signed on to work for the law.'

'Get off my back,' Alex said. 'That was a move you made to protect yourself. Look, I'll go to ten thousand. That's my limit.'

'I can't take your money, Alex.' I tore Elaine's cheque in two.

We were all silent for a moment. Then he said, 'You bastard. You've accepted a better offer. No wonder you're so evasive.'

'As a matter of fact, I did get an offer from the Widow McCloud. She's very well heeled, since the demise of Mr McCloud.'

'You chiselling crook!' Crittenden said. He was livid. 'I thought you were a man of some principle.'

'Stop it, Alex,' Elaine said. 'Don't you see that he's making sport of you?' Her face had a waxen sheen but her mouth looked big and muscular. 'He didn't take that woman's money. He's convinced himself that he's working for justice. But that's all a pose. He's really getting his revenge.'

'I don't get it,' Alex said. 'Revenge against who?'

'Against me!' she said. 'He's never forgiven me for the divorce. After I divorced him, he cracked up. He spent a year in a mental hospital. It finished his glorious military career.'

Alex looked stunned. 'Why didn't you tell me this earlier?'

'I didn't realize his motive until tonight,' she said.

Alex put his notebook away with a flourish. 'You just saved me a nice piece of change, Elaine. We don't have to buy the silence of a certified nut on a revenge kick. If this got to court, Andy Maxwell could discredit his testimony with no sweat.'

'Look how swell it worked out,' I said. 'Ralph is safe from my slander. I no longer have a conflict of interest, and it didn't cost anybody a dime. We should all be satisfied.'

'Not quite yet!' Elaine said, her voice hoarse with loathing. She turned to Alex. 'What if Ralph should show up? Considering Morgan's animosity, I don't want him here. Get rid of him.' She turned and left the room.

Crittenden rose and made an awkward gesture. 'She's really sore. What did you say tonight to get her like this?'

I shrugged. 'Hell hath no fury like a woman unmasked.'

'Sorry I asked,' he said. 'Look, I apologize for that certified-nut remark. But our chief concern now is Ralph's welfare. I think you'd better leave.'

'What if I choose not to leave?'

The apology left his face. 'Then I would call a Mr Ben Murdock in from the garage. He's chief investigator for the lawyer I saw tonight. The lawyer wants Murdock on the premises tonight. If Ralph should show, we want him taken into custody on our terms. But I can have Murdock bounce you out of here if it's necessary.'

'No, I'll go quietly. But have your boy keep an eye out for Vince Sutton. He might drop by tonight looking for Ralph.'

'I'll tell him. Thanks for the tip.' He took a step closer. 'Why not take this cheque? What the hell?'

'Maybe I'll send you a bill,' I said.

I drove back to Cunningham's motel and caught him just as he was leaving his room for dinner. I checked in, and we ate in the motel restaurant in case Sims called from Jericho. Jim thought it was funny about me getting canned and losing all that money. After he finished ribbing me

about it, I related more details about my work in New
York. He was inclined to agree with my evaluation of the
Suttons.

Then we hoisted a couple in the bar, but still no call
from Jericho. Jim wondered if Sims was stalling us. We
decided that if he didn't call by morning, I would go down
there. Then I bid the chief good night and hit the sack.

At six am my phone rang and Cunningham said, 'Rise
and shine, deputy. Maynard's flying home from Tennessee,
and we have to prepare a reception committee.'

CHAPTER XXIV

AT seven am I finished a breakfast of ham and eggs in the
coffee shop at DC National and fired up a stogie over
coffee. Ralph Maynard was due in thirty minutes. He'd
taken the milk run from Nashville, which left at four am,
made three stops, and arrived at seven-thirty. Sheriff
Gilford Sims had learned that Maynard was aboard the
Nashville flight an hour after its departure and had
promptly called Cunningham. Maynard was listed on the
passenger manifesto as Robert Mansfield, the alias he
had used in Crafton.

The airport security chief was co-operating to the hilt.
He had loaned Jim two men to help make the pinch and a
private office for the interrogation. Jim was down there
now working out the final arrangements. Maynard would
never know what hit him.

I paid my cheque and hiked out to the main concourse,
from where I had a fine view east across the runways.
The storm had passed. The light was already good enough
for me to see the Potomac and, beyond it, air traffic at
Bolling Air Force Base. By seven-thirty the light would
be fine. We had him. It was all cut and dried.

So why did I feel as jumpy and out of place as the
proverbial lady of ill repute in the house of worship?

My stogie had gone out. I flung it away, flopped in a
chair to light a fresh one, and at that instant I knew May-

nard was not on the milk run from Nashville. Call it hunch, intuition, or the paranoia of a certified nut, but I was as certain of that fact as I was that the sun was rising over Bolling Field.

I hustled over to the TV screen which showed incoming flights. Yes, just as there had been both a non-stop and a local headed for Nashville last night, they had the same two flights inbound this morning. The non-stop had left Nashville at five-twenty and landed here at six-thirty. Maynard had cleared the airport while I was feeding my face. It was an old fugitive's trick. I should have been warned by the fact that he'd used the Mansfield alias. No one was that stupid. With a good cab driver, he would be almost home by now.

I wasted thirty seconds leaving a message for Cunningham, then ran two hundred yards to where I'd left my car in a police zone. I burned rubber taking off, missing a stewardess in a crosswalk by a foot, and broke half the traffic laws in the state getting across Route 1 and up the Glebe Road to Lee Highway. Fortunately, most of the traffic was headed in the opposite direction. I pared a half-hour drive to half that and entered Maynard's street just as he was climbing into a station wagon parked in his driveway.

I skidded to a stop, blocking his exit. Maynard rocked the wagon forward, reversed, shot backward across the lawn, and sank both rear wheels into a rose garden turned into goo by last night's rain. A calm man could have rocked it out of there, but he jumped on the accelerator, spinning both rear wheels, and sunk it in to the axle.

I started across the lawn. Maynard clambered out with a gun. It looked like the .38 automatic I'd seen in Atlantic City.

He said, 'Hold it, Butler. I'll use this, so help me God.' His face had the fierce, glazed look of a man I'd once seen who had been knocked down by a concussion grenade.

I stopped. 'Put the hardware away, Ralph. Let's talk.'

'No time! I'm taking your car. Don't try to stop me.'

'Either way you'll have to shoot me, Ralph. I'd put the alarm out. You wouldn't get out of the neighbourhood.'

'No, listen! You've got to co-operate. He's got Elaine. He

left a message for me to call him. I just talked to him, and I have to go there. He's threatened her life.'

Now I understood the glazed look. I felt mild shock myself. 'Don't panic, man. Are you telling me Vince Sutton's got her?'

He froze in place. 'So you know about Sutton.'

'Yes, and I know about the gold heist you boys pulled off in the Philippines during the war.'

He took a wild step forward and stopped suddenly, rocking from the torso with momentum. 'I knew that spineless Duncan would talk. All right, then you know the lunatic I'm up against. I have to follow instructions. He's got Alex, too. He'll kill them both!'

'Okay, but if you don't stop waving that gun around, that lady across the street will holler cop anyway.'

'What lady?' He turned halfway toward the street.

I took one long stride and pounced, swinging my fist from overhead like a sledge. I cracked his gun arm just behind the wrist bone. He yelped and the gun spun into the grass. He made the mistake of diving for it. I swung a knee and caught him full in the face as he lunged forward. It made an ugly sound and dumped him. He sat up, bleeding at the mouth. I had the gun.

'Now let's get off the lawn before we're spotted,' I said.

Ralph got up slowly. 'You black-hearted bastard.' He moved sluggishly across the lawn and we entered the house. I made him lean against the wall in the hallway while I frisked him. No iron. He was dripping blood on the rug, so I told him to clean himself up in the lavatory off the living-room and to leave the door open. I carried the phone to a chair from where I could watch him, intending to call Cunningham at the airport. Maynard came out of the bathroom, and before I could move he ripped the phone cord from the wall.

'No police!' he said. 'That was the first thing Sutton warned me about.' He had dropped a bloody towel on the rug. Stooping to retrieve it, he made a gesture of supplication. 'Butler, you loved her once. Let me go. Let me give Sutton what he wants.'

'Exactly what does he want?'

His smile was grotesque. 'He claims he only wants to clear his good name. He wants my written confession to that massacre in the Philippines. He wants it in the presence of witnesses, which is why he took Alex along. Oh, he's a cunning devil. He'll release Elaine once he's got me, knowing she won't go to the police while Alex and I are prisoners. Then after Alex comes out and tells her what I confessed to, she won't want to go. She'd spit on my grave.'

'Then you don't believe Sutton is out to clear himself,' I said.

Maynard made a savage noise. 'He wants the confession because it will give him the names of any others still alive. So he can kill them the way he killed Kelso and McCloud.' He brandished the bloody towel. 'Blood is all that maniac has ever wanted.' He flung the towel aside. 'Not that I blame the poor son of a bitch.'

If he was putting on an act, he rated an Oscar in my book. I said, 'How did Sutton convince you that he has Elaine?'

'He put her on the phone. She told me that Alex fought them, and Sutton roughed him up. Everybody suffers.' He made a fist and clouted himself on the side of the head. He did it again.

'Take it easy. Sutton might not take damaged merchandise.'

'I'm all right.' He looked embarrassed, beat, phlegmatic.

'Fine, then let's hike out to the garage. There was a security man on guard. I want to see if he's still around.'

He led the way out to the garage and turned on the light. The security guard, Ben Murdock, was stretched out in one corner. I knelt beside him. A deep gash at the base of his skull was full of clotted blood, but his pulse felt strong enough.

'He ought to have an ambulance,' I said.

'I've got to get on the road! Sutton gave me a deadline.'

The raw, manic edge in his voice brought me to my feet. He was ten feet from me, but he was leaning like a fullback about to hit the line. He said, 'Butler, either shoot me or give me your car keys and let me go. There's no third

way.' He kept flexing his fists.

'Tell me where he took them, Maynard.'

His face took on a miserly cast. 'I don't trust you enough.'

'Then I'm going in with you, to make sure Elaine gets out.'

'The hell you are,'

'The hell I'm not!' I showed him some teeth and the bore of the .38. 'Either I go, or you take a slug in the leg and tell it from a hospital bed. I've had a skinful of your bungling. You bungled it in Crafton, and you bungled it in Atlantic City. What makes you think you're any better now?'

Instead of arousing his anger, the insult depressed him. He murmured, 'Yes, he's beat us at every turn. I can't deny that.' He wiped his palms on his chest. 'But if Sutton sees you, he'll kill them both. He swore it!'

'He won't see me until I want him to. Can't you get it through your thick skull that this is my trade?'

He sighed. 'Okay. We'll call an ambulance for this guy once we get on the road. I'll drive, and you spell me later.'

We called the ambulance from a roadside phone at the junction of Route 50. Then he headed west. I asked how far we had to go. 'Figure on a two-hour drive,' Maynard said. 'They took Elaine to my Dad's old farm, just across the Pennsylvania line.'

'How did Sutton know about the farm?'

'I didn't ask. Maybe he pried the information from Elaine.'

'You said Sutton left you a note at the house. How did he know you were coming home this morning?'

'I called home about four am, once my plane reservation was set. A woman answered. She said she was the maid, and that Elaine had taken a sedative. She sounded like the maid, damn it! So I told her to tell Elaine I would be home around seven.'

'That must have been Rita Sutton, Vince's sister,' I said.

'How would you know that?'

'I've met the lady. I had a run-in with her, Vince, and their hired man, a fellow named Harry Price. Name mean

anything to you?'

'No. I thought Sutton was working alone.'

'That was a rare piece of luck for them, to have you call in as soon as they took over your house. They must have known you were headed home. Any chance that your buddy Sims tipped them off?'

He jerked a look at me. 'Who told you about Sims? Duncan?'

'Indirectly. Tell me about Sims. He was in on that massacre with you boys back in forty-five, wasn't he?'

'Oh, yes. And he has been on that same massacre every night of his life since.' Maynard gave a weird barking laugh. 'You don't know what that experience did to him. He has dedicated his life to cleansing his soul of that bloody sin, "In the eyes of the Lord and the Prince of Peace." You ought to hear him. He's a religious fanatic, but under perfect control. They say he's a brilliant law-enforcement man. He exorcises evil every day of his life. His share of that loot, every dime, he has ploughed back into good works.'

'If he's all that saintly, why didn't he turn you boys in?'

'We talked about that. He has wrestled with that lion. He measured Vince Sutton's suffering against the suffering that would occur to the wives and families of the men involved, and Sutton lost. But get this : He won't lift a hand against Sutton now. If Sutton catches up with him, he sees it as the judgment of the Lord. It even ran against his grain to outsmart you guys by lying about the plane I was coming in on, but he did it.'

'But he was in that stockade with you others, wasn't he?'

'Yes, for slugging a lieutenant who panicked and dropped some mortar rounds into Sims' CP. But when his CO got out of the hospital, the case was thrown out and Sims was released.'

'But he went on that raid. How does he justify that?'

His knuckles grew white around the steering wheel. 'How does anybody justify that?'

'I know McCloud was the boss, but how did he learn about the gold?'

'I don't want to talk about it.' He bit the words off.

'Yes, you do, Ralph. You've ached to tell this story for over twenty years. Not telling it has been slowly driving you nuts.'

The whine of the motor increased a notch and for a dozen miles he was silent. Then he spoke hoarsely. 'I did have the urge to tell Elaine. I came close a couple of times, and it scared me. It was a strange urge. She's the last person in the world to tell.'

I didn't tell him that it was a perfectly natural impulse to solicit a goddess for salvation. I just waited. He gave me another long exhibition of his driving skill before he talked.

He said, 'Major Bob McCloud, stockade warden—no man was ever in a better position to choose a band of thieves. He did a good job. He wanted combat veterans, malcontents and misfits who had a grudge against the Army, men jumpy from the war who had to go back into it. Oh, he chose well, did Bob McCloud. He offered us something we all wanted. Not the gold, but the chance to give fate a good, swift kick. Of course, his description of the raid was very different from what really happened. We knew the Dutchman was on that island with a few natives. We thought we would breeze in, scare the gold out of the Dutchman, and breeze out. On the way over we joked about it. We were tough and cocky, pirates of a sort, on our way to liberate a little gold. We didn't know about the women, or about the two Navy fliers. And we didn't expect a bloodbath.'

'Skip the gory details. Tell how McCloud knew about the gold.'

His face was glossy with sweat but serene. 'McCloud learned about the gold while he was training in Hawaii. The gold was hijacked from the Philippine government when the Nips invaded. Everybody thought they got it. The irony was that the men who did hijack it got shelled by the Japs. Most of them were killed, and their escape route was cut. One of them knew about this uncharted island with fresh water outside the regular shipping lanes. So they got boats and natives and made the trip. They left the Dutchman to guard the gold for the duration. Only one of the others made it back to Hawaii. Later he began to worry

O

that the Americans might discover the island as they secured the Philippines. So he made the deal with McCloud
to double-cross his old buddy. All he wanted was one-
third of the take—one million in gold.'

I spoke quickly. 'How did you get the gold out? You
didn't pack three million in gold bars in your duffel bags.'

'McCloud solved that problem,' he said. 'I don't know
how.'

'Who was Trader Horn?' I asked.

He grinned, his expression still remote, rapt. 'Trader
Horn was a joke among us, like a code name. Trader Horn
was our boy. He was going to get the gold to Australia,
turn it over to the planter from Hawaii, who would sell it
and put the money into a foreign account. The plan called
for all of us to get paid off exactly one year after the war
ended, in the Palmer House in Chicago. It seemed like a
pipe dream, but it happened. McCloud sent out invita-
tions and we were there to a man, all but two who died in
the war.'

'But not Trader Horn?' I said.

'No, but he got his cut. I've often wondered how the
rascal did get that gold to Australia. Some guys thought he
was a big shot, a general, with a private plane.'

I prodded again. 'You must have some idea who he was.
Duncan tried to send you a message warning you that he'd
seen Trader Horn in Atlantic City. He said the name
would be enough to alert you.'

'Duncan had turned into a jellyfish,' Maynard said. 'You
wouldn't believe what a hardcase he was when he was
sergeant of the guard at that stockade. Men change. They
get old and soft and are never ready for the day of reckoning.' He swerved and passed a truck.

That was the last he had to say for an hour. At Winchester we left 50 and picked up 522 north to Hancock.
Maynard drove with total absorption, as if the mechanics
of driving gave him a grip on reality. Just after Hancock
we crossed into Pennsylvania. Minutes later Maynard
turned off on a macadam road, and we were in the backcountry, the Appalachians. I asked how much farther
we had to go.

'Ten miles.' He looked at his watch. 'Right on schedule.'
'Tell me about your deal with Sutton. How does Elaine get out?'

'Okay. The farm's at the end of a private road. There's a bridge at the foot of the hill below the house. I'm to leave the car there with the key in it and hike up the hill. But they told me to walk past the front gate and up the lane to an old wagon shed. When I show myself in front of that shed, they let Elaine out the front way. She's to drive to Maple Grove, two miles away, take a room at the Red Maple Inn, and wait for Alex and me.'

'But you don't think Sutton will let you go with Alex?'

He twisted his mouth. 'What's the difference? When Sutton sticks a gun in my ear, you'll barge in. The Marines to the rescue.'

'Don't get tense about it now, Maynard.'

'I'm not scared, friend. I just don't want any Boy Scout heroics. Why get your head blown off for me? Or risk getting Alex shot? Hell, this isn't one of Alex's old-fashioned Westerns. When Buck Jones gunned him down, the director yelled cut, and Eric Knight got up and went to lunch. But in this show they're using real bullets. He'll stay dead.' He gave that harsh laugh again. 'In this show you can't tell the guilty from the innocent without a programme.'

'What about Elaine?' I asked.

That sobered him. 'God knows she's innocent.'

'Then think about her. Here's our plan. I'll get out and duck into the woods before the bridge. After Elaine leaves, I'll move in.'

'All right, but do me one favour. Let me take my gun with me.'

'Don't be a fool. Sutton won't let you walk in with a gun.'

'But I've got a perfect place to stash it on the way in, a hiding place I used as a kid. They won't see me. Please.'

'No sale, Ralph.'

'So you don't trust me.' He made a hard left turn at a crossroads, spraying gravel on the underside of the fenders. 'Okay, I don't blame you. I call Sutton a lunatic, but I

feel like a psycho myself.' He drove another mile, then suddenly he slapped the wheel with the flat of his hand. 'Jesus!'

'What is it?'

'There's a roadside park around the next bend. Sutton told me to check in on the pay phone there. I almost forgot.'

'But you didn't. No harm done.'

'Yes, but they could be watching that park to make sure I'm coming in alone. It's only a mile from the house.'

'All right. I'll ride the floor in the back. No funny stuff.'

I took his automatic from my belt and let him see it before I climbed over the front seat and settled on the floor in the back.

As he pulled into the park, he said, 'Nobody in sight.' He stopped the car, opened his door, stepped out, and paused. Then I felt his weight on the seat again and his head appeared above me. 'I used my last dime to call that ambulance. You got one?'

I dipped into a pocket. A shadow like a swooping bird swept over me. Before I could react, he hit me on the side of the head with a howitzer barrel. At least the explosion in my ears clanged like a howitzer, and I seemed to have a view up the rifled barrel to that shiny disc of light at the end of the bore.

Then that light went out, and by some trick of association I was back inside the ice-cold sheet pack in the padded room in San Diego, mummified, chilled to the bone, and helpless.

I came out of it when two tiny jets of flame shot up my nostrils. I grabbed a hairy wrist and could just see the smelling salts.

A voice said, 'Easy does it, Mr Butler. I'm Trooper Wetzel. You took a good lick alongside the head. Any idea who did it?'

I wiped tears from my eyes. A chunky state trooper was hunkered down beside me. I was propped against the picnic bench in the park. My pants were soaked and cold. I looked at my watch. I'd been out for thirty minutes. 'Lucky

you came along.' My speech was slurred.

'No luck involved. A fellow stopped here to answer a call of nature and spotted you in the ditch. He called it in. I checked your ID, found your gun and badge. Little off your beat, ain't you?'

'You found just one gun?' I asked.

'Just the Luger. What's the story, Mr Butler?'

I tried to move. My head hurt like hell. But more alarming was the paralysis in my right arm and leg. Maynard had clubbed the left side of my skull, which controls the motor and sensory nerves on the right half of the body. 'Do you know the Maynard farm?'

'That I do,' he said. 'Is there trouble at Maynard's farm?'

'The worst kind. Help me up. I'll fill you in on the way.'

Wetzel looked sceptical. 'I'll need more facts before I take off at high port, Mr Butler.'

'Okay, how's this? An ex-con is holding Maynard's wife and brother hostage at the farm. Maynard is on his way up there with a gun. Is that enough to get us on the road?'

'Yes, indeedy. Come on.'

I leaned on Wetzel all the way to the car. My right leg was absolutely useless. He soon had us on the macadam, moving fast. After he called it in on the radio, he asked if Maynard had slugged me. I said yes and explained about Maynard's instructions and how I had foisted my company on him. Wetzel was worried about the gun Ralph was toting. He wasn't half as worried as I was. I had unloaded that .38 automatic while Ralph was cleaning up in Sweetbriar Falls. I always unload a weapon I take from an adversary, especially if I plan to use it to cover the man for a while. I knew Ralph hadn't thumbed the clip out for a look, because the seven loose cartridges were still in my coat pocket.

Maynard had lied about the distance from the park to the farm. It was four miles, not one, but Wetzel got us there in five minutes. We parked beside my rented car, which Ralph had left in front of the old wooden bridge below the house. Someone had ripped out several planks from the bridge to prevent anyone driving across it. The

planks hadn't been replaced, which meant that no vehicle had come out over the bridge since Ralph's arrival. Wetzel drew his revolver and said, 'I thought the wife was to drive this car into town.'

'Something went wrong,' I said. 'We'd better have a look.'

'*I'll* have a look. I'd like to pussyfoot, just to be on the safe side. I can't do that with you on my back.'

He was right. 'Okay. Don't be long.'

He showed me how to use the radio in case of emergency, then crossed the bridge and went up the hill. Somewhere near the top he faded into the shrubbery. I experimented with movement, but all that earned me was the loss of my breakfast. Nearly ten minutes passed before Wetzel returned. He leaned on the windowsill beside me.

'When you said trouble, you weren't just whistling Dixie,' he said. 'Two dead—Maynard and a guy named Price. Two alive in the house—the hostages, I'd say. And the marks of heavy-duty tyres going up through the pasture toward the hills. You hit an old logging road up there. I used the phone in the house to call it in. We should cut that vehicle off. Wait while I put the planks back in that bridge, and I'll drive you up there.'

He did the work and drove me up the hill. Ralph Maynard was stretched out forty feet from the front door, shot through the chest. I needn't have worried about the empty .38. The gun in his fist was a .357 Magnum. Harry Price was dead on the front steps, with two bullet holes in him. Elaine and Alex Crittenden were in a bedroom, handcuffed to the exposed pipes in the unfinished walls. They were alive but drugged.

CHAPTER XXV

THE official manhunt for the Suttons was launched just ten minutes after Wetzel and I reached the farm. In Price's wallet we found a rental contract for a 1967 Jeep station wagon, a vehicle likely to be equipped with four-wheel

drive, essential equipment for the old log road Wetzel described. So he called in the make and licence number, plus descriptions of Vince and Rita Sutton furnished by me. Wetzel was confident that the pair would be intercepted at the junction of the log road and Route 220. By his calculation, the Suttons needed an hour to reach that junction, and at best they had had a forty-minute headstart.

But either Wetzel erred in his calculations, or the Suttons had extraordinary luck in traversing the mountain road. We learned later that they cleared the junction at 220 five minutes before the roadblock was set up. Nor did they head north toward the turnpike, where they would have been spotted by a trooper assigned to that post by the APB. They crossed 220 and travelled secondary roads south across Route 40 into Dan's Mountain State Park, where they ditched the station wagon and stole a fisherman's car and trailer. They drove to Fairmont, West Virginia, and abandoned the camping rig two blocks from the Greyhound bus station. By the time they were traced to Fairmont, the trail was cold. The Fairmont report came in early that afternoon, soon after Jim Cunningham arrived on the scene.

By then a great many official vehicles had rolled up the lane to the Maynard farm. The experts had come and gone with their equipment. They had dusted, measured, photographed, collected specimens, and performed their clinical rituals with the dead. Alex and Elaine had been taken to the County Hospital on the Cumberland Road and the bodies of Price and Maynard to the morgue in Maple Grove.

The man in charge of the investigation was Captain Bannister of the state police. He was a six-footer with iron-grey hair and the look of a man who has outlived his capacity for pity and anger and is already focused on his retirement a week from Thursday. He was too busy for the first hour to give me more than a nod.

Meanwhile, I got medical aid from the county coroner, a local GP with a white moustache stained with snuff. He asked a few questions and shone a beam of light into my eyes. The right side of my body still felt leaden, and I had

flashes of double vision. He murmured something about subdural hematoma, then said that the shock of the blow had deadened the synapses and nerve function on that side. He feared there might be ruptured blood vessels or bone splinters in there. He wanted me in the hospital for some stitches and an X-ray. He went over and told Bannister so.

The captain strolled over. 'Butler, I'd like to get a brief statement before Doc Gentry takes you in. You feel up to it?'

'Why not?'

'Good.' He gave an order and Trooper Wetzel appeared with a Sony 800 tape recorder and set it up on a table.

The story I told was accurate, factual, and totally free of any details that might create confusion. I'd taken my cue from Jim Cunningham over the phone an hour earlier. I had located him exactly where a good cop should have been waiting, at the Maynard home in Sweetbriar Falls, and I'd given him the bad news.

'Tough luck,' he said. 'Okay, I'm coming up there. Meanwhile, you'd better give the local law the lowdown. But only the relevant facts. No theories. No speculation.'

'Should I mention Sims?'

'Use your own judgment. I'll see you when I hit town.'

So I'd had an hour to compose my story, and I doctored chapter and verse to suit myself. I abridged the New York part considerably. Beverly Sherwin's name wasn't mentioned, and Susan Wolfe was Mrs McCloud, a widow I interviewed because of the raid on her house. I glossed over my encounter with the Suttons in New York, revealing only that I'd turned up Vince's memoirs. There was no problem about leaving Sims out of it. My appearance at Maynard's house was justified by my concern that the Suttons might show up there. It all hung together pretty well. When I finished, Captain Bannister looked over some notes he'd scribbled down.

He said, 'I gather Sutton thought Maynard was one of that crowd that framed him. Did Maynard say anything that would bear that out?'

Ralph was dead, Elaine was alive, and there was a platoon of reporters down at the bridge licking their chops

over the spread they would get out of this one. I swallowed bitter phlegm and lied. 'He denied it. He thought Sutton was a madman who had him on that list because he was stationed in the Philippines at the right time.'

'Then how do you explain his trip to Crafton?'

'I could only hazard a guess. But you deal in facts.'

'Yes, and here's one fact that bothers me. You say Maynard took a thirty-eight automatic from you. But we didn't find one anyplace. Maynard was armed with a Magnum. Can you explain that?'

'No. He didn't have the Magnum on him at his house.'

'But he hit you with a weapon in the car. Did you see it?'

'No. I think it was something he picked up in his garage this morning, while I was examining that guard.'

Bannister smiled. 'If he could filch a wrench without you seeing him, he could have picked up a revolver.'

'You could be right.' It fascinated me that the Magnum had turned up again. It had to be the same one that had killed Kelso and McCloud. 'I assume you've run a paraffin test on Maynard,' I said.

'Yes. He fired the Magnum. Then somebody got him with a high-powered rifle at close range. The slug went clean through.'

We were interrupted by a trooper who gave Bannister the report about the Suttons switching vehicles in Dan's Mountain Park. The captain stood up. 'Wetzel can run you down to the hospital in your car, Butler. It's been checked out, and your luggage is inside.'

At the County Hospital, Doc Gentry supervised the X-rays of my head, then took me to a treatment room and pricked my scalp twice with a long needle. A nurse cleaned and shaved the area around the wound. They had put me in a wheelchair to move me around, which suited me fine. Soon Gentry returned and put the stitches in. The sound of each one rasped in my inner ear, and I could feel tension in my skull as he pulled them tight. While the nurse was putting on the dressing, I began to get more feeling in my right hand.

This pleased Gentry. He said, 'If you're regaining sensation that fast, you should be back to normal control by tomorrow. So I prescribe a quarter grain of morphine and twelve hours' sleep.'

'Later,' I said. 'I have to talk with a man due any minute.'

'If his name's Cunningham, he's in the solarium,' the nurse said.

'Take me down there, Doc, I may rent that bed later.'

'It's your head,' he said. 'Show him the way, nurse.'

She pointed me toward the solarium, and I wheeled down there. Jim Cunningham was alone in the room. He gave me a grin and stuck out his hand. I had to work to raise my hand high enough.

He said, 'Deputy, I do wish you'd stop getting yourself beat up like this. It gives my department a bad name.'

'I don't even know why you bothered to come up here,' I said.

'That's easy. I came to fire you. As soon as you get your hands on my number-one suspect, you let him get knocked off.'

'Okay, so I'm fired. I didn't much like the hours anyway. I don't suppose you have a drink on you, as severance pay?'

He lifted a hip flask from his briefcase. 'Bourbon okay?'

I drank, and after a minute my head felt slightly less like an over-inflated football. 'How did you know where I was?' I asked.

'I called Maynard's farm. A Captain Bannister said you were here. I thought we should talk before I met the captain.'

'Do you want what I told him, or what I held back?'

'Both. You know my bias. I want to close the book on McCloud. That doesn't mean I intend to give the story to the wire services. Not even if Ralph Maynard is guilty. Which brings us to your bias.'

'I didn't know I had one. Mrs Maynard fired me, remember?'

'I remember. Well, if you think I'm going to give *you* a corny speech about how some nasty bad man despoiled

your turf, you're wrong. The only turf you own is that farm, and the only despoiling you get over there is with horse manure, as I understand it.'

I took another drink from his flask. 'That was a corny speech. I admit it. What's the point, aside from your insults?'

'I told you. I want to close the book on McCloud. Are you still working on it?'

'Hell, you fired me, didn't you?'

'Christ, if you're all that sensitive, you're hired again.'

'That's better. Have a drink.' He took the flask.

'Snap it up. Bannister said he was on his way over here.'

So I told him what had passed between Maynard and me that morning and gave him the version of the case I'd related to Bannister.

He pounced on the same item that had intrigued me. 'That Magnum does get around. Kelso. McCloud. One crack at you. And now here. Could you swear he didn't have it this morning?'

'I'd stake my reputation on it, if I had any left.'

'Hold it up,' Cunningham said. 'We have company.'

Captain Bannister and Trooper Wetzel entered the solarium. I did the honours, and they shook hands all around. Bannister asked how I felt. Much improved, I informed him.

'Good,' he said. 'Mrs Maynard and Crittenden are able to talk now. I thought you gentlemen might want to sit in.'

'Have they been told that Maynard's dead?' I asked.

He looked a little sheepish. 'You being a friend of the family, I thought they might take it easier coming from you.'

It seemed an appointment that had been in the cards from the moment Elaine had appeared at my farm. I said, 'Let's get on with it.' Wetzel wheeled me to the room, but I entered on my feet, limping.

They had cranked Elaine up to a sitting position. Her face had a drawn, starchy look. I introduced Bannister, but Elaine grabbed my hand and said, 'Morgan, tell me what's happened. The last I remember was talking with Ralph on the phone this morning. Then that girl gave me

another shot, and I woke up here.'

'We're still putting the pieces together, Mrs Maynard,' the captain said. 'You can help by telling us about last night.'

Colour flushed her cheeks. 'Alex!' she said.

'He's fine,' I said. 'Now tell us about last night.'

Elaine looked at me bleakly. 'Two of them came into my bedroom around three am—the girl, Rita, and the man called Harry. They had guns. I was petrified. They ordered me to get dressed, then took me down to the living-room. I thought there were just the two of them, and Alex must have thought so, too. He'd heard them and gone down the back stairs to Ralph's study. He burst into the room with Ralph's shotgun, ordered them to drop their guns, and yelled for that guard, Murdock. I thought it was Murdock coming from the kitchen. But it was that monster, the one called Vince. He hit Alex and kept hitting him until Harry made him stop. Then the girl stuck me with a needle. I passed out.'

'How did they learn about the farm?' I asked.

She rubbed her temples. 'I don't know. They could have found Ralph's map of the farm in his study. They went there after guns.'

Then Bannister asked her a few questions about the Suttons, but she couldn't tell much. They had awakened her that morning with coffee and prepared her for Ralph's phone call. Suddenly her nails bit into my wrist. 'Hey! Ralph promised to be at the farm by ten. It's after noon now. Where is he? I want to know!'

'He's dead, Elaine,' I said. 'They shot him at the farm.'

'Oh, no, I can't permit that.' She jerked upright. 'Not dead. Not me as the Judas goat. This I will not endure.' She clawed at my chest and uttered a cry so harsh it threatened to tear her throat.

The nurse bounced in and ordered us from the room. Bannister was frowning. He said, 'Odd way for her to act, as if she betrayed him.'

'She's bound to be confused right now,' I said. I could hardly tell him that only the night before she had all but wished him dead. The deed had followed too closely upon

the heels of the vagrant wish.

'What about Crittenden?' I said gruffly to the captain.

He said, 'He should be back from X-ray now. They say he took some good lumps, including a fractured arm. Let's go.'

Crittenden looked even worse than I'd anticipated. They had repaired a gash on his cheek, but that side of his face was swollen and discoloured, and his right arm was immobilized.

He acknowledged introductions and said to me, 'I know Ralph's dead. I pried it from the X-ray man downstairs. I failed him.'

'Don't blame yourself, Alex,' I said. 'You had a guard posted. And Elaine says you put up a good fight.'

'Don't softsoap me! I had a loaded shotgun in my hands when that big ox charged me last night. I had enough time to shoot him. I screamed at him to stop, like a damn schoolgirl. I couldn't pull the trigger.' He laughed scornfully. 'In the movies they always stop when you've got them covered. I've lived in that damn dream factory too long. The one time in my life when I'm in a spot that calls for real guts, and I'm the original jellyfish.'

'You were out of your element,' Bannister said. 'It has nothing to do with guts. A civilized man has to psych himself pretty fast to blow a stranger's head off. Now I've got a few questions.'

He asked them, and Crittenden confirmed the story Elaine had told. He had little to tell after Vince had knocked him out. He regained consciousness and through a mist of pain saw Rita Sutton forcing Elaine to drink coffee. He heard enough of the phone conversation with Ralph to learn that he was at the old farm. They saw that he was awake when they brought Elaine back, and they gave him a hypo. That was all he knew until he woke up in the hospital.

By then Alex was answering in monosyllables. He looked weary, depressed, and barely acknowledged our departure from the room.

Bannister sent Wetzel to check in with the substation and accompanied Jim and me back to the solarium. I sat in

my wheelchair and took a nip from Jim's flask. I needed
it. The local anaesthetic had worn off, and a dozen wasps
with stingers like fish hooks were energetically building a
nest in the side of my head.

Bannister said, 'Butler, how would you describe Maynard's mental state on your drive up this morning? Erratic?
Unstable?'

'That's a fair description. Why?'

'I'm trying to reconstruct what happened at the farm.
As I see it, Maynard was walking in from the wagon
shed, as instructed, when Price stepped out the front door.
Maynard started blazing away with the Magnum. He
killed Price. Then Sutton shot Maynard from the house.
So Maynard must have gone berserk. Killing Price was
hardly the act of a man concerned about his wife. Any
ideas?'

'Just one. Suppose it was Sutton who went berserk. He
was the boy out for revenge. He might have shot Maynard,
blowing the whole kidnap scheme. Then if Price threatened
to turn him in to save his own skin, Sutton might have
shot Price with the Magnum. Easy enough to put the
Magnum in Maynard's hand and fire it again.'

'That's possible,' Bannister said. 'But what if Maynard
recognized Price as someone from the past who had betrayed him?'

'Why do you say that?'

'That investigator's licence Price carried was a phony.
His New York office was a front rented just a month ago.
We've sent his prints to DC, but no report yet.'

'I can speed that up,' Cunningham said. 'In fact, this
Mr Harry Price is beginning to interest me considerably.'

I asked Bannister what kind of statement he'd given the
press.

'At this stage, we're keeping it simple,' he said. 'Too
early to open up that keg of nails about the Philippines.
All we know is that an ex-con named Sutton and two companions kidnapped Mrs Maynard and Crittenden, and
Ralph Maynard came up here to get them out. There was
a shoot-out, and the Suttons vamoosed. You're not even
mentioned in the statement, Butler.'

'I don't need the publicity,' I said.

Just then Wetzel tramped in with the report about the camping rig the Suttons had abandoned near the bus station in Fairmont, West Virginia. Bannister had to hustle over to the substation and get to work. He invited Cunningham and me to come along.

'You boys go ahead,' I said. 'It's time for my nap.'

They departed, but I kept Jim's flask. I called a nurse and bought that private room Doc Gentry had offered. I declined the shot of morphine until later. I planned to nip on the flask and do a little thinking. But those wasps kept working on my head, and I overdid it with the flask, and before long I went to sleep.

While I slept the good luck the Suttons had enjoyed turned sour on them. Their first piece of bad luck occurred on the bus they had boarded in Fairmont for Pittsburgh. The driver, in violation of company rules, kept a transistor radio hanging beside his seat. He heard the bulletins about the manhunt but didn't think much about it until he made a rest stop at Uniontown and saw the Suttons leave the bus. The driver dug up a foot patrolman who agreed to wait on the platform until the Suttons reboarded the bus.

But apparently the driver had spooked them. Forty minutes later they stole a car from a supermarket parking lot near the edge of town and had their second piece of bad luck. The owner of the car saw them driving off the lot and had the presence of mind to go to a police call box and report the theft. The police blocked every main artery leaving the city. But the Suttons slipped through on secondary roads, hit Route 40 at Farmington, and brazenly drove east. Maybe they thought the police wouldn't dream they would head back toward Cumberland, the vicinity of their crime.

But misfortune wasn't done with them. After thirty miles they had to stop for gas. While the attendant was hanging up the hose, a motorcycle patrolman drifted into the station to put air in a low tyre. Vince Sutton killed the officer with a shotgun before the man got off his bike. The attendant dived under a parked car, then ran for the phone as soon

as the Suttons drove off.

Twenty minutes later a police helicopter spotted them headed north on 219, and three patrol cars cornered them near the town of Berlin, just south of the turnpike. Rita tried to run the roadblock. All seven troopers on hand knew that Vince had killed one of their own. They put nineteen bullets into the Sutton car. Rita ripped out a dozen fence posts and wrapped the Chevy around a culvert. Vince was dead. Rita had a bullet in her spine and was busted up inside and out. They loaded her on the helicopter, and Bannister had her flown back to the hospital near Maple Grove.

I got this play by play from Jim Cunningham. He woke me up an hour after they brought Rita to the hospital.

'Will she make it?' I asked.

'Not a chance. But she's conscious now, and we thought she might respond to you better than to us. Do you feel up to it?'

'Yes. Hand me the clothes out of that closet.'

I walked like a man with a club foot, but I got down the hall and we took the elevator up one floor. Bannister met us at the door to Rita's room. At first I thought she was dead. Her head was bandaged, including one eye, and her mouth had been split and stitched. They were piping plasma into her arm and had a gadget in her nose.

I leaned over the bed and spoke her name. Her good eye opened and focused on me. I asked if she knew me. She nodded.

I said, 'Rita, who shot Ralph Maynard at the farm?'

She spoke in a guttural whisper. 'He deserved to die. He brought cops. The cheat. Is Vince dead?'

'Yes. Did he kill Maynard?'

Her breath whistled through her teeth. 'He was right and I was wrong. We should have killed them all from the beginning.'

'But tell us what happened at the farm. Who killed Price?'

She gargled as if trying to speak. I leaned closer. Her naked eye was like hot pitch. She hawked, spat in my face, and died.

An embarrassed nurse gave me a tissue. I wiped my cheek on the way out. I wiped it twice more on the way back to my room. Jim tagged along. The spot on my cheek burned as if she'd spat acid.

Cunningham flopped in a chair and said, 'When they play those deathbed scenes in the movies, they always confess their sins.'

'Shut up.'

'I hope you're not taking that personally. She was full of pain and hate. You just happened to be within range.'

'I said shut up!'

'I will if you'll stop scrubbing your cheek.'

I wadded the tissue up. 'What bugs me is something I told Rita in New York. She tried to convince me that one of McCloud's gang was killing the others, using Vince as fall guy. I warned her that if she was right, he only had to manipulate them into position one more time, make one more kill, and he was home free.'

'What are you getting at?'

'I hate to be such an accurate prophet without knowing why.'

Cunningham said, 'But Sims is the only one left, and we know he hasn't been out of Jericho County all week.'

I said nothing, and after a while Jim got up. He said, 'I'm going to have a bite to eat with Bannister, then find myself a bed for the night. I assume you'll sleep here with the other invalids.'

'You're right. I'll see you in the morning.'

He left, and before long a nurse drifted in and offered me a sleeping pill. I took it. Not that my head was hurting all that much. But I was in the grip of a childish anxiety that I was on the verge of hallucinating. The pill took me under on a cloud of helium. I hallucinated anyway, but when you can call them dreams you don't worry about your sanity.

CHAPTER XXVI

THE dreams were the usual nonsense, but when a nurse woke me at six to stick a thermometer in my mouth an idea remained in my mind as conspicuous as the Taj Mahal. It stayed with me through the morning routine, and I was still admiring it when Dr Gentry came to stab his little light in my eyes. He was happy to report that my X-rays didn't show any bone splinters piercing my grey matter.

So I got cleaned up and went downstairs to pay my bill. They had a message from Cunningham asking me to meet him at the Red Maple Inn at ten o'clock. I got direction to the inn and drove over there. The day was crisp and brilliant, and I felt chipper.

The inn was one of those rambling, rustic hostelries, with a veranda and Civil War cannons on the lawn. The lobby boasted hand-hewn beams and portraits of Lee and Grant. I bought three papers at the news-stand, left word for Cunningham to meet me in the dining-room, and went in and ordered a big breakfast.

While I ate, I got caught up on my reading. The big shoot-out with Vince Sutton got top billing, although the kidnapping and Ralph Maynard's attempted rescue and death were duly noted. But that part of the story in each paper was full of words like allegedly and purportedly. Only one paper hinted that Maynard had a gun in his hand, and none said a word about the Philippine Islands.

Jim Cunningham arrived on schedule, admired my new bandage, and ordered coffee. He asked what I thought of the news stories.

'Looks like Bannister decided to stick Sutton for all the killings,' I said. 'Ralph shot nobody, according to these accounts.'

'Bannister had good reason for changing his mind,' Jim said. 'He turned up that weapon Maynard clobbered you with, a piece of galvanized pipe. It was in a field behind that roadside park.'

'Any sign of the automatic he took from me?'

'Negative. We figure Sutton took it along, saw it was empty, and gave it the old heaveho.'

'But they did find a rifle on Sutton?'

'Yep. Thirty-ought-six, and a twelve-gauge shotgun. Listen, I've got a bigger piece of news than that to lay on you.'

'Let me guess. You have good reason to believe that Harry Price was none other than Trader Horn.'

'You have to steal my thunder. But how did you know what it took me half the night on the phone to nail together?'

I tapped my temple with a finger. 'The old subconscious. It bit me like a snake first thing this morning. What have you got?'

'For openers, they found a money belt on Price at the morgue that Bannister's men missed at the farm. Price had seven thousand dollars in there. So he didn't need that job with the Suttons.'

'What else?'

'Okay, not only were his credentials phony, so was his name. His real name was Larry Gibson. He was a cop in Chicago back in the thirties, but only for a few years. Then he and a buddy teamed up as private investigators, mostly divorce work for well-heeled clients. Price had a rep as a tough mug and a lady-killer. Which brings us up to the forties.'

'What did he do in the war?'

'Nobody knows. We do know he never served in the armed forces. One story has it that he married one of his rich divorcees, a gal many years his senior, and lived in Mexico to avoid the draft. Another yarn has him in Canada during those years, working the black market. Anyway, he turned up in Mexico after the war, Cuernavaca, with no wife but plenty of scratch. He lived there fifteen years.'

'Which brings us up to the sixties,' I said.

'Right. In sixty-one he sold his hacienda and moved up to Palm Springs. Been living there since, dabbling in real estate.'

'That's all you've got?'

'What did you expect, a typewritten confession?'

'Funny, I thought you'd find something concrete. An item that would tie him in with McCloud or put him in the Philippines.'

'You can't have everything. I think it's plenty that he sold himself to Rita Sutton as a private dick. He knew she'd been to those lawyers, so he knew she had that Crafton lead. What better way to protect himself than to join the Suttons? Once he knew they had tagged Kelso, Kelso had to die. If Kelso had talked, McCloud would have been implicated, and he would have revealed Horn's identity.'

'But killing Kelso didn't solve the problem,' I said.

'No, but I'll bet it was Rita Sutton, not Price, who got those telephone leads to Maynard and Duncan. Too bad you never asked her.'

'Too bad I didn't ask why she never saw that Magnum Price had to be toting around. They had to know a Magnum killed Kelso.'

'I think we can assume that he was slick enough to get away with that. Hey, why are you fighting me on this?'

'I thought I was helping, by caulking up the holes in this theory you're building. I'll even make a contribution. Rita Sutton admitted that in every case where the Magnum was used—on Kelso, McCloud, and the attempt on me— Price had the opportunity.'

'Fine. And with Price as Trader Horn, we have the answer to the question that troubled you the most: How did the killer waltz into Duncan's house and shoot Mc-Cloud, when McCloud was on his guard? It was easy. Trader Horn wasn't the enemy. He was a friend.'

I nodded. 'But why didn't it end with McCloud? McCloud was the only one of the gang who knew Horn by sight.'

'Horn was running scared by then. He had to assume that McCloud had given Duncan his real name. The way Duncan was tortured by having his pills crushed—that could have been Price making him admit that he'd gotten a message off to Maynard about Trader Horn.'

'So then Maynard had to die,' I said. 'Horn would

know that Sims had got religion and would send Maynard packing. So the place to get Maynard was Sweetbriar Falls.'

'By God, I like it!' Cunningham said.

I offered him a stogie and we lit up. 'Now tell me what Price-alias-Horn planned to do at Maynard's farm to wrap up his game.'

Jim blew a smoke ring, gave it a smug look, and said, 'Maybe he planned to kill the Suttons with the Magnum, knock off Maynard when he showed, arrange the bodies, and fade into the sunset.'

'Leaving behind two witnesses who could identify him?'

'Yeah, but who would ever trace him to Palm Springs?'

'What about me? He had to assume I might run him down.'

'Maybe he had plans for you. We'll never know.'

'Fair enough. But what ruined his plan at the farm?' I asked.

'You answered that yourself. One of the Suttons spotted that Magnum—and realized that Price had been doing the killing all along. So Vince killed Price and Maynard, and he and Rita took off.'

I chewed my stogie and said, 'You make a good case. Does it satisfy you enough to close the book on McCloud?'

'It might.' Cunningham cocked his head and squinted at me. 'But I gather you're not satisfied. Why?'

'Well, it does gloss over a couple of details.'

'Such as?'

'Why did it take Duncan so long to figure out that he had seen Horn in Atlantic City?'

'I can plug that hole. Price called Duncan on the phone and tried to set him up for the same play that did McCloud in. But he let something slip that tipped Duncan to the fact that this gink he'd seen hanging around the Sea-breeze was Trader Horn.'

'But how could he justify knowing where to call Duncan?'

'Easy. He could say he had contacted Maynard. That would explain why Duncan assumed Maynard knew Horn's identity.'

'Okay, Jim. But for a guy who improvised the whole

damn show from day to day, Price had an awful lot of luck.'

'Until yesterday,' he said. 'The house odds caught up with him yesterday. Look, you had some bad luck yourself on this one. But you can't expect every case to end with a bang.'

'So I shouldn't whimper, is that it?'

He grinned. 'You figured out that Price was Horn yourself.'

'I have a feeling that you're about to fire me again, Chief.'

'Retire you would be more accurate. I've got to get back on the job. What are your plans?'

'I'll convalesce here for one more day. I'd like to make my peace with Elaine. Also, I have to get my car back from New York.'

'Maybe the Widow McCloud will drive it over,' he said, pursing his lips. 'She called Bannister's office today trying to locate you. What did go on between you two in New York?'

'You have a dirty mind, James. The lady just wants my final report. She had a natural curiosity about who killed her man.'

'For a guy who didn't make a dime out of this, you sure did work for a lot of people.'

'That's me, a soft touch. Everybody's errand boy. Let's go.'

I paid my cheque and we drifted out to the lobby. Cunningham was asking if I cared to stop in the bar for a final drink, when he seized my arm suddenly and said, 'Lo and behold.'

A truly striking woman had just swept into the lobby from the front entrance. She was slender, lithe, almost gaunt in appearance, with a face that seemed all flat surfaces and sharp angles. She had a mane of black hair as shiny as a raven's wing. Her walk, her eyes, the tilt of her chin, all expressed a sensuous vitality barely under control, and she had that authentic look of hauteur that comes only from having mother's milk served with the silver spoon. Her outfit was wool trimmed with fur. All she

needed to complete the effect was a pair of Russian wolf-hounds at her heel. A bellhop trotted behind her with her luggage, looking as if he might choke on his own spittle out of pure humility.

'Who is she?' I said in Cunningham's ear.

'You have led a sheltered life on that farm,' he said. 'She is one of the Beautiful People, the naughty daughter of Old Tidewater Aristocracy. Her family numbers among its ranks various generals and judges and other assorted bigwigs, and this one keeps them a trifle nervous with her peccadilloes. They say she does the scandalous thing with such flair that it becomes the chic thing to do.'

'Like what?'

'Oh, when she was a kid, maybe twenty, she played hooky from her school in Switzerland and acted in a couple of movies they shot on the Riviera. She partied on the notorious Greek's yacht before that became socially acceptable. Her latest shocker was a stunt she pulled a year ago. She modelled a series of new topless gowns for a layout in *Vogue*. She's been married twice, but neither took. For the last ten years she's been playing the field, from famous pro quarterback to celebrated novelist to one of the Young Turks in the Kennedy administration. I was in DC a lot during those years, which is why I got briefed on the lady. But what brings her here?'

'I can answer that,' I said. 'Christine Mellon, isn't it? She's engaged to Alex Crittenden.'

'I admire his courage. You know, she must be at least forty, but she hardly looks thirty. How does she do it?'

'I'll ask her when she invites me over for tea and footsie. Now let's have that drink.'

We had it in the bar and spent a quarter of an hour discussing angles of the case we had previously covered in haste. It was just chatter. Then we said our good-bye without getting too choked up about it. Jim went up to pack his bag, and I went to the desk to rent a room for the night. They had a message for me from Elaine asking me to visit her at the hospital. I drove on over there.

CHAPTER XXVII

At the hospital I learned that Elaine was visiting with Alex on the rear grounds. It was a big piece of real estate, with stately elms, curved walks, and sheltered nooks. I found Elaine and Alex in one of these nooks. I was screened from them by a huge evergreen, and something about the scene froze me in place.

They seemed to be sharing an enchanted moment. Alex was in a wheelchair, well bundled, his bad arm in a sling. Elaine was perched on a chaise longue, leaning toward Alex. She was bareheaded, wearing a tweed pantsuit and a red car coat. He was talking in a low, calm voice. Elaine was totally absorbed, her face lifted toward the sun, her eyes closed. She appeared to be leaning on Alex's presence. I had an eerie feeling that I'd seen them like this before.

Then I realized what image they recalled. In the final, bitter days of our marriage, I had seen Elaine in this same posture more than once. But the man she leaned on then was Major Cartwright.

The association taught me something about her. She could stand instability in anything but her marriage. When that became chaotic, she turned to the most reliable man available for solace, spiritual if not physical. It was an office I had spurned in Atlantic City, when I refused to take her to New York. So it was natural that she had turned to Alex. Now they had a deeper bond. They were fellow mourners.

I rustled branches and walked down the slope into their nook. Elaine turned and rose, moving as if her body were sore with sunburn. She wore no make-up, and her face looked tender, sad. She said, 'Morgan, I'm so glad you came. After the way I behaved the other night, I half expected you to refuse to come. Please sit down.'

We both sat facing Alex. I asked how he felt.

'Better,' he said. 'But it's odd how an experience like this can make you feel old and feeble.'

'A physical beating often has that effect,' I said. 'I'm a little creaky myself today.'

He looked at my bandage. 'I understand Ralph did that. Is it true that you intercepted Ralph and rode up here with him?'

I nodded. 'I thought we had formed a team, but he outfoxed me. Maybe I was thinking too much about how I could outfox him.'

'There wasn't anything about it in the papers,' Alex said. 'In fact, those stories puzzle me. Yesterday that captain hinted that Ralph had shot Price. The papers say Vince Sutton shot him. But why would Sutton kill his own man?'

'The law has a theory that Price wasn't really Sutton's man.'

Elaine spoke up. 'Morgan, I saw no mention in the papers of that business in the Philippines. Was that your doing?'

'Partly. But I'm sure Captain Bannister feels it's tidier that way. With both Suttons dead, it doesn't make much difference.'

'But you must have the inside dope on what happened,' Alex said. 'How about filling me in? Assuming you're not still sore because I threatened to sic Murdock on you the other night.'

'No hard feelings about that,' I said. 'But I don't think this is the time to fill you in. You're going to have a visitor soon. I saw Christine Mellon at the Red Maple Inn a while ago.'

His eyes lit up. 'Christine? How typical. I called her last night and told her to stay away from here. I didn't want her involved. But what can you do with a woman like that?' He tried to smile, but his hurt jaw turned it into a grimace. 'I'd better get up there, or she'll be tossing interns out the window. Butler, if you'll wheel me up the hill, my nurse will take over.'

I wheeled him up to the nurse and walked back down the slope.

Elaine said, 'I'm glad for him. Christine's the medicine he needs. He feels bad about not shooting that man Sutton.'

'He'll get over that. I gather you've met Christine.'

'Yes, last summer. I was prepared not to like her. You know her reputation—neurotic playgirl, tramp of the Jet Set. But she's not like that at all. She has wit, charm, and . . . well, I guess the word is glamour. But for all her sophistication, she's led an insecure life. I think she responds to something solid and durable in Alex. Well, listen to the expert on love and marriage.'

She made a jerky movement and seemed to shiver with pain. I put a hand on her shoulder, and she pressed her cheek against it. She said, 'Sit down. Talk for a minute. Please.'

She drew me down beside her. Her face had a tense, famished look. 'I'm ashamed of the way I treated you the other night. First I tried to crack your skull with that glass. Then I accused you and humiliated you before Alex. I was like a crazy woman. Why?'

'No great mystery. I'd just brought you very bad news.

She cupped my chin with one hand. 'Alex thinks I harboured a resentment against you for years *because* you cracked up. Some people call insanity a form of suicide, social suicide. It's a cruel judgment on a wife to have her husband commit suicide.'

'Alex is a bright guy,' I said. 'Did he tell you that you had a legitimate grudge against Ralph, too?'

'Well, he did point out that Ralph was a murderer and maybe he was trying to absolve himself by having me share the spoils of his crime. So the marriage was something of a fraud.'

'Do you buy that?'

She gave a wan smile. 'No. I don't see Ralph as a murderer.'

'He wasn't. He was a kid chewed up by the war who got conned into taking part in what looked like a prank.' I told her about the cocky band of pirates on their way to liberate a little gold and of Ralph's horror at the killings that had occurred.

Tears stood in her eyes. 'It was good of you to come here and tell me that. It takes the curse off a little.'

'What are your plans now?' I asked.

'I'm going to bury Ralph in the family plot at the farm tomorrow. He wanted that. His parents and Alex's mother are buried there. I plan a simple service, with only the immediate family, plus Sam Brewer and his wife. They'll drive up in the morning. I don't see any reason to delay it, do you?'

'No. Am I invited to the funeral?'

She squeezed my hand. 'Morgan, that's kind, but I have Alex.'

'I wasn't thinking of that. Maybe I'd like to be rein-stated as immediate family, if only in a left-handed sort of way.'

She gave me a studious look. 'You're a strange guy. Of course, you're invited. In fact, you can drop me off in town. I have shopping to do, and certain arrangements to make.'

I dropped her off and drove on out to the Maynard farm. The police had erected a barrier at the bridge, and a state police car was parked beside it. Trooper Wetzel sat in the car, paring an apple.

I walked over and said, 'Having trouble with tourists?'

'Yeah, and souvenir hunters.' He cut a thick slice of apple.

'Mind if I look around up there?' I asked.

'Be my guest. Heck, I'll tag along.'

'Glad to have you. I've got a bone to pick with you anyway.'

We walked up the hill and followed the old wagon road past the front gate and along the hill to where it curved and swung back through the wagon shed. The shed was forty yards from the house. A flagstone path followed the contour of the slope to the front door. Several objects be-tween the shed and the house interested me—a bronze hitching post, a sundial, an old-fashioned well with a shake roof, and a grape arbour between the well and the house.

'So you're still hunting that thirty-eight,' Wetzel said.

I nodded. 'When Maynard tried to coax me to give him the gun, he planned to stash it some place on the way in.'

Wetzel pointed to the wagon shed. 'There's a thousand hiding places in there. Help yourself.'

He was right. One side of the shed was cluttered with old farm machinery. The other side was packed to the roof with furniture from the razed farmhouse. I scratched around in there for a while, then inspected the hitching post and sundial. Next I gave the well a careful inspection. It had long since been filled in and sealed with bricks, and the bucket hanging from the rope had been varnished to keep it from cracking. The grape arbour didn't look promising, but I checked it out, too.

'You're wasting your time,' Wetzel said.

'Loose ends trouble me. Another thing that troubles me is your blunder about how long it took the Suttons to travel that log road.'

Wetzel flushed. 'To hell with that noise! You're the one who goofed on that. You said we hit this farm thirty minutes behind Maynard. I had a patrol car at that junction twenty minutes later. So they made that drive in less than fifty minutes, which I know is impossible. You were wrong about how long you lay in that ditch. You were too groggy to think straight.'

'You could be right,' I said gently. 'But how can you be certain they couldn't drive that road in fifty minutes?'

'Easy. We got a boy named Jake Ferby runs the filling station in town. He's a stock car racer and some wheel man. He's got a Land-Rover he uses for hunting in these mountains, with four-wheel drive *and* compound low. He made a run from this farm to that junction last month, wide open. He did it in forty-five minutes. So no clown who never even saw that road is going to drive it in fifty.'

'Like you say, I could have been wrong about the time.'

'*Had* to be wrong,' he amended and went back down to his car.

I entered the house and poked around for a while. Then I sat in a wicker rocker and lit a stogie, which made my head ache. It was a tranquil place, and after a while I dozed off.

The telephone woke me at twilight. I answered. It was a

person-to-person call from Susan Wolfe in New York City.

'You're a hard man to track down,' she said. 'First I talked to Chief Cunningham in Pearl Beach. Next I called that inn up there, then the state police substation. They gave me this number.'

'Such persistence ought to be rewarded,' I said.

'That's not funny. But Cunningham said you were in a churlish mood. He also said you'd been hurt again. Was it bad?'

'I'll survive. How's your situation? Rough?'

'A lot you care, from the way you keep your promises. You were going to call me when this was finished.'

'Did Cunningham tell you that it was finished?'

'Yes. He said that man Price killed them all.' She paused, then spoke in a more vibrant voice. 'It is finished, isn't it?'

'I never argue with a chief of police. Now stop acting like a jilted schoolgirl, and tell me how you are.'

'All right. You nicked my vanity, making me call you. The truth is, I feel schitzy. The grieving widow's mask . . . well, sometimes it's no mask.'

'That's bound to happen. You lived with the guy ten years.'

'Listen, after the funeral tomorrow I'm flying to Jamaica for a few days. Maybe a week.'

'They say it's great down there this time of year.'

'Don't be obtuse. You could use a little healing in the sun.'

'But I'm going to Maynard's funeral up here tomorrow.'

Her voice cooled. 'I see. Too many widows competing for you. That one is paying you, as I recall. Are you open for bids?'

'I might be. Can I call you tomorrow?'

'Strictly up to you. My plane leaves at three. If you haven't called by then, I'll have your car sent over.' She hung up.

A tempting invitation, but it wasn't the call I was expecting.

That call came through two hours later, while I was dressing for dinner in my room at the Red Maple Inn.

Jim Cunningham said, 'Butler, you are a good prophet. Remember that evidence you wanted confirming Price as Trader Horn?'

'So it turned up?'

'That it did. The New York Police shook down that phony office Price had up there. They found a batch of papers taped to the bottom of the drawer. Meant nothing to them, so they sent the stuff to me.'

'What kind of papers?'

'First, a pack of seven cards with entries typed in some kind of shorthand. I think each card represents one of our boys.'

'What else?'

'The clincher. A letter addressed to Horn, telling him about the two who were killed in the war, and how everybody's cut was raised by a certain percentage. It's signed "The Warden." How do you like it?'

'It verifies your theory. Why so sour?'

'I'm not sure I like the way you predicted we would find it. Tell me, friend, are you holding out on me?'

'I've been doing some thinking. Last night you said Rita Sutton didn't tell us anything on her deathbed. But she did tell us something. She said Maynard had brought the police in with him.'

'He did. He brought you. They knew you toted a badge.'

'But he had dumped me. He wouldn't brag about it to them.'

'Okay, so when they had him under the gun he tried to bluff them with the threat of police. It could be that simple.'

'Uh-huh. Have you closed that book on McCloud yet?'

'Not technically. By God, you do have something! What is it?'

'Only a lie, Jim, a silly, stupid lie. But if I were you, I wouldn't close that book yet.' I hung up fast and left the room.

CHAPTER XXVIII

THEY held Ralph Maynard's funeral at two o'clock the next afternoon. It was a small funeral procession. First came the hearse, followed by the black limousine from the funeral parlour. Elaine, Alex, and Ralph's aunt from Gettysburg rode in the limousine. Next came Sam and Wendy Brewer in their Buick, and finally a Chevy driven by the minister who was to perform the services.

My car wasn't in the procession. I'd driven out that morning, alone, with a basket of provisions. The day was overcast and blustery. I'd built a fire in the fireplace in Ralph's uncompleted house and was on hand to greet the gravediggers when they arrived at nine. They were glad to warm their bellies with a shot of my bourbon before they set to work. They departed at noon and were to return at four to fill in the grave. Next came a young man driving a florist's truck containing several baskets of flowers. He set them up around the grave and drove away. I had the place to myself until the others arrived, and I joined them as they walked up a path to the family plot, a hundred yards from the house. They backed the hearse up the hill, and Sam Brewer, myself, and the drivers served as pallbearers.

The site had been well chosen, the shelf of a small hill sheltered by two giant oaks. The gravediggers had cut the weeds in the plot and had dusted off the headstones on the graves already there. We set the casket on the boards lying over the grave, and the four of us lifted it with the tapes provided. The minister removed the boards, and we lowered the casket into the grave.

The drivers rode the hearse down the hill, and we official mourners stood around the grave, with the minister at the head. Elaine stood to his right, wearing a charcoal-coloured coat. She held Alex's left arm. His right was supported by a black silk sling and his suit was black mohair. Elaine was so pale that her eyes looked unnatur-

ally bright, which helped give her face a brittle, porcelain cast. She seemed oblivious to the cold, too numb to feel it.

The minister was elderly and spry, with prominent veins at his temples. He read a psalm and allowed as how he'd known Ralph as a boy, as well as his folks. He then extemporized a eulogy about Ralph meeting his death in the performance of a heroic act, implying that his Maker would take that into consideration. Then he recited a prayer, waited for the amens, handed Elaine a trowel with which to drop the token clod into the grave, and the deed was done.

I was the first one down the path to the cars. Elaine and Alex lingered by the grave for a moment, then moved down the hill. I intercepted them where the path forked toward the house.

I said, 'Alex, I can give you that information now.'

He looked blank. 'I beg your pardon.'

'You wanted the inside story on the murders. Remember?'

'My God, man! This is no time to go into that.'

'This is the only time we'll have. I leave for Ohio today.'

He shook his head impatiently. 'Look, we're chilled to the bone, and this has been an ordeal for Elaine.'

'I've thought of that,' I said. 'I've got a fire inside, and I brought out refreshments. We'll have privacy for the talk, then I'll drop you two off at the inn. Elaine, do you mind?'

She frowned. Her face still had the porcelain look. 'No, I don't mind.' She squeezed Alex's arm. 'I could really use that fire.'

Alex said, 'Well, it seems such a morbid thing to do.'

'You're the one who wanted the information,' I said. 'I admit I'd like to get it off my chest. I did put in a week's work, and this is the only compensation I'm getting.'

His lip curled. 'You can be a crude man.'

'I prefer eccentric,' I said.

'Please don't quarrel,' Elaine said. 'Let's go in. I'm cold.'

'You two go ahead,' I said. 'I'll tell the others.' I went
down to the cars, related the message, and hiked up to the
house.

Elaine and Alex were seated on an old sofa I'd drawn
up before the fire. I poured sherry for her, bourbon for
Alex and me, and took a seat in the rocker, more or less
facing them.

Elaine sipped her sherry and extended a hand toward the
fire. 'That does feel nice. Morgan, this was a good idea.'

Alex fumbled a cigarette from his case awkwardly with
his left hand and worked his lighter. 'You've got the floor,
Butler.'

'All right. Yesterday you asked why Sutton killed Price,
his own man. Well, Price's real name was Larry Gibson, and
the evidence shows that he was a silent partner in that raid
the boys pulled in the Philippines. He got the gold out.
He was known personally only to McCloud. The others
knew him by a nickname, Trader Horn.'

Elaine was watching me with mild curiosity, but Alex
was alert, attentive. He said, 'But why did he team up
with the Suttons?'

So I gave them the complete version of Cunningham's
theory. I began with Price's phony credentials and background, and Rita Sutton's visits to the lawyers, and how
Gibson-alias-Price must have learned about the lead she
had on Kelso. Then I ran through each of the murders,
showing how Price had had the opportunity in every case
to do his dirty work, including the crack he'd taken at me,
presumably because I had seen his face. I explained why
Price had given Duncan a boost on his passage to the
Great Beyond, learning in the process that Duncan had sent
some kind of message to Maynard implicating Horn. Price
knew where Maynard was. He knew that the man Maynard had gone to for help would turn him down. So he
and the Suttons headed for Sweetbriar Falls to pull off the
kidnapping. He believed that once he killed Ralph, he
would be home free.

My throat was parched. I took a pull on my drink.
Crittenden said, 'But why did he have to kidnap us

Q

and turn the whole thing into such an elaborate production?'

'That was partly for the benefit of the Suttons,' I said. 'Maynard was their last hope, and I guess the kidnap scheme looked surefire to them. But Horn had his own motive. He wanted his final kill to occur in a place like this. He knew Vince had sworn never to go back to prison. With Vince and Rita on the run in this backcountry, wanted for murder, driving a conspicuous vehicle—Horn gets rid of his last two witnesses.'

'He must have been a lunatic!' Elaine said. 'Why didn't he just kill the two Suttons before it all started?'

'I think I can answer that,' Alex said. 'You read that story Rita Sutton put on paper, and we know she had taken it to lawyers. If both Suttons were murdered just after Vince got out of prison, the federal authorities might have started an investigation. Right, Butler?'

'That's how we figure it,' I said.

'But how did he blunder?' Alex asked. 'What did him in?'

I shrugged. 'Cunningham thinks Sutton spotted that Magnum, the gun Price used to kill Kelso and McCloud.' I lit up a stogie.

'But wasn't it stupid of him to keep using that gun?' Elaine asked. 'Wouldn't any gun have served his purpose?'

'Ah, not necessarily,' Alex said. 'If he had killed Ralph with that Magnum and got Sutton on the run, as Butler has suggested, then Sutton would have been blamed for all the murders. You see the continuity? Sutton was in all those cities. Do you agree, Butler?'

'Up to a point. I agree that Trader Horn planned it that way. But not Mr Larry Gibson alias Harry Price.'

'Now I'm confused,' Elaine said. 'I thought Price *was* Horn.'

'That was the bill of goods we were supposed to buy,' I said. 'Personally, I don't believe a damn word of it.'

Just then a log in the fireplace popped very loud. Elaine flinched, but Alex was oblivious to it. He said, 'But what about that evidence you said they found in Price's office

in New York?'

'Planted. Just like the money belt with the seven thousand bucks. Horn had to convince us that he was dead so we wouldn't look for him. In fact, when Horn hired Gibson, this was exactly the fate he had in mind for the man. He needed a man with a background like his, who had been out of the country during the war years, engaged in some shady enterprise.'

'Just a minute,' Alex said. 'Do you expect us to believe that Horn hired Gibson to kill those men, then got Sutton to kill Gibson?'

'Not at all,' I said. 'Gibson alias Price never killed anyone. Vince Sutton didn't kill anyone. Trader Horn killed them all.'

'My God, Morgan,' Elaine said. She jerked to her feet, crossed to the table, splashed bourbon into her sherry glass, and drank.

Alex said, 'That's incredible. What was he, the invisible man?'

'That's a good description, Alex,' I said.

Elaine lit a cigarette and said, 'Morgan, how do you know all this? Why didn't you believe Cunningham's theory?'

'Too many stray pieces just don't fit the theory,' I said. I began to tick them off. 'If I was such a threat to Price because I'd seen his face, why didn't he ever take another crack at me? He had plenty of chances. Then we have that weird business of Duncan taking a full day to realize he'd seen Horn in Atlantic City. Jim had an explanation for that, but it was a flimsy one. Next, we have the odd fact that the message Duncan sent Ralph was meaningless to him.'

'Maybe Ralph lied about that,' Elaine said.

'I doubt it. Another item that troubles me is that Ralph came up here armed with an automatic which was never found. Then I have a problem with the time it took the Suttons to drive over that old log road and avoid the roadblock. A near impossible feat.'

Alex shrugged. 'You're the expert, but none of these

flaws impress me. Hell, you can't expect to have it air tight.'

'He's right, Morgan,' Elaine said. 'You seem to be clutching at straws.' She rubbed her temple, as if I'd given her a headache.

Alex noticed. He said to me, 'You shouldn't have put her through this today. Now will you kindly drive us into the inn?'

'Frankly, I'm insulted,' I said. 'Do you really think I dragged you in here and put you through this to show you what a clever fellow I am at picking holes in Cunningham's theory?'

Elaine gave me a sharp look. Firelight reflected in her eyes made them glow like jade. 'No,' she said. 'You wouldn't have raised those questions if you didn't have the answers to them.'

'That's right,' I said.

She stretched like a cat awakening. 'Tell us, Morgan.'

'All right. Let's be clear on one point. Very little of what happened was improvised on the spot. Horn decided to kill them all a long time ago, except for the man in Tennessee, who was no threat. Horn wasn't going to live his life in anxiety that one of those boys would expose him. He knew Duncan was sick and vulnerable, that Ralph was coming apart at the seams. So he chose Gibson and got him hired by Rita Sutton, and when Vince got out of prison they went to work. He knew McCloud and the others would assume Sutton was on a rampage.'

I got up, poured a fresh drink, and wet my whistle. 'Horn did all the deeds we've credited Price with. He went to Crafton and killed Kelso with Ralph's Magnum, knowing that would scare Ralph to Atlantic City. Over there, just when the Suttons were ready to move in on McCloud, Horn killed him. When Duncan took off, Horn knew where to find him. He'd known about Duncan and the Sherwin girl. He had Price take the Suttons to New York and raid McCloud's house. Meanwhile, Horn was making sure Duncan died. Crushing those pills was a smokescreen, to make it look like Sutton's revenge. Horn knew where

Ralph was, and he knew he would soon be on his way home. So he set up the kidnap scheme, to lure Ralph to the farm to die.'

'This is still cloud-nine stuff,' Alex said impatiently. 'You haven't answered a single one of those questions you raised.'

'Fair enough,' I said. 'Let's start with the first one. Why didn't Horn ever take another crack at me? Answer: It wasn't a case of me being a threat because I'd seen his face, as we'd assumed with Price. I was a threat to Horn because he knew I had a date with Duncan the next day, and he was afraid he couldn't stop it.'

'Wait!' Elaine said. 'You're not saying it was Cunningham?'

'Be patient,' I said. 'Next, what made Duncan realize that a man he'd seen in Atlantic City was Trader Horn? Answer. He saw the same man in New York, in circumstances that revealed his name, a name McCloud had no doubt mentioned to Duncan.'

'But you're still not giving us facts,' Elaine said. '*Who* knew you had a date with Duncan? *Whom* did Duncan see in New York?'

'Don't rush him,' Alex said. 'Get to the next item, Butler. The one about Ralph not understanding Duncan's message.'

'That's easy. Once Duncan knew Horn's identity, he had to conclude that Ralph had known Horn all along. In fact, Duncan probably guessed that Horn entered the picture by coming to that stockade in the Philippines to visit Ralph. Naturally, he would have had to get permission from the warden. And Horn was just the man McCloud was waiting for, the one person who could get the gold to Australia undetected. Maybe Duncan's mistake was figuring that Horn had gone ahead and visited Ralph, after making a deal with McCloud. But Horn wasn't that stupid. Still, even if Duncan didn't count on the visit, it was logical for him to assume that Ralph and Horn had often discussed the gold heist over the years. Given the facts at Duncan's disposal, Ralph had to know Horn's identity.'

They were as immobile as statuary. Alex licked his lips. 'You're saying that Horn was someone close to Ralph,' he said.

'Right in the family, Alex, right in the family. You're Trader Horn, Alex. And Ralph, the poor sap, never even knew it.'

CHAPTER XXIX

'OH, no, Morgan!' Elaine said. 'You have to be wrong.'

'Of course he's wrong!' Alex said. 'You've flipped your lid again, Butler. This is the most asinine charge I've ever heard.'

'I can prove it, Alex. Don't you want to hear how you failed?'

Elaine said, '*I* want to hear it.' Her voice was full of dread.

Alex looked scornful. 'Go ahead, make an ass of yourself, like you did the other night with that crap about Molly Prescott.'

'You blundered that night, Alex.' I said to Elaine, 'Did Ralph ever tell you what name Alex used when he was a Hollywood cowboy back in the thirties?'

She frowned. 'No, not that I recall.'

'Ralph told me the name on our drive up here,' I said. 'It was Eric Knight. That Prescott dame in New York jabbered about Alex being a knight, but I didn't know she was referring to his stage name.'

'So Eric Knight was my stage name,' Alex said. 'What does that prove?'

'That's not the name you tried to foist on me the other night in Sweetbriar Falls,' I said. 'Remember? The entry in the TV guide listed Buck Jones and Victor Ritchie. You claimed to be Ritchie. You emphasized that they had given you billing.'

'You did, Alex,' Elaine said. 'I remember.'

'All right, a silly lie,' he said. 'A piece of vanity. I was

trying to make myself look important. Doesn't mean a thing.'

'Oh, but it does, Alex,' I said. 'You were desperate not to have Eric Knight resurrected. For all you knew, Duncan mentioned that name to the Sherwin girl, and her to me. Because you knew damn well how Duncan identified you. He happened to watch *Rangeland Renegades* on TV. He saw the same face he'd seen in the lobby of his motel only the day before, on a man I had called Maynard's half brother. No doubt he watched the credits after the film. Eric Knight was the name he knew you by.'

Alex said, 'That's pure fantasy, a coincidence.' But he gave Elaine a jerky look, and he was sweating now.

'Is it?' I said. 'Here's another reason you had to keep Eric Knight dead and buried. That was the name you used when you made a USO tour of the South Pacific early in forty-five. When you went to Europe later that year, you used your own name. That's on the record. I'm sure we'll be able to turn up the South Pacific record.'

'I never denied making a South Pacific tour!' he yelled. 'Sure, I made it. And I admit I looked up Ralph's outfit, learned he was in the stockade, and tried to see him. But they wouldn't let me in. You still haven't proved anything.'

'What job did you have with the USO company?' I asked.

'Another guy and I did rope tricks, fast-draw exhibitions, stuff like that. Most of the show was women—singers and dancers.'

'Did you help with the prop trunks?' I asked.

'All the men did.'

'I'll bet. That's how the gold got to Australia.'

'To hell with you!' he said. 'I don't have to listen to this.'

'Sit where you are, Alex!' Elaine said. She pounced to her feet, and her voice made my scalp prickle. 'Maybe Morgan is wrong. I hope to God he is. But we're going to get the truth here and now.' She turned to me. 'If he's Trader Horn, how could he have tried to kill you that night in Atlantic City? He'd already left town.'

'He lied. As soon as he left the Montclair, he got in touch with Price and had him sic the girl on me. Remember, Alex was the boy who knew I had a date with Duncan, and he knew Duncan was under police guard. So after Price left me chained to that bed, Alex slipped in for the kill. I was lucky the Sutton girl didn't give me the knock-out dose Price had ordered.'

'All right,' she said. 'But how could Alex have been in New York the next day to do that to Duncan? He called us from the Coast.'

'A fake. All he needed was a girl to play long-distance operator. I've done it myself. He flew to the Coast from New York.'

'But how do you explain what happened in my house the other night?' she asked. 'Sutton almost killed him.'

'That wasn't in the script,' I said. 'But Price stopped Vince as soon as he could, and it worked out to Alex's advantage. It made his story look better.'

'But they drugged him here in this house that morning,' she said. 'I saw them do it. I'd just come back from the phone.'

'Who gave him the needle?'

'Price! So that was faked, too. But how did they do the rest?'

'They had a nice plan,' I said. 'Ralph was due at a certain time. No doubt Price went to the top of the hill as lookout. Then he dashed back and told the Suttons that Maynard had brought the law in with him. He told them to take the Jeep wagon and hit for the old log road, and he would delay pursuit. The Suttons left. Let's say it took ten minutes for Ralph to stroll up the hill the long way and get close enough for Alex to get him with a rifle. Then Alex shot Price with the Magnum, which Price had prob-ably brought along from your house. How am I doing, Alex?'

He rose to his feet with a show of dignity. 'You said I used a rifle. How could I, with a broken arm?'

'You busted that arm yourself, Alex. After you had done your killing, and before you took that needle Price had saved for you.'

'You're nuts,' he said. He wheeled and walked straight across the room and out the door—precise, dignified, elegant.

Elaine grabbed my arm. 'You can't just let him go!'

'He's not going far. Remember, we have no proof that would hold up in court. That's why I hit him with everything. He's in shock. I think he's going to give us the evidence we need.'

Elaine moved quickly to a window. 'He stopped at the well.'

I joined her. Alex was screened from us by the grape arbour, so we moved to the kitchen window. Alex had a grip on the handle connected to the drum you turn to lower the bucket into the well. He gave the handle a twist and yanked it out. Then he pulled an object from the drum, tucked it into his sling, and came toward us.

Elaine said, 'I think he's got a gun!'

I took her arm and hustled her back to the fireplace. 'Don't be scared. It has to be Ralph's gun, and I unloaded it. Look.' I showed her the cartridges from my jacket pocket. 'Just let him talk.'

Alex entered, still the model of dignity. 'Where's your gun, Butler?' He produced the .38 automatic from his sling.

'I never wear a gun to a funeral,' I said.

'I don't believe you.' He turned the .38, and pain showed in his face when he worked the slide with his bad hand. 'Remove your jacket. Fine. Now throw it on the sofa, and turn around slowly.'

I obeyed, but he still wasn't satisfied.

He said, 'Put your hands on your head, and keep them there.'

I did so and said, 'So that's where you hid Ralph's gun.'

'No, Ralph hid it there. As boys we both hid things in that drum. I found his gun when I was hiding stuff I didn't want found.'

'Yes, the rifle and the syringe,' I said. 'But you didn't answer my question, Alex. Did I have the particulars right?'

He seemed to bristle with contempt. 'One thing you

said was accurate. I planned to kill them long ago. But not for a reason as banal as anxiety. You don't know what happened in the Philippines. McCloud lied to me. He said he knew where some thieves had cached this gold, and it would be easy to pick up. So I bought in. I didn't know about the massacre until I read about Sutton's trial. I didn't know I was conniving with murderers, rapists, scum!'

'But you took your share of the loot, old buddy.'

'Yes, but that didn't make me one of them, even though McCloud insinuated as much on several occasions. That was what I refused to tolerate, having my fate in the hands of men like that. After all, they committed a heinous crime. Their punishment was deserved.'

'Get off it, Alex. You're not the lunatic Elaine called you. You really don't see yourself as the saintly avenger on a big white steed. You had a far better motive than that.'

'What do you mean?'

'I saw your motive come floating into the Red Maple Inn yesterday. You're about to marry into the aristocracy, Alex. You'll hobnob only with the élite, in high society. You'd really be vulnerable up there. You didn't want that scum alive to jeopardize your new standing. In fact, I think you were earning your spurs. It was a ruthless, arrogant piece of work, Alex, worthy of an aristocrat.'

Tilting his head, he gave us a laconic smile. 'There could be something in what you say. But it's all academic now. You've forced me to be ruthless just one more time.'

'Killing us will be hard to explain,' I said. 'There's nobody around to take the rap for you this time.'

'Oh, I don't know,' he said. 'A grief-stricken widow and an ex-mental patient. I would say the ingredients are perfect.'

'But how do you know I didn't tell the police about you?'

Now his smile was arrogant. 'I've watched you, Butler. You fancy yourself a rugged individualist. You scorn help. The night the girl lured you into that trap in Atlantic City, you could have called Cunningham to back you up. You didn't, and I knew you wouldn't. It's a form of

conceit, the big flaw in your character.'

'Okay, Alex. But if you're going to shoot us, you'd better have some thirty-eight ammo. I unloaded that gun personally.'

'That's a cheap bluff, Butler. Hardly worthy of you.'

'Try it, Alex. Pull the trigger.'

He lined it upon my chest, squeezed, and got a dry click. He thumbed the clip out and saw that it was empty. He flung the gun aside and trotted through the doorway, swaying with his cast.

'Stop him!' Elaine said. Her voice was savage, guttural.

'He's just going to the well again for more water.' But I walked out and down the steps. Alex reached the well and rammed his good arm into the drum. He was after the rifle, but he'd had to disassemble it to get it into the drum. First he came out with the stock, then the barrel.

'Give it up, Alex!' I yelled. 'Don't make me hurt you.'

He wheeled toward me, agony on his face.

From the porch behind me Elaine said savagely, 'You filthy, demented murderer! You filthy, demented murderer!'

I turned. She had a two-handed grip on Ralph's automatic. How silly, with an empty gun, was my first thought. My next thought—that she'd taken a cartridge from my jacket and jammed it into the chamber—came too late. The gun roared and bucked, and the slug knocked Alex back against the well.

Elaine had that same look of stark and unrelenting frenzy she had worn the night she threw the glass at me. She held her arms rigid, as if she meant to fire again, her face drained of blood.

I mounted the steps. 'That was a damn good shot for twenty yards, shooting downhill,' I said. I seized the gun, but she was frozen to it, white-knuckled. I shook it and her whole frame shook. 'Give me the gun, Elaine.'

She gave a wretched moan and released it. She had bitten blood from her lower lip. 'Did I kill the monster?' she asked. It was the voice of a girl asking Daddy about something in a dream.

'Easy does it. Let's get you inside, then I'll go see.' She moved woodenly, but I got her to the sofa and left her there.

I walked down to the well. Alex was sitting propped against it. As I knelt beside him a tablespoon of blood spurted from one corner of his mouth and ran down his chin.

He said, 'Jesus Christ,' in a funny, scared voice.

I examined him. The slug had gone through his plaster cast, nicking his fractured arm, then passed neatly between two ribs and lodged in his right lung. I could see the butt of the slug between the ribs. His lung was haemorrhaging from inside, but he wasn't bad off.

'Buck up, aristocrat,' I said. I went into the house, picked up the phone, and dialled. It was answered promptly. I said, 'Come and get him, Bannister. You'd better bring an ambulance. I had to put a slug in him.' I hung up.

I gave Elaine a shot of bourbon. She drank it off, and there was a sneer on her lips. 'You don't have to lie for me. *I* killed him. I heard you lie.' Her voice had a metallic ring.

'You didn't kill anybody. Not that he doesn't need killing and not that you weren't justified. I would call that the most spontaneous act you've ever performed. It was one damn fine shot.'

She ground her teeth together and said, 'I don't understand. What will they do to me now?'

'Nothing. But I'll do something. I'm taking you home.'

She made a face. 'I don't want to go home.'

'I don't mean Sweetbriar Falls. I'm taking you home to the farm. You've cost me a week's delay in harvesting my field corn, and you're going to help bring it in.'

'You must be crazy.' She watched me, and the little girl look faded. 'Will you really take me home to the farm?'

'Yes. But you have to earn your keep. You'll have to work.'

'But I don't know anything about husking corn.'

'You'll learn. Don't worry about that.'

CHAPTER XXX

SHE learned to husk corn, all right, and it was a far cry from a set of tennis at the club. Two days after Ralph's funeral I had her in the field at seven am. The temperature was thirty degrees and the shocks were hoary with frost. I had her outfitted in thermal underwear, Levis, boots with a shoepac, a Mackinaw, and a stocking cap. She wore a glove on her left hand, but on her right she wore a partial glove because she needed those fingers free for the husking peg. The peg has a curved metal blade on the end, which you use to peel the cured husk off the corn. Then you snap the ear from the stalk, toss it into the pile, and grab your next stalk. We all had a piece of canvas to kneel on while we worked.

I gave Elaine a brief lesson, and it took her two minutes to husk her first ear solo. She approached the task with all the decorum of a lady peeling a banana before royalty. In that outfit and that setting, she looked comical.

Johnny King, who husked corn with the precision of a trained juggler, keeping a continuous flow of yellow ears drifting through the air, had to avert his face to hide his smile. But she stuck it out. She nicked gashes on her hand and one arm with the blade of the husking peg, chapped her face with corn leaves from a day of grabbing fresh batches from the shock, got cramps in her hips and tears in her eyes from the cold. But she stuck it out. That night she had a hot bath and a light supper and fell asleep at eight in front of the fireplace.

When I woke her up at six the next morning, she yelled that she refused to get up until the sun rose, that she was not so masochistic that she had to torture herself, and she certainly had nothing to prove to me or to anyone else about her pioneer spirit or her passion for the primitive life.

But twenty minutes later she joined us over hotcakes and sausage, dressed in her work clothes, calm and polite, and she went to the field with us at seven.

The next morning at six she denounced me with the
same fervour but different words. She said that my motive
for bringing her to the farm and working her like a slave
was so transparent it was laughable. I was giving her
occupational therapy, as if she were an inmate in an asylum,
and she was not fooled by my tactics.

Except for these outbursts, which seemed to be her way
of working up a head of steam to propel her from bed, she
didn't talk much during the first four days. But each day
she applied herself to the work with more zeal, and one
change was so obvious it was funny—her appetite. She
began to eat like the field hand she was.

Then she began to loosen up. One evening when Johnny
brought the team and sled out to haul the day's harvest
into the barn, she asked if she might learn to drive the
team. She stood with Johnny on the back of the sled,
gliding over the soft earth, crushing corn stubble. He turned
the reins over to her halfway in, on a downhill run. The
blacks began to jog and she lost her cap and her bright hair
flowed behind her like a pennant. Just before they reached
the barn I heard her laugh. Even I had to admit that on
that day she had husked a pretty fair crop of corn for
an amateur.

It was not that night but the next that she returned to
the living-room at eleven while I was locking up for the
night. She wore a quilted robe and looked fresh from the
bath. She said, 'How about a nightcap? Surely I'm entitled
to a rum ration.'

'Sure. What's your pleasure? I thought you were asleep.'

She stretched languidly and smiled. 'I must be getting
used to it. Scotch and soda, please.'

I mixed two and we sat in front of the fire. She sipped
her drink and said, 'You know, I agree with you.'

'About what?'

'That was a damn good shot, at twenty yards, shooting
downhill.'

'I told you it was.'

'Yes, but now I believe it. I would believe it even if I'd
killed him. I feel righteous and good about it.'

'You should.'

'That's another thing they failed to teach me at Vassar—that in spite of everything, you can get into a situation where the only solution is to shoot the son of a bitch.'

'There aren't any schools where they teach that.'

She rose and moved to the mantelpiece. Looking down into the fire, she said, 'But the sensation of having done it —does that ever leave you? I don't mean just the righteous part.'

'No, not completely. That's the price you pay.'

'I thought not.' She saluted me with her glass and drank. Then she said, 'That's why you brought me to the farm, isn't it? To isolate me and render the fat away and have me learn this.'

'Not me, lady. I brought you to help with the corn. What goes on inside that beautiful head of yours is your own affair.'

She looked amused and proud. 'Have it your own way, farmer.' She put the glass on the mantel and walked over and sat on the arm of my chair. 'Am I earning my keep? Was I good in the field today?'

'You were great.'

'Then kiss me a minute.'

I pulled her on to my lap and kissed her a minute. Then I said, 'You're not wearing anything under this robe.'

'No. We country girls like to be loose and limber. We're a little on the primitive side, we country girls.' She nestled her head into my shoulder. 'What will they do to him?'

'Alex? The State of Pennsylvania will prosecute him for the two murders at the farm. That's their best case. Oh, he told it all when he thought he was dying, but they have their best evidence for those two at the farm. They'll get a conviction.'

We were quiet for a while. I could feel heat from the fire and a vibrant quality in Elaine that seemed part of her scent.

She said, 'Will the corn be done by Thanksgiving?'

'Yes, if you continue to earn your keep.'

'Fine. I'd like to stay until Thanksgiving. We'll celebrate the holiday. Maybe it'll snow by then. We can build a snowman and do other foolish things. May I stay until

Thanksgiving?'

'You can stay as long as you like.'

'Oh, no. That's as long as I dare stay. You don't want me dependent on you for the wrong reasons. I'll go to Michigan and spend some time with the Tycoon and mother.'

'Then what?'

'I don't know. But after Thanksgiving, I'll be sound and salubrious. Ready to tackle anything. If you want to court me, farmer, you'll have to take the initiative.' She turned her face up and smiled impishly. 'I do feel a little smug about one thing. You never did get paid for that week's work.'

'You're wrong. I got a cheque yesterday from the Widow McCloud in New York. Ten thousand dollars, marked "for services rendered".'

'Why on earth did she do that?'

'She wanted me to track down her husband's murderer. I did it. I guess she felt duty bound to pay up.'

'That's odd. Surely you're not going to keep the money?'

I knew that Susan Wolfe believed the same thing. She had sent the cheque in a fit of pique because I hadn't made it to Jamaica. The tricks they pull. Her message was clear. If I tore up the cheque and returned it, we would get together again. If I accepted it, for services rendered, we were through.

I said, 'No, I'm keeping it. I earned it, and it's only a smidgen of McCloud's estate. So I take it as fair payment.'

'You are a mercenary devil,' she said. 'And not above exploiting helpless widows. For shame.'

'Helpless, indeed. If you don't get out of here and get to bed, you'll be my next victim.'

She nestled again. 'I was hoping, just this one night, you might tuck me in. We could start Thanksgiving early this year.'

So I carried her upstairs, and we had early Thanksgiving. She made jokes about the Indians sharing their corn with the Puritans, and jokes about feasting and the anatomy of the turkey. She was full of jokes, vibrant with life, and altogether mortal.

by the same author

THE MIDNIGHT LADY AND THE MOURNING MAN
THE ORGANIZATION

Blood on a Harvest Moon

Lured from his dangerous career as a top private investigator by the promise of a more leisured life as a gentleman farmer, Morgan Butler, ex-Marine captain, is in the midst of harvesting when an unexpected visitor summons him from the fields. Concerned about the mysterious and uncharacteristic disappearance of her second husband, a successful businessman named Ralph Maynard, Butler's still-beautiful ex-wife has come to enlist his aid. Will he track down the missing Maynard?

Routine work for an old pro—until a string of brutal and baffling murders obscures Maynard's trail. Will Maynard be the next victim in this series of ingeniously executed slayings? Or is the threat to Maynard's life an artful deception designed to conceal Maynard's own guilt? Drawn into a subtle and ever-widening circle of deceit and death, Butler himself becomes the prey of a ruthless assassin determined to preserve the bloody secret of a wartime plot in this superbly crafted, high-tension novel of suspense.

D0589592